VOID STALKER

Tolemion advanced, shield high and hammer at the ready. 'Make peace with your black-hearted gods, heretic. Tonight, you will know the–'

Xarl gave a distinctly annoyed snort. 'I'd forgotten how much you heroes liked the sound of your own voices.' As Tolemion drew nearer, the Night Lord gripped his two-handed chainblade in a single gauntlet. In his other hand, Xarl caught the handle of Uzas's damaged chain-axe, as he kicked it up from the deck.

Both blades began to roar as their teeth chewed the air. He'd fought through seven Imperial Space Marines to get back here, and their blood flicked in a light spray from the whirring teeth of his chainsword. Beneath his armour, sweat bathed his skin in a greasy sheen, while amusement danced with the strain of pain and anger in his eyes. The sting of already suffered wounds knifed at him through the rents in his war plate.

'Let's get this done,' he said, still smiling.

By the same author

• **NIGHT LORDS** •
Book 1 – SOUL HUNTER
Book 2 – BLOOD REAVER
Book 3 – VOID STALKER

THRONE OF LIES
A Night Lords audio drama

CADIAN BLOOD
An Imperial Guard novel

THE EMPEROR'S GIFT
A Grey Knights novel

THE FIRST HERETIC
A Horus Heresy novel

BUTCHER'S NAILS
A Horus Heresy audio drama

More Chaos Space Marines from Black Library

IRON WARRIORS: THE OMNIBUS
Graham McNeill
(Contains the novel *Storm of Iron*, the novella
Iron Warrior and five short stories)

WORD BEARERS: THE OMNIBUS
Anthony Reynolds
(Contains the novels *Dark Apostle*, *Dark Disciple*
and *Dark Creed* plus a short story)

A WARHAMMER 40,000 NOVEL

AARON DEMBSKI-BOWDEN
VOID STALKER

A NIGHT LORDS NOVEL

BLACK LIBRARY

A BLACK LIBRARY PUBLICATION

First published in Great Britain in 2012 by
The Black Library,
Games Workshop Ltd.,
Willow Road, Nottingham,
NG7 2WS, UK

10 9 8 7 6 5 4 3 2 1

Cover illustration by Jon Sullivan.

© Games Workshop Limited 2012. All rights reserved.

The Black Library, the Black Library logo, Games Workshop, the Games Workshop logo and all associated marks, names, characters, illustrations and images from the Warhammer 40,000 universe are either ®, TM and/or © Games Workshop Ltd 2000-2012, variably registered in the UK and other countries around the world. All rights reserved.

A CIP record for this book is available from the British Library.

UK ISBN: 978 1 84970 148 8
US ISBN: 978 1 84970 149 5

No part of this publication may be reproduced, stored in a retrieval system, or transmitted in any form or by any means, electronic, mechanical, photocopying, recording or otherwise, without the prior permission of the publishers.

This is a work of fiction. All the characters and events portrayed in this book are fictional, and any resemblance to real people or incidents is purely coincidental.

See the Black Library on the internet at
www.blacklibrary.com

Find out more about Games Workshop
and the world of Warhammer 40,000 at
www.games-workshop.com

Printed and bound by CPI Group (UK) Ltd, Croydon, CR0 4YY

*For the new Mrs Dembski-Bowden.
Well, both of them.*

IT IS THE 41st millennium. For more than a hundred centuries the Emperor has sat immobile on the Golden Throne of Earth. He is the master of mankind by the will of the gods, and master of a million worlds by the might of his inexhaustible armies. He is a rotting carcass writhing invisibly with power from the Dark Age of Technology. He is the Carrion Lord of the Imperium for whom a thousand souls are sacrificed every day, so that he may never truly die.

YET EVEN IN his deathless state, the Emperor continues his eternal vigilance. Mighty battlefleets cross the daemon-infested miasma of the warp, the only route between distant stars, their way lit by the Astronomican, the psychic manifestation of the Emperor's will. Vast armies give battle in His name on uncounted worlds. Greatest amongst his soldiers are the Adeptus Astartes, the Space Marines, bio-engineered super-warriors. Their comrades in arms are legion: the Imperial Guard and countless Planetary Defence Forces, the ever-vigilant Inquisition and the tech-priests of the Adeptus Mechanicus to name only a few. But for all their multitudes, they are barely enough to hold off the ever-present threat from aliens, heretics, mutants - and worse.

TO BE A man in such times is to be one amongst untold billions. It is to live in the cruellest and most bloody regime imaginable. These are the tales of those times. Forget the power of technology and science, for so much has been forgotten, never to be re-learned. Forget the promise of progress and understanding, for in the grim dark future there is only war. There is no peace amongst the stars, only an eternity of carnage and slaughter, and the laughter of thirsting gods.

AUTHOR'S NOTE

REGARDING CONTINUITY, AS more of the Horus Heresy comes to light in the *New York Times* bestselling Horus Heresy series, the lore of the Warhammer 40,000 universe undergoes subtle shifts in scope. In *Soul Hunter*, it was claimed that the Warband of the Broken Aquila had experienced a century of time passing since the Horus Heresy, due to the vicissitudes of the warp.

In keeping with the new revelations and detail regarding the Traitor Legions during the Scouring, I've changed that slightly to maintain consistency. *Void Stalker* contains references to how much time has passed for Talos and First Claw, settling the issue much more firmly in the newly established lore of those ancient, war-torn eras.

It's a minor change, and one I suspect most readers wouldn't even notice, but consistency matters to me – hence this note.

I just wanted to say thanks in advance for your indulgence.

'I have seen a time when the Imperium can no longer breathe.
  When Man's empire chokes on its own corruption,
  Poisoned by the filth and sin of five hundred deluded generations.

On that night, when madness becomes truth,
  The Gate of Cadia will break open like an infected wound,
  And the legions of the damned will spill into the kingdom they created.

In this age at the end of all things,
  Born of forbidden blood and fate's own foul humour,
  Will rise the Prophet of the Eighth Legion.'

– 'The Crucible Premonition'
Recorded by an unknown VIII Legion sorcerer, M32

PROLOGUE
RAIN

THE PROPHET AND the murderess stood on the battlements of the dead citadel, weapons in their hands. Rain slashed in a miserable flood, thick enough to obscure vision, hissing against the stone even as it ran from the mouths of leering gargoyles, draining down the castle's sides. Above the rain, the only audible sounds came from the two figures: one human, standing in broken armour that thrummed with static crackles; the other an alien maiden in ancient and contoured war plate, weathered by an eternity of scarring.

'This is where your Legion died, isn't it?' Her voice was modulated by the helm she wore, emerging from the death mask's open mouth with a curious sibilance that almost melted into the rain. 'We call this world *Shithr Vejruhk*. What is it in your serpent's tongue? *Tsagualsa*, yes? Answer me this, prophet. Why would you come back here?'

The prophet didn't answer. He spat acidic blood onto the dark stone floor, and drew in another ragged breath. The sword in his hands was a cleaved ruin, its shattered blade severed halfway along its length. He didn't know where his bolter was, and a smile crept across his split lips as he felt an instinctive tug of guilt. It was surely a sin to lose such a Legion relic.

'Talos.' The maiden smiled as she spoke, he could hear it in her voice. Her amusement was remarkable if only for the absence of mockery and malice. 'Do not be ashamed, human. Everyone dies.'

The prophet sank to one knee, blood leaking from the cracks in his armour. His attempt at speech left his lips as a grunt of pain. The only thing he could smell was the copper stench of his own injuries.

The maiden came closer, even daring to rest the scythe-bladed tip of her spear on the wounded warrior's shoulder guard.

'I speak only the truth, prophet. There's no shame in this moment. You have done well to even make it this far.'

Talos spat blood again, and hissed two words.

'Valas Morovai.'

The murderess tilted her head as she looked down at him. Her helm's crest of black and red hair was dreadlocked by the rain, plastered to her death mask. She looked like a woman sinking into water, shrieking silently as she drowned.

'Many of your bitter whisperings remain occluded to me,' she said. 'You speak... "First Claw", yes?' Her unnatural accent struggled with the words. 'They were your brothers? You call out to the dead, in the hopes they will yet save you?'

The blade fell from his grip, too heavy to hold any longer. He stared at it lying on the black stone, bathed in the downpour, silver and gold shining as clean as the day he'd stolen it.

Slowly, he lifted his head, facing his executioner. Rain showered the blood from his face, salty on his lips, stinging his eyes. He wondered if she was still smiling behind the mask.

On his knees, atop the battlements of his Legion's deserted fortress, the Night Lord started laughing.

Neither his laughter nor the storm above were loud enough to swallow the throaty sound of burning thrusters. A gunship – blue-hulled and blackly sinister – bellowed its way into view. As it rose above the battlements, rain sluiced from its avian hull in silver streams. Heavy bolter turrets aligned in a chorus of mechanical grinding, the sweetest music ever to grace the prophet's ears. Talos was still laughing as the Thunderhawk hovered in place, riding its own heat haze, with the dim lighting of the cockpit revealing two figures within.

The alien maiden was already moving. She became a black blur, dancing through the rain in a velvet sprint. Detonations clawed at her heels as the gunship opened fire, shredding the stone at her feet in a hurricane of explosive rounds.

One moment she fled across the parapets, the next she simply ceased to exist, vanishing into shadow.

Talos didn't rise to his feet, uncertain he'd manage it if he tried. He closed the only eye he had left. The other was a blind and bleeding orb of irritating pain, sending dull throbs back into his skull each time his two hearts beat. His bionic hand, shivering with joint glitches and flawed neural input damage, reached to activate the vox at his collar.

'I will listen to you, next time.'

Above the overbearing whine of downward thrusters, a voice buzzed over the gunship's external vox-speakers. Distortion stole all trace of tone and inflection.

'If we don't disengage now, there won't be a next time.'

'I told you to leave. I ordered it.'

'Master,' the external vox-speakers crackled back. *'I…'*

'Go, damn you.'

When he next glanced at the gunship, he could see the two figures more clearly. They sat side by side, in the pilots' thrones. 'You are formally discharged from my service.' He slurred the words as he voxed them, and started laughing again. 'For the second time.'

The gunship stayed aloft, engines giving out their horrendous whine, blasting hot air across the battlements.

The voice rasping over the vox was female this time. *'Talos.'*

'Run. Run far from here, and all the death this world offers. Flee to the last city, and catch the next vessel off-world. The Imperium is coming. They will be your salvation. But remember what I said. We are all slaves to fate. If Variel escapes this madness alive, he will come for the child one night, no matter where you run.'

'He might never find us.'

Talos's laughter finally faded, though he kept the smile. 'Pray that he doesn't.'

He drew in a knifing breath as he slumped with his back to the battlements, grunting at the stabs from his ruined lungs and shattered ribs. Grey drifted in from the edge of his vision, and he could no longer feel his fingers. One hand rested on his cracked breastplate, upon the ritually broken aquila, polished by the rain. The other rested on his fallen bolter, Malcharion's weapon, on its side from where he'd dropped it in the earlier battle. With numb hands, the prophet locked the double-barrelled bolter to his thigh, and took another slow pull of cold air into lungs that no longer wanted to breathe. His bleeding gums turned his teeth pink.

'I'm going after her.'

'Don't be a fool.'

Talos let the rain drench his upturned face. Strange, how a moment's mercy let them believe they could talk to him like that. He hauled himself to his feet, and started walking across the black stone battlements, a broken blade in hand.

'She killed my brothers,' he said. 'I'm going after her.'

PART ONE

THE CARRION WORLD

I

THE LONGEST DREAM

'Because we are brothers. We've seen primarchs die to blade and fire, and we've seen our actions set the galaxy aflame. We've betrayed others and been betrayed in kind. We're bleeding for an uncertain future, fighting a war for the lies our lords tell us. What do we have left, if not blood's loyalty? I am here because you are here. Because we are brothers.'

– Jago Sevatarion, 'Sevatar', the Prince of Crows
As quoted in *The Tenebrous Path*, chapter VI: Unity

THE PROPHET'S EYES snapped open, bleaching his vision with the monochrome red of his tactical display. The familiarity was a comfort after the madness of the dream. This was how he'd seen the world around him for most of his life, and the dancing target locks following his gaze were a welcome extension of natural sight.

Already, the nightmare fled before him, elusive and thread-thin, unravelling as he sought to hold onto it. Rain on the battlements. An alien swordswoman. A gunship, shooting up the black stone.

No. It was gone. Shadows remained, images and sensations, nothing more.

That was happening more often, recently. The visions refused to stick with any tenacity, whereas once they'd melded to his memory. It seemed to be a side effect of their increasing frequency, though with no understanding of his gift's genesis and function, he had no way of knowing the truth of the matter.

Talos rose from where he'd collapsed on the floor of his modest arming chamber and stood in silence, tensing his muscles, bunching them and rolling his neck, restoring circulation and checking the interface feeds of his armour. The ceramite suit of layered war plate – some of it ancient and unique, some of it plundered much more recently – whirred and growled in rhythm with his movements.

He moved slowly, carefully, feeling the quivering strain of muscles too long locked. Cramps played along his limbs, all except his augmetic arm which responded sluggishly, its internal processors only now realigning with the impulses from his waking mind. The bionic limb was still the first section of his body to come back into full obedience, despite its halting sphere of motion. He used it, the iron hand gripping at the wall, to haul himself to his feet. Armour joints snarled at even these minor motions.

The pain was waiting for him back in the waking world. It crashed against him now, the same torture that always spiked through his blood like a toxin. He murmured breathless, defiant syllables behind his faceplate, uncaring how the words were vox-growled to the empty chamber.

The dream. Were they destined to be deceived, or destined to be the deceivers? Fate often played them the latter hand. The Exalted had said the words so many times: *Betray before you are betrayed.*

No matter how he reached for the dream, it dispersed ever further. The pain wasn't helping. It flooded back as if filling the hole in his memory. On several occasions in the past, the pain had been severe enough to leave him blind for entire nights. This eve was only just shy of the same torture.

He hesitated as he reached for his blade and bolter. They both rested as they should: racked against the wall and bound in place by strong leather straps. This, however, was rare. Talos was many things, but fastidiously tidy was not one of them. He couldn't recall the last time he'd returned to his room, replaced his weapons in perfect order, and promptly passed out comfortably in isolation. In fact, he couldn't ever recall it happening before. Not even once.

Someone had been in here. Septimus, perhaps, or his brothers when they'd dragged him from wherever he'd been when he fell prey to the vision.

Still, they'd never concern themselves with something as mundane as restoring his weapons to their racks. Septimus, then. That made sense. Uncommon behaviour, but it made sense. It was even laudable.

Talos pulled his weapons free before fastening them to his armour. The double-barrelled bolter mag-locked to his thigh, and the ornate golden blade sheathed at his back, ready to be drawn over his shoulder.

: COME TO THE BRIDGE

The words peeled across his visor display, spelled out in distinct Nostraman runes, clear white on the background red-tint like any other measure of tactical information or bio-data. He watched the cursor flicker at the end of the final word, blinking almost expectantly.

Quintus, the fifth of his slaves, had been rendered mute through battlefield injury. They'd communicated during the serf's years of service via hand signs or text uplink from a hand-held auspex to Talos's armour systems, and usually a fair degree of both at once. Quintus, much like Septimus, was a good enough artificer that a little inconvenience was a small price to pay.

: PROPHET
: COME TO THE BRIDGE

Quintus, however, had never behaved so informally. He was also decades dead, slain by the Exalted in one of Vandred's many crazed outbursts.

Talos's retinal display responded to his desire, opening a vox-channel to First Claw.

'Brothers.'

They answered, but without anything resembling cohesion. Xarl's laughter machine-gunned across the vox-waves, followed by the others cursing and screaming oaths in equal measure. He could hear Mercutian's whisperingly polite swearing coming through clenched teeth, and the throaty chatter of bolters in their fusillade drumbeat.

The channel went dead. He tried several others: the strategium, Deltrian's Hall of Reflection, Septimus's armoury, Octavia's chamber, and even Lucoryphus of the Bleeding Eyes. All dead. All silent. The ship thrummed on, evidently active and running at speed.

He perversely relished these first pricklings of unease. It took a great deal to unnerve any of the Eighth Legion, and the ship's sudden emptiness was a pleasant mystery. He had the amusing feeling of being hunted, and it sent a smile creeping across his pale lips. This must be what his prey felt like, though he'd hardly lose control of his muscles and babble meaningless prayers to false gods the way humans usually did.

: I AM WAITING

Talos drew his sword and left his chamber.

HE WAS FAR from shocked to find the bridge abandoned. It was no more than a minute's travel from his chamber on the deck below, but the *Echo of Damnation*'s central spinal thoroughfares were similarly empty when he'd passed through them.

The strategium was an expansive oval of gothic architecture, populated by leering gargoyles and sculpted grotesques clinging to the walls and ceiling. Here, a mutilated angel with eyes wrapped by barbed wire roared voicelessly at the central throne; there, a bat-winged daemon spread its pinions across the ceiling above the secondary gunnery platforms. The artistry involved in the *Echo*'s construction never failed to captivate him – for all the Eighth Legion's flaws as disciplined warriors, the Night Lords had managed to breed a few scholars and craftsmen with the same skill shown by the artisan-knights of the Emperor's Children and the Blood Angels. No matter their individual skills in craft, most Eighth Legion vessels were decorated with blasphemous relish, depicting tortured divinities and captive daemons across the architecture.

A central throne rose above all else, its immense bulk aimed at the occulus viewscreen. Above the occulus, a Legionary's broken skeleton was bound, crucified in place, hanging on chains.

In concentric circles around it were the banks of navigation, gunnery and operation stations. No robed heretic priests muttered their way between control tables. No uniformed crew relayed orders or adjusted settings. No branded servitors hardwired into their restraint thrones chattered and drawled their status reports in machine voices.

This was surely a dream, though it matched no vision he'd ever seen before. No other explanation fit.

'I am here,' Talos said aloud.

: YOU HAVE BEEN DREAMING MANY DREAMS
: NOW YOU ARE CLOSE TO WAKING ONCE MORE
: SIT BROTHER

He didn't smile. He rarely did, even when amused, though it was most definitely amusing to be told to take a seat in his own command throne. Talos complied, even if only to see what would happen.

: ALMOST CLOSE ENOUGH TO TOUCH

That prickled at the prophet's skin. He looked up at Ruven's crucified remains.

: YOU ARE NOT THE WARRIOR YOU SHOULD BE
: BUT YOU AND I MUST SPEAK
: IT MUST BE HERE AND IT MUST BE NOW
: THERE WILL NEVER BE ANOTHER CHANCE

Talos remained seated, the very picture of stoic

patience. He refused to let his anger or doubts rise to the surface. Targeting reticules slid by without gaining a grip on Ruven's shattered skeleton.

: YOU MADE MY CORPSE INTO THE FINEST DECORATION
: THAT IS ALMOST AMUSING

Talos reclined in the throne the way he did on the true bridge.

'Can even death not render you silent?'

: YOUR OWN LIFE IS MEASURED IN MONTHS PROPHET

The skull, suspended on chains, leered with empty eye sockets. 'Is that so?' Talos asked it. 'And how do you come by this precious lore?'

: DO YOU PRETEND THIS MOMENT HAS NO SIGNIFICANCE
: DO YOU BELIEVE I CANNOT HEAR YOUR HEART BEATING FASTER

Talos stroked the hilt of the relic blade resting at his side. The restraint needed to resist demanding an explanation brought his headache to a crescendo.

'Get on with it,' he said, continuing his facade of bored indulgence. He had to collect his thoughts. At best, this was a trap. At worst, it was sorcery. More than likely, it was both.

That wasn't good.

: YOU REMEMBER NOTHING DO YOU
: YOU HAVE COME TO SEEK A PURE WAR
: A NOBLE WAR
: BUT YOU SHOULD NEVER HAVE RETURNED TO THE EASTERN FRINGE
: OTHERS HAVE BEEN WAITING FOR YOUR RETURN WITH REVENGE IN THEIR HEARTS

The prophet remained as he was, still stroking the blade's wingspread hilt. The Eastern Fringe. He couldn't think of anything that would ever drive him back there.

'I think you lie, husk.'

: WHY WOULD I LIE
: YOU RUN FROM THE EYE
: YOU RUN FROM THE ELDAR
: YOU RUN FROM DOOM AT THE HANDS OF ALIEN WITCHES

: WHERE BETTER TO FLEE THAN THE OTHER EDGE OF THE GALAXY

Perhaps there was truth in that, but the prophet felt no urge to confess it. He remained silent.

: HOW LONG HAVE YOU WAGED THIS WAR TALOS

He shook his head, feeling the sudden need to swallow. 'A long time. The Heresy was the bloodiest decade. Then, the Raiding Years, when we called Tsagualsa home. Two centuries of bitter glory, before the Imperium came for us.'

: AND HOW LONG SINCE WE LEFT THE CARRION WORLD

'For the Imperium?' He narrowed his eyes at the question. 'Almost ten thousand ye–'

: NO
: HOW LONG FOR THE TRAITOR LEGIONS
: HOW LONG FOR YOU TALOS

He swallowed again, beginning to sense where this was leading. The warp stole all meaning from the material realm, even banishing all pretence of physics and temporal stability. The Great Heresy was days in the past for some of the Traitors within the Eye, and fifty thousand years gone for others. All of them, each and every soul to betray the Emperor in that golden age, could claim a different scale of time for the years since.

'A century since we left Tsagualsa.' Less than many, but more than some.

: A CENTURY FOR YOU
: A CENTURY FOR FIRST CLAW
: THAT MAKES YOU OVER THREE HUNDRED YEARS OLD PROPHET

Talos nodded, meeting the skull's hollow eyes. 'Close enough.'

: STILL SO YOUNG FOR A TRAITOR
: STILL NAIVE
: BUT LONG ENOUGH THAT YOU SHOULD HAVE LEARNED CERTAIN LESSONS BY NOW
: AND YET YOU HAVE NOT

The prophet stared up at the wreckage of crucified

bone, and the letters superimposed over it. They flickered across his retinal display almost impatiently, as if awaiting an answer.

'If you find me lacking, revenant, then by all means enlighten me.'

: WHY ARE YOU FIGHTING THIS WAR

The prophet snorted. 'For vengeance.'

: REVENGE FOR WHAT

'To avenge the wrongs done to us.'

: WHAT WRONGS DO YOU SPEAK OF

The Legionary rose to his feet, feeling the skin crawling at the back of his neck. 'You *know* what wrongs. You *know* why the Eighth Legion fights.'

: THE EIGHTH LEGION DOESN'T KNOW WHY IT FIGHTS
: YOU CONCEIVE EXCUSES TO JUSTIFY A LIFETIME OF WASTED HATE
: THE LEGION FIGHTS ONLY BECAUSE IT IS AMUSING AND PLEASURABLE TO DOMINATE WEAKER SOULS

'Unadulterated fantasy.' Talos laughed, though he'd never felt less like laughing. He considered shooting the chained skeleton down from its ungainly crucifixion, though it was doubtful whether the act of spite would achieve anything. 'We rebelled because we had to rebel. The Imperium's pacifism was destined to fail. Order can only be maintained through keeping its souls fearful of retribution. Control, through fear. *Peace* through fear. We were the weapon mankind needed. We still are.'

: THE LEGION NEVER FOUGHT FOR THOSE IDEALS
: YOUR DELUSION WAS NEVER EVEN POPULAR AMONG OUR RANKS
: BUT IT FADED WHEN THE TRUTH CAME
: YOU CLING TO YOUR ILLUSIONS NOW BECAUSE HATE IS ALL YOU HAVE LEFT

'Hate is all I need.' He drew the bolter now, aiming both barrels up at the corpse's shattered ribcage. 'My hatred runs pure. We *deserve* vengeance against the empire that abandoned us. We were *right* to punish those worlds for their sins, and threaten others with destruction if they ever broke our laws. Control. Through. Fear. The systems we pacified…'

: THE SYSTEMS WE PACIFIED WERE BARELY HUMAN ANYMORE
: WE MADE THE POPULATIONS INTO COWERING ANIMALS DISPOSSESSED OF FREE WILL
: LIVING IN TERROR OF BREAKING THE LAW
: LIKE THE WEEPING HERDS OF HUMANS LIVING IN THE BOWELS OF OUR WARSHIPS NOW

'I stand by what I did.' The prophet was aware of his own maddening stance – he couldn't aim for much longer without making good on his threat to fire, but nor did he wish to strike in useless anger. 'I stand by what we all did.'

: MANY OF OUR BROTHERS NEVER CARED FOR ANY OF THOSE IDEALS
: THAT IS NO SECRET
: IT IS WHY CURZE DESTROYED NOSTRAMO
: TO STEM THE FLOW OF POISON INTO THE EIGHTH LEGION
: AND IT WAS WHY WE WERE PUNISHED BY THE IMPERIUM

'The lesson of the Legion.' Talos lowered the weapon. 'The primarch said those words many times.'

: WE BECAME THE VERY THING WE WARNED WHOLE WORLDS ABOUT
: WE WERE THE KILLERS AND THE MURDERERS WE TOLD THEM NEVER TO BE
: FREE TO SLAY AT WILL AND FREE FROM RETRIBUTION

There was a long pause. Talos felt the ship give a shudder, in sympathy to some external torment.

: THE BLOOD RAN COLD IN THAT AGE BEFORE THE GALAXY BURNED
: AND IT RAN IN RIVERS FROM THE VEINS OF THE GUILTY AND INNOCENT ALIKE
: BECAUSE WE WERE STRONG AND THEY WERE WEAK

'He hated us, I know that for certain. Curze loved us and hated us in equal measure.' Talos returned to his throne, his voice softened by contemplation. Ideas danced and died behind his black eyes, hidden beneath the monochrome red of his helm's eye lenses.

Much of it was true, and no mystery to the prophet. Curze had annihilated their home world in a melancholic decree, seeking to end the recruitment of rapists and murderers, but it was far too late by then. Much of the Legion was already given over to the very criminal scum he sought to purge from humanity. This was no secret. No revelation. Merely shameful truth.

But they'd still been right to fight. Pacification through overwhelming force, and ruling forever after by fear. It had worked, for a time. The resulting peace across dozens of systems had been a beautiful thing to behold. A population only dared rise in rebellion when the boot was lifted from their throat. In such cases, it was the fault of the oppressor for showing weakness, not the oppressed for rising up. To resist was human nature. The species couldn't be hated for it.

'Our way was not the way of the Imperium,' Talos quoted the ancient adage, 'but we were right. If the Legion had stayed pure…'

: BUT IT DID NOT

: THE LEGION WAS TAINTED BY SIN THE MOMENT THE FIRST NOSTRAMAN-BORN WARRIOR SWORE HIS OATH OF SERVICE

: AND WE DESERVED THE HATE OF OUR PRIMARCH

: FOR WE WERE NOT THE WARRIORS HE WISHED US TO BE

Another pause. Another tremor quivered through the ship's bones.

'What's happening?'

: REALITY IS SLIPPING THROUGH NOW

: THE ECHO OF DAMNATION ARRIVES AT ITS DESTINATION

: BUT YOU SHOULD NEVER HAVE COME BACK TO THE EASTERN FRINGE

Talos looked up again. The corpse hadn't moved. 'You

said that before. I still don't recall ordering such a thing.'
: YOU ORDERED IT IN SEARCH OF A PURE WAR TO ELEVATE THE WARBAND
: AND SEEK ANSWERS TO THE DOUBTS THAT PLAGUE YOU
: BY WALKING UPON TSAGUALSA ONCE MORE
: NOTHING I SAY NOW IS A REVELATION
: I SPEAK ONLY THE SAME TRUTHS YOU ARE TOO PROUD TO SPEAK ALOUD
: YOU HAVE BEEN HOLLOW FOR A LONG TIME BROTHER

'Why am I seeing this?' He gestured around the chamber, at the body, at himself. 'What... what is all this? A vision? A dream? A spell? The tricks of my own mind, or something from the outside crawling into my thoughts?'

: ALL OF THOSE AND NONE OF THEM
: PERHAPS THIS IS MERELY A MANIFESTATION OF YOUR DOUBTS AND FEARS
: IN THE WAKING WORLD YOU HAVE BEEN UNCONSCIOUS FOR FIFTY-FIVE NIGHTS
: YOU ARE CLOSE TO RISING

He was on his feet again, as the ship began to shake in prophetic earnest. He heard the hull groaning with the sincerity of a gut-shot soldier. Cracks began to lace their way across the occulus, sprinkling glass to the decking. 'Fifty-five nights? That cannot be. How did this happen?'

: YOU KNOW WHY
: YOU HAVE ALWAYS KNOWN
: SOME HUMAN CHILDREN ARE NOT MEANT TO CARRY GENE-SEED
: IT BREAKS THEM APART AT THE GENETIC LEVEL
: SOME DIE FAST
: SOME DIE SLOW
: BUT AFTER THREE CENTURIES OF BIOLOGICAL FLUX YOUR GENETIC INCOMPATIBILITIES ARE FINALLY CATCHING UP TO YOU

'Lies.' Talos watched the ship coming apart around him. 'Lies and madness are all you ever uttered in life, Ruven. The same holds true in death.'

: VARIEL KNOWS THE TRUTH
: CENTURIES OF INJURY
: CENTURIES OF ENDURANCE AND PAIN
: CENTURIES OF THE VISIONS BORN OF POISONOUS PRIMARCH BLOOD
: YOUR BODY CAN TAKE NO MORE PUNISHMENT
: ENJOY WHAT TIME REMAINS TO YOU BROTHER
: DUTY AWAITS IN THE WAKING WORLD AND YOU WILL REMEMBER PRECIOUS LITTLE OF OUR TALK
: RISE TALOS
: RISE AND SEE FOR YOURSELF

II
AWAKENING

Light, muted and bleached by the red of his visor display, filtered into his eyes.

The first thing he saw was the last thing he expected. His brothers. His crew. The strategium, with its two hundred souls engaged in their duties.

'I...' He tried to speak, but his voice was a dehydrated vox-rasp. Talos slumped in his throne, though a chain collar around his throat prevented him from falling too far forward. Voices babbled all around him, along with the growl of armour joints moving closer.

'I am not in my meditation chamber,' he said. He'd never woken from a vision anywhere else, let alone to rise and find himself on the warship's bridge. The prophet was struck by the image of his surroundings, wondering if he'd sat here in his armour the entire time, unconscious and screaming his delusional chants across the vox-network.

Chains rattled around his throat, wrists and ankles as he sought to rise. His brothers had bound him to the throne.

They had much to answer for.

Whispers of 'He returns' and 'He awakens' wove their way through the mortal crew. From his seat of honour on a raised dais at the heart of the bridge, Talos could see them pausing in their assigned duties, face after face turning to regard him. Their eyes were bright with surprise and reverence in equal measure. 'The prophet awakens,' kept leaving their pale lips.

This, he decided with a crawling feeling of spinal discomfort, was what being worshipped must feel like.

His brothers clustered around the throne, each of their faces masked behind their helms: Uzas, with his painted bloody handprint across the faceplate; Xarl, his helm crested by sweeping bat wings; Cyrion's eyes painted with streaking lightning bolt tears; Mercutian's helm topped by brutal, curving horns ringed with bronze.

Variel knelt before Talos, the Apothecary's bionic leg grinding and seizing, making the movement awkward. He alone wore no helm, his cold eyes fixed upon the prophet's own.

'A timely return,' he said. His curiously soft voice held no shade of amusement.

'We have arrived, Talos,' Cyrion qualified. There was a smile in *his* voice, at least.

'Fifty-five nights,' said Mercutian. 'We have never witnessed such a thing. What did you dream?'

'I remember almost none of it.' Talos looked past them all, at the world turning slowly within the elliptical frame of the occulus screen. 'I remember little of anything. Where are we?'

Variel turned his pale gaze upon the others. It was enough to get them to move back a little, no longer crowding the reawakened prophet. As he spoke, the Apothecary consulted his bulky narthecium gauntlet. Talos could hear the auspex scanner crackling with static and chiming with results.

'I administered supplemental narcotics and fluids to keep you in adequate health without activating your sus-an membrane these past two months. You are, however, going to be extremely weak for some days to come. The muscle wastage is minor, but significant enough for you to notice it.'

Talos tensed against the chains again, as if to make a point.

'Ah, yes,' said Variel. 'Of course.' He keyed in a code on his vambrace, deploying a circular cutting saw from his narthecium. The kiss of the saw along the chains was a high-pitched, irritating whine. One by one, the lengths of metallic binding fell free.

'Why was I restrained?'

'To prevent injury to yourself and others,' explained Variel.

'No.' Talos focused on his retinal display, activating a secure vox-link to his closest brothers. 'Why was I restrained here, on the bridge?'

The members of First Claw shared glances, their helms turning to face each other in some unknowable emotion.

'We took you to your chambers when you first succumbed,' said Cyrion. 'But...'

'But?'

'You broke out of the cell. You killed both of the brothers standing guard outside the door, and we lost you in the lower decks for almost a week.'

Talos tried to rise. Variel fixed him with the same glare he'd turned on the rest of First Claw, but the prophet ignored it. The Apothecary had been right, though. He felt as weak as a human. His muscles burned with cramps as blood trickled back into them.

'I do not understand,' Talos said at last.

'Neither did we,' replied Cyrion. 'You'd never acted in such a way while afflicted.'

Xarl took up the explanation. 'Guess who found you?'

The prophet shook his head, not knowing where to begin to make assumptions. 'Tell me.'

Uzas inclined his head. 'It was I.'

That would be a story in itself, Talos reckoned. He looked back at Cyrion. 'And then?'

'After several days, the crew and the other Claws began to grow uncomfortable. Morale, such as it is among we happy and loyal dregs, was suffering. Talk circulated that you'd died or were diseased. We brought you here to show the crew you were still among us, one way or the other.'

Talos snorted. 'Did it work?'

'See for yourself.' Cyrion gestured to the rapt, staring humans around the command deck. All eyes were upon him.

Talos swallowed the taste of something acrid. 'You made me into an icon. That treads close to heathenism.'

First Claw shared a low chuckle. Only Talos was unamused.

'Fifty-five days of silence,' Cyrion said, 'and all you have for us is displeasure?'

'Silence?' The prophet turned to look at each of them in turn. 'I never cried out? I never spoke my prophecies aloud?'

'Not this time,' Mercutian shook his head. 'Silence, from the moment you collapsed.'

'I do not even remember collapsing.' Talos moved past them, leaning on the rail ringing the central dais. He watched the grey world hanging in the void, surrounded by a dense asteroid field. 'Where are we?'

First Claw came to his side, forming up in a line of snarling joints and impassive, skullish facemasks.

'You don't recall your orders to us?' Xarl asked.

Talos tried not to let his impatience show. 'Just tell me where we are. That is a familiar sight, yet I struggle to believe we truly stand before it.'

'It is, and we do. We're on the Eastern Fringe,' said Xarl. 'Out of the Astronomican's light, and in orbit around the world you repeatedly demanded we travel to.'

Talos stared at it as it turned with indescribable slowness. He knew what world it was, even though he could remember nothing of these events his brothers insisted had happened. It took a great deal more effort than he'd expected to resist saying the words 'It cannot be'. Most unbelievable of all were the grey stains of cities scabbing over the dusty continents.

'It has changed,' he said. 'I don't understand how that can be true. The Imperium would never build here, yet I see cities. I see the stains of human civilisation scarring what should be worthless land.'

Cyrion nodded. 'We were just as surprised as you, brother.'

Talos let his gaze sweep across the rest of the bridge. 'To your stations, all of you.' The humans complied with salutes and murmurs of 'Yes, lord'.

It was Mercutian who broke the silence that followed. 'We are here, Talos. What should we do now?'

The prophet stared at a world that should have been long dead, purged of life ten thousand years before and abandoned by all who called it home. The Imperium of Man would never re-seed a cursed world, especially one beyond the holy rim of the Emperor's beacon of light. Reaching this world under standard propulsion would take months from even the closest border planet.

'Ready all Claws for planetfall.'

Cyrion cleared his throat. Talos turned at the surprisingly human gesture. 'You have missed much, brother. There is something that requires your attention before we become involved planetside. Something pertaining to Septimus and Octavia. We were unsure how to deal with it in your absence.'

'I am listening,' the prophet said. He wouldn't admit how his blood ran cold at the mention of those names.

'Go to her. See for yourself.'

See for yourself. The words echoed in his mind, clinging with an unnerving tenacity, feeling somewhere between prophecy and memory.

'Are you coming?' he asked his brothers.

Mercutian looked away. Xarl grunted a laugh.

'No,' Cyrion said. 'You should do this alone.'

HE REACHED HER chamber, appalled at the weakness in his own limbs. Fifty-five nights, almost two full months without the daily training rites, hadn't been kind to him. Octavia's servants lingered in the shadows around her door, hunchbacked royalty in the sunless alcoves.

'Lord,' they hissed through slits in their faces that were once lips. Their bloodstained bandages rustled as they shifted and lowered their weapons.

'Move aside,' Talos ordered them. They fled, as roaches flee a sudden light.

One of them stood its ground. For a moment, he thought it was Hound, Octavia's favoured attendant, but it was too slender. And Hound was months dead, slain in the ship's capture, scarcely twenty metres from this very spot.

'The mistress is weary,' the figure said. Its voice was somehow clenched, as though it strained through closed teeth. It was also a soft voice, too light to be male. She raised a bandaged hand, as if she could possibly bar the warrior's passage with a demand, let alone with her physical presence. The woman's cloth-wrapped face revealed nothing of her appearance, but her stature suggested she was less devolved – at least physically – than most of the others. Bulky glare-goggles covered her eyes, their black oval lenses amusingly insectile, giving the impression of mutation where none was immediately apparent. A thin red beam projected from the goggles' left edge, following the attendant's gaze. She'd welded a red dot laser sight to her facewear – for what reason, Talos couldn't begin to guess.

'Then she and I have much in common,' the prophet stated. 'Move.'

'She has no wish to be disturbed,' the strained voice insisted, growing even less friendly. The other attendants were beginning to return now.

'Your loyal defiance does your mistress credit, but we are now finished with this tedium.' Talos tilted his head down at the female. He had no wish to pointlessly slay her. 'Do you know who I am?'

'You are someone seeking to enter against my mistress's wishes.'

'That is true. It is also true that I am master of this vessel, and your mistress is my slave.'

The other attendants skulked back into the shadows, whispering the prophet's name. *Talos, Talos, Talos*... like the hissing of rock vipers.

'She is unwell,' the bandaged female said. Fear crept into her voice now.

'What is your name?' Talos asked her.

'Vularai,' she replied. The warrior smiled, barely, behind his faceplate. *Vularai* was the Nostraman word for *liar*.

'Amusing. I like you. Now move, before I begin to like you less.'

The attendant moved back, and Talos caught the glint of metal beneath the woman's ragged clothing.

'Is that a gladius?'

The figure froze. 'Lord?'

'Are you carrying a Legion gladius?'

She drew the blade at her hip. For a Night Lord, the traditional gladius was a short stabbing weapon the length of a warrior's forearm. In human hands, it became a sleek longsword. The swirling Nostraman runes etched into the dark iron were unmistakable.

'That,' said Talos, 'is a Legion weapon.'

'It was a gift, lord.'

'From whom?'

'From Lord Cyrion of First Claw. He said I needed a weapon.'

'Can you use it with any skill?'

The bandaged woman shrugged and said nothing.

'And if I'd merely shoved you aside and entered, Vularai? What would you have done then?'

He could hear the smile in her strained voice. 'I'd have cut out your heart, my lord.'

THE CHAMBER OF navigation offered a little more illumination than the rest of the ship's rooms and hallways, lit by the grainy, unhealthy half-light of almost thirty monitors linked to external pict-feeds. They cast their greyish glare across the rest of the wide chamber, bleaching the surface of the circular pool in the centre. The meaty reek of amniotic fluid was thick in the air.

She wasn't in the water. In the months since they'd taken the *Echo of Damnation*, even after half the ship had been scoured and purged clean with flame weapons, Octavia had vowed to only use the amniotic pool for warp flight, when she required her deepest connection to the ship's machine-spirit. Talos, having seen Ezmarellda, the chamber's previous prisoner, could understand all too well why the Navigator refused to spend too long in the nutrient-rich water.

Mixed in with the chemical stink of the thin ooze were the usual smells of Octavia's personal space: the tang of human sweat; the musty edge of her books and parchment scrolls; and the faint – not unpleasant – spice of the natural oil in her hair, even when recently washed.

And something else. Something close to the scent of a woman's monthly blood cycle, with the same rich piquancy. Close, but not quite.

Talos walked around the edge of the pool, approaching the throne facing the bank of monitors. Each screen showed a variant view of the ship's outer hull, and the cold void beyond. A few showed the grey face of the world they orbited, and its contrasting white rock moon.

'Octavia.'

She opened her eyes, looking up at him with the moment's bleariness that follows sleep but precedes comprehension. Her dark hair was bound in its usual ponytail, hanging from the back of the silk bandana.

'You're awake,' she said.

'As are you.'

'Yes,' she admitted, 'though I'd rather not be.' Her lips curved into a half-smile. 'What did you dream?'

'I can recall little of it.' The warrior gestured to the world on the screens before her. 'Do you know the name of this world?'

She nodded. 'Septimus told me. I don't know why you'd want to return here.'

Talos shook his head. 'Neither do I. My memory is in fragments from even before I succumbed to the vision.' He released his breath as a slow sigh. 'Home. Our second home, at least. After Nostramo, there was Tsagualsa, the carrion world.'

'It's been colonised. A small population, so it's a recent colonisation.'

'I know,' he said.

'So what will you do?'

'I don't know.'

Octavia shifted in her throne, still wrapped in her thin cloth blanket. 'This chamber is always cold.' She looked up at him, waiting for him to speak. When he said nothing, she filled the silence herself. 'It was difficult to sail here. The Astronomican doesn't shine this far from Terra, and the tides were blacker than black.'

'May I ask what it was like?'

The Navigator toyed with a stray lock of hair as she spoke. 'The warp is dark here. Utterly dark. The colours are all black. Can you imagine a thousand shades of black, each darker than the last?'

He shook his head. 'You are asking me to envisage a concept alien to the material universe.'

'It's cold,' she said, breaking eye contact. 'How can a colour be cold? In the blackness, I could feel the usual disgusting presences: the shrieking of souls against the hull, and the distant cancers, swimming alone in the deep.'

'Cancers?'

'It is the only way I can describe them. Great, nameless entities of poison and pain. Malignant intelligences.'

Talos nodded. 'The souls of false gods, perhaps.'

'Are they false if they're real?'

'I do not know,' he confessed.

She shivered. 'Where we've sailed before, even away from the Astronomican... those places were still dimly lit by the Emperor's beacon, no matter how far from it we sailed. You could see the shadows and shapes gliding through the tides. Daemons without form, swimming through liquid torment. Here, I can see nothing. It wasn't about finding my way through the storm, the way I've been trained. This was a matter of tumbling forward into blindness, seeking the calmest paths, where the shrieking winds were lessened, even if only for a moment.'

For a moment, he was struck by the similarity between her experiences and the sensation of falling into his own visions.

'We are here,' he said. 'You did well.'

'I felt something else, though. The faintest thing. These presences, warmer than the warp around them. Like eyes, watching me as I brought the ship closer.'

'Should we be concerned?'

Octavia shrugged. 'I don't know. It was one aspect of madness amongst a thousand others.'

'We've arrived. That is what matters.' Another silence threatened between them. This time, Talos broke it. 'We had a fortress here, long ago. A castle of black stone and twisting spires. The primarch dreamed of it one night, and set hundreds of thousands of slaves to making it. It took almost twenty years.'

He paused, and Octavia watched the passionless skull of his facemask, waiting for him to continue. Talos exhaled in a vox-growl.

'The inner sanctum was called the Screaming Gallery. Have any of the others ever spoken of this before?'

She shook her head. 'No, never.'

'The Screaming Gallery was a metaphor, of a kind. A god's torment, expressed in blood and pain. The primarch wanted to reshape the external world to match the sin within his mind. The walls were flesh – humans moulded and crafted into the architecture, formed as much from sorcery as from ingenuity. The floors were carpeted in living faces, preserved by feeder-servitors.'

He shook his head, the memory too strong to ever fade. 'The screaming, Octavia. You have never heard such a sound. They never stopped screaming. The people in the walls, crying and reaching out. The faces on the floor, weeping and shrieking.'

She forced a smile she didn't feel. 'That sounds like the warp.'

He glanced at her, and grunted acknowledgement. 'Forgive me. You know exactly what it sounds like.'

She nodded, but didn't say anything else.

'The foulest thing was the way you'd become immune to the wailing chorus. Those of us who attended the primarch in his last decades of madness spent much of our time in the Screaming Gallery. The sound of all that pain became tolerable. Soon after, you found yourself enjoying it. It was easier to think when surrounded by sin. The torment first became meaningless, but afterwards, it became music.'

The prophet fell silent for a moment. 'That was what he wanted, of course. He wanted us to understand the Legion's lesson, as he believed it to be.'

Octavia shuffled again as Talos knelt by her throne. 'I see no lesson in mindless brutality,' she said.

He unlocked his collar seals with a breath of air pressure, and removed his helm. She was struck, once again, by the thought that he'd have been handsome but for the cold eyes and the corpse-white skin. He was a statue, a scarred demigod of clean marble, dead-eyed, beautiful in his sterility, yet unlovely to look upon.

'It was not mindless brutality,' he said. 'That was the lesson. The primarch knew that law and order – the twin foundations of civilisation – are only maintained through fear of punishment. Man is not a peaceful animal. It is a creature of war and strife. To force the beasts into civilisation, one must remind them that excruciation awaits those who harm the herd. For a time, we believed the Emperor wanted this of us. He wanted us to be the Angels of Death. And for a time, we were.'

She blinked for the first time in almost a minute. In their many long discussions and reflections, he'd never spoken of this in such detail. 'Go on,' she pushed.

'Some say he betrayed us. Once our use was complete, he turned against us. Others claim that we'd merely taken our self-appointed role too far, and had to be put down like animals ourselves, for slipping our leashes.' He saw a question in her eyes and waved it away. 'None of that is important. What matters is how it began, and how it ended.'

'How did it begin?'

'The Legion had taken immense casualties in the Great Crusade, in service to the Emperor. Most of these were Terran. They came from Terra, from the Emperor's wars across humanity's birth planet. But all of our reinforcements came from our home world, Nostramo. Decades had passed since the primarch last walked upon the world's surface, and his lessons of law had long since died. The population slid back into lawless anarchy, with no fear of punishment from a distant Imperium. Do you understand how we were poisoning ourselves? We were repopulating the Legion with rapists and murderers, with children who were the blackest sinners before they'd even tasted adulthood. The primarch's lessons meant nothing to them, meant nothing to most of the Eighth Legion at the end. They were slayers, raised to become demigods, with the galaxy as their prize to plunder. In wrathful desperation, the primarch burned our home world. He destroyed it, breaking it apart from orbit with the firepower of the entire Legion fleet.'

Talos breathed, low and slow. 'It took hours, Octavia. All the while, we remained aboard our ships, listening to vox-calls from the surface, sending their screams and pleas up to us in the heavens. We never answered. Not even once. We stayed in space and watched our own cities burn. At the very end, we watched the planet heaving, breaking apart beneath the fleet's rage. Only then did we turn away. Nostramo disintegrated into the void.

I have never seen anything like it again. I know, in my heart, I never will.'

A moment of foolishness almost made her reach a hand to touch his cheek. She knew better than to give in to that instinct. Still, the way he spoke, the look in his black eyes – he was a child, grown into a god's body without a man's comprehension of humanity. No wonder these creatures were so dangerous. Their stunted psyches worked on levels no human could quite comprehend: simplistic and passionate one moment, complex and inhuman the next.

'It didn't work,' he continued. 'The Legion was poisoned by then. You know that Xarl and I grew up together, murderers even as children. We joined the Legion late, when Nostramo's venom was already rich in the Legion's veins. And believe me when I say that where he and I grew up, among the street wars and the cheapness of human life, it was one of the more civilised regions of Nostramo's inner cities. Much of the planet was in the throes of devolution, lost to urban wastelands and scavenger armies. As the strongest candidates, they were usually the ones chosen for implantation and ascension to the Eighth. They were the ones to become legionaries.'

Talos finished with a smile that didn't reach his eyes. 'By then, it was too late. Primarch Curze was in the throes of degeneration himself. He hated himself, he hated his life, and he hated his Legion. All he craved was one last chance to be right, to show that he'd not wasted his entire existence. The rebellion against the Emperor – that war of myth that you call the Horus Heresy – was over. We'd turned against the Imperium that sought to punish us, and we'd lost. So we ran. We ran to Tsagualsa, a world outside the Imperium's borders, away from Terra's Beacon of Light that he claimed still stung his eyes.'

He gestured at the grey world. 'We ran here, and here is where it ended.'

Octavia's breath left her lips as mist. 'You fled a war you lost and constructed a castle of torture chambers. How noble of you, Talos. I still see no lesson in it.'

He nodded to that, conceding the point. 'You have to understand that by the end, the primarch was riddled through by madness. He cared nothing for the Long War, wanting nothing beyond bleeding the Imperium and vindicating his life's path. He knew he was going to die, Octavia. He wanted to be *right* when he died.'

'Septimus told me of this,' she said. 'But raiding the Imperium's edges for couple of centuries at the behest of a madman, and slaughtering entire worlds, is hardly a lesson of worthy ideals.'

Talos watched her with his soulless eyes unwavering. 'In that light, perhaps not. But humanity has to know fear, Navigator. Nothing else ensures compliance. By the very end, when the Screaming Gallery was the Legion's war room and council chamber alike, the primarch's degeneration had devoured him from within. He was rendered hollow by it. I still remember how regal he looked to us, how majestic our father was to our adoring eyes. But looking at him was like growing used to a disgusting smell. You could forget the foulness, just as you can ignore the scent, but when something reminds you of it, you perceive it with renewed strength. His soul had rotted away by the end, and on some nights you could see it in the flash of his dying eyes, or the bleak shine of his teeth. Some of my brothers asked if he were tainted by some outer power, but most of us no longer cared. What did it matter? The end result was the same.'

The lights chose that moment to flicker and fail. The warrior and the mutant remained in darkness for several heartbeats, illuminated only by the eye lenses of his armour and the grey glare from the screens.

'That's happening more and more lately,' she said. 'The *Covenant* hated me. The *Echo* seems to hate all of us.'

'An intriguing superstition,' he replied. The lights, dim

as they were, came back on. Talos still didn't continue.

'And the assassination?' she prompted.

'The assassination came soon after, when his mad clarity was at its height. I have never seen a creature so placidly delighted by the thought of its own destruction. In death, he would be vindicated. Those who break the law must be dealt with in the most violent, lethal way, as an example to all who would consider betrayal. So he set us butchering across the galaxy, breaking every law against reason and rhyme, knowing the Emperor would prove the point all too well. The assassin came to slay Curze, the great Breaker of Imperial Law, and she did just that. I saw him die, vindicated, pleased for perhaps the first time in centuries.'

'That's grotesque,' she said. Her heart quickened at the thought he would take offence, but her fear was unfounded.

'Maybe so,' he nodded again. 'The universe has never seen a living being that loathed being alive as much as my father. His life was broken in seeking to prove how humanity could be controlled, and his death was a sacrifice to prove that the species was ultimately wretched.'

Talos withdrew a hololithic orb from his belt pouch, and thumbed the activation rune. A life-sized image of flickering blue light manifested before them both. A figure rose from an unseen throne, its hunched, feral posture still not entirely stealing the beauty of its muscled physique, or the savage nobility in its movements. The distortion robbed the image of clarity, but the figure's face – a wraith's visage of black eyes, gaunt cheekbones and filed fangs – was set in a vicious grin of sincere amusement.

The image died as Talos deactivated the orb. For a long time, neither of them said another word.

'Was there no one to lead you after his death?'

'The Legion broke down into companies and warbands, following individual lords. The primarch's presence was what inspired unity within us. Without him, the raiding parties sailed farther from Tsagualsa, staying away for longer periods. As the years passed, many stopped returning at all. Many captains and lords claimed they were the Night Haunter's heir, but each claim was refuted by the others. No one soul can bind a Traitor Legion together now. It is simply the way of things. As much as I loathe him, Abaddon's success is what sets him apart – and above – the rest of us. His is the name whispered across the Imperium. Abaddon. The Despoiler. The Chosen. *Abaddon*. Not Horus.'

Octavia shivered. She knew that name, she'd heard it whispered of in the halls of Terran power. Abaddon. The Great Enemy. The Death of the Imperium. Prophecies of his triumph in the final century of mankind were rampant among the psychically-gifted in thrall to the Emperor's throne.

'There was only one,' Talos said, 'who could have held the title without his brothers betraying him. At least, there was only one who would have survived his brothers' betrayals, but even he would have struggled to hold the Legion together. Too many ideologies. Too many conflicting desires and drives.'

'What was his name?'

'Sevatar,' the prophet said quietly. 'We called him the Prince of Crows. He was killed in the Heresy, long before our father.'

She hesitated before speaking. 'Mercutian has spoken of him.'

'Mercutian comes to speak with you?'

The Navigator grinned. Her teeth were whiter than any of the crew's, from so few years spent in the filth of slavery. 'You are not the only one with tales to tell, you know.'

'What does he speak of?'

'He's *your* brother. And one of the ones you don't spend your time trying to kill. You should be able to guess what he speaks of.'

The prophet's black eyes glinted with some repressed

emotion. She couldn't tell if it was amusement or annoyance.

'I still do not know Mercutian well.'

'He speaks of the Heresy, mostly. He tells me stories about brothers that died in the Siege of the Emperor's Palace, or the Thramas Crusade against the Angels, and the centuries since. He likes to write about them, recording their deeds and deaths. Did you know that?'

Talos shook his head. He'd had no idea.

'What did he say about the Prince of Crows?' he asked.

'That Sevatar wasn't killed.'

The words brought the ghost of a smile to the prophet's lips. 'That is an entertaining fiction. Every Legion has its conspiracies and myths. The Eaters of Worlds claim that one of their captains is the chosen of a bloodthirsty god.'

Octavia didn't smile. 'When will you make planetfall?'

'My brothers wished for me to see you first.'

She raised an eyebrow, smiling as she clutched her blanket tighter. 'To give me a history lesson?'

'No. I do not know what they wished. They mentioned some problem, some flaw.'

'I don't know what they could mean. I'm tired, but the flight here was hellish. I think I earned a little sleep.'

'They said it concerned Septimus, as well.'

She shrugged again. 'I still can't guess. He hasn't been lax in his duties, and neither have I.'

Talos thought for a moment. 'Have you seen him often, recently?'

She looked away. Octavia might have been skilled at many things, but she was a poor deceiver. 'I do not see him much, these nights. When are you making planetfall?'

'Soon.'

'I've been thinking about what comes next.'

He regarded her with a curious expression; one she'd never seen before that wasn't quite puzzlement, nor was it exactly interest or suspicion. It seemed to be all three.

'What do you mean?' he asked.

'I thought we would make a run for the Eye of Terror.'

He chuckled. 'Do not call it that. Only mortal starsailors, frightened of their own shadows, call it that. We simply call it the Eye, or the Wound, or... home. Are you so keen to drift into those polluted tides? Many Navigators lose their sanity, you know. It is one of the reasons so many of our vessels rely on sorcerers as guides in the Sea of Souls.'

'It is the last place in the galaxy I would like to go.' Octavia narrowed her eyes as she smiled. 'You're avoiding the question. Just like every other time I ask it.'

'We cannot return to the Eye,' Talos replied. 'I am not avoiding the question. You know why I am reluctant to sail there.'

She did know. At least, she could make a decent guess. 'The eldar dreams,' she said, not quite a question.

'Yes. The eldar dreams. Worse than before, now. I will not return there just to die.'

Octavia was quiet again for a time. 'I'm glad you're awake again.'

Talos didn't answer her. He didn't understand why he'd been sent here. For several seconds, he merely glanced around the chamber, listening to the ripple of the water, the thrumming pulse of the hull's rumble, and...

...and the two heartbeats.

One was Octavia's, a steady *thump, thump, thump* of wet thunder. The other was a muffled stutter, almost quick enough to be a buzz. Both came from within her body.

'I am a fool,' he said, rising to his feet in a snarl of armour joints.

'Talos?'

He drew in a breath, seeking to quell a surge of anger. His fingers were trembling, the micro-servos in his knuckles whirred as his hands clenched into fists. Had he not been so weary and his senses so dulled, he'd have heard the two heartbeats immediately.

'Talos?' she asked again. 'Talos?'

He walked from her chamber without a word.

III

HOMECOMING

As soon as the door opened, Septimus realised he was probably going to die.

He had half a second to draw breath before the hand was at his throat, and another half-second to croak out a denial. The gauntlet closed around his neck with enough strength to choke off any breath, let alone speech, and he struggled as he was lifted off the decking.

'I warned you,' the intruder said. Septimus tried to swallow, and gagged instead. In response, the Night Lord hurled him across the chamber. He hit hard, crashing against the wall and sinking to the floor in a heap of slack, shivering limbs. Blood marked the black iron where his head had struck.

'I warned you,' the warrior said again, filling the room with the sound of armour joints and bootsteps. 'Was I somehow not clear enough? Was my warning something to be ignored merely because I was unconscious for fifty-five nights?'

He hauled Septimus up by the hair, and threw him against the opposite wall. The slave went down again, this time without a sound. The warrior kept advancing, kept speaking, his voice twisted into machine-like impassivity by his helm's vocaliser grille. 'Did I perhaps fail to express my meaning in absolute terms? Is that it? Is that where this savage breakdown in communication has occurred?'

Septimus struggled to rise. For the first time in his life, he drew a weapon on his master. At least, he tried to. With a snort that might or might not have been a laugh, the towering warrior thudded a boot into his slave's side – not a battlefield kick, but rather the scuffing of refuse from underfoot. Still, the modest, messy chamber echoed with the twig-snaps of breaking ribs. Septimus swore through clenched teeth, reaching for the pistol he'd dropped.

'You son of a...' he began, but his master cut him off.

'Let us not compound disobedience with disrespect.' The Night Lord took two steps forward. The first crushed the laspistol into pieces, grinding them along the deck in a mangled spray of abused metal components. The second rested on Septimus's back, slamming him face-first onto the decking and knocking the wind from his lungs.

'Give me one reason not to kill you,' Talos snarled. 'And make it *incredibly* good.'

Breath sawed in and out of the human's lungs, through the heavy, jagged obstructions of broken ribs. He could taste blood at the back of his throat. Through all his years of captivity, all the years they'd forced him to serve and aid them in their heretical war, Septimus had never once begged for mercy.

He wasn't about to start now.

'Tshiva keln,' he grunted through the pain. Pinkish spit painted his lips as he fought to breathe.

It was a night for first occurrences. Septimus had never before drawn a pistol on his master, and Talos had never before had one of his slaves tell him to 'eat shit'.

The prophet hesitated. He felt his malign concentration suddenly broken by a short burst of bemused laughter. It echoed hollowly around the small chamber.

'Ask yourself this, Septimus: does it seem wise to annoy me even further?' He dragged the bleeding human up by the back of the neck, and threw him a third time against the sloping iron wall. When Septimus went down this time he didn't curse, or resist, or do much of anything at all.

'That's better.' Talos stalked closer, and knelt by his barely breathing slave. Septimus's facial augmetics were damaged, the eye lens split by an ugly crack. Spasms quivered through him, and it was clear from the angle of his left arm that it'd been wrenched from its shoulder socket. Blood bubbled from the man's swollen lips, but no words came forth. That last fact was probably for the best.

'I warned you.'

Septimus turned his head slowly, facing the voice. He either couldn't say anything, or intelligently chose not to. His master's boot pressed down on his back, a veritable weight of absolute threat. It would take no effort at all to stamp down and reduce the human's torso to a pulp of disordered meat and bone.

'She is the most precious thing on this ship. We cannot sail the Mad Sea with her health compromised. *I warned you*. You are fortunate I do not skin you and hang your bones from New Blackmarket's ceiling.'

Talos lifted his boot from the slave's back. Septimus hissed in a slow breath, rolling onto his side.

'Master…'

'Spare me any false apologies.' Talos shook his head, the skull-painted faceplate passionless in its red-lens gaze. 'I have broken between fourteen and seventeen of your bones, and your cranial bionics need maintenance. The focusing retinal lens also has a longitudinal crack. Consider that punishment enough.' He hesitated, looking down at the prone human on the deck. 'You are also fortunate I do not order surgery to eunuch you. On my soul, I swear these words are true, Septimus: if you touch her again, the merest brush of skin against skin, I will let Variel flay you. Then, while you are still alive as a skinless, weeping husk, I will pull you apart with my bare hands, and let you watch your own limbs being fed to the Bleeding Eyes.'

Talos didn't bother to draw weapons to heighten the threat. He merely stared down. 'I own you, Septimus. I have afforded you many freedoms in the past because of your usefulness, but I can always train other slaves. You are only human. Defy me again, and you will live just long enough to beg for death.'

With those words, he left in a thrum of whirring armour joints. In the sudden silence, Septimus dragged in a wracking breath and began to crawl across the deck of his chamber. Only one thing would have roused his master's ire like that. The very thing he and Octavia had feared had evidently come to pass, and the Night Lords had sensed the changes in her biology. The revelation wasn't quite drowned in the sea of pain from the beating he'd received.

Septimus spat out two of his back teeth, and the man who would soon be a father promptly lost consciousness.

TALOS GATHERED THE Claws in the war room around the long hololithic council table. Eighty-one warriors in total, each standing in midnight clad. Many were bloodied, or yet bore armour scars from the purgation duties still taking place in the bowels of the *Echo of Damnation*. Stealing the ship back from the Red Corsairs had only been the first step. Cleansing a warship of this size would take years, with flamer teams incinerating the worst touches of Chaos taint – where the hull was corroded with foulness, or worse, where the metal had mutated into living tissue.

The *Echo of Damnation*, much like the *Covenant of Blood* before it, was essentially a city in space, carrying a crew of over fifty thousand souls. She was, in all ways, a grander beast and a greater beauty than the Standard Template Construct cruisers and barges of the Adeptus Astartes that patrolled the heavens of the modern Imperium. The *Echo* had first tasted the void in the Great Crusade ten thousand years before, when the warriors of the Legiones Astartes claimed the finest vessels for themselves, and sailed their warships at the vanguard of expansionist fleets. A strike cruiser of yesteryear wasn't always equal to its Imperial counterpart, and the *Echo* showed how they often eclipsed their newer cousins in size and firepower.

Fifty thousand souls. Talos had never grown used to the number, even as they toiled for decades below his boots. His life was among the ever-diminishing elite, and their most favoured slaves.

On the rare occasions he descended into the ship's dank reaches, it was for the duty of purging any insidious taint that threatened the ship's optimal function, or for the more plebeian desire for murder. Most of the slave-caste workers dwelled in the deepest reaches and lowest bowel-decks of the immense warship, toiling their lives away in the darkness, working as engine crews and the other menial tasks suitable for human cattle. Hunting for skulls and screams among the mortal chattel was merely one of the traditional paths of training. It was undeniably the most pleasurable.

Talos regarded his brothers, the eighty-one warriors pulled together by fate into a fragile alliance, drawn from the remnants of the Night Lords' Tenth and Eleventh Companies. However he'd intended to begin the war council was discarded once he saw them all gathered. One thing was abundantly clear from their ragged ranks, with some squads reduced to two or three surviving members.

'We must restructure the claws,' he said to them.

The warriors shared glances. Neck joints hummed as they turned to one another.

'The infighting ends here, brothers. First Claw will remain six-strong. The other claws will reform as close to full strength as they are able.'

Xeverine, a warrior never without his ornate chainglaive, raised his voice to speak. 'And who leads these new claws, Soul Hunter?'

'Honour duels,' answered Faroven, wearing a similar

ceremonial helm to Xarl. The winged crest dipped as he nodded. 'We should commit to honour duels. The victors lead the seven new Claws.'

'Honour duels are for the weak and fearful,' said one of the scarred veterans nearby. 'Murder duels should settle an issue of leadership.'

'We do not have the numbers to bleed away in murder duels,' replied Carahd, leader of Faroven's claw.

Arguments broke out among the gathered squads, each seeking to shout the others down.

'No one is reaching for a weapon yet,' Xarl said quietly, 'but give it time, and we'll be wading through a bloodbath.'

Talos nodded. This had gone on long enough.

'Brothers,' he said. He kept his voice coloured by nothing but patience. Sure enough, one by one they fell silent. Eighty helms regarded him, variously painted with skulls, Nostraman runes, crested with high wings, or darkened by battle damage. To First Claw's left, the five remaining Bleeding Eyes vox-buzzed and hissed amongst themselves, but Lucoryphus favoured the prophet with his full attention. The Raptor lord was even standing up, his foot-claws unsuited to the posture, watching Talos with his sloped daemon-mask.

'Brothers,' Talos said again. 'We have eleven squad leaders, with enough warriors to make seven full claws. All who wish an honour duel to claim leadership are free to do so.'

'And murder duels?' asked Ulris.

'Murder duels will be fought against Xarl. Anyone who wishes to kill a brother for the honour of leading a claw is free to challenge him. I will grant a full claw to anyone that slays him.'

Grumbling simmered between several of the claws.

'Yes,' said Talos, 'that is what I thought you would say. Now enough of this, we have gathered for a reason.'

'Why did you bring us back to Tsagualsa?' one of the warriors called out.

'Because I am such a sentimental soul.' Bitter, mirthless laughter broke out across the chamber in answer. 'For those of you that have not heard, the planetary sweeps have detected cities capable of housing a population of over twenty-five million, principally spread across six major cities.'

Talos gestured to a tech-adept, who stepped forward to the table. Deltrian, his skeletal form robed as always, deployed a plethora of micro-tools through the tips of his fingers. One of them, a neural interface trident-pin, clicked within the table console's manual socket. A sizeable hololithic image of the grey world appeared in the air above the table, fraught with eye-watering flickers.

'I am operating under the primary hypothesis that the world's past requires no explanation to the legionaries of the Eighth.'

'Get on with it,' muttered one of the Night Lords.

Such disrespect. It galled Deltrian to think of the ancient bonds of allegiance between the Martian Mechanicum and the Legiones Astartes, now degraded to this degree. All the oaths that had been sworn, and all the rituals of respect – reduced to ashes.

'Honoured adept,' said Talos. 'Please continue.'

Deltrian hesitated, fixing the prophet with his dilating eye lenses. Without realising he still possessed such a curiously human habit, Deltrian reached up to adjust his hood, and sank his metallic features deeper into shadow.

'I will vocalise the principal factors in the defence array. First, the–'

The Night Lords were already speaking over one another. Several shouted their objections.

'We cannot attack Tsagualsa,' said Carahd. 'We cannot set foot upon that world. It is cursed.' Murmurs of agreement grew in chorus.

Talos gave a short bark of a laugh, the sound shaped for mockery. 'Is this really the time for idiotic superstition?'

'It is cursed, Soul Hunter,' Carahd protested. 'All know

it.' But the agreeing mutters were fainter this time.

Talos leaned his knuckles on the desk, watching the gathered warriors. 'I am willing to allow this world to rot, forgotten on the edge of space. But I am *not* willing to walk away when the world we called home for so many decades is infested with Imperial filth. *You* may run from this, Carahd. *You* may weep over a curse ten thousand years old, and long grown cold. *I* am taking First Claw down to the surface. *I* will show these intruders the unforgiving nature of the Eighth Legion. Twenty-five million souls, Carahd. Twenty-five million mouths to scream, and twenty-five million hearts to burst in our hands. You truly wish to remain in orbit while we bring this planet to its knees?'

Carahd smiled at that. 'Twenty-five million souls.' The prophet could already see the glint of avarice in the warrior's eyes.

'Is a world cursed simply because we left it in a moment of indignity? Or is the curse a beautifully convenient masquerade to conceal our shame at running from our second home world?'

Carahd didn't answer, but the answer was clear in his colourless eyes.

'I am pleased that we understand one another,' finished Talos. 'Now, Deltrian, please continue.'

Deltrian reactivated the hololithic image. It bred a ghostly gleam across the dark armour-plating of the gathered warriors. 'Tsagualsa is as lightly defended as most Imperial frontier worlds. We have no data on the frequency or size of Naval patrols in the subsector, but given the location, viable projections indicate minimal and irregular presence of the Imperial war machine. Three Chapters of the Adeptus Astartes are known to hold protectorates in approximate regions. Each of these claims descent from Thirteenth Legion gene stock. Each of these was also present in the year–'

Talos cleared his throat. 'The vital details, please, honoured adept.'

Deltrian repressed a blurt of irritated binary. 'The world is undefended from orbit, as is common among frontier worlds, with the exception of any Imperial void patrols that are willing to risk venturing this far from the Astronomican. Without the Emperor's warp beacon to guide their Navigators, destruction within the Sea of Souls is a significant threat. I struggle to process the reasons the Imperium would even establish a colony this far into the Eastern Fringe. The cities on the surface are likely to be self-sustaining society-states, almost certainly adapted to depend on global resources rather than the infrequent imports from the wider Imperium.'

'What of military movements upon the surface?' asked one of the warriors.

'Analysing,' Deltrian said. He turned his hand as though turning a key in a lock. The neural interface link clicked in the console, and the hololithic stuttered, several sections of the world now flashing red. 'We have monitored satellite vox-traffic for the last sixteen hours, since arrival. It was initially remarkable in that so little communication takes place at all. The world is almost silent, suggesting devolution and/or a primitive grasp of technology.'

'Easy prey,' another Legionary grinned across the chamber.

Cease interrupting, Deltrian thought. 'Three point one per cent of planetary vox communication was military in nature – or could be interpreted as such, in matters of city-state security and law enforcement – suggesting two things: firstly, that this world maintains a minor – perhaps infinitesimal – garrison of conscripts for planetary defence. Secondly, it suggests that despite its reasonable population statistics by the standards of Apex Degree frontier worlds, it levies no regiments for service in the Imperial Guard.'

'Is that unusual?' asked Xarl.

Cyrion chuckled. 'What does he look like, an Imperial recruiter?'

Deltrian ignored the misguided attempt at wit. 'Twenty-five million souls could sustain an Imperial Guard Founding, but frontier worlds seem to be marked for other tithes. The remote location of Tsagualsa makes it increasingly unfavourable and unlikely for Guard recruitment. It should be noted that the planet's inhospitability renders it detrimental – almost hostile – to human life. Auspex readings indicate settlements capable of sustaining the stated numbers, but actual populations are likely to be lower.'

'How much lower?' another warrior asked.

'Conjecture is useless. We will see for ourselves soon enough. The world is undefended.'

'In short,' Talos said, 'this world is ours, brothers. We need only to reach out our claws and take it. We will divide before planetfall,' Talos explained. 'Each Claw will take a section of the city, to do with as they please.'

'Why?'

All eyes turned to Deltrian. 'You have something to say?' Talos asked him.

The tech-adept took a fraction of a second to frame his thoughts into a verbal formation and tone calculated to offer the least offence.

'I would ask, lord, why you seek to make planetfall here at all. What does this defenceless world offer us?'

Talos didn't look away. His black eyes drilled into the tech-adept's cowl, locking to the glimmering lenses therein.

'This is no different to any other raid, honoured adept. We are raiders. We raid. This is what we do, is it not?'

'Then I would form a further query. Why did we travel across a quarter of the galaxy to reach this location? I suspect I need not process the number of worlds in the Imperium and calculate the percentage that offer potential raid targets. So I would phrase my query thusly: Why did we come to Tsagualsa?'

The Night Lords fell silent again. They watched the prophet in wordless patience, for once.

'I want answers,' Talos said. 'I believe I will find them here.'

'Answers to what, Soul Hunter?' one of the warriors asked. He could see the question mirrored in many of their eyes.

'To why we are still fighting this war.'

As expected, his answer was met with laughter, with the answers 'To win it' and 'To survive' mixed in with the amusement. That suited Talos well enough. Let them believe it was a veteran's joke, shared with his kindred.

It took three hours for Xarl to speak the words Talos had been expecting.

'You shouldn't have said that.'

The arming chamber was a hive of industry, as Septimus and several servitors machined First Claw's war plate onto their bodies.

Cyrion glanced at the human serf helping to drill his shin guard into its locking position.

'You look like death,' he pointed out. Septimus forced a smile, but said nothing. His face was a palette of bruised swelling.

'Talos,' Xarl said, 'you shouldn't have said that in the war council.'

Talos closed and opened his fist, testing the workings of his gauntlet. It purred in a muted orchestra of smooth servos.

'What, exactly, should I not have said?' he asked, though he already knew the answer.

Xarl shrugged his left shoulder as a servitor drilled the pauldron into place. 'No one respects a maudlin leader. You are too thoughtful, too introspective. They considered your words to be a jest, and that was a saving grace. But trust me, brother, none of the Claws would wish to descend onto that cursed world purely to satisfy your desire for soul-searching.'

Talos nodded, agreeing easily while checking his bolter. 'True. Their only reason for making planetfall is to spread terror through the population, is it not? There's no place for nuance or deeper emotion in such shallow, worthless psyches.'

First Claw looked at their leader in silence for several moments.

'What is wrong with you?' Xarl asked. 'What bitterness grips you these nights? You were speaking like this before you fell into the long dream, and have been twice as bad since awakening. You cannot keep shouting out against the Legion. We are what we are.'

The prophet locked his bolter to his thigh plating along the magnetic seal. 'I am tired of merely surviving this war. I want to win it. I want there to be meaning behind fighting it.'

'We are what we are, Talos.'

'Then we must be better. We must change and evolve, because this stasis is worthless.'

'You sound like Ruven before he left us.'

The prophet's lips curled in a snide sneer. 'I have carried this bitterness for a long time, Xarl. The only difference is that now I wish to speak of it. And I do not regret it. To speak of these flaws is like lancing a boil. I already feel the poison bleeding from me. It is no sin to wish to live a life that matters. We are supposed to be fighting a war and inflicting fear in the name of our father. We are sworn to bear his vengeance.'

Xarl didn't hide the confusion taking hold of his pale features. 'Are you insane? How many among the Legion truly paid heed to the rantings of a mad primarch spoken so long ago?'

'I am not saying the Legion has heeded those words,' Talos narrowed his eyes. 'I am saying that we *should* heed them. If we did, our lives would be worth more.'

'The Legion's lesson is taught. It was taught when he died. All that remains is to survive as best we can, and wait for the Imperium to fall.'

'And what happens when it falls? What then?'

Xarl looked at Talos for a moment. 'Who cares?'

'No. That is *not* enough. Not for me.' His muscles bunched as he clenched his teeth.

'Be calm, brother.'

Talos moved forward, immediately restrained by Mercutian and Cyrion, who struggled to hold him back.

'It is *not* enough, Xarl.'

'Talos…' Cyrion grunted, seeking to drag the prophet back with both arms.

Xarl watched with wide eyes, unsure whether to reach for his weapon. Talos still sought to throw his brothers free. Fire danced in his dark eyes.

'It is *not* enough. We stand in the dust at the end of centuries of useless sin and endless failure. The Legion was poisoned, and we sacrificed an entire world to cleanse it. We failed. We are the sons of the only primarch to hate his own Legion. There, again, we failed. We swore vengeance on the Imperium, yet we run from every battle where we don't possess overwhelming force over a crippled enemy. We fail, again and again and again. Have you ever fought a battle you'd struggle to win, with no hope of running away? Have any of us? Have you ever, since the Siege of Terra itself, drawn a weapon with the knowledge you might die?'

'Brother…' Xarl began, backing away as Talos took another step closer, despite Cyrion and Mercutian's best efforts.

'I will not see my life whored away without meaning. Do you hear me? Do you understand me, prince of cowards? I want vengeance against a galaxy that hates us. I want Imperial worlds to cower when we draw near. I want the weeping of this empire's souls to reach all the way to Holy Terra, and the sound of suffering will choke the corpse-god on his throne of gold.'

Variel had joined in, restraining Talos from getting any closer to Xarl. Only Uzas stood apart, watching with dead-eyed disinterest. The prophet thrashed in their grip, managing to kick Cyrion away.

'I will cast a shadow across this world. I will burn every

man, woman and child so the smoke from the funeral pyres eclipses the sun. With the dust that remains, I will take the *Echo of Damnation* into the sacred skies above Terra, and rain the ashes of twenty million mortals down onto the Emperor's palace. *Then* they will remember us. *Then* they will remember the Legion they once feared.'

Talos hammered his elbow into Mercutian's faceplate, knocking his brother back with a crack of ceramite. A fist into Variel's throat sent the Apothecary sprawling, until no one stood between Xarl and the prophet. Talos aimed Aurum's golden blade at his squadmate's left eye.

'No more running. No more raiding to survive. When we see an Imperial world, we will no longer ask if it is worth attacking for plunder, we will ask how much harm its destruction would cause the Imperium. And when the Warmaster calls us for the Thirteenth Crusade, we will answer him. Night by night, we will bring this empire to its knees. I will cast aside what this Legion has become, and remake it into what it should be. Do I make myself clear?'

Xarl nodded, his eyes locked to the prophet's. 'I hear you, brother.'

Talos didn't lower the blade. He breathed in the stale, recycled air of the shipboard ventilation, tinged with the musk of weapon oils and Septimus's fear-sweat.

'What?' he asked the slave.

Septimus stood in his beaten jacket, his scruffy hair loose around his face, not quite hiding the damaged optic lens. He held his master's helm in his hands.

'You are bleeding from your ear, lord.'

Talos reached to check. Blood marked the fingers of his gauntlets. 'My skull is aflame,' he admitted. 'I have never felt my thoughts running clearer, but the trade in pain is extremely unpleasant.'

'Talos?' one of his brothers said. He wasn't sure which one. Through blurring vision, they all looked the same.

'It is nothing,' he told the faceless crowd.

'Talos?' a different voice called. He was struggling with the realisation that they couldn't understand what he was saying. His tongue had turned thick. Was he slurring his words?

The prophet stilled himself, taking a deep breath.

'I am fine,' he said.

Each of them looked at him with doubt in their eyes. Variel's cold gaze was keenest of all.

'We must speak in the apothecarion soon, Talos. There are tests to be run, and suspicions I hope are not confirmed.'

'As you wish,' he conceded. 'Once we return from Tsagualsa.'

IV

THE THREAT OF WINTER

THE CITY OF Sanctuary barely deserved the title, and it deserved its name even less. By far the largest of the settlements on the far-frontier world Darcharna, it was a mongrel cityscape formed from landed explorator ships, half-buried colonist cruisers, and simple prefabricated structures risen against the howling dust storms that blanketed the planet's face in place of real weather.

Walls of cheap rockcrete and corrugated iron ringed the city limits, patchworked by flakboard repairs and armour-plating pried from the beached spaceships.

The lord of this spit-and-bonding-tape settlement looked out at his domain from the relative quiet of his office. Once, the room had been the observation spire aboard the Ecclesiarchy pilgrim hauler *Currency of Solace*. Now it stood empty of the pews and viewing platforms, housing nothing beyond the archregent's personal effects. He called it his office, but it was his home, just as it had been the home of every single archregent for the last five generations, since the Day of Downfall.

The window-dome was thick enough to suppress the gritty winds into silence, no matter how they thrashed and raged at the settlement below. He watched the gale's shadow now, unable to see the howling winds but forever able to see their influence in the flapping of ragged flags and the crashing of armoured windows slamming closed.

Will we go dark, he wondered. *Will we go dark again? Is this the first storm of yet another Grey Winter?*

The archregent pressed his hand to the dense glass, as though he could feel the gale blowing through the bones of his junkyard city. He let his gaze drift upward, to the thin cloud cover and the stars beyond.

Darcharna – the *real* Darcharna – was still out there somewhere. Perhaps the Imperium had despatched another colonist fleet to replace the one that had been lost with all souls in the deepest depths of the warp, only to find itself vomited back into real space in the Eastern Fringe. What little contact existed between this Darcharna, the Darcharna they called home, and the wider Imperium was limited, to say the least. It was also not a matter for the populace. Some things had to be kept secret.

The last had been several years before – another garbled vox message from a distant world, relaying the signal from deeper beyond. Throne only knew how it had reached them. The automated response to several centuries of pulsed calls for supplies and extraction was blunt to the point of crudity.

You are protected even in the darkness. Remember always, the Emperor knows all and sees all. Endure. Prosper.

The archregent breathed slowly as the memory curdled in his thoughts. Its meaning was clear enough: *Remain on your dead world. Live there as your fathers did. Die there as your fathers did. You are forgotten.*

During his rule, he'd personally spoken to only two souls off-world. The first was the magos captain of a deep-space explorator vessel, with no interest in any dialogue beyond cataloguing the world's usefulness and moving on. Finding little of worth meant the ship had left orbit after a handful of hours. The second soul was a lord among the sacred Adeptus Astartes, who had informed him this region of space came under the protectorate of his warriors, the Genesis Chapter. They sought a fleeing xenos fleet outside the Emperor's light, and while the Imperial Space Marine lord had professed sympathy with the unwilling colonists of Darcharna, his warship was no place for, in his words, 'the tread of ten million mortal boots'.

The archregent had said he understood, of course. One did not argue with warriors of heroic mythology. No, indeed – especially not when they displayed such a thin veneer of patience.

'Do you have no astropaths?' the Space Marine lord had pressed. 'No psychic souls with the power to call out into the void?'

Oh, they did. Incidents of psychic occurrence were perhaps a little too common on Darcharna; a fact the archregent had considered wise to conceal from the Adeptus Astartes lord. Half of the psychically-aware men and women born to the colony cities suffered mutation or deviance beyond tolerable allowance. As for the other half, many were put down in peace when they showed signs of failing their training. What passed for an Astropathic Guild in Sanctuary was a collection of shamans and interpreters of dreams, forever whispering to ancestor-spirits only they could see, and insisting on worshipping the sun as a distant manifestation of the Emperor.

Those leaders who donned the mantles of Ecclesiarchs – the archregent and abettor among them – sympathised with the solar reverence on this darkest of worlds. Despite most of the cities' populations having access to the old archives, a huge number of them considered themselves among the faithful.

Even so, there were limits. At best, the Astropathic Cult was a den of deviancy waiting to happen, with little to no ability to actually communicate off-world. At worst, they were already heretics in dire need of purging, just as they'd been culled by former archregents in previous generations. How many times had they called out into the void never to receive an answer, never to even know if their cries were loud or strong enough to reach other minds?

The archregent stood at his window for some time, watching the stars decorating the sky. In his reverie, he didn't even hear the dull grind of the door opening on low power.

'Archregent?' came a tremulous voice.

He turned then, to be met by the thoughtful eyes and perpetual frown of Abettor Muvo. The younger man was slender to the point of ill health, and his bloodshot eyes and yellowing skin told of organs working poorly. In this regard, he was no different from any of the population in Sanctuary, or any of the other settlements across Darchana. Crude hydroponic plantations in the sunless bowels of beached void cruisers sustained the surviving descendants of the first colonists, but hardly enriched them. There was – the archregent had decided long ago – surely a difference between living and simply being alive.

'Hello, Muvo,' the ageing man smiled. It deepened the lines of his thin face. 'To what do I owe the pleasure of your company?'

'The storm-scryers have sent word from the east hills. I thought you'd want to know.'

'I thank you for your diligence. Am I to assume Grey Winter falls once more? It feels early this year.' But then, it felt earlier every year. One of the curses of getting old, he thought.

The abettor's scowl softened for a rare moment. 'Would you believe, we actually have an uplink?'

The archregent didn't bother to conceal his surprise. Vox and pict communication beyond Sanctuary's walls, and often within it, were so unreliable the technology bordered on being abandoned. He could count on one hand the number of times he'd spoken over a vox in the last two years, and even then, all three of those times had been within Sanctuary's city limits.

'I would like that very much,' he said. 'Visual?'

The abettor gave an abrupt grunt and said nothing.

'Ah,' the archregent nodded. 'I thought not.'

The two men moved to the archregent's battered desk, looking into the dead screen set in the wooden face. Several dials needed re-tuning before anything like a voice resolved itself.

Rivall Meyd, the son of Dannicen Meyd, was a technician in the same vein as his father. He carried the official rank of storm-scryer, which gave him no small pride, but travelling up into the hills and predicting weather patterns was only a small part of his duties. Most of the people walled up back in Sanctuary and the other encampments knew little of his work.

He was content with their ignorance. Using his heirloom meteorological auspex scanners was more glamorous to layfolk than the truth, which was that he spent most of his time bandaged and goggled against the grit of the dust plains, looking for things that didn't exist and wasting time on things that couldn't be repaired.

They needed metal. The people of Sanctuary needed metal almost as much as they needed food, but there was almost none to be found. Any veins of ore he found in his travels were hollow and worthless. Any scrap metal from damaged ships on the Day of Downfall had been vultured up by his predecessors decades ago.

The vox towers and storage bunkers were another matter, but enjoyed the same measure of failure. The first generation of colonists, fresh from the Day of Downfall, had clearly been optimistic and enterprising souls. They'd built relay networks of communication towers across the plains, binding each city by the dubious reassurance of vox contact. Bunkers had been established beneath the ground, to refuel and resupply travellers making the overland journey between cities and satellite settlements. Even from their first landing, it was little trouble to brew and refine promethium fuel for wheeled vehicles, though flyers and void-worthy vessels were grounded – thirsty for fuel and unable to sustain flight in the winds anyway.

Rivall stood at the cliff's edge, brushing dust from the lenses of his macrobinoculars and looking back at Sanctuary as a stain on the horizon. Most of the city stood empty now. The fleet had come to Darcharna with almost thirty million souls cramped in the confines of pilgrim carriers and repurposed troop ships serving as colonist vessels. Planetwide estimates now numbered them at fewer than a third of that, in the four hundred and seventieth year since the Day of Downfall.

'Meyd, get over here.'

'What is it?' He lowered the macrobinoculars and moved over the rocks back to his partner. Eruko was wrapped as he was, no skin showing against the abrading wind. His friend was crouched by the backpack vox-caster, working the dials.

'It's only the bloody archregent,' Eruko said. 'If you're not too busy staring at the horizon.'

Meyd crouched with him, straining to hear the voice.

'...fine work, storm-scryers,' it was saying between distortion crackles. '...Winter?'

Meyd was the one to answer. 'The scanners register a drop in temperature, as well as an increase in winds, over the last week. The first storms are coming, but Grey Winter is still a few weeks away, sire.'

'Repeat please,' the voice returned.

Meyd breathed in deep, and lowered the cloth strips wrapped around his face, baring his lips to the scratching wind. He repeated himself, word for word.

'Good news, gentlemen,' replied the archregent.

'So we're gentlemen now?' asked Eruko quietly. Meyd smiled back.

'Sire?' Meyd spoke into the speech-handle. 'Any word from Takis and Coruda?'

'Who? I am afraid I'm not familiar with their names.'

'The...' Meyd had to pause to cough glassy grit from his throat. 'The team responsible for the next eastern boundary. They went to scout last night's asteroid for iron.'

'Ah. Of course. No word yet,' the archregent replied. 'My apologies, gentlemen.' Rivall Meyd liked the old man's voice. He sounded kind, always patient, like he genuinely cared.

'I assume this contact is only possible because you managed to repair the erosion damage to East Pylon Twelve.'

Meyd smiled, despite the grit stinging his lips. 'It is, sire.' He didn't add that they'd needed to junk an old dune-runner buggy to get it done.

'A rare victory. You have my thanks and admiration, both of you. Come to my office when your rotation ends. I will offer you a glass of whatever passes for alcoholic finery in my admittedly limited cellar.'

Neither Meyd nor Eruko replied.

'Gentlemen?' the archregent's voice rang out. 'Ah, have we lost the link?'

Eruko hit the ground first, his cheek breaking against the stone. He said nothing. He did nothing, except bleed in silence. The blade through his heart had killed him instantly.

Meyd wasn't dead when he fell. He reached a bleeding hand to the vox-caster's emergency rune button, but lacked the strength to push it. Bloodstained fingertips smeared meaningless patterns over the button's plastek surface.

'Gentlemen?' asked the archregent again.

Meyd drew the last breath of his life, and used it to scream.

The archregent looked at the abettor. The younger man toyed with the hem of his brown robe's sleeves.

'I would like you to tell me that was interference,' the archregent said.

The abettor sniffed. 'What else would it have been?'

'It sounded to me like someone was crying out, Muvo.'

The abettor attempted to force a smile. It wasn't entirely successful. With respect to the older man, his hearing wasn't what it once was. They both knew how often Muvo had to repeat himself for the archregent.

'I believe it was interference,' the abettor said again.

'Maybe so.' The archregent ran his hands through his thinning white hair, and took a breath. 'I would still feel more comfortable sending out a search team if those gentlemen have not restored contact within the hour. You heard the wind, Muvo. If they fell from those cliffs…'

'Then they're already dead, sire.'

'Or in need of help. But dead or alive, we are recovering them.' He felt curiously energised for a moment. The dust plains had taken too many of them over the years, and Eruko and Meyd were close enough to recover in a few days, if the dust storms were really going to stay away a while longer.

The vox-channel crackled live again, as though the channels were being tuned. The abettor gave a joyless smirk of triumph. The archregent smiled in response.

'Interference, indeed. You win this round,' the old man said, but his fingers froze before they touched the dial. The voice rasping from the speakers wasn't human. It was too low, too guttural, too cold.

'You should never have settled on this world. Our shame is our secret to keep. Tsagualsa will be clawed clean of life once more. Hide in your cities, mortals. Lock your doors, reach for your weapons, and wait until you hear us howl. Tonight, we come for you.'

V

A PURE WAR

DANNICEN MEYD HAD noted his fifty-eighth birthday a month before, and on Darcharna that made him practically ancient. The grit in his bones from a life on the dust plains meant that it ached to move and it ached to lie still, and these days he did a lot more of the latter than the former.

The plains gave a man a serious beating over the years. There were the skin abrasions to deal with, which came with their own infections soon after. Then you had black lung to worry about from the grit getting into your mouth and nose, eventually losing lung tissue to decay or infection, and spending most of your time coughing up bloody phlegm.

Sore eyes were a constant misery – always leaking, yet somehow always dry – and his vision was clouded over by years of particulates dulling his sight. He didn't hear so well, either. The Emperor only knew what decades of ashy grit had done to his ear canals, but when his blood was up and his heart beating fast, everything was muted and faint, like he was hearing things underwater.

His heart hurt worst of all. Now it rattled and raged at him every time he walked for more than a few minutes.

All in all, he was a man with every right to his complaints, yet he had very few. Dannicen Meyd wasn't a man given over to musing over misery. He'd tried to talk Rivall out of the plains life, though. That hadn't worked out so well. It went almost exactly the same as it'd gone when Dannicen's own father had tried to say the same words to him, way back in a life before all these aches and pains.

He was giving in to that often-replayed memory when the city's sirens started up their discordant wail.

'You're not serious,' he said aloud. Storms were starting damn early this year. Last he'd heard from Rivall, they were supposed to have a few weeks yet, maybe even a month.

Dannicen hauled himself from the couch that served as his bed, sucking air through his teeth as his knees crackled in chorus. Both joints came awake with needling jabs beneath the bone. *Nasty, nasty. Getting old is a bitch, make no mistake.*

A shadow passed his window. He looked up just as fists started pounding on the flakboard plank that served as his door.

'Throne of the bloody Emperor,' he grunted as his knees gave another protest, but he was up and walking no matter what they had to say about it.

Romu Chayzek was on the other side of the door. Romu Chayzek was also armed. The battered Guard-issue lasrifle hadn't been new this side of the millennium's turning, but as Watchman for South-43 Street down to North/South Junction-55, he had the right to bear arms in his patrols.

'Going hunting for dust rabbits?' he almost laughed, gesturing to the gun. 'A little early to be shooting looters, kid.'

'The sirens,' Romu was panting. He'd obviously run here, down the muddy alley that served as a street for the prefabricated bunkerish buildings.

'Storms are early.' Dannicen leaned out of the door, but any view of the horizon was stolen by Sanctuary's broken-tooth skyline. Families were pouring from their homes, milling through the street in every direction.

Romu shook his head. 'Come on, you deaf old bastard. To the sub-shelters with you.'

'Not a chance.' The Meyd house had stood up to every Grey Winter so far, as had most of those in this section of the city. South Sector, 20 through 50, had the choicest picks of the troop landers way back at the Day of Downfall. All that armour did the deed when it came to keeping out the worst of the dust storms.

'Listen to me, it ain't the storms. The archregent's under attack.'

For a moment, Dannicen didn't know whether to laugh or go back to bed. '...he's what?'

'This ain't a joke. He could be dead already, or... I don't know what. Come on! Look at the sky, you son of a bitch.'

Dannicen had seen the panic in Romu's eyes before, on the faces of those he'd served with outside the walls. That animal fear of being lost on the plains, turned about and directionless as a dust blizzard bore down. Helplessness – sincere, absolute helplessness – painted across a man's face, turning it sick and ugly.

He looked to the west, towards the distant archregent's tower, where a faint orange gleam illuminated the evening sky behind the rows of awkward urban stalagmites serving as a cityscape horizon.

'Who?' he asked. 'Who would attack us? Who even knows we're here? Who even cares?'

Romu was already running, blending in with the crowd. Dannicen saw him reach a cloth-wrapped hand to help a young boy back to his feet, and shove him into the press of bodies.

Dannicen Meyd waited another moment, before he took his aching knees and arthritic hands back inside his house. When he emerged, he carried his own lasrifle – and this one worked just fine, thank you very much. He'd used it in his own days as a volunteer Watchman, shooting looters in the Grey Winters after his retirement from storm-scrying.

He kept to the edge of the crowd, walking west as they pressed east. If the archregent was under attack, to hell with running and hiding. Let it never be said that Dannicen Meyd didn't know how to do his bloody duty.

He looked down, just briefly, to check his lasgun. That was the moment he heard the dragon.

The crowd, every one of them, screamed and crouched, covering their heads as the beast roared overhead. They looked up with terrified eyes as the roar hurt their ears. Only Dannicen remained exactly as he was, his bloodshot eyes wide in awe.

The dragon was black against the grey sky, screaming above them on howling... engines. Not a dragon at all. A flyer. A gunship. But nothing had flown on Darcharna for centuries. The crowd was screaming now, thin parents carrying their even thinner children and hiding their eyes.

It banked above them, streaming fire from its thrusters as the wind rattled grit against its armour-plating. Its own momentum had it drifting as it hovered in the air, fighting the wind raging against the dark hull. Its leering prow seemed to watch the panicking people below before the gunship slowly veered away. Buildings shivered and cracked as its thrusters gave a thunderous boom, kicking the flyer across the sky and into the distance in the time it took Dannicen to blink.

He broke into a run, the pain in his joints all but forgotten. 'Let me through,' he said when he needed to, though the crowd parted and was fleeing in the opposite direction with little encouragement from him. The gunship had been more than enough.

He made it three streets before his knees gave up the fight. He leaned against a shack wall, cursing at the needles in his joints. His heart felt no better, racing to the point of strain, sending tendrils of tightness through his chest. Dannicen thumped a fist against his breastbone, as if anger would soothe the spreading fire.

More orange glows were showing stark against the clouds now. More of the city was burning.

He caught his breath, and forced his knees to obey

him. They shivered but complied, and Dannicen stumbled forward on shaking legs. He made it another two streets before he had to stop and let his breathing catch up to him.

'Too old for this foolishness,' he coughed as he slumped against the wall of a grounded Arvus industrial shuttle now serving as a family home.

Legiones Astartes power armour makes a distinctive thrum: the loud, violent hum of immense energy waiting to be released. The armour joints, not coated in layers of ceramite, are still armoured against harm and filled with servos and fibre-bundle cabling in imitation of living muscles. They snarl and whine with even the most modest movement, from a tilt of the head to a clench of fist.

Dannicen Meyd didn't hear any of this, despite it taking place mere metres away from where he stood, struggling to catch his breath. His blood was up, and his ears deaf to all but the ragged drumbeat of his own heart.

He saw the street clearing of life as people fled. Many were looking back at him, their eyes and mouths wide in screams Dannicen couldn't quite hear. His teeth itched now, and his gums ached. There was a tremor in the softness of his eyes, as though an aggressive, subsonic sound pulsed nearby. Something he couldn't hear, but could feel like an unwanted caress.

He blinked, wiping away the sting of his watering eyes, and lifted his head at last. What he saw crouching on the roof of the shuttle was enough to tear the thin walls of his heart at last.

The figure wore ancient battle armour, contoured ceramite the colour of midnight. Lightning bolts marked the armour-plating in clawed streaks. Slanted red eyes stared down at him from their place in a skull-faced helm. Spikes and spines knifed up from the figure's bulky armour, glistening with moisture in the moonlight. Blood coated the thing, from its face to its heavy boots.

Three heads, their ripped necks still leaking, were tied to its shoulder guard by their own hair.

Dannicen was already on his knees, his burst heart losing all rhythm. Instead of blood, it pumped pain. Bizarrely, his hearing faded back into being.

'You are suffering heart failure,' the crouching figure told him in a deep, emotionless rumble. 'The constriction in your chest and throat. The breath that will not come. This would be more amusing if you feared me, but you do not, do you? How rare.'

Dannicen raised his lasrifle, even through the pain. The figure reached down to take it from his hands, as though stripping a toy from a child. Without looking, the warrior crushed the barrel in his fist, mangling it and casting it aside.

'Consider yourself fortunate.' The figure reached next to lift the ageing man by his grey hair. 'Your life ends in mere moments. You will never feel what it is like to be thrown into the skinning pits.'

Dannicen breathed out a strangled, wordless syllable. He was soiling himself, without feeling it, without realising, as he lost control of his body at the edge of death.

'This is our world,' Mercutian told the dying man. 'You should never have come here.'

TORA SEECH WAS seven years old. Her mother worked in a hydroponics basement, her father taught sector children to read, write and pray. She hadn't seen either of them in several minutes, since they'd run into the street and told her to wait in the single room that served the family as a house.

Outside, she could hear everyone shouting and running. The city's sirens were wailing loud, but there'd been no storm warnings before this. Usually her parents gave her a few days to pack and get ready to head to the shelters before the sirens started up.

They wouldn't have left her here. They wouldn't have run away with everyone else and left her here alone.

The growl started from far away, and came closer each time her heart beat. It was a dog's growl, an angry dog fed up with being kicked. Then the footsteps followed it. Something blocked the pale light from her window, and she dragged her thin blanket higher. She hated the sheet, it had fleas that brought her out in itchy lumps, but it was too cold without it. Now she needed it to hide.

'I see you under there,' said a voice in the room. A low, snarling voice with a crackle, like a machine-spirit come to life. 'I see the heat of your little limbs. I hear the beat of your little heart. I taste your fear, and it is sweet indeed.'

The bootsteps thudded slowly closer, making her bed shiver. Tora squeezed her eyes shut. The sheet was a whisper against her skin as it was dragged away, leaving her cold.

She screamed for her parents when the cold metal hand gripped her ankle. The shadow hauled her from her bed, holding her upside down. She saw the brief flash of a long silver knife.

'This will hurt,' Cyrion told her. His red eyes stared at her without emotion, without life. 'But it will not last long.'

GERRICK COLWEN SAW one of them when he went back for his pistol. At first he thought his street was empty. He was wrong.

His first clear glance was of a figure almost a metre taller than a normal man, wearing spiked armour drawn from the depths of mythology. A skinless, bleeding body hung over each shoulder, raining dark fluid onto the dark armour-plating. Three more cadavers trailed along behind in the dust, hooked to the walking warrior by bronze chains pushed into their spines. Each of them had been skinned in the same crude rush, the skin peeled and torn from their body in indelicate rips. Dusty soil coated them now like false skin, painting the exposed musculature dark with ash.

Gerrick raised his pistol, in the bravest moment of his life.

Variel turned to him, a bloody flesh-saw in one hand and an ornate bolt pistol in the other. A sourceless peal of thunder boomed between them.

Something hit Gerrick in the stomach with the force of a truck crash. He couldn't even shout, so fast did all air leave his lungs, nor did he have time to fall before the bolt in his belly detonated, taking him apart in a flash of light.

There was no pain. He saw the stars spinning, the buildings tumbling, and fell into blackness just as his legless torso struck the mud road. The life was gone from his eyes before his skull cracked open on the ground, spilling its contents into the dirt, leaving him long dead before Variel started skinning him.

Amar Medrien pounded his fists on the sealed door.

'Let us in!'

The shelter entrance for three streets of his subsector was in the basement of the Axle Grinder, a dive bar set on a tri-junction. He never drank there, and the only time he'd spent more than five minutes in the place was the Grey Winter four years before, when most of his district had endured three weeks underground during dust storms that ravaged their homes.

He stood outside the sealed bulkhead with a tide of others, locked out of their assigned emergency shelter.

'They locked it too early,' voices were saying, back and forth.

'It's not a storm.'

'Did you see the fires?'

'Why did they seal the doors?'

'Break them down.'

'The archregent is dead.'

Amar ran his fingers along the door's seams, knowing he wouldn't find any sign of weakness, but with nothing left to do in the press of bodies from behind. If they kept packing the basement – and the flood showed no sign of slowing – he'd be crushed against the old iron before long.

'They're not going to open it...'

'It's already full.'

He shook his head as he heard the last remark. How could it be full? The bunker had room for over four hundred people. Close to sixty were still out here with him. Someone's elbow dug into his side.

'Stop pushing!' someone else shouted. 'We can't get it open.'

Amar grunted as someone shoved him from behind. His face thumped against the cold iron, and he couldn't even get enough room to throw an elbow back to clear some space.

The tinny whine of the door release was the most beautiful song he'd ever heard. People around him cheered and wept, backing away at last. Sweating hands gripped at the door's seams, pulling it open on hinges in dire need of oiling.

'Merciful God-Emperor...' Amar whispered at the scene within. Bodies littered the bunker's floor, each one mutilated beyond recognition. Blood – a slow river of the thick, stinking fluid – gushed out across Amar's boots and over the ankles of those waiting behind him. Those who couldn't see what he saw were already shoving against those in the front rows, eager to get into their false solace.

Amar saw severed limbs cast in every direction; blood-spattered fingers gently curled as they dipped into the bloody pools across the floor. Body upon body upon body, many strewn where they had fallen, others heaped in piles. The walls were flecked with graceless sprays of red over the dark stone.

'Wait,' he said, so quiet that he couldn't even hear himself. The shoving from behind didn't cease. 'Wait...'

He stumbled with the pressure, staggering into the

chamber. As soon as he crossed the threshold, he heard the roar of a chainblade revving up.

Streaked with blood, most notably a fresh palm-print on the faceplate of his helm, Uzas rose from his hiding place beneath a cairn of corpses.

'Blood for the Blood God.' He spoke through lips stringed by spit. 'Skulls for the Eighth Legion.'

THE ARCHREGENT LOOKED down at the fires, and wondered how metal ships could burn. He knew it wasn't the hull itself catching flame, but the flammable contents within the vessel's body. Still, it seemed strange to watch smoke and flame pouring from ruptures in the walls of his grounded ship. The wind couldn't steal all the smoke. Great plumes of it choked the air around the observation spire, severing his sight beyond the closest buildings.

'Do we know how much of the city is burning?' he asked the guard by his desk.

'What few reports we've had suggest most of the population is making it to their assigned shelters.'

'Good,' the archregent nodded. 'Very good.' *For whatever it's worth*, he thought. If their attackers had come to kill them, hiding in the subterranean shelters would achieve nothing beyond herding the people together like animals for the slaughter. Still, it reduced the chaos on the streets, and that made it progress of a kind.

'The lockdown list, sire,' another guard said. He wore the same bland uniform as the first, and carried a dataslate in one gloved hand. The archregent glanced at it, noting the number of shelters reporting green light lockdowns.

'Very good,' he said again. 'If the raiders make demands, I want to be informed the moment the words have left their lips. Where is Abettor Muvo?'

Providence answered, as Muvo entered before any of the twelve guards could reply.

'Sire, the western granaries are burning.'

The archregent closed his eyes. He said nothing.

'Landers are coming down in the western districts, deploying servitors, mutants, machinery and... Throne only knows what else. They're excavating pits and hurling the bodies of our people into the holes.'

'Have we managed to send word to the other settlements?'

The abettor nodded. 'Respite and Sanctum both sent acknowledgements of warnings received.' He paused for a moment, his bloodshot eyes flicking to the scene beyond the glass dome walls. 'Neither of them will have any better chance at defending against this than we do.'

The archregent took a breath. 'What of our militia?'

'Some of them are gathering, others are heading into the shelters with their families. The Watchmen are organising shelter retreats. Should we call them off storm protocol?'

'Not yet. Spread word through the streets that all Watchmen and militia should gather at their assigned strongholds as soon as the shelters are locked down. We have to fight back, Muvo.'

He looked at his two guards, and cleared his throat. 'With that in mind, might I have a weapon, young man?'

The guard blinked. 'I... sire?'

'That pistol will do, thank you.'

'Do you know how to fire it, sire?'

The archregent forced a smile. 'I do indeed. Now then, Muvo, I need you to... Muvo?'

The abettor raised a shaking hand, pointing over the archregent's shoulder. Every man in the chamber turned, facing a huge vulture silhouette in the smoke. The dome was dense enough to drown out all sound, but the amber flare of the gunship's engines cast myriad reflections across the reinforced glass. They watched it rise higher, an avian wraith in the mist, until it hovered above the dome's ceiling. Fire washed down against the dome, spilling liquid-like over the surface, beautiful to behold from below.

The archregent saw the gunship's maw open, a ramp lowering into the air, and two figures fall from the sky. A flash of gold from one of their hands speared downward, splitting the dome with brutal cracks from the impaling point.

Both figures' boots struck the cracks as they fell, shattering the dome's ceiling in a storm of glass. Razor diamonds rained into the centre of the chamber, coupling with the breathy roar of the gunship's engines, no longer held silent by the transparent barrier.

The figures fell twenty metres before thudding down onto the deck with enough force to send tremors through the chamber. For a moment, they knelt in the dent they'd caused, crouched in their impact crater with their heads lowered. Glass hailstones broke almost musically against their armour.

Then they rose. One held an oversized chainsword, the other a golden blade. They moved in predatory unison, animalistic without intent, walking towards the desk. Each of their steps was a resonating thump of ceramite on iron.

Both of the archregent's guards opened fire. In the same moment, both armoured warriors threw their weapons. The first died as the golden sword speared him through the chest, dropping him to the floor in a twitching heap. The second went down as the chainsword smashed into his face and torso, the live teeth eating into his flesh. Streaks of warm meat and hot blood splashed across the abettor and archregent. Neither man had moved.

The archregent swallowed, watching the armoured figures approach. 'Why?' he asked. 'Why have you come here?'

'Wrong question,' Xarl smiled.

'And we owe you no answers,' said Talos.

The archregent raised the borrowed pistol and sighted down the barrel. The warriors kept walking. Next to him, Abettor Muvo was interlacing his fingers, seeking to quell their shaking.

'The Emperor protects,' the archregent said.

'If he did,' replied Talos, 'he would never have sent you to this world.'

Xarl hesitated. 'Brother,' he voxed, ignoring the old man with the gun. 'I am getting a signal from orbit. Something is wrong.'

Talos turned back to the other Night Lord. 'I hear it, also. Septimus, bring *Blackened* along the eastern edge of the spire. We must return to the void at once.'

'Compliance, master,' was the crackling reply. Within moments, the gunship was hovering by the dome's edge, gangramp lowering like an eagle's hooked maw.

'The Emperor protects,' the archregent whispered again, trembling now.

Talos turned his back on the mortal. 'It would seem that on rare occasions, he really does.'

Both Night Lords dragged their swords clear from the dead bodies as they ran, and drew bolters mid-sprint, opening fire on the reinforced glass. Their armoured forms crashed through the damaged barrier, taking them into the smoke and out of sight. The archregent watched their silhouettes vanish into the darkness of the gunship's innards, still unable to blink.

'The Emperor protects,' he said a third time, amazed that it was so very, tangibly true.

TALOS HELD HIS head in his hands. The pain was a rolling throb now, pushing at the back of his eyes. Around him, First Claw were readying their weapons, standing and holding to the handrails as the gunship climbed back into the sky.

'Is it a Navy vessel?' Cyrion was asking.

'They think it's an Adeptus Astartes cruiser,' Xarl held a hand to the side of his helm, as if it would aid his hearing. 'The vox reports are exciting, to say the least. The *Echo* is taking a beating.'

'We outgun any of their cruisers.' Mercutian was kneeling as he refitted his heavy bolter, not looking up at the others.

'We outgun them when they don't break into the system and knife us in the spine from a perfectly executed ambush,' Cyrion pointed out.

Talos drew breath to speak, but no words left his lips. He closed his eyes, feeling tears in his eyes and hoping it wasn't blood again. He knew it would be, but holding to hope prevented his temper from flashing free.

'The Sons of the Thirteenth Legion,' he said. 'Armour of scarlet and bronze.'

'What is he saying?'

'I...' Talos began, but the rest of the sentence fled from him. The sword hit the deck first. The prophet collapsed to his hands and knees a moment later. Behind his eyes, the darkness was returning in a tidal roar, hungry for his consciousness.

'Again?' Xarl sounded angry. 'What in hell's name is wrong with him?'

'I have my suspicions,' answered Variel, kneeling beside the prone warrior. 'We have to get him to the apothecarion.'

'We have to defend the damned ship when we reach it first,' Cyrion argued.

'I hear sirens,' Talos said, and fell forward once more into the yawning maw of nothingness.

VI

ASSAULT

He woke laughing because of Malcharion. The war-sage's deep, rumbling declaration from over a year before rattled through his aching head, when the Dreadnought had woken with the words *'I heard bolter fire.'*

He could hear bolter fire too. There it was, that unmistakable drumbeat – the heavy, juddering chatter of bolters opening up against one another. The distinctive thuds of fired shells and the echoing crash of them detonating against walls and armour set up a familiar cacophony.

The prophet dragged himself to his feet, smacking a hand to the side of his helm, forcing the retinal display to re-tune. He stared at his surroundings: the confined troop bay of his own Thunderhawk gunship.

'Fifty-three minutes, master,' said Septimus, relaying the exact duration of his unconsciousness. Talos turned to see his servant, clad in his usual ragged flight jacket, low-slung pistols at his hips.

'Tell me everything,' the warrior ordered. Septimus was already handing him his weapons, one after the other. The human needed both hands to lift each one.

'I know little. All claws were recalled before a brief void battle began. We've been boarded by the enemy. I do not know if our shields are still down, but the enemy cruiser isn't firing with their own men on board. We came into the cortex hangar, under Lord Cyrion's orders. He wished to be close to the bridge for the defence.'

'Who boarded us?'

'Imperial Space Marines. I know nothing more. Did you not dream of them?'

'I do not remember what I dreamed. Just the pain. Stay here,' Talos ordered. 'My thanks for watching over me.'

'Always, lord.'

The prophet descended the gangramp, into the hangar. Mute servitors and skull drones watched him impassively, as if expectant he might offer them orders.

'Talos?' one of his brothers voxed.

'Was that Talos laughing?' came another voice.

'Fall back!' That was Lucoryphus. That was definitely Lucoryphus, he could tell from the bass-edged rasp. 'Fall back to the second concourse!'

'Stand your ground!' Cyrion? Yes... Cyrion. The vox made it hard to tell. *'Stand your ground, you carrion-eating bastards. You'll leave us without support.'*

From there, the vox-network degenerated back into a melee of conflicting voices.

'Is that Talos laughing?'

'This is Xan Kurus of Second Claw...'

'Where is that damned Apothecary?'

'This is Fourth Claw to First, we need Variel immediately.'

'Falling back from the tertiary spinal. Repeat, we've lost Spinal Tertius.'

'Who was laughing?'

'Talos? Is that you?'

The prophet heaved breath in through a throat that felt atrophied from disuse. 'I am awake. First Claw, status report. All claws, report in.'

He didn't receive an answer. The vox broke apart in a fresh gale of bolter fire.

Talos staggered from his small hangar, weapons loose in fists that still spasmed with residual pain. He followed the sounds of bolter fire, and made it no more than five hundred metres down the winding corridors before he found its closest source.

Indeed, he staggered on weak limbs right into the middle of a firefight, and promptly took a shell to the side of the head.

IT LEFT HIM blind for a moment. The shell that cracked against the side of his helm was deflected by the angle, but hit with enough force to scramble the delicate electronics for an irritating cluster of seconds. Vision returned in a static-laden wash of red-tinted sight and flickering runic displays.

'Stay down,' warned a voice. Mercutian stood above him, hands shaking with the kickback from his bolter cannon. Bolt weaponry offered little in the way of muzzle flash, but the ignition from every self-propelled shell flickered a splash of amber across Mercutian's midnight armour.

'This is Mercutian of First Claw,' he voxed. 'The Bleeding Eyes have broken ranks. We are cut off in the primary concourse, strategium deck. Requesting immediate reinforcement.'

A voice crackled back, 'You are on your own, First Claw. Good hunting.'

Talos turned as Cyrion moved into view. His brother held a gore-wet gladius in one hand, and his bayoneted bolter in the other. Cyrion cracked off three shots, one-handed, barely aiming.

'Nice of you to wake up,' he commented with commendable calm, never once even glancing at Talos. Cyrion threw his gladius into the air, reloaded with smart precision, and caught the sword as it fell back into his grip. Several dozen metres down the corridor, the vague figures of their foes never moved from cover. The reason for their tactical concealment was Mercutian. Or, more accurately, Mercutian's booming heavy bolter.

'We're going to die here,' Mercutian grunted over the

cacophony of his pounding weapon. He never stopped firing, the cannon kicking in bellowing three-round bursts, bathing himself in stark, amber flashes.

'Oh,' Cyrion agreed amiably, 'no doubt.'

'Those *kalshiel* Bleeding Eyes,' Mercutian swore as he dropped to one knee, reloading as fast as he could. Cyrion took up the screen of fire, bolter shells detonating down the length of the corridor.

'They'll charge any moment, Talos,' he warned. 'You could use that pretty bolter of yours, you know. There's no better time for it.'

Talos half-dragged himself into cover behind a wall arch. Both his blade and bolter were on the decking by his boots. These, he retrieved with a grunt at his unclear vision and the pain weaving its way down his spine. It took him two attempts to level his massive bolter, before he added its weight to the chorus of gunfire. Torrents of explosive shells barked down the yawning corridor. Thirty seconds passed in the stuttering melody of drumming gunfire.

'What happened?' he asked. 'Who boarded us? What Chapter?'

Cyrion laughed. 'You don't know? You dreamed this, didn't you? You said "armour of scarlet and bronze" before you lost consciousness.'

'I recall nothing,' Talos confessed.

'Reloading,' Mercutian called out. He dropped to one knee again, eyes still fixed on the tunnel, hands moving in dark blurs. A crunch, a click, and the heavy bolter sang its throaty song once more.

'What happened?' Talos repeated. 'Blood of the False Emperor, *someone* tell me what's happening.'

Cyrion's explanation broke off as Uzas crashed into the middle of the corridor. He dropped from the ceiling, falling from a crew ladder with his hands around the throat of a red-armoured Imperial Space Marine. Both warriors tumbled through the line of fire, causing the opposing squads to break off their attacks, even if only for a moment.

'Idiot,' Mercutian breathed, finger idling by his trigger.

The Imperial warrior threw a fist to Uzas's faceplate, snapping the Night Lord's head back with a bone-jarring echo. As their brother staggered, the rest of First Claw cut the Space Marine down with a blistering hail of bolter fire.

The Space Marine fell with a cry of his own. Unimpeded now, the enemy squad at the other end of the corridor advanced, bolters up and crashing with the same *thud, thud, thud* as First Claw's kicking guns. Shells exploded around Talos's cover, showering him with debris.

Uzas ran, and for once he maintained enough sense to run in the saner direction, back toward his brothers. Talos watched the warrior stagger as a shell took him high in the spine, and another clipped the back of his leg. Uzas smacked against the wall at Mercutian's side, rebounding from the steel in a hideous squealing crackle of abused ceramite. When he sank to the decking, his helmeted head crashed against the floor with the ringing finality of a funeral bell.

'Idiot,' Mercutian repeated, his heavy bolter rumbling. The enemy squad reached halfway along the corridor, leaving their dead and dying on the deck behind them. And still, they kept to the cover of the gothic-arched walls.

Talos's retinal display showed First Claw's vital signs still beating strong. With more trouble than he cared to confess, he moved to Uzas's side, dragging the twitching fool into cover. His brother's armour was scorched black, the shreds of flayed flesh serving as his cloak now burnt to cinders. Uzas had been drenched in flamer promethium more than once in the recent past. The chemical stink rose from his blackened battle plate in a miserable tang.

'Son of a...' Uzas mumbled, and fell into a coughing fit. His heaving chokes were sickly wet.

'Where's Variel?' Talos asked. 'Where's Xarl? I'll kill

you myself if you don't start answering me.'

'Xarl and Variel are holding the rear tunnels.' Cyrion was reloading again. 'These wretches had already engaged the *Echo* in orbit before we docked. One way or another, the Imperium was waiting for us.'

Mercutian retreated a couple of steps as a lucky shell detonated against his shoulder guard, spraying all three of them with ceramite wreckage.

'Genesis Chapter,' he growled. 'Boarded us an hour ago. Scum-blooded cousins to the Ultramarines.'

'Perhaps we left the warp too close to Newfound before we drifted into the Tsagualsa system,' Cyrion admitted. 'I doubt it, though. More likely that they tracked us from warp beacons left by their Librarius division. Cunning fellows, these thin-bloods.'

'Very cunning,' Mercutian grumbled.

'You can blame your Navigator, of course,' Cyrion remarked. The wall by his head burst in a spread of sharp fragments. 'She should have sensed the beacons these tenacious dogs left in the warp.'

Talos slammed back into cover as he reloaded. 'She said she sensed something, but she had no idea what they were,' he said. 'We need to fall back. This corridor is lost.'

'We can't fall back from here; we're the only defenders on this arc. If they get onto the bridge, we'll lose the ship. The void shields are still down, as well. Deltrian is sweating oil and blood trying to repair the primary generator.'

'And we can't run,' Mercutian muttered. 'The Bleeding Eyes were holding the southern walkways. The Imperials are closing on us from behind now, too.' Mercutian cursed and fell back another few steps. 'Oh, hell. *He* looks dangerous.'

The prophet left Uzas slouched and bleeding against the wall, moving to his brothers and aiming down the corridor they were generously feeding with explosive fire. His vision had fully re-tuned at last, targeting locks flickering and zeroing in on individual enemies. He could make out the ornate chains and tabards draped across the foes' armour, and the emblems inscribed, worn with righteous pride. One warrior stood out above all, walking closer with inevitable purpose.

'Oh,' Talos said. What followed were several multi-syllabic curse words in Nostraman, with no literal Gothic translation. They were not fit for polite society, or even the less decadent tiers of impolite society.

Cyrion fired with his bolter at his cheek, laughing as he replied. 'At least we'll be killed by a hero.'

The void shields weren't down. That wasn't the problem.

'Analysing,' the tech-adept said aloud. 'Analysing. Analysing.' He stared through ream upon ream of runic figures streaming through his mind. The link to the generator's cogitator was strong and fluid, but the amount of information was taking an unacceptable amount of time to filter.

The problem wasn't that the void shields were down. The problem was they had dropped for three minutes and nine seconds, and the ship had suffered an as yet unknown degree of infestation exactly forty-eight minutes and twelve seconds previously. In the battle with the enemy ship, those precious seconds of vulnerability had been enough for the enemy to board them in heavy numbers.

The thought of all those Imperial Space Marines tearing the *Echo* apart from within would have made Deltrian's skin crawl, had he any skin remaining.

The shields revived, but the generator itself was strained to the point of damaging itself. This led to a further problem: that unless he managed to bring the generator back to a semblance of stability, it might flicker-fail again if the enemy fleet fired another barrage. Perhaps it was unlikely they would, with scores of their own troops on board, but Deltrian hadn't achieved something close to immortality by relying on supposition and assumption. He was a creature that didn't play the odds. He weighted them in his favour.

To extrapolate further, a second flicker-fail would potentially cost them the ship if the shields didn't revive quickly enough. Worse, it could lead to a complete failure, which would not only cost them their ship, but also their souls.

Deltrian had no intention of dying, especially not after investing so much time and meticulous care into resculpting so much of his biological frame into this artifice of mechanical perfection. Nor did he wish his immortal soul to spill out into the transmogrifying ether, to be pulled apart at the amused mercies of daemons and their mad gods.

That, as he was so fond of saying, would not be optimal.

'Analysing,' he said again.

And there it was. The bruise of flawed code, mixed in with the generator's scrambled cogitations, lost and found within a thousand thoughts per second. The damage was minimal, and focused around several of the external projector arrays on the starboard hull. They could be repaired, but not remotely. He'd need to send servitors, or go in person.

Deltrian didn't sigh. He registered his irritation with a non-linguistic blurt of machine-code, as if belching in binary. With an exaggerated patience he didn't possess, the tech-seer activated his epiglottal vox by simulating the act of swallowing.

'This is Deltrian.'

The vox-network replied with an overwhelming miasma of shouting and gunfire. Ah yes, the defence effort. Deltrian had quite forgotten. He disengaged from the terminal and re-tuned into his surroundings.

He considered the scene for a moment. The Void Generatorum was one of the largest chambers on the ship, with its walls layered in clanking power facilitators forged from bronze and sacred steel. All of these secondary nodes fed the central column, which itself was a black iron tower of throbbing plasma, with the churning liquid energy visible from the outside through the eyes and open mouths of gargoyles sculpted onto the pillar's sides.

Only now, as his focus returned to the external world, did he see the madness had ceased. The chamber around him, so recently alive with crashing gunfire and vox-altered screaming, was now beautifully silent.

The enemy boarders – or rather, the fleshy, broken things that had until so recently been the enemy boarders – lay in a ruptured carpet of blood-soaked ceramite across the chamber. Deltrian's olfaction sensors registered a severe level of vascular and excretory scents in the air, enough to make mortal digestive tracts rebel in protest. The smell of the slain was nothing to Deltrian, but he recorded the charnel house stench for the sake of completion in the reference notes he planned to compile later that evening.

His attackers hadn't come anywhere near him. That was because Deltrian, like many adepts of the Machine Cult, was first and foremost a believer in preparation to cover all contingencies, and secondly, a practitioner in the habit of overwhelming force. As soon as the void shields had failed for that split second, he knew the Night Lords would be scattered across the ship, defending every deck against the anomalous outbreak. So he took his safety into his own hands.

Admittedly, three-quarters of his servitors hadn't survived. He paced the chamber, taking stock of the variances in slaughter. Those still standing were slack-faced automatons, lobotomised past personality, their left arms amputated in favour of bulky heavy weaponry. Bionics covered at least half of their skin and replaced a great deal more of their internal functioning. Each one was a labour of faith, if not quite love, and required unswerving attention to detail.

He didn't thank them, nor offer congratulations on

their victory. They'd never register it, either way. Still, to slay ten Imperial Space Marines was no mean feat, even at the cost of... (he counted in a heartbeat) ...thirty-nine enhanced servitors and twelve gun-drones. A loss like that would inconvenience him for some time.

Deltrian paused a moment to regard the emblem on a dislocated shoulder guard. A white triangle, crossed by an inverted sigil. Their armour was a proud, defiant red.

'Recorded: Genesis Chapter. Thirteenth Legion genestock.' *How delightful. A reunion, of sorts.* He'd last encountered these warriors – or their genetic forefathers, at least – in the Tsagualsan Massacre.

'Phase One: complete,' he said aloud, as he pulsed the affirmation code to the surviving servitors' waiting minds. 'Commence Phase Two.'

The cyborgs fell into step, continuing the execution of their previously laid out order rotation. Half of the dozen remaining would move through the ship in a pack, carrying out seek-and-destroy subroutines. The other half would walk with Deltrian, back to the Hall of Reflection.

The ship quivered, hard enough for one of his servitors to miss its footing and emit an error message from its cybernetic jaw. Deltrian ignored it, tapping back into the vox.

'This is Deltrian to Talos of First Claw.'

Bolter fire answered, distant and crackly over the vox. 'He's dead.'

Deltrian hesitated. 'Confirm.'

'He's not dead,' came another voice. 'I heard him laughing. What do you want, tech-priest?'

'To whom am I speaking?' Deltrian asked, not bothering to inflect his voice with any aural signifiers of politeness.

'Carahd of Sixth Claw.' The warrior broke off, replaced for a moment by bolter chatter. 'We're holding the port landing platform.'

Deltrian's internal processors required a fraction of a

heartbeat to recall Carahd's facial appearance, Legion record, and every modification made to his battle armour in the last three centuries.

'Yes,' he said, 'your situational update is fascinating. Where is Talos of First Claw?'

'First Claw is engaged on the primary concourse. What's wrong?'

'I have discovered and analysed the flaw in void shield function. I require the lord's order, and an escort, to–'

Carahd's vox-link deteriorated, breaking apart with the sound of furious screaming.

'Carahd? Carahd of Sixth Claw?'

Another voice took over. 'This is Faroven of Sixth Claw, we're falling back from the landing bays. Anyone still breathing in the sternward concourses, link up with us in New Blackmarket.'

'This is Deltrian, I require a Legion escort to–'

'For the love of all that is sacred, *shut up*, tech-priest. Sixth Claw falling back. Carahd and Iatus are down.'

Another voice crackled in reply. 'Faroven, this is Xan Kurus. Confirm Carahd is down.'

'I had visual confirmation. One of these aquila-bearers took his head off.'

Deltrian listened to the legionaries as they defended the ship. Perhaps their disrespect was excusable, given the circumstances.

Walking around the organic refuse that had once been loyal soldiers of the Golden Throne, and the mortuary of modified bodies that had been his own weaponised minions, Deltrian decided to take matters into his own hands yet again.

LUCORYPHUS OF THE Bleeding Eyes wasn't limited to the decking in the same way as his lesser kindred. He couldn't run though, not as he once might have done. His retreat was a surprisingly agile and unarguably feral race on all fours, his hands and foot-claws clanking on the deck grilles in bestial rhythm. He ran as an ape would, or a wolf, or – as he was – a warrior who'd not been fully human in many years, thanks first to Imperial genetic redesign, and later to the shifting tides of the warp.

Lucoryphus, perhaps more than most of his brothers, wanted to live. He refused to die for their cause, and refused to stand his ground in a hopeless battle, let alone one he was ill-suited to fight in the first place. Let the madness of futile last stands be something his brothers embraced. He lived his life, twisted as it was, by a code of abject rationality. Thus, as he fled, he felt nothing in the way of shame.

Responding to his feverish need for self-preservation (one couldn't call it fear, especially when it lay closer to anger), the thrusters on his back trailed thin, bleak coils of smoke. They were eager to breathe flame and howl loud, carrying him up into the sky. He was eager to give in to it. All he needed was somewhere to soar. Trapped on board the dying *Echo*, it wasn't a likely prospect.

Over the vox, First Claw were still berating the Bleeding Eyes for retreating.

'Let them whine,' Vorasha chuckled, his laughter a hissing '*Ss-ss-ss*'. Both of them were clinging to the ceiling as they fled. The other Bleeding Eyes, whittled down these last months to the most stubborn and brutal survivors, clawed their way across the walls and floor.

The ship shuddered again. Lucoryphus had to cling to the metal for a moment with his hands and foot-claws, to prevent being shaken free.

'No,' he hissed back. 'Wait.'

The Bleeding Eyes halted with inhuman union, each of them holding motionless, clinging to the walls around their leader: a pack meeting in three dimensions. Vorasha tilted his sloping helm, watching as a bird might. Each of them regarded their champion with the same tear-trails painted upon their daemonic iron faceplates.

'What? What is it?'

'You go.' Lucoryphus punctuated his order with an

irritated shriek. 'Fall back to the second concourse. Reinforce Fourth Claw.'

Their muscles tensed as the instinct to obey ran through them. 'And you?' Vorasha hissed back. Lucoryphus gave a wordless cry, the call of a carrion crow, as he turned and moved back the way they'd come.

The Bleeding Eyes regarded each other as their leader tore back down the corridor, running along its ceiling. Instinct pulled at them: the pack hunted together, or not at all.

'*Go,*' Lucoryphus voxed back to them

Without sharing a word, they reluctantly obeyed.

FROM HIS BIRTH on an orderly, respected feudal world at the edges of Ultima Segmentum, the warrior had risen among the ranks of his Chapter through a liberal measure of discipline, focus, skill and peerless tactical acumen. None of his brothers had bested him in an honour duel for close to four decades. He'd been offered a company captaincy on three occasions – to assume the mantle of mastery over a hundred of the Emperor's chosen warriors – and had refused with humility and grace each time.

One shoulder guard was given over to the white stone majesty of the Crux Terminatus, the other bore the symbol of his Chapter carved in blue-veined marble and black iron.

To his brothers, he was simply Tolemion. In the archives of his Chapter, he was Tolemion Saralen, Champion of the Third Battle Company. To the enemies of Terra's Throne, he was vengeance incarnate clad in carnelian ceramite.

His armour was an ablative suit of composite metals, layered and reinforced through hundreds of hours of consummate craftsmanship. His helm, with its ornate faceguard and bronzed grille, was an imposing and crested relic from a bygone era, forged in the age of humanity's interstellar apex. One red gauntlet clutched a trembling thunder hammer, its power field charged to a teeth-aching whine. The other held a huge tower shield out ahead, the barrier's shape that of an aquila in profile, one golden wing spread to protect the bearer.

The order he growled to his kindred was a mere two words.

'Boarding blades.'

The warrior's remaining three brothers advanced alongside him, slinging their bolters and drawing pistols and short swords.

First Claw watched this implacable advance, pouring fire down the corridor, watching everything they had shatter harmlessly against the champion's tower shield.

Mercutian dumped his heavy bolter with a disgusted crash.

'I'm dry.' In mirror image of the closing Space Marines, he drew a bolt pistol and the gladius sheathed at his shin. 'I never thought I'd *want* to see Xarl,' he added.

Talos and Cyrion drew their blades a moment later. The prophet helped Uzas to his feet, expecting no word of thanks, and stunned when he actually received a grunt of acknowledgement.

In the moment before the squads came together, the Imperial shield-bearer growled through his amplifying vox-grille.

'I am the End of Heretics. I am the Bane of Traitors. I am Tolemion of the Genesis, Warden of the West Protectorate, Slayer of–'

First Claw didn't wait to be charged. They were already running forward.

'Death to the lackeys of the False Emperor!' Uzas cried. 'Blood for the Eighth Legion!'

VII

DEADLOCK

First Claw had one chance to survive the next few minutes, and they reached for it with everything they had left. The four of them hurled their weight forwards as one, shoulder-charging in a mass of midnight armour. Talos and Mercutian bore the responsibility of the vanguard, and both of them thudded their sloping, spiked shoulder guards against the half-aquila shield with a shared cry of wordless anger.

Tolemion braced against them, his boots chewing sparks from the decking as he was sent slowly skidding backwards. He had the shadow of a second to swing his hammer, pounding the maul into Mercutian's back-mounted power generator, discharging its gathered storm of force in a burst of energy and light.

Mercutian's backpack exploded, blasting debris in every direction. The hammer's concussive force threw him to the decking in a clatter of deactivated armour, to be trampled beneath the grinding feet of both squads. Talos saw Mercutian's life signs wipe blank from his retinal display, powered down before even registering a flatline.

Even as Mercutian was falling, Uzas took his place against the shield, sending the champion staggering backwards. Cyrion pounded into his brothers' backs, adding his strength and weight to the jury-rigged phalanx.

It turned the tide. First Claw and their majestic victim went down in a fighting tumble, cursing and spitting.

Cyrion was the first to rise, the first to face the Genesis Chapter's blades. His gladius punched into the abdomen of the closest Imperial Space Marine, eliciting an irritated, pained gurgle. The Space Marines hacked at his armour, their scoring blades leaving silver smears where they cleaved paint from the ceramite, and ceramite from the subdermal layers.

Uzas didn't even bother to rise. He cleaved with his chainaxe, severing one of the enemy at the knees. For his efforts, he was rewarded with another of the enemy warriors ramming a short sword into his back.

Talos, pinned atop Tolemion's shield, couldn't reach the champion through the aquila barricade. He caught an incoming sword from above with his augmetic hand, and yanked to pull the bearer off-balance. The Genesis warrior fell forward, his proud breastplate of beaten bronze meeting the rising gold of Talos's Blood Angel blade. A crunch. A squeal of metal on metal. The hiss of bubbling blood on charged iron.

The prophet rolled aside, kicking the dying Imperial's legs out from under him.

Two down. His senses thrumming in response to heightened synapses and reflexes, Talos scrambled up and launched at the last Genesis Space Marine in the same moment as Cyrion. Both Night Lords bore the warrior to the decking, slaking their blades' thirsts with each puncturing stab.

We are not soldiers. We are murderers first, last, and always.

Who wrote those words? Or spoke them? Was it Malcharion? Sevatar? Both were prone to those dramatic turns of phrase.

He was dizzy now. His vision watered as he dragged his sword from its scraping sheath in the Space Marine's collarbone. He'd never had to fight so soon after a prophetic dream. Tolemion rose on snarling armour joints, smashing Uzas aside with the edge of his shield. The Legionary staggered back into his brothers, his helm mangled beyond recognition.

Mercutian lay unmoving at the champion's feet. The three Genesis warriors were down and just as dead. Talos, Uzas and Cyrion faced Tolemion, all of their bravado – in short supply even at the fight's beginning – now gone. Uzas and Talos were barely able to stand. In First Claw's infamous, not-quite-illustrious history, few battles had ever looked so one-sided.

'Come then,' the Space Marine intoned. They each heard the cold amusement in his voice, distorted as it was by the waspish buzz of vox-growl.

Despite the challenge, Tolemion didn't wait for them to charge, nor was he willing to risk them trying to flee. His crested helm dipped as he advanced, the hammer emitting its migraine whine as it made ready to fall.

Aurum, the Blade of Angels, caught the first blow. Gold scraped against gunmetal grey, with the prophet locked against the champion. Tolemion broke the deadlock with only the scarcest effort, levelling a second blow against the sword's crosspiece. The thundercrack was deflected enough to miss a direct strike, but pounded into the Night Lord's joined wrists. Talos lost hold of the blade, and Tolemion kicked the prophet against the arched wall, finishing him with a backhanded blow to the chest. The broken aquila on Talos's chestpiece burned black with scorch damage, while chasm-cracks ripped out in an unintentional star.

'Down you go, heretic.'

As Talos collapsed, joining Mercutian on the decking, Cyrion and Uzas descended as one. The former hurled himself onto the weighty shield, his gauntlets clawing at the edges. If he could tear it from Tolemion's grip, or even lower it enough, Uzas could deliver the death blow.

He realised his mistake as soon as he latched onto the ornate shield. Uzas, at his best, was sloppy beyond belief when it came to pack tactics. Desperation didn't focus him the way it did his brothers. And Tolemion was no fool; he recognised the threat as soon as it came near, and bashed Cyrion back against the wall the moment the Night Lord had a grip.

The pressure was somewhere close to falling beneath a Land Raider's treads. Cyrion voxed nothing beyond strangled breaths as he felt himself slowly crushed into the wall. Reaching around the shield's edge with his pistol allowed him to crack a shot into the champion's knee, which did nothing but scar the ceramite.

Tolemion used his backswing to finish the damage he'd already begun to inflict on Uzas. As the axe-wielder came in for a second strike, he met the thunder hammer face-on. It broke through his weak guard, pounding a half-second later into his breastplate. Lightning played across Uzas's armour in sick delight, even as the warrior toppled backward, dead-limbed, onto the decking next to his brothers.

With the others finished, Tolemion released Cyrion. The Legionary staggered forward, weapons falling from numbed hands. A third and final shield bash rocked him back to his heels, sending him down to the deck in a weak heap.

'Your impurity sickens me.' The angry hum of Tolemion's armour was a rumbling percussion to the snarl of his words. He moved to stand over Cyrion, pressing a boot onto the Night Lord's chestplate. 'Was it worth it, to fall from the Emperor's grace? Do all of your viperous achievements validate your cancerous existence, now that your life comes to an end?'

Cyrion's laughter was broken by coughing, but it was laughter all the same. 'The Thirteenth Legion... always gave... the best battle sermons.'

Tolemion raised the hammer, his expression hidden by the dense metal facemask.

'Behind you,' Cyrion was still laughing.

Tolemion was no fool. Even an initiate wouldn't be

deceived by such crude trickery. That fact, coupled with the noise of chatter from the boarding squads in constant communication over the vox, was why he was taken completely by surprise when Xarl came at him from behind.

Cyrion was the only one of First Claw to witness the duel that followed. What he saw stayed with him until the night he died.

They didn't engage at once. Xarl and Tolemion stared at each other for several moments, each taking in the trophies and honour markings displayed across their rival's suit of armour. Tolemion was a vision in Imperial accoutrement, with wax purity seals, honour scrolls and aquilas decorating his ornate war plate. Xarl stood in filthy reflection, his armour adorned with skulls and Imperial Space Marine helms hanging from rusted chains, with swatches of flayed skin in place of parchment scrolls.

'I am Tolemion of the Genesis, Warden of the West Protectorate. I am the End of Heretics, the Bane of Traitors, and a loyal son of Lord Guilliman.'

'Oh,' Xarl chuckled through his voxsponder. 'You must be very proud.' He tossed something round and heavy onto the decking between them both. It rolled to knock gently against Tolemion's boot. A helm. A Genesis Space Marine's helm – the eye lenses put out, the faceplate smeared with blood.

'You'll scream just as he did,' Xarl said with a smile.

The Champion showed no reaction. He didn't even move. 'I knew that warrior,' he said with solemn care. 'He was Caleus, born of Newfound, and I know he died as he lived: with courage, honour, and knowing no fear.'

Xarl swept his chainsword across the scene, gesturing at the prone forms of First Claw. 'I know all of these warriors. They are First Claw, and I know they'll die as they lived: trying to run away.'

It was the laughter that did it. His mockery of the Genesis Champion's demeanour wasn't quite enough to incite the Imperial wretch to rage, but Xarl's laughter served as the coffin's final nail.

Tolemion advanced, shield high and hammer at the ready. 'Make peace with your black-hearted gods, heretic. Tonight, you will know the–'

Xarl gave a distinctly annoyed snort. 'I'd forgotten how much you heroes liked the sound of your own voices.' As Tolemion drew nearer, the Night Lord gripped his two-handed chainblade in a single gauntlet. In his other hand, Xarl caught the handle of Uzas's damaged chainaxe, as he kicked it up from the deck.

Both blades began to roar as their teeth chewed the air. He'd fought through seven Imperial Space Marines to get back here, and their blood flicked in a light spray from the whirring teeth of his chainsword. Beneath his armour, sweat bathed his skin in a greasy sheen, while amusement danced with the strain of pain and anger in his eyes. The sting of already suffered wounds knifed at him through the rents in his war plate.

'Let's get this done,' he said, still smiling. 'I look forward to letting our slaves use your helm as a shitbucket.'

DELTRIAN DIDN'T NEED to breathe – that is, to respire in the conventional sense – but his remaining internal organics required an oxygenated system to function, and could only be slowed by necessity for so long. The augmetic equivalent of holding one's breath was to manipulate his inner chronometry, forcing it to operate at a fraction of optimal speed. It left him slower, near sluggish, but it meant he could operate in the void for up to three hours, by his closest prediction.

His robes drifted around him as he walked. Beneath his clawed feet, the ridged hull of the *Echo of Damnation* stretched out for kilometres both ahead and behind. To look in any other direction was to stare out into the far reaches of space, and the stars winking an infinity's distance away. The enemy vessel circled the *Echo of Damnation* with rapacious patience, casting shadows across the larger cruiser's hull as it eclipsed the distant sun. The ship was a battlemented void-cutter, a strike cruiser with the inscription *Diadem Mantle* along its prow. Almost against his will, he considered it a singularly beautiful name for a warship.

Deltrian took another step, making his cautious way across the outer hull, leading a phalanx of those in his service. Most wore environment suits and full rebreathers. Several were robed, as resistant to the void as Deltrian himself. The pack traversed brutalised sections of the ship's armoured skin, moving through craterous holes and across wrenched-steel terrain. A warship would endure an eternity of external damage with no concern, but a handful of unfortunate shots against certain sections, and havoc was the result.

'Your Reverence, please,' one of Deltrian's lesser adepts began over the vox. Lacking the human lexicon to continue in a formal complaint, the robed priest blurted a pulse of offended code over their communications link. Deltrian turned to face the other adept, his skullish face peering from beneath his red cowl with glittering eye lenses. While Deltrian's appearance was a calculated artifice to inspire discomfort in biologicals, his Mechanicum kindred could read the displeasure in the subtle kinetics of his facial movements, even down to the shutter-guarded glare of his focusing lenses.

The adept was already preparing to apologise when Deltrian spoke.

'Lacuna Absolutus, if you distract me with further objection, I will have you rendered down to your component pieces. Pulse me acknowledgement signifying your comprehension.'

Lacuna Absolutus transmitted a spurt of affirmative code.

'Good.' Deltrian returned his focus to his duty. 'Now is not the time to cite optimal operational specifics.'

It took the Mechanicum repair party exactly twelve minutes and two seconds to reach the first shield generation spire. The damage was immediately apparent: the pylon, reaching out six times as high as an unaugmented man, was a mangled tower of scrap iron in a crater of damage eaten into the metal meat of the hull.

'Analysing,' he said, devoting his sphere of attention to the damage he beheld. What required immediate maintenance? What was superficial hull-scoring, and could wait until dry dock?

'Sixteen composite metal girders to replace the focusing spire's damage.' Four servitors shambled to obey, their mag-locked boots sending minute tremors along the hull. Deltrian's eye lenses whirred as he sought to perceive through the outermost layers of the hull. He pressed his hand to the twisted metal, pulsing ultrasound into the damaged floor. 'The damage does not extend to any significant depth. Internal team, move ahead.'

'Compliance,' came the dead-voiced reply, from over a dozen metres beneath his feet.

'Your Reverence?' one of his adepts voxed.

Deltrian didn't turn. He was already walking into the crater, beginning the hike to the next spire.

'Vocalise, Lacuna Absolutus.'

'Have you determined the probability of the enemy craft detecting the attempted repairs on their narrow-band auspex sweeps?'

'Detecting us is irrelevant. The void shields are active. We are working to ensure they remain active. I had not realised the situation was beyond your cognition.'

'Your Reverence, the void shields are active *now*. If they fall again before we complete the repairs, the enemy will surely seek to interfere with our actions, will they not?'

Deltrian resisted the urge to emit an expletive. 'Be silent, Lacuna Absolutus.'

'Compliance, your Reverence.'

* * *

Xarl caught another hammer blow in the crossed blades. His own sword – the unimaginatively-named Executioner – was already reduced to ruin. In flashes of insight between blocking blows and swinging to kill, he sincerely doubted Septimus would be able to restore it to full working order.

If Septimus was even still alive. The ship was taking a hell of a beating, and the crew with it.

He'd miss this sword, no doubt there. Assuming he survived, of course. He trusted his skills in battle above any of First Claw (above any Night Lord except Malek of the Atramentar, if he was being perfectly honest), but duelling an Adeptus Astartes Company Champion was no laughing matter, especially not one this well armed and armoured.

Xarl knocked the thunder hammer aside with Uzas's damaged axe, lashing another fruitless strike against Tolemion's dense armour with his own blade. The chainsword, now almost toothless, skidded along the layered ceramite, leaving nothing but scratches. With so few teeth, it had almost no grip. No chain weapon could stand up to a protracted duel with a thunder hammer. Xarl cast it aside with a curse.

Three crashing strikes against Tolemion's shield drove the warrior back as far as Xarl needed. He repeated his kicking move, flipping Talos's stolen Blood Angel power sword off the deck and catching it in his spare hand. Clenching the grip was enough to activate it. The sword hissed and spat with lethal lightning dancing along its golden length, crackling as the energy discharged into the air.

Everything changed the moment he held the blade, for he had a weapon that could reliably parry the devastating maul. Xarl used both weapons to smash into the hammer's haft, knocking its descent aside. Conflicting power fields met with angry, snarling sparks. When Tolemion's shield came high, readying for a crushing bash, Xarl's axe hacked into the top rim. The Night Lord pulled the hooked axe, tearing the shield from the Space Marine's grip.

They backed away once more. Xarl kept both weapons live, one boot on the half-aquila of the fallen boarding shield. Tolemion gripped his hammer in both hands.

'You have done well, traitor, but this ends now.'

'I think I'm winning.' the Night Lord grinned behind his faceplate. 'What do you think?'

DELTRIAN REACHED THE third damaged generator pylon. This one, half a kilometre from the first, was a ruined stump of melted metal. Its severed nub scarcely poked from the ship's scorched armour-skin. The hull underfoot was a pitted, dissolved desert of abused steel, having suffered heavy damage in the last cannonade.

For the first time in several decades, Deltrian felt something akin to hopelessness. The emotion was simply too powerful, too sudden, to swallow back down in traditional Mechanicum repression of the mortal, the flawed, the organic.

'Lacuna Absolutus.'

'Your Reverence?'

'Take the last team ahead to the final damaged spire. I will deal with this one myself.'

Lacuna Absolutus stood next to his master, his own red hood drifting in the airless void. His face was a chrome-plated simulacrum of an ancient Terran death mask, expressionless, yet not without judgement. His voice issued forth from a coin-sized vocaliser tablet sutured into his throat.

'Understood. But how will you deal with this, your Reverence?'

Deltrian grinned, because he always grinned. His features left him no choice in the matter. 'You have your orders. Begone.'

A shiver wormed its way down his spine as he received information from his link to the ship.

'No,' he said aloud.

'Your Reverence?'
'No, no, no. The generator was stabilised.'
'Void shields,' came the voice across his uplink bond, *'failing.'*

VIII

TURNING THE TIDE

Xarl heaved with the blade, each of his grunted breaths rasping blood flecks into the inside of his helm. The duel had lasted no longer than a handful of minutes, during which both warriors had melted into blurs of movement, each landing blows and smashing others aside with feverish desperation. All elegance had fled, coming down now to two warriors wishing nothing more than to kill the other.

It grieved him to realise it, but Xarl was already exhausted. Being hit with a tank-cracking thunder hammer was little different from being hit by a tank itself. His left arm was slack and useless, the pauldron broken along with the shoulder beneath it. Each breath was effort, rendered into needling torment from the way his destroyed breastplate had pierced his chest in several places.

'Just *die*,' he breathed, and heaved with the blade yet again. This time it came clear, ripping free of Tolemion's stomach with a spray of cleaved armour shards moistened by gore.

The Champion sagged, his armour reduced to similar wreckage, the cast-iron hammer now dragging against the decking.

'Heretic,' the Space Marine snarled. 'For your… impurity…'

Xarl's backhand ended the threatened chastisement,

snapping the loyalist's helm to the side. 'I know, I know... You already said all that.'

The Night Lord staggered back himself, dropping the sword so his one good hand could claw at his collar locks. He had to disengage his helm's seals. He had to get the helmet off so he could see, and so he could breathe.

It came free with the *snap-hiss* of depressurising air. As soon as his eyes were clear of the blood-smeared lenses, Xarl raised Talos's blade again. The ship was shaking around them.

'Your shields are down.' Tolemion barked a harsh laugh. 'More of my brothers will be boarding.'

Xarl didn't reply. He charged forward with all the strength he could muster, muscles fuelled as much by anger as the adrenal sting of combat narcotics. Sword met hammer again and again, crashing and flashing as their opposing power fields protested each impact. Their blows were blurs as the wounded warriors spat and cursed, bleeding the last of their energy into the duel's final moments.

Tolemion gave no ground. Retreat was simply not within him. Xarl's blade cracked against his armour-plating, cutting cold and deep, each carve leeching precious portions of what little strength he had left. In return, his hammer was a slow, clumsy maul that rarely struck his opponent – but when it did, it echoed with vicious finality, throwing the Night Lord back against the wall.

Xarl jumped to his feet again, feeling split sections of his outer armour falling free. He shuddered to think how long these repairs were going to take First Claw's artificer, and stumbled, almost falling again as he stepped over Cyrion's body. The other Night Lord was trying to rise himself, to no avail.

'Xarl,' Cyrion growled through his helm. 'Help me up.'

'Stay down,' Xarl was panting. A single glance at his

brother's prone form told him all he needed to know: Cyrion was too weak to do anything, anyway. 'I will be done in a moment,' he said.

Hammer and blade fell in the same moment, meeting midway between the bloody, swearing warriors. The flash was enough to leave a retinal bruise playing over Xarl's eyes, while his vision danced with flickering after-images.

He wasn't going to win this if it stayed a fair fight, and his options to cheat were getting thinner with each drop of blood that ran from his body. The bastard's armour was too thick, and one more hammerfall would keep him down long enough for Tolemion to finish the job.

The Genesis Space Marine drew breath for another chastisement. Xarl chose that moment to head-butt him.

A life of bloodshed and battle meant Xarl was no stranger to pain, but pounding his bare forehead against the riveted, dense helm of an Adeptus Astartes Company Champion immediately ranked as one of the most agonising moments of his existence. Tolemion's head snapped back, but Xarl wouldn't let him go. He leaned closer, around their waspishly buzzing weapons, and powered his head against the Space Marine's faceplate a second time. Then a third. The impacts made the corridor echo like a forge, and his nose gave way with a sickening snap on the fourth. On the fifth, something cracked in the front of his skull. Two more followed it. He was breaking his own face apart, and the feeling was both distantly indescribable, and painful beyond words.

Blood sheeted into his eyes. He could no longer see, but he could feel Tolemion's muscles loosening, and hear the gargling of a throat injury. He spat, then. A stringy gobbet of blood-diluted acidic saliva splashed against Tolemion's left eye lens, eating its hissing way into the flesh beneath.

An eighth head-butt was enough to send both of them reeling: Tolemion stumbling back against the wall, Xarl losing his balance and collapsing to his knees for several heartbeats. Talos's sword fell from his grip. Blinded, he felt along the floor for the fallen weapon.

He sensed the shadow rising above him, and heard the tense growl of wounded power armour. He knew the Genesis Space Marine was raising the hammer high, its distinctive thrum was unmistakable. Xarl's fingers closed around the hilt of Talos's energised sword. With a scream of effort, he rammed it upwards.

It bit, and bit deep. Xarl didn't hesitate – he started carving as soon as it sank in. His clumsy, brutal hacksawing tore through armour, flesh and bone with equal relish. Gore rained onto him, populated wormishly by the looping ropes of Tolemion's intestines. He felt them splash over his shoulders and circle his neck like oil-slick snakes. At any other time, he'd have been amused at the foul display.

Xarl yanked the sword free, hauling himself to his feet in a surge of renewed vitality. His next chop cleaved the champion's hammer-hand at the wrist, letting the weapon fall at last.

'I am taking your helm,' Xarl panted, 'as a trophy. I think I earned it.'

Tolemion swayed on his feet, too strong and too stubborn to collapse. 'For... For the... Emp–'

Xarl took a step back, spun with all the strength he could muster, and powered the golden blade through his enemy's neck. It went through without slowing, as though it had nothing to chop but clean air. The head fell one way, the body another.

'To the abyss with your Emperor,' Xarl sighed.

DELTRIAN HAD NEVER worked faster, even with the relative limitations opposed by his slowed internal chronometry. He'd deployed his four auxiliary arms, activating them and letting them uncurl from their sockets in his resculpted back. These replicas of his skeletal main arms each gripped a blocky signum device, shaped as wire-encrusted rods. The adept couldn't trust his servitors to work with the speed and precision the moment required, and thus it fell to Deltrian to slave them to his more efficient output.

The four servitors responded in service to the merest movement of the signum controls in his hands, their every tic and breath controlled by his will. In a morbid ballet of lobotomised unity, the bionic slaves lifted girders into place, sealed them with fusing strips, and worked to rebuild the destroyed power pylon's external focusing spire.

Linking the spire's foundations to the flash-fried electronics being replaced in the hull itself was a much more difficult task. To that end, Deltrian multisected his visual receptors, seeing with a fly's segmented vision through the eyes of the four servitors outside on the hull with him; through his own perspective as overseer at the crater's edge; and through the eyes of two of the servitors on board the ship, several metres below his feet. They were cramped into the crawlspace tunnels, their corpse-like flesh leaking its oily sweat as they laboured with fingertip micro-tools, re-bonding and rewiring the damage done.

Deltrian was a man (in the loosest sense) that usually enjoyed his work. Challenge motivated him, resulting in something akin to a pleasant emotive response as well as increased productivity. A fleshier creature would probably call it inspiration.

This, however, was an exercise in manipulation and haste far beyond preferred operational parameters. He'd fought wars with less effort than this.

The void shields had flicker-failed again, snapping out of existence for two minutes and forty-one seconds. During that time, as Deltrian multisected his attention between six servitors, he'd also looked out into the void and watched the distant red smear of the enemy ship in its far-ranged orbit of the wounded *Echo of Damnation*. Zooming his eye lenses had diverted even more of his precious attention span, but he had to know if the enemy cruiser was risking an attempt to deploy more warriors while the *Echo*'s shields were down.

The crew of the Genesis strike cruiser had surely been tempted to fire, but would never do so with so many of their loyal warriors on board. Instead, it launched another two boarding pods, surely now representing the warship's entire complement of Imperial Space Marines spent.

Deltrian had watched the pods diving closer, burning through the void. The *Echo*'s main broadside weapon batteries had no hope of shooting down such minute targets, but the servitor-manned defence turrets began spitting hard tracer fire into the void the moment the pods entered range. One had popped in silence, coming apart in the barrage, spilling its organic cargo into space. Deltrian hadn't seen the Imperial Space Marines and their pod's debris strike the hull with lethal inertia, but he'd allowed himself a brief imagining of the mess such an impact had likely made.

The second pod struck home in the ship's belly, far from the tech-adept's visual sphere. He pulsed a vox-screed detailing his estimated location for the pod's breaching, and hoped at least one of the claws defending the ship would pay heed to it.

Seven minutes and thirty-seven seconds later, when the void shields were back up and his work on the reconstruction was nearing forty per cent complete, a shadow ghosted behind him. Deltrian reluctantly began to spare it a fraction of his attention, and was halfway turned when something with the force of a Titan's kick hammered into his side, detonating in a flash too fast for the human eye to follow. His ocular implants were technically capable of registering the spherical detonation as it dispersed at otherwise untrackable speeds, spreading its force into the void with no resistance to counter it. He didn't manage to track anything, however. The explosion against his ribcage blasted him from his grip on the hull, sending him skidding along the ship's outer skin.

As he tumbled away, several hands reaching out to latch onto the hull and arrest his fall, his cogitation processor did the following things: firstly, it catalogued an instant display of the damage his physical form had sustained; secondly, it felt all six of his servitors go mind-dead, defaulting to their slower, simpler behaviour; thirdly, it spared the runtime to pulse a warning to the other repair teams on the outside of the ship; and lastly, it allowed him a moment to wonder how in the infinite hells any of the Imperial Space Marines had survived their disintegrating pod, and managed to walk their way along the hull to shoot him in the back. That level of resilience was irritating when found in one's enemies.

All of this took less than a second. Deltrian's skidding, clawing slide ended three seconds after his cogitations, as he drifted out of reach from the hull, turning and spinning into the void. The stars twisted, unfocused, in his spiralling vision.

With no method of thrust or creating inertial force, he was almost certain to drift away until his death. This... this was not optimal.

Something caught his robe, jerking him in place. He turned in the weightless, airless nothingness, seeing the hand clutching the very edge of his cloak, and the warrior that the gauntlet belonged to.

The Night Lord regarded him through curving eye lenses. Tears, painted in red and silver streaks, ran down the daemonic faceplate.

'I heard you on the vox,' said Lucoryphus of the Bleeding Eyes.

'Praise be to the beneficence of the Machine God,' Deltrian sent back over the communication link.

The Raptor pulled the adept back onto the hull, without bothering to be gentle about it.

'If you say so,' Lucoryphus rasped. 'Remain here. I will slit your ambusher's throat. Then get back to your repairs.'

The engines housed on his back cycled into silent life, their roars stolen by the airless void. With a burst of manoeuvring thrusters, the Night Lord kicked off from the ship's skin and boosted over to the damaged pylon.

Deltrian watched him depart, so overcome with relief he decided not to record the Raptor's disrespect for later archiving.

This time.

XARL DROPPED THE sword, and with almost insane patience, he moved to lean against the arched wall. He remained there for a timeless span, cataloguing his hurts, catching his breath. The blood leaking through his breastplate smelled too rich, too clean. Heartsblood, he knew. That wasn't good. If one of his hearts was sundered, he'd be laid up for weeks adapting to an augmetic replacement. He couldn't move one arm, and the other was numb from the elbow, the fingers starting to seize up. One knee was refusing to bend, and the pain in his chest was getting colder, spreading farther.

He grunted again, but couldn't move away from the wall just yet. *Another minute, perhaps.* Let his regenerative tissues catch up to the damage. That's all. That's all he needed.

Cyrion was the first to rise, pulling himself up by the opposite wall. His armour looked almost as ruined as Xarl's, and rather than help the others, he lifted the now-dead hammer in his hands.

'Its power cells are depleted to eighty per cent now. Perhaps it was hitting us harder than it hit you.'

Xarl didn't reply. He kept leaning against the wall.

'I've never seen a duel like that,' Cyrion added. He moved to where his brother stood.

'Get away from me. I need a moment to breathe.'

'As you wish.' Cyrion moved over to Talos, who still lay paralysed on the deck. A vial of chemical stimulant injected into the prophet's neck sent his muscles into spasm, and he rose, choking, a moment later.

'I have never been hit with a thunder hammer before. Variel will bore us all with details of what it does to a nervous system, but I never want to feel it again.'

'Be glad the blow was glancing.'

'It did not feel glancing,' Talos replied.

'If you're still alive, then it was glancing.'

One by one, First Claw rose to their feet.

'Xarl,' Talos said. 'I can't believe you killed him.'

The other warrior faced his brothers with an amused sneer. 'It was nothing.' He caught his helmet when Talos tossed it to him. For a moment, Xarl stroked his fingers along the winged crests – the ceremonial Legion decoration – looking down at the bitter visage he presented to the galaxy.

His eyes were clear of blood, but his skull was a shattered mash of bone and flesh. Even rolling his eyes in their sockets bred enough pain to drive him to his knees, but he wouldn't allow such weakness to show. Blinking was an agony so fierce he lacked the imagination to describe it even to himself. He didn't even want to know how much of his face was left. The others were looking at him with worry in their eyes, and that only made him angrier.

'Can you still fight?' Talos asked.

'I've felt better,' replied Xarl. 'But I can fight.'

'We need to move,' Mercutian said. He was the weakest of them all. Without power, his armour was almost useless, adding nothing to his strength or reflexes. The joints didn't whirr, and the backpack didn't hum. 'We need to link up with one of the other claws if we're being boarded again.'

'Xarl,' Talos said again.

The warrior looked up. 'What?'

'Take the hammer. You earned it.'

Xarl lifted his helm back into place. It clicked once, sealing to his collar locks, and his voice left his vocaliser in its usual vox-altered snarl.

'Talos,' he said. 'My brother.'

'What is it?'

'I regret arguing with you before. It is no sin to wish for a life with meaning, or a way to win this war.'

'We will speak of this later, brother,' said Talos.

'Yes,' he replied. 'Later.'

Xarl took a single step closer. His head rolled forward in a slow nod, and his body followed in a boneless topple. He collapsed into the prophet's arms, utterly limp, his armour broadcasting the tuneless whine of a flatline signal.

IX

REPULSION

'I have broken a hundred oaths. Some by design, some by chance, some by misfortune. One of the few I still seek to honour is our pledge to the Mechanicum. No Legion can stand without the foundations provided by the exiles of Mars.'

– Konrad Curze, the Night Haunter,
Primarch of the Eighth Legion

TALOS DRAGGED THE body onto the bridge. Xarl's armour growled along the decking, the ceramite grinding every step of the way.

'Leave him,' Mercutian said. He was bareheaded now, his powerless suit no longer tied into the vox. 'Talos, leave him. We have a battle to fight.'

The prophet hauled Xarl's body to the side of the chamber, leaving his brother lying by the western doors. When he rose, he took in the sight before him through impassive eyes. The bridge was deep in its usual bustle of noise and organised chaos, with officers and servitors calling back and forth, running between their stations. First Claw, what remained of them, moved to the eastern doors, checking their weapons as they walked. Humans scattered before them, all gestures of respect going ignored.

Only Talos lingered by the command throne. 'Why aren't we engaging the enemy ship?'

'You don't want it as plunder once we've beaten these dogs into their graves?' Cyrion voxed back.

Talos turned to the occulus, watching the scarlet strike cruiser drifting with excruciating patience. 'No,' he said, 'No, you should have known I would not.'

'But we can't board them with every squad engaged.'

'Are you insane? I don't want to board them,' the prophet said. 'I want them to burn.'

'They're half a system away, hanging back out of weapons range. They pulled away as soon as they released boarding pods.'

Talos looked at his brothers, then at the crew, as if they were deluded beyond comprehension. 'Then *chase them.*'

As the ship warmed up around them, Cyrion cleared his throat. 'You want to destroy that ship? Truly?'

The prophet shook his head, not in denial but confusion. 'Why is that so hard to understand?'

'Because it is hardly the province of pirates to annihilate any reward from their raids.' Cyrion looked at the distant ship. 'Think of the ammunition reserves on that cruiser. Think of the thousands of crew, the resources, the weapons we could take as plunder.'

'We have all we need on board the *Echo*. I do not want plunder. I want revenge.'

'But...' Cyrion trailed off as Talos watched him for a moment, his face without expression.

'No,' the prophet said. 'It burns. They die.'

The eastern doors opened on dense hydraulics. Variel limped in, his augmetic leg giving off sparks from its locked knee. Blood washed the flayed leathery flags of skin draped across his armour. The symbol of the Corsair's fist was a hammer-broken ruin on his shoulder guard, while the other pauldron showed the Legion's winged skull with bloodstained pride.

'Fifth Claw has purged the principal habitation decks,' he said. 'The Genesis warriors are bleeding us, but the tide is turning.'

Talos said nothing.

'Xarl?' Variel asked him.

'Dead.' Talos didn't glance at the body. He sat in the command throne, grunting at the pain of his wounds. Combat stimulants were holding off the worst of it, but he needed to get out of his armour soon. 'Take his gene-seed later.'

'I should harvest it at once,' Variel replied.

'*Later*. That is an order.' He looked over to his brothers, stood in a pack. 'The other claws need Variel. Get to the Hall of Reflection and defend Deltrian at all costs. I will ensure all squads fall back to you once their killing is done.'

Cyrion stepped forward, as if to protest. 'What about you?'

Talos nodded to the occulus. 'I will join you, as soon as I finish this.'

THE RAPTOR WAITED at the crater's edge. Deltrian paid the warrior little heed, casting his attention back into the difficulties of multisecting vision. The replacement pylon was being capped by the conduction orb, while the deck crews worked to fuse the tower's electronics to the ship's main systems.

Despite the absence of nerves, and the resulting lack of pain, Deltrian's wound was a troubling one. He'd leaked precious haemo-lubricant oils in place of blood, and his minimal organic components were triggering internal alarms along his retinal displays. Worse, the straining organs were now putting increased pressure on his augmetic systems to keep him functional.

Time was more of a factor than ever. Thankfully, work was almost complete.

Blood crystals clattered gently against his deployed arms as he worked. The fate of Deltrian's ambusher had apparently been an unpleasant one. The body was gone, but crystalline evidence remained, frozen in the void.

He could hear Lucoryphus fighting again, hear it by

the grunts and dull thumps over the vox, but the adept spared the Raptor no significant attention.

At that moment, the ship gave a colossal tremor beneath his feet. The stars began to turn in the night sky, and Deltrian lost several precious seconds watching the void dance before his eyes.

The ship was moving. An attack run, surely. He couldn't envisage a scenario where the Night Lords would run from a smaller vessel, especially not when it had arrived to guard the world they wished to take for themselves.

'This is Deltrian to the strategium. The shields will be secured within four minutes standard.'

'This is Talos,' came the crackling reply. 'The shields are already active.'

'I am aware of that. But they are unsecured, due to external pylon damage. They may yet fail again, and the probability rises to a near-certainty if kinetic force is a factor. Do not engage until the void generators are at a secure operational capacity. Four minutes. Acknowledge understanding of this critical proviso with an immediate response.'

'Understood, adept. Work fast.'

THE SHIP SHOOK around her. Octavia remained in her throne, watching the stars drift by on her wall of pict-feed monitors.

'They're running,' she said. 'The Genesis warship is trying to maintain distance.'

Septimus stood next to the throne, his wounds still bandaged, the bruises discolouring his face now at their ripest.

'Should you even be here?' Octavia asked, unwittingly sounding more like a Terran aristocrat than ever.

He ignored the question. 'I don't see how you can tell they're running,' he said, his throat tight and his voice scratchy. 'It's just a red speck in the blackness.'

She didn't lift her eyes from the screens. 'I can just tell.'

Several of her attendants bustled on the other side

of the fluid pool, guarding the bulkhead door. One of them approached, the footsteps echoing around the humid chamber.

'Mistress.'

Octavia turned to glance at the bandaged, cloaked figure. 'What is it?'

'The door is sealed. Word from Fourth Claw promises this deck is safe from intrusion.'

'Thank you, Vularai.'

The figure bowed, and moved back to its brethren.

'You are treating them better,' Septimus pointed out. He knew she still missed Hound.

She smiled, patently forced, and looked back to the screens. 'We're catching up, but too slowly. The engines are taking too long to burn hotter. I can almost picture the enemy captain, watching us as we watch him, hoping his boarding teams will take our bridge before we reach his ship. And they might, for this chase will take hours. Maybe several days.'

'Octavia,' came a bass rumbling voice from the gargoyles carved into the chamber walls. Their wide maws were sculpted to hold vox-emitters.

She reached to the armrest of her throne and worked the cranking lever. It settled with a crunch.

'I'm here. How is the battle going?'

'Victory will have a high price. I need you to ready the ship for immediate warp entry.'

She blinked twice. 'I… what?'

'The void shields will be secured in two minutes. You will jump the ship shortly after. Understood?'

'But we're in orbit.'

'We are leaving orbit. You can see that.'

'But we're so close to the planet. And the enemy isn't even running to the system's warp beacons. They're not going into the Sea of Souls.'

'There is no time to debate this, Octavia. I am ordering you to engage the warp engines as soon as the void shields are secured.'

'I'll do it. But what's the destination?'

'Nowhere.' He sounded impatient now, which she found a rare change. 'Jump closer to the enemy. I want to... to shunt the ship through the empyrean, and ambush the enemy strike cruiser. I am not wasting days chasing these fools across the stars.'

She had to blink again. 'You're talking about ripping a hole in space to leap through the narrowest slice of the empyrean. The engines will barely be live before we'll need to kill power to them. It will be a jump of less than a second, and even then, we may overshoot by a long way.'

'I did not say I cared how it was done.'

'Talos, I'm not sure this *can* be done.'

'I did not ask that, either. I just want you to do it.'

'As you wish,' she said. Once she'd worked the lever back, cutting off her vox-link to the bridge, Octavia took a deep breath. 'This will be interesting.'

'CONSTRUCTION COMPLETE.'

Deltrian began to retract his augmetic arms, while the servitors fell back into a hear/obey pattern around him.

'Orders?' one of them voxed to him.

'Follow me.' Deltrian was already moving, his magnetic boots pounding along the hull in silent shivers. 'Lucoryphus?'

The Raptor waited at the crater's edge, three red helms in his clawed clutch. 'You are finished, at last? We must regain immediate access to the ship.'

Lucoryphus lifted from the decking on a gentle surge of thrust. Gone was the crawling, awkward creature – out here, freedom altered him into something much more lethal. Guidance thrusters breathed little jets of soundless pressure, keeping him suspended in place.

'Why?'

'Because Talos intends to jump the ship.'

'That is incorrect terminology.'

Lucoryphus merely snorted. 'It is still happening.'

'When?'

Deltrian didn't stop walking. He strode past the hovering Raptor, head down, eye lenses focused on the closest bulkhead set into the ship's skin. It was still over three hundred metres away.

'Must I truly answer that question with a detailed chain of events? He intends to engage the warp engines as soon as the void shields are secured. I have repaired the final pylon. Thus, they are secured. Thus, to clarify further, he intends to jump the ship now. Have you ever borne witness to a living organism left unprotected in the warp?'

Deltrian could hear something wet over the vox. He suspected it was the Raptor's smile.

'Oh yes, tech-priest. I most certainly have.'

The ship rumbled beneath the adept's boots, building strength and momentum the way a beast draws breath to roar.

Deltrian cycled through his epiglottal vox-triggers. 'Lacuna Absolutus?'

'Your Reverence?'

'Inform me of your location at once.'

A spurt of amused code fed back over the link. 'Do I detect trace amounts of concern in your query, Revered One?'

'An answer, if you please.'

'My team is between sixteen and twenty seconds' journey from our closest maintenance bulkhead, approximately six hundred metres roll-ward and prow-ward from your position. I believe the...' His words washed away in a flow of static.

'Lacuna Absolutus. Finish vocalisation.'

Static remained the only reply.

'Hold,' Deltrian ordered. The servitors obeyed. Lucoryphus did not, he was already at the next bulkhead, claws gripping the hull as he keyed in the access cipher.

'Lacuna Absolutus?' the adept tried again. The white noise continued unabated, until Deltrian applied audio filters to the vox-channel, scrambling through the chaos. It rendered one sound clearer than all else.

'Lucoryphus,' Deltrian said.

The Raptor hesitated, in the middle of hauling the circular bulkhead door wide open. 'What is it?'

'My subordinate, Lacuna Absolutus, has been engaged. I have deciphered the sound of servitor death across the vox-link.'

'So?' The Night Lord swung the door wide, peeling back the steel to expose the crawlspace within. Beneath their boots, the ship gave a premonitory shudder, its engines gaining power. 'Build another assistant, or whatever it is you do to engineer your slaves.'

'He is...' Deltrian trailed off, feeling the vibration through the ship's bones. They were less than a minute away from entry into the warp.

'He is already dead,' Lucoryphus reasoned. 'Get inside.'

'Your Reverence,' crackled Lacuna Absolutus's voice over the reconnection. '...Astartes...'

Logic and emotion warred within the ancient adept. He had several auxiliaries and subordinates, but few were as gifted as Lacuna Absolutus. Few also retained the same sense of personality and drive, which were aspects to be admired – at least when they blended with efficiency and ambition in that rare mesh of perfect fusion. More than the inconvenience involved in training a replacement, more than the vastly increased workload it would force him to endure – on a small, subtle and personal level it would also grieve Deltrian to lose his favoured aide.

The truth was an awkward one. Affection bred a cold, alien discomfort within his core. In an entity with more flesh to feel with, the sensation might be called a chill.

'I will not abandon him.'

Deltrian turned and made it seven steps before he heard Lucoryphus's disgusted sigh.

'Get inside.' The Raptor soared past him, thrusters

trailing ghost-fire as he raced over the hull. 'I will deal with your lost friend.'

Lucoryphus of the Bleeding Eyes covered the distance in a matter of heartbeats. The hull flashed beneath him in a streaking blur the same colour as his armour, while his target stood out in the stark illumination of external siren lights.

A single red-armoured warrior guarded the maintenance hatch, clearly in the process of entering when he'd seen the adept's servitor pack approaching. Filthy Throne-worshippers. It was bad enough having them worming through the ship's bones, let alone having to endure them crawling over the *Echo*'s skin as well.

The hull veered beneath him with a slow, serene urgency. Enough of this. He would not be trapped outside when the *Echo* entered the warp. That was no way for a leader of the Bleeding Eyes cult to meet his end.

Lucoryphus turned in the void, angling his dive to bring him down atop the Genesis Space Marine. The warrior reared back, only in time to take both of the Raptor's clawed feet in the chest. Lucoryphus gripped with his hands, clutching at the Space Marine's helm while he kicked with his foot-talons, shredding the ceramite breastplate, the subdermal muscle cabling, and the soft flesh beneath. A vicious wrench broke the Space Marine's neck – Lucoryphus felt the muted, popping snaps of the vertebrae giving way even through the armour that separated him from his prey.

The Genesis warrior went slack, still standing straight with his boots mag-locked to the hull. Blood left his torn chest in a crystallised cascade.

Lucoryphus boosted up, twisting in space to land on the hull several metres back with his pistol drawn. A single bolt shell hammered into the Space Marine's breastplate, knocking the body from its magnetic perch, sending it tumbling into the nothingness.

Only then did Lucoryphus turn to find Lacuna

Absolutus. The adept was cowering behind a ridged rise of hull armour, holding a laspistol. The safety settings were still showing as active along the weapon's side – not that such an insignificant weapon would enjoy much luck against an Imperial Space Marine even at the best of times.

'Have you never modified yourself for battle?' Lucoryphus asked, reaching for the adept's throat and hauling him out of hiding.

'Never.' The adept dangled in the warrior's grip. 'But after the events of this night, I plan to rectify that failing.'

'Just get inside,' the Raptor growled.

'TELL ME THAT worked,' Talos said to his crew.

While Octavia was heaving her guts up after the jump, purging the liquefied contents of her stomach, and while the warband's claws were at last forming together to isolate and slay the final remnants of the enemy boarding parties, the *Echo of Damnation* trembled with the pressures of returning to real space. The warship burst back into reality, streaming the migraine-coloured unsmoke of the deep ether from its spinal battlements, after what was assuredly the shortest warp jump in Legion history.

The engines had flickered live for less than a single second, ripping a rift in the void at the vessel's prow. Even as the *Echo*'s entrance rip was sealing, another opened tens of thousands of kilometres away, disgorging the warship back into space.

No warp transit came without cost, but neither did the laws of logic apply when rushing through the hell behind the veil. A short flight was no guarantee of safety, and the ship's emergence mere heartbeats after entry still left it juddering, its Geller field made visible by the clinging pollutant mists.

The shaking bridge had the added rattling melody of chains clashing together as they dangled from the ceiling. The Night Lords occasionally used them to hang bodies – Ruven wasn't the only decoration.

'Speak to me,' Talos ordered.

'Systems realigning,' one of the bridge officers called back. 'Auspex live. I... It worked, lord. We're thirteen hundred kil–'

'Come about,' interrupted the prophet. 'I want that cruiser dead.'

'Coming about, sire,' called the Helmsmistress. The gravitic generators whined at the strain as the ship banked hard, and the occulus reactivated with a blast of static, resolving into a view of the distant red warship.

Talos spared a glance for the hololithic display, still scrambled and showing little of worth. They were too far ahead for any of their weapons to reach yet – still, it was an improvement over lagging so far behind. He had another idea, one that would work now.

'All power to the engines.'

'All power, aye.' The Master of Propulsion reached for his vox-caster, dialling the code for his subordinates on the enginarium control deck. 'All power to the engines,' the veteran officer said into the speech horn. 'We need every one of the reactors burning like a sun's core. Don't spare the slaves.'

Seven replies overlapped into one mess of agreement. Not all of the voices were human.

The *Echo of Damnation* kicked forward, tearing through space in pursuit of its prey.

Talos knew he wasn't a void warrior. He lacked the Exalted's patience, and he was a self-confessed creature of sensation – he waged war with a blade in his hand and blood on his face – the salty reek of an enemy's fear-sweat in his senses focused him, spurring him on. Void warfare required a measure of tolerance he'd never acquired. He knew it, and didn't berate himself for the deficiency. One couldn't be an expert at all things.

To that end, Talos spared no time after taking the *Echo*, almost immediately investing a great deal of trust in his mortal crew. Some of them were survivors from the *Covenant of Blood*, others were veterans of the Red

Corsairs' fleet. When they spoke, he listened. When they advised, he considered their words. When he acted, it was with their counsel.

But patience had its limit. One brother had already died this day.

Another look at the resolving hololithic spoke of the shortening distance between the runes denoting both ships.

'We will catch them,' Talos said.

'They're running for the system's jump locus,' the Master of Auspex called out.

Talos turned to the hunchbacked former Corsair slave. The eight-bladed star blackened his face in a vicious burn marking.

'I do not believe they are. They are running to hide, not to flee.' He ordered the occulus to pan across the expanse of space, finally resting its gaze on a distant moon.

'There,' Talos said. 'They seek to purchase time, pulling further away from us to hide on the other side of that rock. They need only wait long enough for their boarding parties to take control of the ship, or for confirmation that the assault has failed. Then they can return or flee, whichever they deem necessary.'

The Master of Auspex was working his multi-jointed fingers along the clicking console keys. Each brass button clacked like some ancient typing machine.

'You may be correct, lord. Before the warp jump, such a manoeuvre would have bought them approximately seven hours.'

Talos felt his gaze drawn to Xarl again. He resisted it, knowing his brother would still be slouched against the wall. Nothing could be gained by staring at his corpse. 'And now?' he asked.

The robed officer scratched at the weeping sores that marked the edge of his lips. 'We will catch them in perhaps two hours.'

Better. Not good, but at least it was better. Still, a

discomforting thought gnawed at him. Talos mused aloud, 'What if they realise their assault has failed beyond recovery?'

The robed man drew in a sticky breath. 'Then we will not catch them. The warp jump gave us a chance at an honest engagement. No more, lord. No less.'

Talos watched the ship running for respite, burning its engines hot as it made for the temporary sanctuary offered by the dead-rock planetoid. It didn't matter. His idea would work.

'Nostramo,' he whispered. Memory and imagination bred a fire in his dark eyes, though it was lost behind the skullish faceplate and slanted red eye lenses.

'Sire?'

The prophet took several moments to answer. 'Let them run. We are close enough now for the Shriek to work. Pursue, but let them reach orbit on the other side of that rock. Let them come close to it, believing they can buy a few more hours.'

'My lord?'

Talos gestured to the vox-mistress. 'Find Deltrian, if you please.'

The officer – heavily augmented, her remaining flesh pitted by acid scars – worked her console, and nodded a moment later. 'Ready, sire.'

'This is Talos to Deltrian. You have ten minutes to activate the Shriek. It is time we won this fight.'

When it came, the tech-adept's reply was overridden by Lucoryphus's husky drawl. 'We are in the starboard terminus arc. It will take us ten minutes to even reach the adept's chambers.'

'Then move swiftly.' Talos gestured for the Vox-mistress to terminate the link, and released a heavy breath. 'Master of Arms.'

The officer looked up from his console, his sleek and elegant uniform faded by time. 'My lord?'

'Ready cyclonic torpedoes,' the Night Lord ordered.

'Lord?' was the stunned reply.

'Ready cyclonic torpedoes,' he repeated in exactly the same tone.

'Lord, we only have five warheads.'

Talos swallowed, clenching his teeth and closing his eyes as if he could contain his anger by sealing the portals of his face.

'Ready cyclonic torpedoes.'

'Sire, I believe we should save them for–'

The human said nothing more. The front of his face came free with a sickly *crack*, the flesh and jagged bone crunching in the Night Lord's fist. Talos ignored the body as it toppled, spilling the insides of its halved skull onto the decking.

No one had even seen him move, such was the prophet's speed, clearing ten metres and vaulting a console table in the time it took a human heart to beat once.

'I am trying to be reasonable,' he said to the hundreds of watching crew members. His vox-voice carried across the chamber in a guttural, malign whisper. 'I am trying to end this battle so that we might all return to our insignificant lives, still wearing our skin around our souls. I am not, by nature, a choleric creature. I allow you to speak, to advise… but do not see my indulgence as weakness. When I order, you will obey. Please do not try my patience this night. You will regret it, as Armsmaster Sujev is so aptly demonstrating.'

The body at Talos's feet was still twitching, still leaking. The prophet handed his fistful of bloody facial wreckage to the nearest servitor.

'Dispose of this.'

The servitor watched him with dead-eyed devotion. 'How, my lord?' it asked in a monotone murmur.

'Eat it for all I care.'

The prophet stalked back to his throne, tracking through the organic filth running from Sujev's corpse. All the while, he resisted the need to cradle his aching head in his hands. Something inside his mind threatened to break out, shattering his skull with the strain.

The gene-seed is killing you. Some humans are not meant to survive implantation.

He looked up, where Ruven's remains hung on rusting chains.

'I killed you,' he told the bones.

'Sire?' asked a nearby officer. Talos looked over at the man. Mutation had ruined him, leaving one side of his body seized and muscle-locked, giving his face the perpetual leer of a stroke victim. He wiped his drooling, stretched lips on the back of his hand, frozen as it was into a half-claw.

Is this what we have fallen to? the prophet wondered.

'Nothing,' said Talos. 'All stations, ready for deployment of cyclonic torpedoes. When the Shriek is live and our torpedoes cannot be intercepted or tracked, destroy the moon.'

X

REVENGE

'Xarl is dead,' Mercutian said to the darkness. 'I can scarcely believe it. He was unkillable.'

Cyrion chuckled. 'Evidently not.'

The lights around them failed with a crack of overloading circuitry, and the ship groaned strangely beneath their boots. The air itself seemed to cling to them for a moment, pushing and pulling at their limbs.

'What was that sensation?' Variel asked. His shoulder-mounted lamp pack flared in response to the dimming lights, cutting a beam through the blackness. The slice of light panned across the empty iron tunnel ahead.

Even though their retinal displays filtered to compensate, the other Night Lords instinctively turned their eyes from the sharp glare.

'Deactivate that,' Cyrion said softly.

Variel obeyed, amused without possessing the grace to actually smile. 'Please answer my question,' he said. 'That sound, and the ship's shiver. What caused it?'

Cyrion led the remnants of First Claw through the tunnels, moving deeper into the ship. 'It was the inertial adjustment from releasing cyclonic warheads. Talos is doing something either very clever, or very, very foolish.'

'He is angry,' Mercutian added. His brothers, still wearing their helms, didn't pause to look back. They led the way, weapons in their fists. 'Talos will not take Xarl's death with any grace,' he continued. 'I could see it in the way he moved. He is wounded over this. Mark my words.'

Uzas breathed through his speaker-grille. 'Xarl is dead?'

The others ignored him, all but Mercutian. 'He died an hour ago, Uzas.'

'Oh. How?'

'You were there,' Mercutian said quietly.

'Oh.' The others could almost sense his attention sliding across the surface of the conversation, failing to hold.

Cyrion led the depleted claw around another corner, descending the spiralling walkway to the next deck. Crew members scattered before them, like roaches fleeing a sudden light. Only a few of them, robed menials and beggars alike, remained to kneel and weep at the boots of their masters, pleading to be told what was happening.

Cyrion kicked one of them aside. First Claw made its way past the others. 'This ship is the size of a small city,' he said to his brethren. 'If the Genesis wretches go to ground, we may never dig them out. We've only just managed to cleanse the worst of the taint left over from the bastard Corsairs.'

'Did you hear what they found on deck thirty?' Mercutian asked.

Cyrion shook his head. 'Enlighten me.'

'The Bleeding Eyes reported it in a few nights before we arrived at Tsagualsa. They said the walls are alive down there. The metal has veins, a pulse, and sheds blood when cut.'

Cyrion turned his head to Variel, his disapproving sneer hidden behind the glaring helm. 'What did you tainted fools do to this ship before we stole it back?'

The Apothecary stomped on, his augmetic leg pistoning and hissing as its servos mimicked human joint structure as best they could.

'I have seen Night Lord vessels infinitely more corrupt than you seem to imply. I am hardly one of the faithful, Cyrion. I have never once spoken in reverence to the

Powers That Be. The warp twists what it touches, I do not deny it. But do you pretend there were no poisoned decks on board your precious *Covenant of Blood*?'

'There were none.'

'Is that so? Or did you merely linger around the least-populated decks, where the touch of the Hidden Gods was lessened? Did you walk among the thousands of slaves toiling in the ship's engine-bowels? Was it all as pure and unchanged as you claim, despite all your decades in the Great Eye?'

Cyrion turned away, shaking his head, but Variel wouldn't let it lie. 'I loathe hypocrisy more than all else, Cyrion of Nostramo.'

'Be silent for a minute, and spare me your whining. I will never understand why Talos saved you on Fryga, nor will I understand why he allowed you to come with us when we left Hell's Iris.'

Variel said nothing. He was not a soul inclined to long arguments, nor did he feel a burning need to get the last word in a dispute. Such things mattered little.

As they descended to another deck, it was Mercutian who spoke, his voice accompanying their clanking tread. More slaves scattered before them – ragged and wretched things, all.

'He is with us because he is one of us,' Mercutian said.

'If you say so,' Cyrion replied.

'You think he isn't one of us, simply because sunlight doesn't hurt his eyes?'

Cyrion shook his head. 'I don't wish to argue, brother.'

'I am sincere when I say this,' Mercutian insisted. 'Talos believes it, too. To be Eighth Legion is to have a focus, a... dispassionate focus not shared by any of our kindred. You do not have to be born of the sunless world to be one of us. You merely need to understand fear. To take pleasure in inflicting it. To relish the salt-piss smell of it, emanating from mortal skin. You must think as we do. Variel does that.' He inclined his head to the Apothecary.

Cyrion cast a glance over his shoulder as they walked, his painted lightning tears splitting his helm's cheeks with what seemed like jagged relish.

'He is not Nostraman.'

Mercutian, never given to laughter, actually smiled. 'Almost half of the primarch's Chosen were Terran, Cyrion. Do you remember when First Captain Sevatar fell? Do you recall the Atramentar breaking up into scattered packs, because they refused to serve Sahaal? There is an example in this. Think on it.'

'I liked Sahaal,' said Uzas, from nowhere. 'I respected him.'

'As did I,' Mercutian allowed. 'I had no affection for him, but I respected him. And even when the Atramentar disbanded after Sevatar's death, we knew their resistance to Sahaal was born from something more than simple prejudice. Some of the First Company *were* Terran, the oldest warriors in the Legion. Even Malek was Terran. There was more to it than Sahaal's birth world. Being Terran, Nostraman, or born of any other world has never mattered to most of us. The gene-seed blackens our eyes the same, no matter the world of our birth. We divide because with the primarchs gone, that is every Legion's fate over time. We are warbands in a shared cause, with a shared legacy and ideology.'

'It is not so simple.' Cyrion wouldn't be moved. 'Variel's eyes are not black. He carries Corsair gene-seed in his throat and chest.'

Mercutian shook his head. 'I am surprised you cling to the ancient prejudice, brother. It will be as you wish, for I am done with this discussion.'

But Cyrion wasn't, not yet. He vaulted a guardrail, dropping the ten metres to the platform below. His brothers followed in a pack.

'Tell me something,' he said, his voice less edged now. 'Why did the First Company refuse to follow Sahaal?'

Mercutian drew in air between clenched teeth. 'I had little chance to speak with any of them. It didn't seem to be because of any flaw with Sahaal as Sevatar's replacement, and more due to the fact *no one* would ever live up to the true First Captain. No one *could* live up to him. The Atramentar would serve no other leader after Sevatar died; he'd made them into what they were, a brotherhood that couldn't be broken any other way. Just as the Legion would serve no single captain after the primarch died. It is not our way. I doubt we'd even follow the primarch now. It has been ten thousand years of change, of war, of chaos, of pain and survival.'

Uzas was trailing the inactive blade of his chainaxe across the iron wall, breeding a scraping shriek of metal on metal.

'Sevatar,' he said. 'Did Sevatar die?'

The others shared chuckles and snorts as First Claw's wounded remnants walked on, deeper into the darkness that filled their home.

TALOS WATCHED THE moon come apart. In times past, he might have marvelled at the power he commanded. Now he watched in silence, trying not to overlay the image of the disintegrating moon with the memory of Nostramo dying in the same way.

Rubicon-grade cyclonic torpedoes weren't enough to annihilate an entire world, but they ate into the small moon with voracity and speed.

'I want to hear the Shriek,' he said as he stared.

'Aye, lord.' The Vox-mistress tuned the bridge's speakers to project the aural aspect of Deltrian's jamming field. Sure enough, the sound matched its name. The air was filled with ululating cries of sonic resonance, hateful and somehow organic. Beneath the cries, beneath the screams of rage and vox-crackling torment, a lone man's voice fuelled it all.

The tech-adept had been exquisitely proud of designing the interference projector, and Talos was accordingly grateful for it. The Shriek made hunting so much easier, when enemy vessels were rendered auspex-blind, feeling their way through the cold void without scanners. The power drain was significant, though. The Shriek cloaked them in their prey's blindness, but suckled strength from every generator on the ship. They couldn't fire their energy weapons. They couldn't move at anything less than a half-speed crawl. They certainly couldn't raise void shields – the deflector screens operated on similar tuning to the Shriek itself, and siphoned power from the same sources.

Talos wondered what had happened on the enemy bridge, once the Shriek had caressed their systems. Secure in the cover of the moon's shadow, had the Chapter serfs panicked when they lost contact with their masters in the boarding parties? Perhaps, perhaps not, but no Adeptus Astartes vessel would be crewed by weaklings. Those officers and servants would be the pinnacle of unaugmented human possibility, trained in war academies reminiscent of those on the worlds of Ultramar.

The entire operation was flawlessly conducted according to their wretched Codex Astartes, from the precision first strike, through the meticulous and savage deck-by-deck fighting, to the cruiser's withdrawal to buy its warriors more time.

Victory would come by changing the nature of the game. Talos knew this, and never hesitated to cheat. Some cyclonic-grade weaponry ignited a planet's atmosphere when used in conjunction with other orbital bombardment. This moon had no atmosphere to speak of, and no population to burn, making such weapons useless even if the *Echo of Damnation* had possessed them.

Other cyclonics buried melta or plasma charges into a world's core, triggering fusion effects to either force cataclysmic tectonic activity, or birth a lesser sun at the heart of the world. Either way, no world would survive. Most died within minutes, taking their populations with them.

Rubicon-grade torpedoes were lesser examples of this latter breed. They were all Talos required. One would almost certainly be enough, but two would ensure the deed was done.

First, he had blinded the enemy by the Shriek. They had no way of tracking the torpedoes cutting towards them, and no way of sensing their impact on the moon until it was too late. Within minutes, the burrowing missiles had done their work. He'd seen no need to destroy the entire moon in a pinpointed spherical detonation at its core. To that end, the cyclonics had struck high in the northern hemisphere, drilling into the salt flats of the barren polar caps. Rather than detonate in the planetoid's core, they'd tunnelled through the moon's scalp, inspiring tectonic instability as they exploded in a series of timed chain reactions close to the world's far side, facing the enemy ship.

The moon came apart. Not neatly, by any means. A quarter of its surface shattered, bursting out into the void with such speed that the *Echo*'s own hololithic display lagged in displaying the changes taking place. No more than three minutes after the torpedoes struck the moon's surface, huge chunks of debris began to break free. Ravine-cracks cobwebbed across the satellite's surface, disgorging an atmosphere of dust into the moon's nearspace.

'Kill the Shriek,' Talos ordered. 'Raise shields, arm weapons. All ahead full.'

The *Echo* shivered as it came back to life, pushing though space with a shark's hunger. The strategium deck fell into its familiar organised chaos as officers and servitors attended to their battle duties. The rattle and clank of levers mixed with the murmur of voices and the clatter of fingers on clicking keys.

'Any sign of the Genesis cruiser?' Talos asked from his central throne. On the occulus, the scalped moon was a sorry looking ruin, already half-surrounded by its new asteroid field.

'I see them, sire.' The Master of Auspex drew in a wet breath through his rebreather mask. 'Rendering on the hololithic now.'

At first, Talos couldn't make out the vessel from the debris. The hololithic flickered with its usual unreliability, offering a scene with hundreds of targets. The moon's ruptured edge was a ragged curve at the image's side. Rocks of all shapes and sizes decorated the space above, along with a hazy mist representing particulate debris too small for focus on individual locks.

There they were. The telltale forked prow of an Adeptus Astartes warship, and the runic signifiers of its weapons firing into the void. Talos watched the hololithic ship as it manoeuvred, suddenly finding itself at the heart of an asteroid field, unloading its weapons on the surrounding rocks as it sought to cut its way free.

He was almost disappointed they'd not been destroyed in the initial burst, but at least he could witness it firsthand now.

'I cannot help but feel a moment of pride,' he said to the crew, 'You have done well, all of you.'

The drifting rocks tumbled through space, crashing into each other and shattering into yet more rubble. Talos watched the hololithic display as several large chunks collided with the flickering ship. The primitive imaging program displayed little of the immense damage such impacts must be inflicting.

'Bring us in for a visual confirmation.' Talos knew that would involve a wait of several hours to close the distance, and an idea took root to pass the time and tip the odds further against the Genesis warriors on board.

'Hail the enemy ship, and filter the feed so every vox outlet on the ship transmits the words we speak.'

Vox-mistress Auri did as she was told. The bridge had fallen quiet after the Shriek was deactivated. Now it rang again with the voices carrying from the enemy cruiser. Monotone servitor voices formed a background chorus to the crumpling thuds of rocks impacting on the hull, and a resonant voice speaking breathlessly.

'I am Captain Aeneas of the *Diadem Mantle*. I will not listen to your taunts, heretic, nor to your temptations.' An explosion cut the Space Marine's words off for a moment, punctuated by distant screams.

'This is Talos of the warship *Echo of Damnation*. I will speak no taunts, merely truths. Your assault has failed, as has your flight from our vengeance. We are watching you die on our auspex hololiths even as we speak. If you have any last words, speak them now for posterity. We will remember them. We are the Eighth Legion, and our memories are long.'

'Filthy, accursed traitors,' crackled the reply.

'He sounds angry,' a nearby officer joked. Talos silenced him with a wordless glare.

'Talos?' came the captain's voice again.

'Yes, Aeneas.'

'May you burn in whatever hell awaits the damned and the deceived.'

Talos nodded, though his counterpart had no hope of seeing the gesture. 'I am sure I will. But you will reach there before I do. Die now, captain. Burn and be mourned, for a wasted life.'

'I fear no sacrifice. The blood of martyrs is the seed of the Imperium. In Guilliman's name! Courage and hon–'

The link went dead. On the hololithic display the runic symboliser of the enemy warship blinked out of existence at the core of the brutal asteroid storm.

'The *Diadem Mantle*,' said the Vox-mistress, 'lost with all souls.'

'Bring us closer to the debris field, and annihilate whatever remains with a volley from our prow armaments.'

'Aye, lord.'

Talos rose from his throne, weary and aching. 'The entirety of our speech was broadcast across the ship?' he asked.

'Aye, lord.'

'Good. May it dishearten the Genesis bastards still alive, to hear their captain die and their warship burn.'

'Lord,' began the Master of Auspex. 'The use of torpedoes... That was a fine plan. It worked beautifully.'

Talos paid him scarce heed. 'As you say, Nallen.' He gestured to the closest officer. 'Kothis. You have the bridge.'

The named officer didn't salute. The masters paid no attention to such formalities. Still, he knew better than to sit in the lord's throne. Instead, he stood by it, taking control over those hunched below him.

Talos moved to the edge of the strategium, and lifted Xarl's corpse onto his shoulders.

'I am going to bury my brother. Summon me only if the need is dire.'

IT TOOK ALMOST an hour for First Claw to reach any of the other squads. Their journey through the *Echo*'s labyrinthine decks took them through chamber after chamber, tunnel after tunnel. At times they passed through crowds of idling slaves hiding in the dark, while other chambers were filled with the bustle of efficiency, as the Legion's servants went about their duties. Minor repair crews and teams of menial slaves were in the majority. Several they passed looked mauled from encounters with the Genesis Chapter, and Cyrion had the uncomfortable feeling that the final crew casualty lists would number in the thousands.

Mercutian was clearly thinking the same. 'They hit us even harder than the Blood Angels hit the *Covenant*.'

Cyrion nodded. Given the numbers of crew lost that night at Crythe, he'd not been keen to witness another boarding assault. Still, the *Echo* had the resources and manpower to compensate for such a grievous mauling; the *Covenant* hadn't.

As they walked, each of them grew aware of a moist, soft sound crackling over the vox. Uzas was licking his teeth again.

'Stop that,' Cyrion warned him.

Uzas either didn't hear or didn't care. His blood-palmed helm didn't even turn to regard the others.

'Uzas.' Cyrion resisted the urge to sigh. 'Brother, you are doing it again.'

'Hnh?'

Despite Mercutian's earlier lecture on prejudice, Cyrion didn't think of himself as a petty creature. However, the endless run of Uzas's tongue along his teeth was enough to make him grind his own.

'You are licking your teeth again.'

Variel cleared his throat with gentle politeness. 'Why does that cause you irritation?'

'The primarch did it. After he'd filed his teeth to points, he'd ceaselessly lick his teeth and lips while thinking, like some kind of animal. He'd often cut his tongue as he did it, and the blood would flow over his lips, driving us on edge with the scent.'

'Intriguing,' the Apothecary noted, 'that a primarch's blood should have such an effect. I have never envied you your existence in their shadows, but that sounds fascinating.'

The others said nothing, showing just how much they cared to discuss that particular subject again.

'I smell intestines,' Uzas grunted as they entered another chamber.

'I smell the Bleeding Eyes,' said Cyrion.

'Hail to First Claw,' cawed a voice from above.

They raised their bolters as one, aiming into the roof of the domed chamber. The room itself was a hollowed-out mess, signs of abandonment in every direction. A supply room or crew barracks, was Cyrion's guess. Four hunched figures squatted in the rafters, barely visible between the tendrilous forest of chains hanging from the ceiling.

Six Genesis warriors dangled, limp as broken marionettes, from hooks on the dirty chains. Their armour was torn open across each stomach – power cables split and layered ceramite shredded, pulled open by clawed hands. The flesh beneath was similarly mutilated, allowing their innards to rain in a slopping spill onto the decking below. Blood still dripped from three of them.

Against his instincts, Cyrion lowered his bolter. These wretches were barely his brothers, but they were murder in a fight, and the warband was fortunate to have them. The problem was keeping them in the fights they joined. *First in*, they always claimed, and that was true enough. The fact was also true that they were also *first out.*

'You have been busy,' he said. Despite the distance, he caught a glimpse of one of them without its helm on. Blood coated its hands and what little he could see of its face, as it fed upon the organs of the hanging warriors. A scalp of black veins and misaligned bone was immediately covered by the traditional sloping, daemon-shrieking helm.

'Throne of Lies,' he swore.

'What?' Mercutian asked, keeping his voice low.

'The warp beats in their blood more than I realised.'

The Raptors shared a series of clicks and growls, passing as discussion between the pack. One of them hissed at the Night Lords below, the sound breaking off into a rasping vox-cackle.

'This deck is clean, First Claw. We cleaned it of enemy heartbeats.' The Raptor's head jerked twice, on a twitching neck. 'You seek Lucoryphus?'

Cyrion shook his head. 'No. We are moving through to the Hall of Reflection. We seek Deltrian.'

'Then you seek Lucoryphus. He stands with the machine-speaker.'

'Very well. Our thanks to you.' Cyrion waved his brothers forward. First Claw walked around the hanging bodies, giving them a wide berth. The Bleeding Eyes never reacted well to others interfering with their kills, or with the feasts that followed.

As First Claw passed, one of the Raptors ignited the thrusters on its back, diving down from the ceiling with a thrust of smoky engine flare, sinking his claws into the exposed meat of a dead warrior's torso. First Claw paid no heed, and moved ahead without a word.

THE MAN WAS only a man in the loosest, most physiological sense. He had no comprehension that he'd ever possessed a name, nor was he truly sentient beyond an ability to express the same tortured emotion over and over again. His existence was divided into two planes of experience, which his strangled mind interpreted as Torpor and Scourging.

In moments of Torpor, which lasted for oceans of time between Scourges, he drifted in a milky haze of numbing sensation, doing nothing, seeing nothing, knowing nothing but an eternity of weightlessness and the taste of salty chemicals in his lungs and throat. The only thing that could be generously interpreted as thought was the faint, distant echo of anger. He didn't feel fury itself, but rather the memory of it: a recollection of once knowing rage, without knowing why.

When the Scourging came, it came in a storm of pain. The anger rose again, sparking through the veins of his head like misfiring power cables. He'd feel his jaws opening, his tongueless mouth silently screaming into the cold nothingness that cocooned him.

After a time, the pain would fade, and the false anger it brought would drift away with it.

It was happening now. The man once known as Princeps Arjuran of the Titan *Hunter in the Grey* breathed the cold liquid of his chemical womb, inhaling fluid and excreting filth as his ravaged body was at last allowed to rest.

Lucoryphus of the Bleeding Eyes stood before the glass tank containing the tortured man. He didn't like to stand upright, but some things bore closer investigation. The Raptor tapped a claw on the glass.

'Hello, little soul,' he rasped in a smiling whisper.

The body within the suspension tank had been

hobbled, its legs ending below the knees and its hands amputated at the wrists. Lucoryphus watched the crippled figure writhing in the fluid, lost in whatever inner torments drifted through its drugged mind.

'Do not touch the glass,' Deltrian's toneless voice still conveyed his disapproval.

Lucoryphus jerked twice, his helmed head twitching on his neck. 'I will break nothing.'

'I did not ask you to break nothing. I asked you to refrain from touching the glass.'

The Raptor cawed a short whine and dropped back down to all fours. He watched the excruciation needles withdrawing from the prisoner's temples, and turned his attention to the tech-adept.

'This is how you make the Shriek?'

'It is.' Deltrian's chrome face was hidden in his hood, as he worked on powering down the pain engines feeding into the suspension tank. 'The prisoner was a gift from First Claw. They tore him from his throne in a Titan's mind-chamber.'

Lucoryphus hadn't heard the tale, but he could guess the details easily enough. In truth, the Shriek fascinated him. To render an enemy vessel's scanners inert and useless, to drown them in a voxed screed of tormented scrapcode... such technology was rare enough, but still possible in any one of a hundred ways with the right genius and the right materials. But to breed electronic interference from the pain of a single human soul, to filter organic agony through the ship's systems and use it to harm the enemy – that was poetry the Bleeding Eyes leader could sincerely appreciate.

He tapped the glass again, uttering a low snarl that wasn't quite a laugh.

'How much of your brain-flesh is still human?' he asked.

Deltrian paused, his multi-jointed fingers hovering over the console keys. 'That is a matter I have no desire or motivation to discuss. Why do you ask?'

Lucoryphus inclined his sloping daemon helm to the

amniotic tank. 'Because of this. This is no cold, logical creation. This is the work of a mind that understands pain and fear.'

Deltrian hesitated again, unsure whether to process the Raptor's words as a compliment. It was always difficult to tell with the Bleeding Eyes. He was prevented from a need to answer, as the doors opened on grinding hydraulics. Four figures stood silhouetted by the red emergency lights beyond.

'Hail,' said Cyrion.

THE HALL OF Reflection was more museum than workshop, and within its walls Deltrian was monarch of all he surveyed. Cyrion watched him for a while, canting binary orders to his menials, directing their efforts to unknowable projects.

The Night Lord walked around the chamber, ignoring the bustle of robed adepts and mumbling servitors. His gaze fell upon the weapons being repaired, and the great Dreadnought sarcophagi chained to the walls, housing the Legion's revenants, forever awaiting reawakening.

The last of these armoured coffins depicted the triumphant image of Malcharion, rendered in burnished gold, as he'd been in life. He stood with the helms of two Imperial champions in his hands, crucified by the rays of a moonrise over Terra's most holy battlements.

'You,' Cyrion turned to a nearby adept.

The Mechanicus worker nodded his hooded head. 'My name is Lacuna Absolutus, sire.'

'Is work still proceeding on reawakening the war-sage?'

'The battle interrupted our rituals, sire.'

'Of course,' Cyrion said. 'Forgive me.' He crossed the chamber to where Deltrian stood. 'Talos ordered us here to protect you.'

Deltrian didn't look up from the console. His chrome fingers clicked and clacked at the keypad. 'I need no protection. Furthermore, reports from all claws report the enemy resistance is ended.'

Cyrion had been listening to the same vox reports. That wasn't exactly what they'd said. 'It is not like you to be so imprecise, honoured adept.'

'Hostilities are almost at their conclusion, then.'

Cyrion was smiling now. 'You are annoyed, and trying not to let it show. Tell me why.'

Deltrian emitted an irritated blurt of code. 'Begone, warrior. Many demands press upon my time, and the array of my attention is limited.'

Cyrion laughed. 'Is this because your requests for assistance weren't answered? We were engaged in battle, honoured adept. If we'd had the time to walk on the ship's hull with you, I assure you we would have done as you asked.'

'My work was critical. The repairs had to be made. If we had committed to a void battle with the enemy cruiser–'

'But we did not,' Cyrion rejoined. 'Did we? Talos tore the moon apart instead. Beautiful overkill, that. The primarch would have laughed and laughed, loving every moment of it.'

Deltrian deactivated his vocabulator, preventing any response based on a moment of emotional temper. He merely nodded to indicate he'd heard the warrior's words, and continued his work.

It was Lucoryphus that answered, from his vigil by the torture tank. 'It does not matter. I answered his call.'

Cyrion and the rest of First Claw turned to the Raptor. 'Yes, after you fled with your rabid pack, leaving us to fight alone.'

'Enough whining.' The Raptor's head jerked on the servos in his neck. 'You survived, did you not?'

'No,' Cyrion replied. 'Not all of us.'

HE WORKED ALONE, with his brother's blood on his hands.

'Talos,' a voice carried over the vox. He ignored it, not even paying heed to whom it belonged.

The extraction of gene-seed wasn't a complicated process, but it required a degree of delicacy and efficiency made easier with the right tools. More than once in recent years, Talos had ruined gene-seed organs in the heat of battle, cutting them from a corpse with his gladius and pulling them free with his bare hands. Desperate times called for desperate measures.

This was different. He wasn't carving open one of his distant brothers under enemy fire.

'You were always a fool,' he told the dead body. 'I warned you it would see you dead one night.'

He worked in the stillness of his own meditation chamber, silent but for the humming of his armour joints and the wet-meat sounds of a blade going through flesh. His own narthecium was long gone, lost in a fight decades ago, yet he had no desire to allow Variel to do this.

Splitting the breastbone beneath the black carapace was the most difficult obstacle. The biological augmentations that rendered a Legionary's bones stronger than a human's were also a bane to easy surgery. He briefly considered widening the wound close to Xarl's primary heart, but it would involve burrowing and pulling more meat free.

Talos hefted his gladius, testing the weight a few times. He brought the pommel orb down on Xarl's solar plexus once, twice, and a third time with a dull thud punctuating each impact. On the fourth, he pounded the pommel down with more strength, cracking the breastbone in a ragged split. Several more thumps widened the crack enough for Talos to curl his fingers around the ribcage, opening his brother's body like a creaking, cracking book. The smell of burned flesh and bare organs soon thickened the air in the small chamber. He reached a gloved hand into Xarl's chest cavity, pulling the first globular node free. It resisted at first, tightly bound to the nervous system; the heart of a mesh of veins and muscle meat.

He poured the handful of cold blood and stringy flesh into a medicae canister. In better times, there had been words to say and oaths to speak. None of them felt right now.

Talos clutched Xarl's limp head, turning it to the side. Moving the body caused a rattle of breath to leave the corpse's open mouth and exposed lungs. Despite his training, despite all the things he'd seen in his centuries of life, the sound caused his hands to freeze. Some instinctive responses were too human, too tightly bound to a warrior's core, to go ignored. Bodies breathing was one of them. He felt his blood run cold, just for that moment.

The progenoid organ in Xarl's throat was much easier to recover. Talos used the tip of his gladius to carve through the skin and sinewy muscle, making a wide wound in the dead flesh. He pulled out another handful of bloody tissue and vein-stringy meat, placing it in the canister with the first.

A twist, a seal, and the medicae canister locked tight. A green rune activated along its side.

For several slow breaths, Talos knelt next to his brother's body, saying nothing, thinking nothing. Xarl's mutilated remains scarcely resembled the warrior in life – he was a defeated, broken thing of ripped flesh and ruined ceramite. The traitorous thought entered his mind of scavenging his brother's armour, but Talos suppressed the vulture's urge. Not Xarl. And in truth, there was little remaining worth the effort of plunder.

'Talos,' the vox insisted. He still ignored it, though the voice pulled him from his dead-minded reverie.

'Brother,' he said to Xarl. 'A hero's burial awaits.'

Talos rose to his feet, moving to his weapon rack. An ancient flamer rested as it had for years, cleaned of all rust and corrosion, its unlit nozzle emerging from a brass daemon's wide maw. He'd never liked the weapon, scarcely even used it since first tearing it from the hands of a dead warrior of the Emperor's Children five decades before.

A click of his thumb activated the pilot light. It hissed in the chamber, an angry candle flame casting a sharp glare in the gloom. He slowly aimed the weapon at Xarl's body, breathing in the scent of his brother's ruptured flesh and the chemical tang of old promethium oil.

Xarl had been there when Talos first took a life: a shopkeeper slain by a boy in the lightless Nostramo night. He'd stood with him as the gang wars swept the cities, always cursing with gutter invective; always first to shoot and last to ask questions; always confident, never regretting a thing.

He was the weapon, Talos thought. Xarl had been First Claw's truest blade, and the controlled strength that formed their backbone in battle. He was the reason other claws had always backed down from facing them. While Xarl lived, Talos had never feared First Claw losing a fight. They had never liked one another. Brotherhood asked for no friendship, only loyalty. They'd stood back to back as the galaxy burned – always brothers, never friends; traitors together unto the last.

But none of it seemed right to say. The flamer hissed on in the spreading silence.

'If there is a hell,' Talos said, 'you are walking there now.' He aimed the weapon again. 'I believe I will see you there soon, brother.'

He pulled the trigger. Chemical fire breathed out in a sudden roar, washing over the body in short bursts. Ceramite darkened. Joints melted. Flesh dissolved. He had a last sight of Xarl's blackening skull, the bones resting in a silent, eyeless laugh. Then it was lost in the smoke choking the air.

The fire quickly spread to the chamber's bedding and the scrolls on the walls. The spoiled-meat reek of burning human flesh turned the cloying air even fouler.

Talos washed the body in a final spread of liquid

fire. He stowed the flamer over his shoulder, locked the medicae canister to his thigh, and reached for his weapons last of all. Talos took Xarl's helm with one hand and his own bolter with the other. Without looking backwards, he strode through the smoke and engaged the door release.

Thick, coiling smoke poured into the hallway beyond, and with it came the smell. Talos walked from the chamber, sealing the door behind him. The fires would die out soon enough, starved of oxygen and fuel in the chamber.

He'd not expected anyone to be waiting. The two humans stood quietly, their cupped hands shielding their mouths and noses from the thinning smoke.

Septimus and Octavia. The seventh and the eighth. Both tall, both dressed in dark Legion uniforms, both permitted, as so few slaves were, to carry weapons. The former stood with his damaged facial bionics clicking each time he blinked or moved his eyes. His long hair framed his face, and Talos – who had little gift for reading human expression beyond terror or anger – could make no sense of the emotion on Septimus's features. Octavia had her hair bound in its usual ponytail, her forehead covered by her bandana. She was getting thin now, and unhealthily pale. This life wasn't being kind to her, nor was her own biology, as her strength faded to be fed to the child growing inside her.

He recalled his order that the two humans remain apart, and his more recent demand that Septimus remain in the hangar. In this moment, neither seemed to matter.

'What do you want?' Talos asked them. 'There is nothing to salvage from Xarl's wargear, Septimus. Do not ask.'

'Variel ordered me to find you, lord. He requests your presence in the apothecarion as a matter of urgency.'

'And it took both of you to deliver this message?'

'No.' Octavia cleared her throat, lowering her hands. 'I

heard about Xarl. I'm sorry. I think... by your standards, by the Legion's ideals, I mean... he was a good man.'

Talos's exhalation became a snort, which in turn became a chuckle.

'Yes,' he said. 'Xarl was a good man.'

Octavia shook her head at the warrior's sarcasm. 'You know what I mean. He and Uzas saved me once, just as you did.'

The prophet's chuckle became laughter. 'Of course. A good man. A heretic. A traitor. A murderer. A fool. My brother, the *good man*.'

Both humans stood in silence as, for the first time in many years, Talos laughed until his black eyes watered.

XI

FATE

Chaos reigned in the Primary Apothecarion. On the *Covenant of Blood*, the Legion's medicae sanctum had been more a morgue than a surgery, becoming a place of stillness and silence – a chamber of cold storage vaults, old bloodstains on the iron tables and memories hanging in the sterile air.

The opposite was true on the *Echo of Damnation*. Variel walked from table to table, through a sea of wounded humanity, his unhelmed face betraying no emotion. Human crew and legionaries alike cried out, reaching for him, filling the air with the reek of sweat, the heat of escaping life and the stink of chemical-rich blood.

Hundreds of tables lined the chamber in rows, almost all of them occupied. Mono-tasked lifter servitors hauled corpses from the slabs, dragging living wounded onto the tables in replacement. Drains in the floor suckled at the blood sloshing across the dirty tiles. Medicae servitors and crew members trained in surgery were sweating as they worked. Variel strode through it all, a gore-streaked conductor overseeing a wailing orchestra.

He paused by one gurney, glancing down at the tangled crewman's body laying there.

'You,' he said to a nearby medicae servitor. 'This one is dead. Remove his eyes and teeth for later use, before incinerating the remains.'

'Compliance,' murmured the bloodstained slave.

A hand gripped his vambrace. 'Variel...' The Night Lord on the next table swallowed blood before he spoke. His clutch tightened. 'Variel, graft the new legs onto the stumps and let's be done with it. Do not keep me here, when we have a world to conquer.'

'You need rather more than new legs,' Variel told him. 'Now remove your hand.'

The warrior gripped tighter. 'I have to be on Tsagualsa. Don't keep me here.'

The Apothecary looked down at the wounded legionary. The warrior's face was half-lost in a wash of blood and burned tissue, baring the skull beneath. One of his arms ended at the bicep, and both legs were fleshy stalks leaking fluid from the ravaged ceramite where his knees had once been. The Genesis Chapter had almost killed this one, no doubt about it.

'Remove your hand,' Variel said again. 'We have discussed this, Murilash. I do not like to be touched.'

The grip only grew tighter. 'Listen to me...'

Variel clenched the warrior's hand with his own, prying the fingers back and holding tight. Without a word, he deployed the laser cutters and bone saw from his narthecium gauntlet. The saw bit down.

The warrior cried out.

'What did you just learn?' Variel asked.

'You wretched bastard!'

Variel tossed the severed hand to another servitor. 'Incinerate this. Ready a bionic left hand with the rest of his planned augmentations.'

'Compliance.'

In the corner of the apothecarion, where they leaned against the wall watching the organised chaos, Cyrion chuckled and voxed to Mercutian.

'You were right,' he said. 'Variel really is one of us.'

'I would have cut out Murilash's heart,' Mercutian replied. 'I've always loathed him.' The two warriors lapsed into silence for a time.

'Deltrian reported they're back to working on reawakening Malcharion.'

Mercutian's reply was to sigh. Through the vox, it was a breathy crackle.

'What?' Cyrion asked.

'He will not thank us for awakening him a second time. I would give much to know why Malek of the Atramentar spared the war-sage's existence.'

'I would give much to know where in the infinite hells the Atramentar are. Do you believe they went down with the *Covenant*?'

Mercutian shook his head. 'Not for a moment.'

'Nor I,' Cyrion agreed. 'They didn't evacuate with the mortals, nor in a Legion gunship. They never reached the *Echo of Damnation*. Which leaves only one choice – they boarded an enemy vessel. They teleported onto a Corsair ship.'

'Perhaps,' Mercutian allowed. His tone walked the border between thoughtful and doubting. 'They would never be able to take a Corsair ship alone.'

'Are you truly this naive?' Cyrion grinned behind a faceplate that wept painted lightning. 'Look how the Blood Reaver treats his Terminator elite. They're his Chosen. I'm not suggesting the Atramentar mounted an assault on the Corsairs, fool. They betrayed us to them. They *joined* them.'

Mercutian snorted. 'Never.'

'No? How many warriors have cast aside the bonds of the First Legions? How many find them irrelevant as the years become decades, and the decades twist into centuries? How many are legionaries only in name, after finding a more satisfying, more purposeful path instead of eternally whining over a final vengeance never taken? Every one of us has his own path to walk. Power is a greater temptation for some than ancient, lofty ideals. Some things matter more than old bonds.'

'Not to me,' Mercutian said at last.

'Not to most of us. I am merely saying–'

'I know what you are saying. I am saying I have no wish to speak of this.'

'Very well. But there is a tale behind the Atramentar's disappearance, brother. One we may never know.'

'Someone knows.'

'That they do. And I would enjoy excruciating the truth from them.'

Mercutian didn't reply, and Cyrion allowed the discussion to wane into an awkward lull. Uzas, standing a few metres away from them, was looking down at his red-painted gauntlets.

'What's wrong with you now?' Cyrion asked.

'My hands are red,' said Uzas. 'Sinners have red hands. The Primarch's Law.' Uzas lifted his head, turning his bruised and bloody face to Cyrion. 'What did I do wrong? Why are my hands painted in sinners' scarlet?'

Mercutian and Cyrion shared a glance. Another moment of rare clarity from their degenerating brother caught them by surprise.

'You killed many of the *Covenant*'s crew, brother,' Mercutian told him. 'Months ago. One of them was the father of the void-born girl.'

'That wasn't me,' Uzas had bitten his tongue, and blood flowed over his lips, slowly raining down his white chin. 'I didn't kill him.'

'As you say, brother,' Mercutian replied.

'Where is Talos? Does Talos know I did not do this?'

'Peace, Uzas,' Cyrion rested a hand on the other warrior's shoulder guard. 'Peace. Do not let yourself grow aggravated.'

'Where's Talos?' Uzas asked again, slurring now.

'He will be here soon,' said Mercutian. 'The Flayer has summoned him.'

Uzas half-lidded his black eyes, drooling saliva and blood in equal measure. 'Who?'

'Talos. You just... You just asked where he was.'

Uzas stood slack-jawed. Blood bubbled at the corner of his thin lips. Even without Legion modification, even had he been left alone as a human boy and never swollen into this broken, avataric living weapon stitched back together after hundreds of battlefields, Uzas would have been a singularly unwholesome and unattractive creature. Everything in the years since only made him fouler to look upon.

'Uzas?' Mercutian pressed.

'Hnnh?'

'Nothing, brother.' He shared another glance with Cyrion. 'It is nothing.'

The three warriors remained silent as the minutes passed on. Again and again, the northern doors opened on grinding tracks. More packs of crew members were arriving each minute, dragging and carrying their wounded.

'It is surprising to see so many mortals flocking here,' Mercutian mused.

With medicae stations on many decks, the crew knew that the Primary Apothecarion was the Flayer's haunt, and few would willingly put themselves beneath his cold gaze and the pressing cuts of his blades.

'They know their own expendability,' Cyrion nodded. 'Only desperation drives them here.'

Talos entered with the latest batch. The prophet ignored the humans around his boots, crossing straight to Variel. Septimus and Octavia trailed him in. The former immediately moved to one of the tables, working to assist the medicae attendant there.

'Septimus,' the surgeon grunted in greeting. 'Start stitching the stomach wound.'

Octavia watched him working, knowing better than to try and offer her help. The mortal crew flinched back from her at all times, no matter her intentions. The curse of the third eye, even when it was hidden beneath her grimy bandana. They all knew what she was, what she did for their lords and masters. None of them wanted to look her way, let alone touch her. So she followed Talos, hanging back what she judged a respectful distance.

Talos walked to Variel, the damage to his armour showing starkly in the apothecarion's harsher light.

'Where is Xarl's corpse?' the Apothecary asked.

Talos handed him the sealed cryo-canister. 'That is all you need,' he said.

Variel took it, his fingers subtly twitching. He disliked others doing inexpert work when he could have performed it to perfection. 'Very well.'

'Is that all?' Talos looked over to Cyrion, Uzas and Mercutian, ready to join them.

'No. We are long overdue a discussion, prophet.'

'We have a world to bring to its knees,' Talos reminded him.

Variel's eyes – ice-blue to the Nostraman's inky black – still flitted around the chamber, drinking in the details. It was the one way Talos thought Variel still differed from the Nostraman-born Night Lords. Whether by genetic legacy or simple habit, a great many Eighth Legion warriors would stare in autistic silence, gazing at those they were speaking to. Variel's attention was altogether more fractured.

'We also have half of our warriors dead or dying,' the Apothecary pointed out, 'along with hundreds of mortal crew. There is gene-seed to harvest, and augmetic grafting to perform.'

Talos fingered his temples. 'Then do what needs to be done. I will take the others down to the surface.'

Variel said nothing for a moment, absorbing the words. 'Why?' he said at last. Around him, men and women were still weeping, moaning, screaming. It put Talos in mind of the primarch's Screaming Gallery, with all the shivering hands reaching out from the walls in fruitful torment. He felt like smiling, really smiling, without knowing why.

'Why what?' asked Talos.

'Why attack Tsagualsa? Why attack it in the first place? Why rush down there to finish the deed now? You have been less than forthcoming with answers on the matter.'

The blue veins beneath Talos's cheeks twisted like lightning, following the contours of his scowl. 'To let the hounds slip the leash and torture as they desire. To let the Eighth Legion be itself. And above all, for the symbolism. This was our world, and we left it barren of life. It should remain that way.'

Variel breathed slowly, his eyes settling on Talos for a long, rare moment. 'The populace of Tsagualsa, such as it is, are now cowering in their storm shelters, fearful of the nameless wrath that attacked their capital city. They know it will return, and yes – I suspect you are correct – once the Legion slips its leash and toys with the lives of those souls on the surface, every warrior will be energised by the infliction of fear and the wanton slaughter to inevitably follow. But that is not a good enough answer. You are dreaming without recalling what you see. You are acting on visions you scarcely remember, and barely understand.'

Talos remembered the first moment of awakening once more, finding himself chained in the command throne, with the occulus showing Tsagualsa's grey face from the silent safety of orbit.

'Where are we?' he'd said.

First Claw had walked to his side, forming up in a line of snarling joints and impassive, skullish facemasks.

'You don't recall your orders to us?' Xarl had asked.

'Just tell me where we are,' he'd demanded.

'The Eastern Fringe,' Xarl had answered. 'Out of the Astronomican's light, and in orbit around the world you repeatedly demanded we travel to.'

Variel broke through the prophet's reverie with a murmur of displeasure. 'You have not been the same since we took the *Echo of Damnation*. Are you aware of this?'

They could have been alone, discussing such things in the stillness of a meditation chamber rather than the abattoir of the Primary Apothecarion.

'I do not know,' Talos confessed. 'My memory is a jagged thing of plateaux and shadows, ripe one moment, hollow the next. I am no longer sure I even see the future. What little I remember is tangled, like fate's skeins matted together. It is no longer prophecy, at least not as I understand it.'

If any of this surprised Variel, he didn't let it show. 'You told me months ago why you wished to travel here, brother. You told me you'd dreamed of human life on Tsagualsa's face once more, and that you wished to see it with your own eyes.'

Talos moved aside as two members of Third Claw dragged a slain brother onto a table.

'Soul Hunter,' one of them greeted him. Talos gave him a withering look, and led Variel away from them both.

'I recall no such dream,' he told the Apothecary.

'It was months ago. You have been slipping for a long time, but the rate of degeneration is accelerating. Focus on this fact, Talos: you wanted to sail back into these skies. Now we are here. Now those same humans you dreamed of crawl into the earth, weak and weaponless, wailing that we have returned. And even as you fulfil your desire, you are still hollow, still void of memory. You are breaking apart, Talos. Fracturing, if you will. *Why* are we here, brother? Focus. Think. Tell me. *Why?*'

'I do not remember.'

Variel's reply was to strike him. The blow came from nowhere, the back of the Apothecary's gauntlet smashing backhanded into the side of Talos's face.

'I did not ask you to remember. I asked you to use your gods-damned mind, Talos. *Think.* If you cannot recall, then work out the answer from what you know of yourself. You brought us here. Why? What benefit is there? How does it serve us?'

The prophet spat acidic saliva onto the floor. When he turned back to Variel, a viperous smile played across his pale, bloody lips. He didn't strike back. He did nothing but smile with bleeding gums.

'Thank you,' he said as the moment passed. 'Your point is taken.'

Variel nodded. 'I had hoped it would be.' He met the prophet's dark eyes. 'I apologise for striking you.'

'I deserved it.'

'You did. However, I still apologise.'

'I said it is fine, brother. No apology is necessary.'

Variel nodded again. 'If that is the case, would you ask the others to cease aiming their weapons at me?'

Talos looked around the chamber. Both members of Third Claw had their bolters raised. First Claw was a mirror of the image, their own guns lifted and aimed. Even several Night Lords on tables awaiting surgery were holding their pistols level and ready to fire.

'Ivalastisha,' said Talos. 'Peace.'

The warriors lowered their weapons at once, in slow unison.

Variel gestured to one of the side chambers. 'Come. There are tests on your blood that I must–'

'The tests can wait, Variel.'

Variel's cold eyes flickered with something, some unknowable emotion never given the grace to flash in full across his features.

'I believe you are dying.' He lowered his voice. 'I have saved you before. Let me analyse you now, and we will see if I can save you a second time.'

'A trifle melodramatic,' Talos replied, though his blood ran cold, feeling like a flush of nerve-killing combat narcotics.

'Your body is rejecting the modifications wrought by the gene-seed. As you age, as you take wound after wound, your regenerative processes are breaking down. You can no longer heal the damage Curze's blood is doing to your body. Some humans are simply unsuitable for gene-seed implantation. You are one of them.'

Talos said nothing for a moment. Ruven's dream-words replayed through his mind, in savage chorus with

Variel's. The prophet's marble visage turned to the rest of the chamber.

'This is conjecture,' he said.

'It is,' Variel admitted. 'I have had little experience in dealing with the physiology of first-generation Legiones Astartes. But I was able to sustain my Lord Blackheart's life for centuries, through a mix of ingenuity, ancient science, and working with fools who practised powerful blood magic. I know my art, Talos. You are dying. Your body no longer functions as it should.'

Talos followed him as he spoke. In the side chamber, the Apothecary gestured to an excruciation table replete with chains. The room's ceiling was given over to a multi-limbed arachnid machine, with various scanners, cutters and probes at the end of each jointed iron limb.

'There is no need to lie down at first. The more detailed tests will come after these preliminaries, but I wish only to draw blood from the veins in your throat for now. Then we will scan your skull. Only then will we proceed deeper.'

Talos acquiesced in silence.

ANOTHER ONE DIED beneath Septimus's hands. He swore in Nostraman.

The surgeon he was working with wiped bloody hands across his own face, as if it would clean away the stains already there rather than add to them.

'Next,' the man said to the closest servitors. They dragged a writhing woman in a filthy crew uniform onto the table. She'd lost a leg to a bolter round, but the tourniquet at her thigh had spared her a cold, shivering death from blood loss. Septimus winced at the biological ruin left of her leg below the knee. Her eyes were wide, the pupils narrow. She hissed air in and out through clenched teeth.

'Who are you?' he asked gently, in the same moment the medicae said 'Name and role.'

'Marlonah,' she said to Septimus. 'Starboard tertiary

munitions deck. I'm a loader.' She squeezed her eyes closed for a moment. 'Don't servitor me. Please.'

'He won't,' Septimus told her.

'Thank you. Are you Septimus?'

He nodded.

'Heard about you,' she said, and lapsed back onto the table, covering her eyes against the bright glare of the lights above.

The medicae wiped his face again, clearly weighing the effort and value of the diminishing cheap augmetic supplies he had at his disposal. Only officers could count on their chances of a bionic organ or limb, but she was hardly underdeck scum.

'She can't do her duty with one leg,' Septimus said, sensing this game was already lost.

'Another could perform a loader's duties just as easily,' the medicae replied. 'Menials are hardly difficult to replace.'

'Primaris,' Marlonah said, the words hissed through the pain. Sweat bathed her in feverish droplets. 'Primaris qualified. Not... not just a hauler. Cart driver, too. Cannon loader.'

The surgeon tightened the tourniquet, eliciting a fresh grunt. 'If I find out you're lying to me,' he told her, 'I will inform the Legion.'

'Not lying. Primaris qualified. I swear.' Her voice was growing weaker now, and her eyes unfocused.

'Record her for omega-grade augmentation after the crisis is over,' the medicae said to his attendant servitor. 'Stabilise her, and pitch the stump until then.'

Marlonah was unconscious now. Septimus suspected that applying hot pitch to her raw stump to prevent any future bleeding would rouse her, though. He released a pent-up breath, cursing the Genesis Chapter for their fanatical assault. Throne in flames, they'd given the ship a beating.

The medicae moved away, seeking another patient on another table, in this endless supply of them. As

Septimus followed, his glance fell on Octavia across the room. She stood at the heart of carnage's aftermath, her pale skin ungraced by the blood marking the dead and dying around her.

He watched her retying her ponytail, seeing the hesitance in her fingers as she walked from table to table, careful not to touch anyone. She only paused by the unconscious ones, resting her fingers on their skin, saying a few words of comfort or checking their pulses.

In the middle of this stinking den of dying heretics, Septimus smiled.

Variel tapped the display monitor, overlaying the hololithic charts.

'Do you see the correlation?'

Talos stared at the distorted hololithic of conflicting charts and hundreds of rows of runic symbols signifying numbers.

He had to shake his head. 'No, I do not.'

'It is difficult to believe you were once an Apothecary,' Variel told him, in a rare moment of pique.

Talos gestured to the overlaid readings. 'I can see the flaws and failings in the body's kinetics. I can see the impairment and the unwarranted spikes in cortical activity.' How easy it was, to speak of his own degeneration so impartially. The idea almost made him bare his teeth in a smile that would have done Uzas proud. 'I am not saying I cannot understand what I am seeing, Variel. I am saying I do not see what you find so unique in it.'

Variel hesitated, trying a new tack. 'Do you at least recognise the spikes in limbic activity, and see the other signs listed as potentially terminal?'

'I recognise the possibility,' Talos allowed. 'It is hardly conclusive. This suggests I will be in pain for the rest of my life, not that my life will be cut short.'

Variel's exhalation trod perilously close to a sigh. 'That will do. But look here.'

Talos watched the looping results flicker and restart,

again and again. The rune-numbers cycled, the charts flowed in some hololithic dance, devoid of all rhythm.

'I see it,' he said at last. 'My progenoid glands are... I do not know how to describe it. They are too active. It seems they are still absorbing and processing genetic markers.' He touched the side of his neck, recalling the removal of Xarl's gene-seed only hours before.

Variel nodded, allowing himself the smallest of smiles. 'Mature progenoids will always react with a subsistent level of activity – a base level of processing genetic matter, collating a biological record of the experiences and traumas of the warrior they serve.'

'I know how progenoids function, brother.'

Variel raised a hand to placate the prophet. 'That is my point. Yours have always been overactive, as we already knew. Much too efficient. They rendered your physiology unstable and were, perhaps, the cause of your prophetic vision. Now, however, they are in rebellion. Previously, they were still trying to *improve* you, from human to one of the Legiones Astartes. But that development was a dead end. You could improve no more. You were already one of us. Their overefficiency has now passed a critical juncture. In many cases, the implanted organs would wither and die within the body. Yours are too strong. They are affecting the host, rather than withering themselves.'

'As I said: pain while I still draw breath, but it is not terminal.'

Variel conceded the point with a flash of thought in his pale eyes. 'Perhaps. Either way, removal of the progenoids is no longer an option. It would make no difference, for your organs are already–'

Talos interrupted with an irritated wave of his hand, as if giving the order to fire. 'Enough. I can read the accursed hololithic. Come, Variel. Deal with the wounded, and let us retake Tsagualsa.'

The Flayer exhaled slowly. The dim illumination of the side chamber painted the skinned faces across his pauldrons in a greasy, pallid light.

'What is it?' asked Talos.

'Were you to die, and a suitable host be found for your gene-seed organs, there is a chance the new host would carry the same curse as you – but with the ability to control it. Your gene-seed is uncorrupted, but unsuited to you. In a better host, with true symbiosis, they would be…'

'Be what?' His dark eyes flickered with thought now, possibilities playing out in their depths.

Variel was staring at the charts. 'Powerful. Imagine your prophetic gift without the false visions that increase as time passes, or the headaches that drive you to your knees, or the unconsciousness that lasts weeks or months. Imagine it without the broken memory, or the other debilitating symptoms that plague you. When you die, brother, you will leave a powerful legacy for the future.'

'The future,' Talos said, his black eyes unfocusing. He almost smiled. 'Of course.'

Variel turned back from the hololithic. 'What is it?'

'That is why we are here.' Talos tongued his split lip, tasting his own blood – a lesser reflection of Uzas and the dead primarch. 'I know what I want from this world.'

'I am pleased to hear it. I had hoped this discussion would have that effect on you. Am I to assume you have changed your perspective, or are you still content to allow the Legion to slip its leash and slaughter everyone on the world below?'

'No. The pure war is not enough. This is Tsagualsa, Variel. The carrion world… now with life tenaciously clinging to its scabbed surface. We can claw more than some tawdry, bloodthirsty satisfaction from this.'

The Apothecary disengaged the hand scanner, letting it power down. 'Then what, Talos?'

The prophet stared past Variel, stared past the chamber's walls, looking at something only he could see.

'We can reforge the Legion. We can lay down an example for our brothers to follow. We can cast aside the hatred between warbands, with these painful first steps. Do you see, Variel?'

He turned at last, his black eyes shining. 'We can make it glorious, this time. We can begin again.'

The Apothecary wheeled several of his full-body scanners into place. Buttons and dials on his narthecium gauntlet activated the jointed arms reaching down from the ceiling. Chemicals sloshed in glass vials.

'Lie down,' he said.

Talos complied, still staring with unfocused eyes. 'Will I lose consciousness?'

'Without a doubt,' Variel replied. 'Tell me, is Tsagualsa the right place to begin such a reforging?'

'I believe so. As an example, as a… symbol. Have any of the others told you what happened when we left this world?'

'I have heard of the Tsagualsan Retaliation, yes.'

Talos was seeing past him again, staring now into memory rather than the paths of possibility.

'That makes it seem so placid. No, Variel, it was much worse than that. With the primarch gone, we'd been decaying for years – scattering to the stars, guarding our own supplies from the claws of our brothers as much as from the preying hands of our enemies. But at the end of it all, when the grey sky caught fire with the contrails of ten thousand drop-pods, that was the day a Legion died.'

Variel felt his skin crawling. He loathed being near any expression of emotion, even the bitterness of old memory. But curiosity forced his tongue.

'Who came for you?' he asked. 'What size was the force to dare attack an entire Legion?'

'It was the Ultramarines.' Talos lowered his head, surrendering to the memory now.

'A thousand warriors?' The Apothecary's eyes widened. 'That's all?'

'You think in such small terms,' Talos chuckled. 'The Ultramarines. Their sons. Their brothers. Their cousins.

The entire Legion, reborn after the Heresy, wearing hundreds of icons proclaiming their new allegiances. They called themselves the Primogenitors. I believe their descendants still do.'

'You mean the Ultramarines' kindred Chapters?' Variel could almost picture it now. 'How many of them?'

'All of them, Variel,' Talos said softly, seeing the sky once again on that distant day. 'All of them.'

PART TWO

THE LAST DAY

XII

THE PRIMOGENITORS' RAGE

He knew he was dreaming.

It didn't help. It didn't make anything less real. The smells were no weaker, the pain was no fainter.

'Get to the ships,' he said aloud. He could sense Variel moving around the chamber, though he could see nothing outside the pictures his mind was painting. The tests being run on his blood, on his brain, on his heart... none of it meant anything, for he felt nothing at all.

'Get to the ships.'

'Peace, Talos,' came Variel's voice, from a great distance. 'Peace.'

He couldn't remember a time of peace. There had never been peace in the purgatory of Tsagualsa.

His first memory of the last day was the sunrise.

THEY CAME FOR vengeance as the weak sun rose.

Tsagualsa's star was a cold heart at the system's core – a source of anaemic, thin light that scarcely brightened the lone world in its care. Its pale radiance spread across the planet's lifeless surface, at last painting bleak illumination across the battlements of a black stone fortress. On the plains, a dust storm was brewing. It would crash over the fortress within the hour.

Before Mercutian, before Variel, before Uzas – there was Sar Zell, Ruven, Xarl and Cyrion.

Sar Zell was the one to come running. His boots

pounded across the battlements as the heavens caught fire.

'They're here,' he voxed to Talos. 'They've come at last.'

In a moment of divine atmospheric poetry, it started to rain from an amber sky.

In the years following the primarch's death, more and more warbands cut loose from Tsagualsa's skies and took their raiding deeper into the Imperium. Many were already carving out havens in the Great Eye with the other Legions, spending as much time waging war against former kin as against the minions of the False Emperor.

A battlefleet of staggering size rested above the grey world's barren face, each warship marked by the winged skull of the Eighth Legion. Here was a fleet that could devastate entire solar systems. It had done so before, many times.

Across the Tsagualsan System, rifts in reality tore open in the silence of the void. They bled foul, daemonic matter into the clean silence of real space, while shuddering battleships strained their way back into the material universe. As with almost all warp flight, there was little cohesion, no alignment of arrival vectors and formations maintained through the rage of empyrean flight. Instead, one by one, the invaders burst from the warp and powered towards the grey world.

At first, they matched the Night Lords' numbers. Soon, they overshadowed them. As the battle began, by the time the skies of Tsagualsa started to burn, they eclipsed the Eighth Legion fleet completely. More warships arrived with each passing minute, vomited from the warp and streaming trails of poisonous mist.

They needed no formation. They needed no strategic assault plan. That many ships needed nothing else to win a war. The Primogenitor Chapters, the Thirteenth Legion in all but name, had come to end the cancer of heresy once and for all.

Captains and commanders filled the vox-net with recriminations; with orders no one else was following; with tactics few souls were willing to hear.

Talos remained on the battlements, listening to the thousands of screaming voices. Always in the past, the screams were those of their prey. Now the cries were torn from the mouths of brothers, brothers that had survived the Heresy and the two centuries of warfare since.

One order was damning in its repetition. He heard it over and over again, screamed and cried and yelled. *Get to the ships. Get to the ships. Get to the ships.*

'We have to defend the fortress,' Talos voxed back to his commander.

The Exalted's voice was a bass drawl, rasping and wet over the scrambled vox. 'You do not see the madness taking place up here, prophet. The Thirteenth Legion will crucify us if we remain.'

'Vandred, we cannot abandon all of the fortress's resources…'

'There is no time for this, Talos. Dozens of our warships are already running. We are more than outnumbered; we are at risk of being overwhelmed. Get back to the ship.'

The prophet activated his narthecium gauntlet, tracking First Claw's armour runic signifiers. Xarl and Cyrion were close, perhaps in one of the armouries nearby. Sar Zell waited only a few metres away, listening in to the vox-chatter. Ruven was deeper in the fortress, doing the gods only knew what.

'Vandred,' said Talos. 'We are already seeing droppods coming down. The sky is aflame with engine wash.'

'Of course it is. They outnumber our ships five to one. We can barely keep them from orbital bombardment, do you think we have any chance of preventing them making planetfall?'

Talos watched the pods raining down, trailing fire from the sky.

'This is Talos to all Tenth Company claws.' His voice

was merely one of many, strangled in the miasma of conflicting vox traffic. 'All claws, get to the gunships. We have to reach the *Covenant*.'

'As you command, Soul Hunter,' replied several squad leaders.

Soul Hunter, he thought, with a cringing sneer. The name given by his father, for the killing of a single soul – avenging his primarch's murder. Talos earnestly hoped that the ludicrously theatrical title would fade out of use in the years to come.

THE FORTRESS WAS not without defences. Even as enemy gunships shrieked over the battlements, even as drop-pods plunged through the scorching atmosphere and impacted in the ash wastes, along the walls, and in the courtyards – the fortress itself resisted the assault.

Anti-air turrets spat hard shells into the sky, hurling Thunderhawks to the ground in flames. Servitor-manned weapons platforms aimed at the landers coming down on the ash wastes, launching missiles and eye-aching streams of laser fire at the vehicles grinding their way overland towards the high walls.

Talos ran across the battlements, Sar Zell a step behind. As they passed turret platforms, their helm's audio sensors parsed down the crashing chatter of auto-cannon fire, as well as the strangely monotone shouts of gun-slaved servitors mumbling their aiming vectors aloud. The black stone beneath the legionaries' boots shook with the rage of the fortress's response.

'The gunship is in the western quadrant, secondary hangar,' Sar Zell voxed. 'That's if it's not stolen by another company before we reach it.'

'I–'

The explosion from nowhere hurled them from their feet. Talos stumbled forward, smashing headfirst into the rampart wall. Sar Zell tumbled across the stone, slipping over the battlement's edge.

Chunks of servitor and weapon battery rained down,

clattering off Talos's armour as he hauled himself back to his feet. Above them, the enemy gunship – its hull painted in royal blue and clean, imperial white – angled away as its rocket pods reloaded. A thunderclap of thrust sent it streaking through the sky again, seeking more turret platforms to destroy.

'Sar Zell,' he voxed, blinking to clear his senses. His retinal display re-tuned to pierce the smoke, but a more tellingly mundane disorientation clouded his eyes for a moment.

The only reply he received over the vox was a grunt of effort. Talos saw the hands gripping the battlement's lip. He offered his own, as his brother hung there two hundred metres above the desert below. The weight of the immense lascannon chained across Sar Zell's back prevented the warrior from pulling himself up with ease.

'My thanks,' Sar Zell voxed back, as his boots thudded on the cold stone again. 'That would have been a singularly ignoble way to die.'

'Perhaps you should leave the cannon,' Talos said.

'Perhaps you should stop speaking madness.'

The prophet nodded. Hard to argue with that.

THEY MET XARL and Cyrion in the armoury level of the closest spire. The walls shook around them as the tiers of autocannons rattled and banged, filling the air with noise. Gunships whined overhead, several ending in the piteous wails of engines spiralling down to the ground.

Xarl wore his wing-crested ceremonial helm, in the midst of looting the armoury. A crate of replacement chainsword teeth-tracks was weighed against one hip.

'I can't find any melta charges,' he told Cyrion, without looking away from his plundering.

Cyrion nodded to Talos and Sar Zell. 'Tell me you have a plan.' The chamber gave a horrendous shudder in time to the tectonic thunder of battlements giving way nearby. 'And tell me it doesn't involve fighting our way across half of the fortress to get to *Dirge*. These

Imperial dogs are inside the walls; we won't survive a long journey.'

Talos drew his chainsword. 'In that case, I think it best if I remain silent. Where is Ruven?'

Xarl finally turned from his looting. 'Who cares?'

Get to the ships. The vox-chatter was a repetitive storm of voices all saying the same thing. *Get to the ships. Get to the ships.*

'With the Legion scattered, the fortress will fall,' said Sar Zell. 'We were fools not to remain united.'

Talos shook his head. 'The fortress was always going to fall one night. Unity was never an option with the primarch gone. We are fools, but only for still being here when so many of our brothers have already taken to the stars.'

THEY MET RESISTANCE three levels down, as their boots hammered across the black stone floor of a primary thoroughfare corridor. Dead slaves lined the walls, some wearing the Legion's blue uniform, others in the rags that made up their only remaining possessions. Each of the bodies lay in burst repose, broken apart by bolter shells. Blood lined the walls in an uneven layer of greasy, stinking paint.

Talos held up a fist and opened his fingers, making the hand signal to spread out. As his armour's kinetic systems recognised the gesture, corresponding runes flashed on First Claw's retinal displays, relaying the order.

'The invaders decorate the same way we do,' Cyrion noted, eyeing the bodies as the squad moved apart.

'Focus,' Xarl grunted in reply. Cyrion lowered his bolter and withdrew his auspex. It crackled as it tuned into their surroundings.

'Contact,' he announced. 'Dead ahead, and moving back this way. They've either got scanners, or they heard us coming.'

Talos checked his bolter as he crouched by a gore-streaked wall. 'Sar Zell,' he said.

Without a word, the warrior braced against the weight of his lascannon and lifted it to aim down the corridor.

'Are we shooting this out?' Xarl asked.

'No.' The prophet listened to the approaching bootsteps. 'Charge after the initial burst.'

Talos felt his teeth itching, alongside the telltale ache in his tongue and gums as the lascannon drew in power. The consistent thrum made the hair on the back of his neck rise, despite the sanctity of his armoured suit.

Their foes were disciplined veterans, too canny to fall prey to easy traps. They fanned out at the corridor's junction, taking cover where the hallway joined a large chamber beyond.

Both squads immediately started the crashing exchange of bolter fire. Chunks of stone flew through the dusty smoke of shell impacts.

'They're bringing up a heavy bolter,' Cyrion voxed, his autosenses filtering through the smoke. 'He's moved behind the left wall.'

'Sar Zell,' Talos said again.

The lascannon drew in one final exhalation of energy before roaring down the corridor with a discordant *freem* of unrestrained blue-white power. The blade-beam of crisp, sun-bright force burned through one of the stone walls, disintegrating a hole clean through the torso of the warrior taking refuge behind it.

'They're not bringing up a heavy bolter anymore,' Cyrion noted.

'Until someone else picks it up,' Talos replied. 'Another volley, then charge.'

The lascannon shuddered in Sar Zell's hands, rattling and steaming with the expulsion of force. Another of the distant enemies clattered down in a heap of ceramite-clad limbs.

First Claw drew their blades and started running.

No more than three minutes later, they almost ran headlong into another enemy squad. Another Claw was pinned down at the far end of a sparring chamber, returning a decreasing level of fire as the Imperial Space Marines gunned them down.

Talos dropped into a crouch, leaning by the wall and raising his bolter. Where Guilliman's sons worked and fought with absolute efficiency, First Claw moved with the shadowed, ragged remnants of discipline. Talos gave no order to fire this time. He didn't need to. Their bolters opened up with throaty barks, utterly without unity, picking their targets with impunity. Of the seven remaining, three went down under the fresh hail of fire.

The four Imperial Space Marines turned to face this new assault, half the squad moving to divide their fire with inhuman precision. Their armour was a clashing mix of grey and green, their shoulder guards marked by eagles of silver.

Sar Zell leaned around the corner long enough to unleash a single shot, blasting a tank-killing stream of laser through the groin and thighs of the squad's grey-helmed sergeant, annihilating him below the waist.

Three left.

'I remember these bastards.' Sar Zell lowered his cannon, brushing away stone debris from its power tubing. Pressurised air, scalding enough to melt skin, vented in a hissing cloud from the weapon's bulky generator.

Talos remembered them, as well. The Silver Eagles and the Aurora Chapter had beaten elements of the Eighth Legion back from a series of targeted void raids only a handful of years before.

'We need to do this quickly,' Xarl voxed, holstering his empty pistol and revving his chainblade. 'Who's with me?'

Sar Zell shook his head. 'A moment.'

He braced again, lifting the cannon and leaning around the corner while First Claw gave covering fire. The lascannon bucked in his fists, thumping back with violent recoil as it screamed out a beam of savage light. The torrent cleaved through one of the last Imperial warriors, disintegrating his head, shoulders and chest.

Two left.

'Ready,' he said, lowering the overheating cannon. Stress vanes along the weapon's side were protesting now. The barrel would need replacing soon.

First Claw charged forward as one, chainswords grinding down against ceramite and pistols kicking at lethal range. Xarl and Talos took the kills, the former decapitating his enemy, the latter tearing his foe's helmet off and feeding him the muzzle of a bolt pistol.

The sergeant, bisected by lascannon fire, still lived. He dragged his way across the floor, nothing more than a legless torso.

Cyrion and Xarl circled him, looking down and sneering.

'No time for games,' Talos warned them.

'But…'

Talos's pistol banged once. The shell blasted the sergeant's head and helm to shrapnel, clattering against their boots and knee-guards.

'I said *no time for games.*'

First Claw moved across the chamber, through the wreckage of sparring equipment, to the squad they'd saved. Only one remained. He was crouched by the bodies of his brothers looting them for weapons, ammunition and trinkets.

'Sergeant,' Talos greeted him.

The Legionary sucked in air through his teeth, lifting a chainaxe from a warrior's lifeless fingers. He cast his broken bolter aside, and stole another from a second corpse.

'Sergeant,' Talos said again. 'Time is short.'

'Not a sergeant, anymore.' The Night Lord rested a boot on the back of a slain warrior. With the axe, he severed the corpse's head, and dragged the helmet free. 'I lost a duel to Zal Haran.'

He placed the helmet on his head and sealed the seams at his collar. 'Now I have Zal Haran's helm, and he is carrion. A poetic cycle.' The warrior looked at them for a long moment, while the fortress shook to its foundations around them. 'First Claw,' he said. 'Soul Hunter.'

'Uzas,' Talos said to him. 'We have to go.'

'Hnh,' he grunted, uncaring of the saliva stringing down from the edge of his lips. 'Very well.'

XIII

LEGACY OF THE THIRTEENTH LEGION

And still he dreamed.

He thought not of the blood analysis taking place, nor of the drills opening his skull to the cold air and the press of curious blades.

He thought only of the time before, when the enemy had come to Tsagualsa ten thousand years ago, bringing punishment for so many sins.

AFTER AN HOUR had passed since the sky first caught fire, Talos had to admit the fatigue was getting to him. The vox was alive with brutal reports of walls falling to enemy artillery; of tanks spilling into the fortress through holes blown in the barricades; of drop-pods crashing through the parapets to disgorge hundreds of enemy squads into the castle's outer districts.

He'd lost all contact with the fleet above, beyond the choppiest, most nonsensical eruptions of curses and screams. He was no longer even sure the *Covenant* was in orbit.

First Claw had quickly abandoned their headlong flight through the fortress, moving to take subsidiary corridors, ventilation shafts, slave tunnels and maintenance crawlways in order to avoid the enemy flooding through their haven.

The vox, what little of it still made any sense, spoke of a bleak picture. Casualties were more than high;

the Legion forces still on the ground were being devastated. Squads of enemy Space Marines were fighting with an efficiency that had no place on such a vast scale. Legion claws were shouting of enemy soldiers linking up with their brethren with vicious frequency, forming overwhelming numbers as they stormed through the primary chambers, forcing the defenders into an ever-heightening state of disorder and retreat. Every Night Lord counter-attack was met with waves of reinforcements, as the Imperials fell back in organised withdrawals, sinking to fall-back points already being reinforced by their freshly landed brethren.

The squad halted in a maintenance duct, so confined that they had to crouch, and for some stretches, move on all fours. Cyrion's auspex wavered in and out of readable resolution.

'We're lost,' Xarl mumbled. 'Accursed servitor tunnels. We should've stayed on the concourses.'

'And be dead like the others?' Sar Zell asked from the rear. He was dragging his lascannon behind him, as careful as he could be with the relic weapon. 'I will take sanity over madness, thank you. I want to live to fight another day, in a war we can win.'

'This is like fighting a virus,' Talos breathed over the vox. 'Like fighting a terminal infection. They're everywhere. They know how best to counter us as soon as we do something. They studied us before committing to this attack. This was all planned to the last detail.'

'Who were the first ones we killed?' asked Sar Zell.

'Before the Silver Eagles? The ones in armour the same green as Rodara's sky were the Aurora Chapter. We fought them at Spansreach. I do not know many of the others,' Talos confessed. 'The vox is alive with names I've never heard. The Novamarines. The Black Consuls. The Genesis Chapter. Titles of the Chapters whose protectorates we've been raiding and punishing for decades. This was what our father felt, before he died. Our sins have come home to roost, just as his did.'

'It doesn't matter,' Xarl interrupted. 'They're all Ultramarines. They bled in the Great War. They'll bleed now.'

'He has a point,' said Sar Zell. 'Better the Thirteenth than the gods-damned Blood Angels, with all their screaming kith and kin.'

'Is *now* truly the time for this argument?' Talos asked quietly. The others fell silent.

'This way,' said Cyrion. 'The hangar isn't far.'

First Claw emerged into relative quiet. The cacophony of thudding bolters and roaring engines hadn't faded completely, but at least here the halls were free of shrieking slaves and the bootsteps and gunshots of conflicting squads.

'We missed the battle here,' Talos voxed to his brethren. Bodies already littered the floor – some in Eighth Legion ceramite, others in the colours of the Primogenitor Chapters. 'Praetors of Orpheus,' he said. 'I recognise their colours.'

It wasn't hard to make out the scene's details. The invaders had breached the fortress at countless points nearby, rather than risk running directly against the hangar's immense defence batteries. From their intrusion points, they'd focused their aggression inwards, splitting their landing forces between penetrating deeper into the bastion and slaughtering all who fled for the safety of the hangar on this level.

The prophet narrowed his eyes, imagining the same scene playing out on every level, through all of the hangars around the fortress, imagining the breaches in every wall.

'They will have left a rearguard,' he warned. 'They are too precise to forget such a thing.'

'No life signs,' Cyrion replied.

'Even so.'

Talos was the one to defile the stillness, kicking out a ventilator grille and dropping to the deck below. Despite the negative scans, he panned his bolter across the scene.

'Nothing,' he said. 'No one. This place is a tomb.'

Cyrion's voice was coloured by a smile over the vox, 'Cowardice has never been so rewarding.'

'We are not safe yet,' said the prophet.

THE HANGAR STRETCHED out before them. Despite being one of the fortress's more modest launch platforms, the western quadrant's secondary hangar bay still housed over two dozen gunships and storage shuttles. At capacity, the workforce would number over two hundred souls; servitors and slaves alike engaged in the duties of maintenance, refuelling, rearming and repair.

Talos breathed out slowly, and swore under his breath. The ground was littered with the remains of the slain. Half of the gunships and shuttles were wrecked by sustained weapons fire. Several were now little more than smoking hulls, while others had had their landing gear carved out from under them, now resting crashed down onto the deck.

'There's no need for a rearguard when they were this thorough,' said Sar Zell. 'Come on.'

The gunship *Dirge* nestled at the far end of the hangar, still held ten metres above the ground in its docking clamps. Speckles of tracer fire dotted the gunship's armour-plating, but the principal damage wasn't to the flyer itself.

'Oh no,' Sar Zell complained. 'No, no, no.' The others stood in silence, watching for a moment.

'Focus,' Talos ordered them. 'Stay alert.'

First Claw, still accompanied by Uzas, fanned out through the hangar, their bolters up. Talos remained with Sar Zell, and gestured to the gunship. 'We need to get off this world, brother.'

'We're not leaving in that,' Sar Zell replied. The Thunderhawk had escaped most of the harm inflicted upon the rest of the bay, but the sabotage was still complete. The docking clamps gripping the gunship were shattered; the fact they still held the Thunderhawk aloft was a miracle in itself.

'We can destroy the docking clamps,' Talos said. '*Dirge* will survive a ten metre fall.'

Sar Zell nodded, though it was vague and almost devoid of actual agreement. 'The rotating platforms along the deck are inactive. The control chamber is ruined.' He gestured to a raised deck overseeing the hangar's operation below. More bodies lay across the consoles – many of them scorched husks of charred meat – and every machine in sight was gouged by blades or darkened by flamer wash.

'We can take off with the positioning carousels,' Talos breathed slowly.

Sar Zell turned his gesturing arm to take in the wreckage lying across the hangar floor, many of the hulks reaching halfway to the ceiling.

'And what do you want to do with all of this detritus? Blast it aside with rocket volleys at suicidal range? I can't fly a gunship through this. We need the hangar systems operational to clear the way. Without them, it will take days.'

Talos held his tongue as he scanned across the husks and wounded gunships. 'There. That one. That will fly.'

Sar Zell's gaze lingered on the burned husk for several seconds, his keen eyes flickering over the condition of the hull. The Thunderhawk stood close to the hangar bay doors, ruthlessly stitched by heavy-calibre fire that had clearly and cleanly punched through its layered armour-plating. Its midnight paint was left charcoal grey-black, the crow-like hull entirely seared by flamer weapons. Even the reinforced windows had melted, leaving the cockpit unprotected. Smoke breathed from the shattered window, evidence of earlier internal grenade detonations.

'It might,' Sar Zell said at last. 'It will mean taking off through the dust storm, and the smoke rising from the burning fortress. The engines may suffocate in the ash.'

'Better than dying here,' the prophet replied. 'Get to work.'

Weighed down by his lascannon, Sar Zell made his way across the hangar and went to find out if the gunship would fly, one way or the other.

THE HANGAR'S FUNEREAL serenity lasted a handful of minutes before it was breached by Imperial soldiers in white livery.

Sar Zell was already in the pilot's throne, relieved by the sound of the engines cycling up to readiness. The gunship had taken a beating, but it would fly.

Admittedly, he knew they'd be without heat-shielding when they went through the atmosphere (solvable, by sealing themselves outside of the cockpit, behind the bulkhead, leaving the gunship's machine-spirit to take over), and in vacuum once they reached the void (no real threat, if their armour was sealed), but first things first, at least the Thunderhawk would take off.

'More Praetors,' Sar Zell voxed.

The rest of First Claw came running. Five of the enemy left the odds close to even, and both squads took cover among the endless opportunities within the wreckage. Talos crouched with Cyrion, checking his ammunition reserves.

'We are cursed,' he said. 'No one alive should have our luck.'

'No?' Cyrion blind-fired over the debris they were hiding behind. 'If anyone deserves to die for their crimes, brother, it's *us*.'

Talos lifted his bolter to add his fire to Cyrion's. In the same moment, all firepower from the enemy ceased.

Talos and Cyrion exchanged glances. Both of them slowly looked above their barricade, letting their bolters lead the way.

All five of the Praetors had left the safety of their cover. All five stood in the open, their limbs locked tight, shuddering as spasms wracked their bodies. As

First Claw watched, two of them dropped their weapons. Their unburdened fingers trembled and curled, all control lost.

A figure stepped into view behind them. Horns curled in an elegant rise from his skull-faced helm, and his T-shaped visor looked upon the scene in expressionless silence. In one armoured fist, the figure held an ancient bolter; in the other, a staff of mercury-threaded black iron, topped by a cluster of human skulls.

The Praetors' shaking helms clicked with flawed vox signals, as they tried to vocalise their torment. Smoke hissed from their melting armour joints, and their epileptic quivers redoubled. As holes appeared in their armour-plating, the screams finally broke free from the molten decay.

One by one, they collapsed to the hangar decking, liquidised organic filth spilling in slow gushes from each armoured suit.

The figure lowered its staff, and walked calmly towards First Claw.

'You weren't thinking of leaving without me, were you?' asked Ruven. His voice lacked even the shadow of emotion.

'No,' Talos lied. 'Not for a moment.'

WIND ROARED IN through the sundered cockpit window. Uzas's cloak of flayed skin flapped in the rushing gale, and the skulls hanging on Xarl's armour-chains rattled in bony chorus. Sar Zell sat in the pilot's throne with the comfortable lean of a soul born to be there.

From the air, the fortress was a stain across the landscape – a castle in the first throes of becoming devastation incarnate. Smoke poured from its broken battlements, with rows of defence batteries aflame and the outer levels ravaged. Scars across the stone showed the impact craters of drop-pods, while a haze of whining, roaring gunships and landspeeders swarmed through the burning skies in an insectile cloud.

First Claw's stolen gunship juddered as it climbed, its intake valves breathing in smoke and its engines exhaling raw fire. It took no more than a few heartbeats to boost up into the pall of smoke now hanging over the fortress. Tracer fire chattered past them from below, knocking on the hull as it scratched home.

'We're fine,' Sar Zell voxed over their shared link.

'It did not sound fine,' Talos ventured, from his own shaking restraint throne.

'We're in the smoke. We're fine now, at least until the ash slays the engines.'

Talos pointed ahead of their ascent. 'What is that?' the prophet asked. A bright blur, fierce as a second sun, blossomed in the black smoke-clouds above them. Veins of fiery light spread in every direction from its white-hot core.

'It's a–' Sar Zell never finished the sentence. He wrenched the control columns, banking the gunship so sharply that every bolt and plate within its construction heaved in torment.

The second sun flashed past them with a carnodon's roar, still streaming atmospheric fire on its insane descent.

Talos released a breath he'd not realised he'd been holding. The drop-pod plummeted from sight.

'That was close,' Sar Zell admitted.

'Brother...' Talos gestured the same moment the proximity alarms caught up and started their tuneless pulse. 'Something else.'

'I see it, I see it.'

Whatever it was, it strafed alongside them – a mirror image in ascension – streaming the same fire from its engines. For a moment, the avian shadow broke through the plumes of smoke, just long enough to reveal the markings along its hull, visible even through the char damage.

'Ultramarines Thunderhawk,' Talos warned.

'I said *I see it*.'

'Then shoot it down.'

'With what? Curses and prayers? Did you have time to load the turrets before we left, and simply chose not to tell me?'

Talos's skulled helm snapped around to face the pilot. 'Will you shut your mouth and just get us into the void?'

'The engines are choking with ash. I told you this would happen. We're not going to clear orbit.'

'Try.'

In the same moment, more tracer fire zipped across their prow, tinnily hammering into the gunship's nose. Half of the control console went dark.

'Hold on,' Sar Zell muttered, an ocean of bizarre calm.

The Thunderhawk banked in a hard roll, driving them all against their restraint thrones. The shaking – already brutal – magnified tenfold. Something burst outside on the hull with a rattle of metal.

'Primary engines are dead,' said Sar Zell.

'The worst... pilot in... all of... Tenth Company...' Cyrion managed to vox through the crushing gravitational forces.

Talos watched the smoke cloud twisting in all directions, feeling the gunship lurch beneath him again. A second detonation was a muffled *crump* on the edge of hearing.

'Secondary engines are dead,' intoned Sar Zell.

There was no single serene moment where the Thunderhawk hovered at the apex of its flight before gently beginning a plummet. They rolled and shuddered in a powerless freefall, listening to the piteous machine-scream of the ash-choked engines. Each of them was shouting over the vox to be heard, even their audio-receptors unable to filter out the storm of noise.

'We're dead in the air,' Sar Zell called, still hauling on the levers to drag some stability back from their death-dive.

'Jump packs,' Talos shouted over the chaos.

First Claw locked their boots to the deck and rose

from their restraint thrones. Step by halting step, they made their way to the crew bay, magnetic bootsteps thumping. Loose debris crashed against their armour-plating. Xarl's crate of replacement chain-teeth shattered on Ruven's helm, eliciting a muttered curse over the vox.

Talos was the first to reach the racked jump packs. He locked the harness over his shoulder guards, secured the seals to his armour, and readied to thud his armoured fist into the bay door release.

'We're going to die today,' Cyrion voxed, sounding more amused than anything else.

Talos hit the ramp release, and stared out into the roaring wind, choking smoke, and the horizon spinning beyond sanity.

'I have an idea,' the prophet replied with a shout. *'But we'll need to be careful. Follow me.'*

'The ash will choke our jump pack engines,' Sar Zell called out. *'We'll have a minute, maybe two. Make it count.'*

Talos didn't reply. He unlocked his boots from the deck and started running, leaping out into the burning sky.

XIV

COVENANT OF BLOOD

First Claw had gathered.

'When will he awaken?' one of them asked. 'The humans below are still in their shelters, but we should act soon.'

'He will be awake within the hour. He is close to the surface now.'

'His eyes are open.'

'They have been for hours, yet he cannot see us. His mind is unresponsive to most external stimuli. He may be able to hear us. The analysis on that matter is inconclusive.'

'You said he was going to die. He said he was going to live, but suffer pain. Which one of you is right?'

'I believe he was correct. His physiology is in flux, and it may not be terminal. But the pain will destroy him over time, one way or another. And his prophetic gift is no longer reliable. There is no distinguishable brain pattern between his natural nightmares and his visions now. Whatever biological miracle, whatever mix of genetic coding bestowed the gift upon him is beginning to fade from his blood.'

Talos smiled without smiling. He would weep no tears if he lost his foresight. Perhaps freedom would even be worth the price of pain.

'We've sensed it for a while now, Flayer. He was wrong about Faroven on Crythe. Since then, he's been wrong more and more often. He was wrong about Uzas killing me in the shadow of a Titan. He was wrong about all of us dying at the hands of the Eldar. Xarl's already dead.'

For a time, the dreamer heard no more voices. The silence seemed important somehow; bloated with tension.

'His gene-seed still manipulates his body more aggressively than it should. It also ingurgitates more of his genetic memory and biological distinctiveness.'

'...ingurgitates?'

'Absorbs. Soaks up, if you will. His progenoid glands are receptors for the unique flaws in his genetic code. In another host, those flaws may not be flaws at all. They might make a legionary of vicious, vicious quality.'

'I do not like that look in your eyes, Variel.'

'You like nothing about me, Cyrion. Your thoughts on the matter are meaningless to me.'

Once more, a pregnant silence reigned.

'The Legion has always said that Tsagualsa is cursed. I feel it in my blood. We will die here.'

'Now you sound like Mercutian. No jokes, Nostraman? No toothed smile to hide your own sins and instability from your brothers?'

'Watch your tongue.'

'You do not intimidate me, Cyrion. Perhaps this world is indeed cursed, but a curse can bring clarity. Before he fell into this slumber, Talos spoke of knowing what to do with the world beneath us. We will linger only long enough to achieve our goals.'

'I hope that you are right. He is no longer mumbling or screaming in his sleep.'

'That was prophecy. This is a memory, not a vision. What was, not what will be. He dreams of the past, and the part he played within it.'

THE ULTRAMARINES THUNDERHAWK shuddered on its hover jets, drifting over the fortress's battlements in lethal serenity. Its rocket pods were empty, its squads deployed, and it hovered on-station, sweeping its bow across the fortress's defence platforms, raking them with merciless fire from its heavy bolters. Every thirty seconds, the gunship's spinal turbolaser discharged a beam of force, annihilating another of the weapons platforms in a bolt of blue light.

Brother Tyrus of the Demes Collegiate saw through flickering pict-screens as the gunship moved in another hulking drift. With his gauntlets on the control levers, he forced the bolter cannons to chew through one of the last remaining servitor weapons teams still alive on the castle's parapets.

'Kill confirmed,' he voxed to the pilot. 'Sabre defence platform, two servitor crew.'

Brother Gedean of the Arteus Collegiate didn't turn from the view through the gunship's blastshield. 'Ammunition reserves?' he voxed back.

'Remain on-station for another six strafing runs,' said Tyrus. 'Advise rearmament thereafter.'

'Understood,' the pilot replied.

There was a distinctive, undeniable bang of metal on metal from above. The pilot, co-pilot, gunner and navigator – each of them Ultramarines drawn from separate training collegiates throughout the worlds of distant Ultramar – all looked up in the same moment.

A second thud sounded from above. Then another, and another.

Brother Constantinus, enthroned in the navigator's seat, drew his bolt pistol. 'Something is–' he began, though he was interrupted by two more thuds on the ceiling above. The thuds made their way down the side of the hull in a feral, hurried drumbeat.

Constantinus and Remar, the co-pilot, disengaged their throne-locks at once, moving from the flight deck and descending via crew ladder into the loading bay.

As soon as they entered, they were greeted by the sight of the external bulkhead being wrenched from its hinges with a tearing whine of abused metal. The crash and boom of the siege poured in with the air outside, and the enemy came in with it.

'Emergency boarding protocol,' Brother Remar voxed to Gedean in the cockpit above. The Thunderhawk immediately started to climb, boosting high on angry engines. Remar and Constantinus kept their backs to the crew ladder, raising their weapons.

The first thing to enter was a broken chainaxe, the adamantine teeth snarled into ruin by chewing through the bulkhead hinges. It crashed onto the deck, tossed inside with casual abandon. The second thing to enter was a warrior of the Eighth Legion, his skull-faced helm leering through the smoke as he slid into the bay with almost serpentine desperation. The huge jump pack turbines on his back made his entrance through the bulkhead altogether less graceful.

Constantinus and Remar opened up with their pistols, taking the warrior down even as he twisted to present his reinforced shoulder guard to protect his head. Before the first boarder had even hit the floor, others were spilling in through the hole. They came armed, their own bolters lashing back with a greater storm of fire.

Both Ultramarines went down – Remar dead, his armour and flesh pulped against the crew ladder behind; Constantinus haemorrhaging from terminal wounds to his chest, throat and stomach.

'Move, move,' Xarl voxed. He led Uzas and Ruven up the crew ladder. Cyrion hesitated, turning back to where Talos remained crouched by their last brother. Blood and broken armour lay in a smear across the floor where Sar Zell had fallen.

'He's dead,' the prophet said. He didn't deploy his reductor to begin harvesting Sar Zell's gene-seed, nor did he make any move to follow the others up the ladder to the cockpit. He remained where he was, Sar Zell's broken helmet in his hands. Blood streaked what was left of the warrior's face.

Cyrion could hear the shouts and blade-grinds from above. He almost resented Talos for making him miss it.

'Leave him,' he said. 'Xarl can fly the gunship.'

'I know.' Talos hauled the body to the side of the bay, leashing it with binding straps. Cyrion helped, albeit belatedly. The gunship juddered as it climbed higher.

'He was a fool to go in first,' Cyrion continued. 'We should have sent Uzas in after he carved the door open. Then–'

Three bolt shells hammered into Cyrion's side, blasting armour wreckage against the bay walls with ringing resonance. The warrior staggered back with a pained cry across the vox, and crashed against the bulkhead's edges before falling from the gunship.

The dying Brother Constantinus still held the empty bolt pistol in a trembling hand. He clicked the trigger three more times, aiming at the remaining Night Lord. In reply, Talos rammed his chainsword through the Ultramarine's spine, letting the teeth chew through everything they could find to bite. For what it was worth, Constantinus died in bitter, angry silence, never once howling in pain.

'Cyrion,' he voxed as he tore his sword free. 'Cyrion?'

'I can't... He hit my jump pack,' was the hissed reply.

Talos ran to the sundered bulkhead, gripped the edges, and hurled himself out into the sky again.

Xarl's voice crackled in his helmet mic. 'Did you just–'

'Yes.' Talos's retinal display flickered as he fell, the runes cycling as they recorded his dropping altitude. Responding to his fevered attention, his target lock pinpointed the tiny figure of Cyrion, detailing a host of life sign bio-data in Nostraman runic script. Talos ignored it, and fired the turbines on his back. He just wasn't falling then, but powering towards the ground. The fortress, faint behind a gauzy veil of smoke, lurched closer as the thrusters kicked harder. He ignored the landspeeders and gunships raging over the battlements.

Nearer now, he could see Cyrion's jump pack flaring with sparks and false thrust. A Thunderhawk in the green of the Aurora Chapter heaved past, unconcerned with such small targets as it strafed the battlements.

And still, Cyrion tumbled through the smoke. The ground surged up to meet them. Too fast, far too fast.

'I thank you...' Cyrion grunted, '...for making the attempt.'

'Brace,' Talos warned, and his straining engines gave another coughing burst of thrust, propelling him downward. Three seconds later, they collided in mid-air, ceramite screeching as they crashed together.

Their contact was utterly devoid of grace. Talos smashed into his brother, his gauntleted fingers scrabbling for purchase, at last clutching Cyrion by the shoulder guard. The other Night Lord reached up, and their hands slammed closed, gripping one another's wrists.

Talos focused on shifting his thrust, forcing the jump pack's antigravitic suspensors to prime along with the adjusted turbines. It made little difference. The two of them tumbled through the sky together, slowed by Talos's jump engines. The thruster pack – despite the archaic design better designed for sustained flight – was already straining from its journeys through the ash storm and clouds of smoke. Talos had the briefest moment of selfish panic: he could let go and save himself dying in a smear across the Tsagualsan dust plains. None of the others would know.

'Drop me,' Cyrion voxed, his lightning-streaked helm facing up to his brother.

'Shut up,' Talos voxed back.

'This will kill us both.'

'Shut up, Cy.'

'Talos...'

They plunged into another column of smoke, the runic numbers on the prophet's retinal altitude chiming red. In the same moment, Cyrion released his grip. Talos clutched harder, cursing in breathless anger.

'Drop me,' Cyrion said again.

'Lose... the... jump pack...'

Cyrion restored his grip with a curse that mirrored his brother's a moment before. With his free hand, he disengaged the seals that bound the boosters to his backpack. As the turbines fell free, the lessened weight pulled them from their freefall.

Slowly, much too slowly, they began to rise.

'We're going to be shot to pieces,' Cyrion voxed, 'even if your engines don't fail in the ash.'

The prophet struggled to keep them steady as they ascended, his gaze ticking back and forth between the burning sky above and the thrust gauge at the edge of his vision. Gunships and land speeders slashed past, some zipping by hundreds of metres away, others roaring by much closer. Wake turbulence threw the brothers around, buffeting them in the air as an armoured landspeeder sliced past, almost close enough to touch.

'They're coming back,' Cyrion voxed.

Talos spared a glance over his shoulder. Cyrion was right; the speeder banked into a skyborne swerve, racing to come about on an attack run.

'No one deserves our luck,' Talos said, for the second time in less than an hour. He fired at the swooping craft despite its distance, the bolter shells going wide in the wind. It bore down on them, turbines howling, the underslung multi-barrelled assault cannon already spinning, winding up to fire.

Tracer fire slashed from above in a flaming hail. The speeder jinked, evading the first streams of the sudden barrage, but the falling firepower shattered through the craft's hull with explosive force.

Trailing fire, the speeder's wreckage hurtled past the defenceless Night Lords, screaming on its way to the ash plains below.

An Ultramarines Thunderhawk darkened the sky before them, its bulky, active engines causing the air itself to throb. Slowly, the forward gangramp started to lower, a vulture's beak opening to shriek.

'Are you finished?' voxed Xarl. 'Can we get the hell out of here now?'

* * *

ONCE THEY CLEARED the ash cloud, the true scale of the invasion force became agonisingly apparent. Talos leaned forward in the co-pilot's throne, watching the sky twist from clouds of fire to become a heaven of stars and steel. Next to him, Xarl gave a soft curse.

The void above Tsagualsa was wretched with enemy vessels, cruisers and barges of standardised classes, deadlocked in the sky with the Legion's remaining fleet. The Imperial Space Marine fleet dwarfed the Night Lords' in numbers and scope, but the Legion's primary warships eclipsed the loyalists' vessels in size by vast degrees. Smaller cruisers ringed the Legion battleships, trading fire against rippling, iridescent void shields.

'The Codex Astartes in action,' Ruven smirked. 'Surrendering their largest and finest warships to the newborn Imperial Navy. I pray that today the Thirteenth learn a lesson in whoring away their most potent firepower to lesser men.'

Talos didn't take his eyes from the fleet engagement filling the heavens. 'The Codex Astartes was responsible for our fortress falling in the most brutally efficient assault I have seen since the Siege of Terra,' he said quietly. 'I would watch your tongue until you're certain we will survive this, brother. The Navy will be blockading the system's outer reaches, one way or another.'

'As you say,' Ruven conceded with an unpleasant smile in his voice. 'Find the *Covenant*, Xarl.'

Xarl was already watching the gunship's primitive hololithic auspex display. Hundreds of runes conflicted across its surface.

'I think it's gone. The Exalted must have run.'

'A fact that will surprise none of us,' Cyrion remarked from the navigator's seat. The bodies of the dead Ultramarines pilot and gunner lay at his feet, where Xarl, Uzas and Ruven had dumped them. Uzas watched the others, saying nothing, his finger occasionally squeezing the trigger of his chainaxe, causing the teeth to chew air.

'That is Sar Zell's axe,' Talos said.

'Sar Zell is dead,' Uzas replied. 'Now it is my axe.'

Talos turned back to the scene beyond the cockpit windshield. Xarl abandoned any false hope of keeping his distance from the battle, taking the gunship through the drifting hulks and doing his best to veer around any storms of battery fire.

'This is First Claw, Tenth Company, to any Legion ships taking survivors.'

A dozen immediately voices crackled back, all asking after Talos. Some were concerned for his safety; the others earnestly appealing that he lie dead in the fortress below.

'Oh,' Ruven chuckled without any amusement, 'to be one of the Night Haunter's Chosen.'

'You could have hunted down our father's killer,' Talos rounded on him. 'I am weary of your whining, sorcerer. Do not hate me because I was the one to avenge the primarch's murder.'

'Vengeance against the primarch's own wishes,' Ruven snorted.

'But it was still *vengeance*. That was enough for me. Why do you still hiss and spit over it?'

'So you gain renown and infamy in equal measure, purely for disobeying our father's last wish. How wonderful for you. Never before has a lack of discipline granted such glory.'

'You...' Talos trailed off, tired of the old argument. 'You speak like a child, deprived of its mother's milk. No more whining, Ruven.'

The sorcerer didn't reply. His creeping amusement was as palpable in the small cockpit as condensation on the walls.

Talos didn't answer the vox. He knew that outside Tenth Company, he was hardly regarded with any real universal admiration – he guessed the same number of his brothers wanted him dead as those that admired him – but avenging the primarch's murder had earned him savage notoriety. He suspected their disregard was more from their own shame at not hunting down the Night Haunter's killer. It was certainly the case with Ruven.

Xarl was the one to reply. 'Yes, yes, the Legion's good luck charm is still breathing. I need a list of ships in a position to take survivors.'

Almost thirty transponder codes bled across the relay monitor in the course of the next sixty seconds.

'That's the *Covenant*'s code,' Talos tapped the monitor. 'They're still here...'

They stared out into the orbital view, seeing the immense bulks of battleships gliding past each other. Ahead, above, and in every direction besides, the two fleets were meeting in the eerily silent, sedate fury of a void war.

'...somewhere,' Talos finished, a little lamely.

Xarl switched from atmospheric thrust to orbital burn, kicking the gunship forward. Something deep in the Thunderhawk's bowels gave an unpleasant rumble.

'This is why Sar Zell flies,' Cyrion pointed out.

'I am not piloting for the claw in the future,' Xarl replied. 'You think you can leave me behind on raids while you have all the fun? We'll train a slave to do this. Quintus, maybe.'

'Perhaps,' Talos allowed.

Small enough to escape notice, the gunship powered on. The stellar ballet of orbital battle played out before them. There, the massive, dark hull of the *Hunter's Premonition* rolled in agonisingly slow motion, its void shields splashing with bruised colour; and there, two Primogenitor strike cruisers shuddering away from the crippled *Loyalty's Lament*, their incidental fire blasting wreckage out of their paths as they escaped the larger ship before it could detonate.

Wings of Eighth Legion fighters, piloted by servitors and naval slaves, swarmed the Primogenitor cruisers, miniscule weapons sparking against the warships' shields. Carriers and battleships alike, resplendent in midnight clad, bore the brunt of enemy fire in return. Ships that had seen service for centuries ceased to exist with the passing of each moment, collapsing in on themselves before their wreckage flew apart on concentric rings of force, born of destabilised power cores. Others fell silent and cold, ruined to the point of drifting hulks, the fires that would lick at their hulls unable to survive in the airless void.

Xarl banked close to the hull of the *Premonition*, racing across its superstructure, weaving through the spinal battlements. A cacophony of light burst on all sides as the warship fired its backbone armaments at the lesser ships above. Xarl cursed at the brightness, flying with clenched teeth.

'I can't do this,' he said.

'We die if you don't,' replied Talos.

Xarl's agreement was a noncommittal grunt.

'Break left,' Cyrion called, staring at the hololithic display. 'You're heading towards the–'

'I see it, I see it.'

'Left, Xarl,' urged Talos. 'Left now…'

'Do you fools want to fly this thing? Shut your mouths.'

Even Uzas was on his feet now, staring out of the windshield. 'I think we should–'

'I think you should *shut up.*'

The gunship boosted faster, breaking away from the *Premonition*'s spinal ramparts, cutting towards two huge cruisers drifting closer together. To port, the Night Lords' warship *Third Eclipse*; to starboard, the Aurora Chapter battle-barge *In Pale Reverence*. Both vessels exchanged withering hails of fire as they readied to pass by.

The Thunderhawk bolted between them, its engines screaming and shaking the cockpit.

'There…' Xarl breathed, facing ahead again.

And there it was. The great ship burned, rolling in space, ringed by lesser cruisers that lashed their fire against its unprotected hull. Its spinal structures and broadside batteries spat back, forcing the invaders to drift away and regroup for another attack run. Along its midnight hull, the Nostraman script read, in immense letters of beaten bronze, *Covenant of Blood*.

'This is Talos to the *Covenant*.'

'You still live,' drawled the Exalted. 'This is a day of so many surprises.'

'We are in a Thirteenth Legion Thunderhawk, approaching the prow. Do not shoot us down.'

The warrior on the other end of the vox gargled something like a laugh. 'I will see what I can do.'

'Vandred is getting worse,' Uzas mused aloud in a dead voice. 'He doesn't blink now. I noticed that.' And then, apropos of nothing and in the same lifeless tone: 'Talos. When you jumped to save Cyrion, Ruven told us not to come back for you.'

'I'm sure he did.' The prophet almost smiled.

Talos opened his eyes. The apothecarion's lights glared down, forcing him to turn his head and shield his sight.

'Am I going to die, then?' he asked.

Variel shook his head. 'Not today.'

'How long was I gone?'

'Exactly two hours and nine minutes. Not long at all.'

The prophet rose, wincing at pains in his joints. 'Then I have a world to make an example of. Are we finished here?'

'For now, brother.'

'Come. We are going back to Tsagualsa, you and I. I have something to show you.'

PART THREE

A SONG IN THE DARK

XV

BEACON IN THE NIGHT

THE PEOPLE REMAINED as they were, lingering in their underground storm shelters. The few that stayed above ground crouched in hiding or set up street-end barricades, ready to defend their territory with iron bars, tools, pylon spears and limited numbers of small arms. They were the first to die when the Night Lords returned. Their bodies were the first cast into the skinning pits.

Servitor excavation teams pulled up entire sections of streets, digging ever-expanding holes to pile the skinless dead. Floating servo-skulls and the Night Lords' own helm-feeds recorded the carnage, archiving it for later use.

The archregent never left his desk. Dawn, as weak as it was on this world, was only an hour away. With the attackers returned, he intended to get some answers, one way or another. If today would see him die, he wouldn't go in ignorance.

Abettor Muvo hurried into the chamber, his shaking hands clutching printed reports as his robe swished across the sooty floor. No servants remained above ground to sweep the debris away.

'The militia is practically gone,' he said. 'The vox is... There's no reason to listen to it any more. It's just screaming, sire.'

The archregent nodded. 'Stay with me, Muvo. All will be well.'

'How can you say that?'

'A bad habit,' the older man confessed. 'All will not be well, but we can face it with dignity nevertheless. I believe I hear gunfire on the decks below.'

Muvo crossed to the desk. 'I... I hear it, too. Where are your guards?'

The archregent took his seat, steepling his fingers. 'I sent them to the closest shelter hours ago, though they did seem likely to remain out of some admirably foolish desire to do their duty. Perhaps that is them deeper in the ship, selling their lives to delay this meeting by a handful of seconds. I hope it's not them, though. That would be quite a waste.'

The abettor gave him a sideways glance. 'If you say so, lord.'

'Stand straight, Muvo. We are about to have guests.'

First Claw walked into the chamber, their armour still decorated in the blood of the tower's defenders. Talos led them in, immediately dropping a red helm onto the archregent's desk. It sent cracks through the wood.

'This desk is an heirloom,' the old man stated with admirable calm. The archregent's hands didn't even tremble as he leaned back in his chair. Talos liked him immediately – not that it would affect the Legion's actions one iota. 'I take it,' the statesman continued, 'that this is the helmet of an Imperial Space Marine belonging to the Genesis Chapter?'

'You presume correctly,' came the warrior's voice, in a snarl of brutal vox. 'Your defenders came to interfere with our plans for this world. It was the last mistake they ever made.'

The warrior turned away, walking around the observation dome, staring out over the city stretching in every direction. He finally looked back at the archregent, the skull helm staring without remorse, but curiously, without the hot-blooded shadow of malice – it was a cold, hollow visage, betraying nothing of the thoughts of the creature wearing it.

The archregent sat straighter and cleared his throat. 'I am Jirus Urumal, Archregent of Darcharna.'

Talos tilted his head. 'Darcharna,' he said without inflection.

'The world had no Imperial designation. *Darcharna* was the name of the first ship from our fleet to land h–'

'This world is called Tsagualsa. You, old man, are archregent of a lie. Tsagualsa had a king once. His throne stands empty at the heart of a forgotten fortress, and he needs no regent.'

The prophet looked back across the city, listening to the music within both mortals' heartbeats. Both were accelerating now, the wet drum tempo increasing in speed, and the salty tang of fear-sweat was beginning to reach his senses. Humanity always smelled its sourest when afraid.

'I will tell you why the Imperium has never come for you,' Talos said at length. 'It is the same reason this world bore no name in Imperial record. Tsagualsa once sheltered a Legion of arch-heretics, in the years after a war now lost to legend. The Imperium wishes only to forget about this world, and all those who walked upon it.

He turned back to the archregent. 'That includes you, Jirus. You are tainted by association.'

The archregent looked at each of them in turn – the skull trophies and ornate weapons; their red eye lenses and thrumming battle armour powered by the bulky backpack generators.

'And what is your name?' he asked, amazed that his voice didn't strangle in the tightness of his throat.

'Talos,' the towering warrior's vox-voice growled. 'My name is Talos of the Eighth Legion, master of the warship *Echo of Damnation*.'

'And what do you hope to accomplish here, Talos?'

'I will bring the Imperium to this world. I will drag them back to the world they so ardently wish to forget.'

'We have been awaiting Imperial rescue for four centuries. They don't hear us.'

The Night Lord shook his head, making the servos in his damaged armour buzz. 'Of course they hear you. They merely choose not to answer.'

'We are too far from the Astronomican for them to risk travel.'

'Enough excuses. I have told you why they abandoned you here.' Talos breathed slowly, weighing his next words with care. 'They will answer this time. I will make sure of that. Do you have an Astropathic Consortium in this husk of a society?'

'A... guild? Yes, of course.'

'And other psychically gifted souls?'

'Only those within the guild.'

'You cannot lie to me. When you lie, your body betrays you in a thousand subtle signals. Each of those signs is a clarion call to me. What are you seeking to hide?'

'There is mutation, at times, among the psychic. The guild deals with them.'

'Very well. Bring this guild to me. Now.'

The archregent made no attempt to move. 'Will you let us live?' the old man asked.

'That depends. How many draw breath upon this world?'

'Our last census collated ten million, across seven settlements. Life is unkind to us here.'

'Life is unkind everywhere. The galaxy has no love for any of us. I will let some of you live, to eke out an existence in the ruins while you wait for the Imperium. If none survived, there would be no one to speak of what they saw. Perhaps one in every thousand will live to greet the Imperium's arrival. It is not necessary, but it will be amusingly dramatic.'

'How... How can you speak of such dest–'

Talos cleared his throat. Through his helm's vocaliser, it sounded like a tank changing gears.

'I am bored of this conversation, archregent. Comply with my wishes, and you may still be one of those who survives the night.'

The old man rose to his feet. 'No.'

'It is a fine thing, to see a man with a backbone. I admire that. I respect it. But dubious courage has no place here, now, in this moment. I shall show you why.'

Cyrion stepped forward, his hand closing with a fistful of the abettor's lank hair. The man cried out as his boots left the floor.

'Please…' the man stammered. Cyrion drew his gladius, drawing it in a workmanlike carve along the abettor's belly. Blood gushed in a torrent, while looping innards threatened to spill out, held inside the body by nothing more than the man's own fingers. His pleading immediately warped into worthless screaming.

'This,' the prophet said to the archregent, 'is happening right now, across the stain of wreckage you call a city. This is what we are doing to your people.'

Cyrion, still holding the abettor aloft by his greasy hair, shook the man in his grip. More screaming, now punctuated by the wet slops of reeking intestinal meat slapping onto the decking.

'Do you see?' Talos's eyes never left the archregent. 'You fled to the shelters, trapping yourselves with nowhere to run. Now we will find all of you, and my brothers and I will do as we always do with those who flee like verminous prey.'

He reached for the man in Cyrion's grip, taking the convulsing, still-living figure in an iron hold around the throat. Without ceremony, he dumped the bleeding body on the archregent's desk.

'Comply with me, and one in a thousand of your people will avoid this fate. You will be one of them. Defy me, and not only will I no longer spare any of the others, you yourself will die now. My brothers and I will skin you, while you still live. We are masters of prolonging the experience, so the prey only dies in the hours after the surgery is performed. Once, a woman lived for six nights, wailing throughout the hours of crippling agony, only dying at last from infection in her filthy cell.'

'Your finest work,' Cyrion mused aloud.

The old man swallowed, trembling now. 'Your threats mean nothing to me.'

The Night Lord pressed his gauntleted fingers to the archregent's face, cold ceramite fingertips following the contours of the weathered skin and fragile bone beneath.

'No? The human body does wondrous things when its mind feels fear. It becomes an avatar of the pressure within a single paradox: to fight, or to flee. Your breath sours from the chemicals at work in your system. The clenching of internal musculature affects digestion, reflexes, and the ability to concentrate on anything but the threat. Meanwhile, the heart's wet rhythm becomes a war drum, beating blood for your muscles to use in order to escape harm. Your sweat smells different, muskier, like an animal trembling in terror, hopelessly marking its territory one last time. The edges of your eyes quiver, answering hidden signals from the brain, caught between wanting to stare to see the source of your fear, or to seal shut, hiding your vision from having to see what threatens you.'

Talos clutched the back of the archregent's head, his skulled faceplate centimetres from the old man's face.

'I can sense all of that on you. I see it in every twitch of your soft, soft skin. I smell it peeling off your body in a thick stink. Do not lie to me, human. My threats mean *everything* to you.'

'What…' The archregent had to swallow again. 'What do you want?'

'I have already told you what I want. Bring me your astropaths.'

As they waited, the archregent watched his city die.

The enemy lord, the one naming himself Talos, stood by the edge of the observation dome, in constant communication with his brethren across Sanctuary. His voice was a low, feral murmur, updating squads on each others' positions and mapping their progress. Every few minutes he would fall silent for a time, and simply watch the fires spread.

One of the other warriors, the one with the bulky heavy bolter slung on his back, activated a handheld hololithic emitter. He altered the scene it displayed each time Talos ordered him to focus upon the pict-feeds from a different squad.

Abettor Muvo had fallen silent. The archregent had closed his friend's eyes, choking on the smell rising from the split corpse.

'You get used to it,' one of the warriors had said with a black laugh.

The archregent watched the hololithic feed, seeing Sanctuary's death playing out clearly enough despite the visual distortion. The armoured warriors projected before him, silent in their hololithic incarnation, tore through shelter bulkheads and ripped through the huddled masses within. He watched them drag men, women and children by the hair out into the street, to be skinned and carried away by servitors, or crucified on the side of buildings, to mark that the closest shelter had been raided and cleaned out of all life. He saw the bodies hauled into the skinning pits; great mounds of flayed corpses stacked higher and higher – monuments of raw flesh in honour of nothing more than suffering and pain.

He saw one of the legionaries catch an infant by the leg and swing it against a building wall. Hunched, clawed warriors with thruster packs on their backs fought over the broken remains, though the image cut to another squad just as the victor began to devour his prize.

'Why?' he whispered, without realising he'd spoken aloud.

Talos didn't turn from watching the city burn. 'Some of us do it because we enjoy it. Some of us do it simply because we can. Some of us do it because this is our empire, and you do not deserve to live within it, enslaved to a lie.'

The slaughter didn't cease when the sun rose. Some primitive, foolish part of the archregent's hindbrain had hoped against hope that these creatures would vanish with the coming of the light.

'Do you have communication with the other cities?' Talos asked.

The archregent gave a weak nod. 'But it is infrequent at best. The astropaths sometimes manage to communicate with other guild members in the other cities. But even that is rare enough.'

'It is rare because they have no focus. I will deal with that. We have Mechanicum adepts among our crew – they will make planetfall and attend to your flawed equipment. We will then broadcast these images to the other cities, as a sign of what comes for them.'

The archregent's mouth was dry. 'You will give them time to organise resistance?' There was no hiding the hope in his voice.

'Nothing on this world is capable of resisting us,' answered Talos. 'They are free to prepare however they wish.'

'What is the Mechanicum?'

'You would know it by their slave-name: the *Adeptus Mechanicus.*' Talos fairly spat the cult's Imperial title. 'Cy?'

Cyrion walked over, his eyes never leaving the burning city. He hungered to be down there – they all did – and it showed in the movement of every muscle.

'You are enjoying this,' he said, seeing no need to make it a question.

Talos's nod was subtle enough to almost go unseen. 'It reminds me of the days before the Great Betrayal.'

And that was true enough. In that age, in the farthest, shadowed reaches of the Emperor's Light, the Eighth Legion had slaughtered whole cities to 'inspire' the other settlements across a given world into obedience of Imperial Law. 'Peace through justice,' Talos said. 'And justice through fear of punishment.'

'Aye. It reminds me of the same. But most of our brothers down there are doing it for the thrill of the hunt, and the pleasure of slaughtering terrified mortals. Remember that, before you graft a false layer of high ideals over what we do here.'

'I am no longer so deluded,' Talos admitted. 'I know what we are. But they do not need to share my ideals for my plan to work.'

'*Will* this work?' Cyrion asked. 'We are on the wrong side of the Imperium's border. They may never know what we do here.'

'They will know,' said Talos. 'Trust me, they will hear this, and come running.'

'Then my advice is this: we should not be here when they arrive. We are down to four Claws, brother. After this, we have to return to the Eye, and link up with whatever Legion forces we can ally with there.'

Talos nodded again, but said nothing.

'Are you even listening to me?' Cyrion asked.

'Just get me the astropaths.'

THEY NUMBERED ONE hundred and thirty-eight in total. The astropaths marched in as a disorderly pack, dressed in the same ragged clothing so typical of Sanctuary's citizens and the detritus caste of humanity found on frontier worlds across the Imperium's edges.

Yuris of the newly-organised Second Claw led them in. Blood marked his armour in dry splotches.

'There was a struggle,' he admitted. 'We tore our way into their guild shelter, and seven of them died. The rest of them came without a fight.'

'A ragged conclave,' Talos noted, walking around the prisoners. An equal mix of men and women; most of them were filthy. Several were children. Most interesting of all, none of them were blind.

'They still have their eyes,' Yuris said, noting Talos's stare. 'Will they still be of use to us if they've not been soul-bound to the False Emperor's Throne?'

'I believe so. They are not a true choir, and enslavement to the Golden Throne has not refined their power. In truth, they are barely worthy of the name *astropaths*. These are closer to telepaths, dabblers, witches and wyrds. But I can still make their powers work as we require.'

'We will return to the city,' Yuris said.

'As you will. My thanks, brother.'

'Good fortune, Talos. *Ave dominus nox*.'

Second Claw left the chamber in a loose pack, no more organised than the prisoners they'd brought in.

Talos faced the wretches, his targeting reticule flicking from face to face.

'Who leads you?' he asked. One woman stepped forward, her ragged robe seeming no different to any of the others.

'I do.'

'My name is Talos of the Eighth Legion.'

Confusion momentarily shone through the dullness of her eyes. 'What is the Eighth Legion?'

Talos's black eyes burned. He inclined his head, as if she had somehow proved a point.

'I am in no frame of mind to provide a lesson in history and myth,' he said, 'so let us simply say that I am one of the original architects of the Imperium. I hold to its founding ideal: that the species must know peace through obedience. I aim to bring the Imperium back into these skies. A lesson was once learned on this world. I find an amusing poetry in using this world to teach a lesson in return.'

'What lesson?' she asked. Unlike many of the others, she showed little overt fear. On the cusp of middle-age, she was likely at the height of her powers, not yet bled dry by them. Perhaps that was why she led them all. Talos didn't care, either way.

'Seal the doors,' he voxed to First Claw. Uzas, Cyrion, Mercutian and Variel moved to guard the chamber's two exits, their weapons clutched in loose fists.

'Do you know of the warp?' he asked the leader.

'We have stories, and the city's archives.'

'Allow me to guess. To you, the warp is the afterlife; a sunless underworld where those disloyal to the Emperor are punished for their faithless ways.'

'This is what we believe. All the archives state–'

'I do not care how you have misinterpreted your records. You are the strongest of your guild, are you not?'

'I am.'

'Good.'

Her head burst in a rupture of blood and bone. Talos lowered his bolter.

'Close your eyes,' he said. 'All of you.'

They didn't obey. The children drew close to their parents, and panicked murmurs broke out, as did intermittent weeping. The guild mistress's body hit the decking with a bony clang.

'Close your eyes,' Talos repeated. 'Commune with your power in whatever way works best. Reach out now, and feel for the soul of your dead leader. All who can hear her spirit still shrieking in the air around us, step forward.'

Three of them stepped forward, their eyes uncertain, their limbs quivering.

'Only three?' Talos asked. 'How very disappointing. I would hate to have to start shooting again.'

Another dozen stepped forward. Another handful followed.

'That is better. Tell me when she falls silent.'

He waited in silence, watching the faces of those who claimed to hear their dead mistress. One woman in particular winced and cringed as if suffering tics. When all others claimed to hear her no longer, she only relaxed a full minute afterwards.

'Now she is gone,' she said, scratching her thin, lank hair. 'Thank the Throne.'

Talos drew his gladius, tossing it and catching it three

times. As it smacked into his palm on the last catch, he turned and hurled it across the chamber. One of the men who'd stepped forward sank to the deck, gasping soundlessly, his eyes wide and his mouth working like a fish deprived of air. The sword impaling through his chest made a gentle, tinny sound as it tapped on the deck with each spasm.

At last, he lay still.

'He was lying,' Talos told the rest. 'I saw it in his eyes. He could not hear her, and I do not like being lied to.'

The air around the crowded guilders was charged now, alive with overlapping tiers of ripe tension.

'The warp is nothing so mundane. Beneath what we see of the universe is a layer we do not. Through this unseen Sea of Souls, an infinity of daemons swim. They are, even now, digesting the spirits of your murdered kin. The warp is not sentient, neither is it malicious. It simply *is*, and it responds to human emotion. Most of all, it responds to suffering, to fear, to hatred, for in such moments humanity is at its strongest and most honest. Suffering colours the warp, and the suffering of psychic souls is like a beacon. Your Emperor uses that suffering as fuel for his Golden Throne, to project the Astronomican.'

Talos could see few of them followed his words. Ignorance stunted their intellects, and fear blinded them to the nuance of his explanation. This, too, he found grimly amusing, as his red eye lenses drifted from face to face.

'I will use your suffering to breed a beacon of my own. The slaughter and torture of this city's people is merely the beginning. You can already feel the pain and death pressing against your minds. I know you can. Do not resist it. Let it saturate you. Listen to the screaming of souls as they dissolve from this realm into the next. Let their torment ripen within you. Carry it with you as an honour, for together you will become an instrument no different from your beloved, distant Emperor. You, like he, will become beacons in the endless night, bred from agony.

'To do that, I will break each one of you. Slowly, so very slowly, so that madness breeds within the pain. I will take you up into our warship, and over the course of the coming weeks, I will have you crippled, flayed, excoriated and excruciated. I will consign your ruined, pained forms – kept alive by our expert grace – to prison-laboratories where your only company will be the skinned carcasses of your children, your parents, and the corpses of others from your dead world.

'With the pain I give you, with your prolonged agonies, I will choke the warp at the Imperium's edge. Fleets will come to investigate, fearing nearby worlds may succumb to daemonic intrusion. Mankind's empire will ignore Tsagualsa no longer, and will learn an old lesson. It is not enough to force criminals and sinners into exile. You must make an example of them, and crush them utterly. Leniency, mercy, trust – these are weaknesses that the Imperium must pay for. The Imperium should have destroyed us here when it had the chance. Let them learn that once more.

'Your lives are over, but in death you will achieve something almost divine. You have prayed for so long to leave this world. Be pleased, for I am granting you that wish.'

As he fell silent, he watched the dawn of horrified disbelief on their faces. They could scarcely imagine what he was saying, but no matter. They'd understand soon enough.

'Don't do this,' came a voice from behind.

Talos turned to face the archregent. 'No? Why should I not?'

'It... I...' the old man trailed off.

'Strange.' Talos shook his head. 'Your kind never has an answer to that question.'

XVI

SCREAMING

Septimus made his way through the dark corridors without any obvious effort. His pistols were holstered at his thighs, and his repaired facial bionics no longer clicked each time he blinked, smiled, or spoke. He could see clearly enough with his augmetic eye piercing the gloom, and a photo-contact lens over the iris of the other – yet another perk of being one of the more valuable slaves on board.

His hands ached though, right to the knuckles. Nine hours of armour maintenance would do that. In the three weeks since Talos had returned from Tsagualsa, he'd managed to repair most of the damage to First Claw's armour. A treasure trove of salvage and spare parts from the Genesis Space Marines and slain Night Lords left the artificer spoiled for choice. Trading with artificers who served the other claws had never been easier, nor as fruitful.

An hour ago, Iruk, one of Second Claw's slaves, had spat something brown between his blackening teeth while they'd traded for torso cabling.

'The warband's dying, Septimus. You feel that? That's the wind of change, boy.'

Septimus had tried to avoid the conversation, but Iruk wouldn't be swayed. Second Claw's arming chamber was on the same deck as First Claw's, and just as chaotic with all the junked armour and weapon parts lying everywhere.

'They're still following Talos,' Septimus said at last, looking for a way out of the discussion.

Iruk had spat again. 'Your master makes them crazy. You should hear Lord Yuris and the others speak about him. Lord Talos is... They know he's not a leader, but they follow him. They know he's losing his mind, but they listen to every word he speaks. They say the same things about him and the primarch: broken, flawed, but... inspiring. Makes them think of a better time.'

'My thanks for the trading,' said Septimus. 'I have work to do.'

'Oh, I'm sure you do.'

He didn't like the amused glint in Iruk's eye. 'You have something to say?'

'Nothing that needs speaking out loud.'

'Then I'll leave you to your work,' Septimus said. 'I'm sure you have as much to do as I have.'

'I do indeed,' Iruk replied. 'But my "work" doesn't involve stroking that three-eyed witch's pale arse.'

Septimus made eye contact for the first time in several minutes. The kit bag full of spare parts slung over his shoulder suddenly felt heavier – as weighty as a weapon.

'She isn't a witch.'

'You want to be careful,' Iruk smiled, showing several missing teeth among the darkened ones remaining. 'Navigator spit is supposed to be poisonous, they say. Must be a lie though, eh? You're still breathing.'

He turned from Second Claw's crew, moving away and hitting the door release.

'Don't take it so hard, boy. She's lovely to look at, for a mutant. Has your master allowed you to start sniffing around her heels again?'

He genuinely considered braining Iruk with the sack and drawing his pistols to shoot the older man on the floor. Worse, it felt like the easiest, most satisfying answer to the man's idiotic barbs.

With teeth clenched, he walked from the chamber, wondering at what point in his life murdering someone became the easiest solution to a moment's discomfort.

'I've been with the Legion too long,' he'd said to the darkness.

An hour later, with servitors left to deal with the final work on Lord Mercutian's chestplate, Septimus was drawing close to what Octavia unsmilingly called her 'suite' of chambers. He could hear screaming from some directionless distance. The *Echo of Damnation* was named well: its halls and decks rang with faint screams, generated from mortal mouths elsewhere on the ship and carried wherever the *Echo*'s steel bones and cold air willed.

He shivered at the sound, still not used to its infrequent rise from nowhere. He had no desire to be illuminated on whatever the Legion was doing to those astropaths, or what they were inflicting on the countless other people brought up from the cities.

Rats, or things like them that he felt no need to examine closer, scampered off ahead of him through the darkness, skittering into side passages and maintenance ducts.

'You again,' said a voice ahead, by the main bulkhead leading into Octavia's chambers.

'Vularai,' Septimus greeted her. 'Herac, Lylaras,' he greeted the other two figures. All three were wrapped in filthy bandaging, clutching weapons. Vularai held her Legion gladius resting on one cloaked shoulder.

'Not supposed to come anymore,' the shortest of the figures hissed.

'And yet, Herac, here I am. Move aside.'

OCTAVIA SLEPT IN her throne, curled up in the huge seat and blanketed against the chill. She awoke at the sound of bootsteps approaching, instinctively reaching to check her bandana hadn't slipped.

It had. She adjusted it quickly.

'You shouldn't be here,' she said to her visitor.

Septimus didn't answer at once. He looked at her,

seeing the bandana over her third eye; seeing her reclining in a throne made for its mistress to use in sailing the Sea of Souls. Her clothes were filthy, her pale skin unwashed, and she'd aged a year for every month she'd been on board the *Echo* and the *Covenant* before it. The dark rings of sleep debt decorated her eyes, and her hair – once a cascade of black silk – was bound back in a straggly and frayed rat's tail.

But she smiled, and she was beautiful.

'We have to get off this ship,' Septimus said to her.

Octavia took too long to laugh. It betrayed more surprise than amusement. 'We… what?'

He'd not meant to say it out loud. He'd scarcely even realised he was thinking it.

'My hands ache,' he said. 'They ache every night. All I ever hear is gunfire and screaming, and orders spat at me by inhuman voices.'

She leaned on her throne's armrest. 'You lived with it before I joined the crew.'

'I have something to live for, now.' He met her eyes. 'I have something to lose.'

'How rare.' She didn't seem overly impressed, but he could see the hidden light in her eyes. 'Even in your atrocious accent, those words bordered on being romantic. Did our master give you another head wound, for you to speak so strangely?'

Septimus didn't look away as he usually would. 'Listen to me. Talos is driven by something I cannot comprehend. He is arranging… something. Some grand performance. Some great point to prove.'

'Like his father,' Octavia pointed out.

'Exactly. And look what happened to the primarch. His tale ended in death through sacrifice.'

Octavia rose to her feet, casting the blanket aside. She was still not showing, though Septimus had too little experience to know if her belly should be beginning to round yet or not. She seemed unconcerned, either way. He felt a brief, guilty flush of thanks that she was strong enough for the both of them, sometimes.

'You think he is leading us towards some kind of last stand?' Octavia asked. 'That seems unlikely.'

'Not intentionally. But he has no desire to lead these warriors, and nor does he wish to return to the Eye of Terror.'

'You're just guessing.'

'Perhaps I am. It doesn't matter, either way. Tell me you want our child born on this ship, into this life. Tell me you want him taken by the Legion and shaped into one of them, or to grow in the darkness of these decks, starved of sunlight his whole life. No, Octavia, we have to get off the *Echo of Damnation*.'

'I am a Navigator,' she replied, though there was no longer any amusement in her eyes. 'I was born to sail the stars. Sunlight is overrated.'

'Why is this a joke to you?'

The wrong words. He knew it as soon as he'd spoken them. Her gaze flashed as her smile became glass.

'It is not a joke to me. I merely resent your patronising assumption.' In all her time there, she'd never sounded quite so like the aristocrat she'd once been. 'I am not so weak that I need *saving*, Septimus.'

'That is not what I meant.' But that was the problem. He wasn't sure what he meant. He'd not even meant to speak the thought aloud.

'If I wished to leave the ship,' she said, lowering her voice, 'how could we do it?'

'There are ways,' said Septimus. 'We'd think of something.'

'That's very vague.' She watched him as he moved around her chamber, absently tidying away old food ration containers and data-slates her attendants had brought her as entertainment. Octavia witnessed the bizarre domestic ritual with her arms crossed beneath her breasts.

'You are still filthy,' he said, distracted.

'So you say. What are you thinking?'

Septimus stopped for a moment. 'What if Talos knows more than he's telling his brothers? What if he's seen how this all ends, and works now to his own plan? Perhaps he knows we'll all die here.'

'Even one of the Legion wouldn't be that treacherous.'

He shook his head, watching her with those mismatched eyes. 'Sometimes, I swear you forget just where you are.'

She wasn't blind to the change within him tonight. Gone was his cautious, endearing tenderness, as if fearful she would either break at a touch or kill him with an accidental glance. Gone was his vulnerability. In place of his patient virtues, frustration left him raw and curiously bare before her.

'Has he spoken to you recently?' Septimus asked her. 'Is there anything different in his words?'

She moved over to her bank of monitors, reaching for several tools in a nearby crate. 'He's always spoken like someone expecting to die sooner rather than later,' she ventured. 'Everything from his mouth is like some painful confession. I've always seen it in him – he never became what he wanted to be, and instead hates what he's become. The others… deal with it better. First Claw and the others – they enjoy this life. But he has nothing but hatred, and even that is growing hollow.'

Septimus sat next to her throne, closing his human eye in thought. His augmetic eye sealed closed in response, like a picter lens whirling shut. Screams filled the silence: distant but resonant, anonymous but so very human. He was no stranger to the sounds on an Eighth Legion vessel, but too much had changed now. He couldn't tune it all out the way he'd done for years before. Now, no matter what he did, no matter where he worked, he could still hear the pain in those crying voices.

'Those poor bastards being skinned alive – do they deserve it?'

'Of course they don't,' she replied. 'Why would you even ask such a stupid question?'

'Because it was the kind of question I'd stopped asking years ago.' He turned to look at Octavia, holding her gaze for several long moments. 'This is your fault,' he told her. 'Maruc understood, but I tried to ignore him. You did this to me. You came here, and made me human again. The guilt, the fear, the desire to live and feel and...' He trailed off. 'You brought it all back. I should hate you for this.'

'You are welcome to do so,' she said as she worked on rewiring one of her external viewfinder monitors. Octavia was hardly in love with the work, but the little tasks of maintenance helped pass the time. 'But you'll be hating me because I returned something valuable to you.'

Septimus gave a noncommittal grunt.

'Do not huff and sigh at Terran aristocracy,' she said. 'That's childish.'

'Then stop... I don't know the words in Gothic. *Yrosia se naur tay helshival*,' he said in Nostraman. 'Smiling to mock me.'

'You mean "teasing". And I'm not teasing you. Just say what you want to say.'

'We need to get off this ship,' he said again, watching her as she worked, sat there with a wire-stripping tool between her teeth.

Octavia spat it out, using it with one dirty hand. 'Maybe we do. That doesn't mean we'll be able to do it. The ship can't go anywhere without me. We'll hardly get very far before they realise we're gone.'

'I'll think of something.' Septimus moved over to her, embracing her from behind. 'I love you,' he said, speaking into her hair.

'*Vel jaesha lai*,' she replied.

AN HOUR LATER, she was making her way through the *Echo*'s tunnels at the head of her attendants, loosely clustered behind her in a ragged pack. The screams were omnipresent now, echoing through the air and travelling through the walls with the same insistence as a natural wind.

The excruciation chambers were several decks down, and hardly a short walk. In terms of territory on board the warship, she knew they were deeper in more dangerous sectors, where the crew weren't as valuable, and life was accordingly cheaper.

'We come with mistress,' one of her attendants had said.

'We'll all come,' Vularai amended, resting her hand on the prized Legion sword she wore at her hip.

'Whatever you wish,' Octavia had said, though she was secretly glad of their devotion.

A pack of equally ragged deck-dwellers fled before her group – the third to run rather than remain. Several had watched her pass, hissing in Gothic, Nostraman, and languages she couldn't even guess let alone comprehend. One pack had challenged her advance, demanding their tradable possessions.

'My name is Octavia,' she'd told the grimy leader with the laspistol.

'That means exactly nothing to me, girl.'

'It means I'm the ship's Navigator.' She'd forced a smile.

'That means as much to me as your name does.'

Octavia had taken a breath, glancing at Vularai. Most of humanity, in all its huddled, unenlightened masses, might be essentially blind to the existence of Navigators, but she had no desire to explain her heritage – or worse, demonstrate it – here.

That's when he made his mistake. The pistol held loosely in his hand was a concern, but hardly a threat. When he waved it in her direction, however, her attendants stiffened. Their whispers overlapped into a serpentine layer of 'Mistress, mistress, mistress...'

The gang leader didn't conceal his unease as well as he'd hoped. He was outnumbered, and as he learned from the solid-slug shotguns being pulled from filthy robes, he was outgunned as well. The iron bars and chains carried by most of his kindred suddenly seemed less impressive.

'You're not deck vermin,' he said. 'I see that now, all right? I didn't know.'

'Now you do,' Vularai rested the oversized gladius on her shoulder, where its edge caught what little light existed.

'Just leave,' Octavia told him. Her hand strayed to her stomach without conscious thought. 'There's already enough death on this ship.'

Although her attendants moved on in peace, their blood was up now. They didn't bother hiding their weapons as they walked on, deeper into the ship.

No one challenged them again.

She found Talos in one of the excruciation chambers, just as she'd expected.

Before entering, she'd placed her hand on the sealed door, ready to go in.

'Stop looking at me like that,' she chided Vularai. 'Navigators keep a hundred secrets, Vularai. Whatever waits behind these doors is nothing compared to the secrets kept in the sublevels of the Navis Nobilite's spires.'

'As you say, mistress.'

The door opened on grinding hydraulics. She saw Talos for less than a second, and then she saw nothing at all. The smell that struck her was strong enough to have an obscene physicality – it quite literally hammered against her the moment the bulkhead rolled open. Her eyes squeezed closed, stinging like salt in an open wound. The reek seeped into the soft tissue of her eyes, choked her throat, cramped her lungs, and lashed at her skin with a disgusting, damp warmth. Even her sworn curse was a mistake, for the moment the air hit her tongue, the stench became a taste as well.

Octavia collapsed to her hands and knees, throwing up onto the deck. She had to get out of the room, but her eyes wouldn't open, and she couldn't catch her breath between her spasming lungs and rebelling stomach.

Talos watched this spectacle from his place by the surgery table. His attention remained rapt as she vomited a second time.

'I am given to understand,' he said, 'that it is common for females in your... condition... to regurgitate as part of the natural process.'

'It's not that,' she breathed, before her guts clenched again, forcing her to heave out another tide of thin, sour gruel.

'I have almost no experience with such things,' he admitted. 'We studied little of the human condition in regards to gestation of children.'

'It's not that,' she wheezed. Inhuman fool, he had no idea. Several of her attendants were similarly struck down, gagging and choking on what they could see and smell.

She crawled from the chamber, half-dragged by Vularai and one other. Only when they had her outside did she manage to rise to her feet, catching her breath as her eyes watered.

'Seal the door...' she panted.

'Mistress?' one of her attendants asked, confused. 'I thought you wished to come here?'

'Close the door!' she hissed, feeling her stomach heave again. Three of the other attendants still hadn't recovered either, but they'd made it out of the room.

Vularai was the one to obey. The bulkhead leading into the excruciation chamber rumbled closed. Despite the mask of bandages, she was gagging and choking herself, barely able to speak.

'Those people on the tables,' she said. 'How are they still alive?'

Octavia spat the last of the bile from her lips, and reached back to re-tie her ponytail.

'Someone get me a rebreather. I'm going back in.'

'WE HAVE TO talk,' she said to him.

The body on the surgery table moaned, too breathless

and ruined to scream anymore. So little of it remained that Octavia could no longer determine its gender.

Talos looked over at her. The blades in his hands were wet and red. Four bodies, skinned and dripping, hung from dirty chains around the central table. He saw her eyes flicker to the hanging bodies, and explained their presence in a voice of inhuman calm.

'They are still alive. Their pain bleeds into this one's mind.' The Night Lord stroked the bloody knife along the prisoner's flayed face. 'It ripens now, swollen with agony. They no longer beg for death with their throats, tongues and lungs… but I can hear their whispers stroking inside my skull. Not long now. We are so very close to the end. What did you want to speak of, Navigator?'

Octavia took a breath through the rebreather mask over her mouth and nose. 'I want the truth from you.'

Talos watched her again, while the bodies drip, drip, dripped.

'I have never lied to you, Octavia.'

'I'll never understand how you can make a credible attempt at sounding virtuous while standing in an abattoir, Talos.' She wiped her eyes; the sick heat bleeding from the ruptured bodies was making them water.

'I am what I am,' he replied. 'You are distracting me, so I would ask you to make this quick.'

'And the manners of a nobleman,' she said softly, trying not to look at the butchery hanging on display. Blood trickled into a gutter grille beneath the table. She didn't want to guess where it led. She suspected something, somewhere down there on a lower deck, was feeding.

'Octavia…' he warned.

'I need to know something,' she said. 'I need to know the truth about all of this.'

'I have told you the truth, including what I expect from you.'

'No. You got it into your head that we had to come here. Now there's this… carnage. You know more than you're telling us. You know if the Imperium comes to answer these atrocities, it will come in force.'

He nodded. 'That seems likely.'

'And we may not escape.'

'That also seems likely.'

Octavia's rebreather clicked at the zenith of each slow breath. 'You are doing what he did, aren't you? Your primarch died to prove a point.'

'I do not plan to die here, Terran.'

'No? You don't *plan* to die here? Your plans aren't worth a damn, Talos. They never are.'

'The raid on Ganges Station seemed to go well enough,' he pointed out. 'And we sent the Salamanders running at Vykon Point.'

His amusement only fuelled her temper. 'You're supposed to be our leader. You command thousands of souls, not just your handful of warriors.'

He growled a laugh. 'Throne in flames, do you truly think I care about every single creature that draws breath on this ship? Are you mad, girl? I am a legionary of the Eighth. Nothing more, nothing less.'

'You could have killed Septimus.'

'And I will, if he defies me again. The moment his usefulness is outweighed by his defiance, he dies skinless and eyeless on this very table.'

'You're lying. You're evil, heart and soul, but you're not the monster you pretend to be.'

'And you are trying my patience, Terran. Get out of my presence before I lose the last vestiges of my tolerance for your irritating ethical theatrics.'

But she was going nowhere. Octavia took another calming breath, trying to control her stubborn anger.

'Talos, you are going to kill all of us unless you're careful. What if the Imperium's answer isn't some ship of salvation to carry the survivors away to tell some awful story, but a vast Navy battlefleet? It'll likely be both. We're as good as dead if they find us nearby.' She gestured to the quivering wretch on the table. 'You want to poison the warp with their pain and annihilate any hope of safe flight through the Sea of Souls, but it will be as much of a struggle for me. I cannot guide us through broken tides.'

Talos said nothing for several seconds. 'I know,' he finally replied.

'And yet you're going through with this?'

'This is one of the precious few times since the Great Betrayal that my brothers and I have felt like the sons of our father again. No longer raiding, no longer merely surviving – we are once more doing what we were born to do. It is worth the risk.'

'Half of them are just killing for the sake of it.'

'True. That, also, is the Eighth Legion way. Nostramo was not a wholesome birthworld.'

'You're not listening to me.'

'I listen, but you speak in ignorance. You do not understand us, Octavia. We are not what you think we are, because you have always misunderstood us. You judge us by human morality, as if we have ever been chained to those ideals. Life means something different to the Eighth Legion.'

She closed her eyes for a long moment. 'I hate this ship. I hate this life. I hate you.'

'Those are the most intelligent words you have ever said to me.'

'We're going to die here,' she said at last. Her hands bunched into helpless fists.

'Everyone dies, Octavia. Death is nothing compared to vindication.'

XVII

GAMBITS

CYRION WAS ALONE, now that his latest victim lay dead.

He sat with his back to the wall, breathing through spit-wet teeth. The gladius in his hand clattered to the stained decking. Shivers still rippled through him; pleasant aftershocks as the man's death played out again in his mind. Real fear. Real terror. Not the dull haze of pain that was all that remained among the astropaths and their other victims. This had been a vital, strong man with no desire to die. Cyrion had cherished the look in his eyes as the gladius hacked and carved. He'd been scared to the bitter end: a dirty, unwarranted death, replete with begging, deep in the ship's lower decks.

The Night Lord had needed it – water to a parched man after all the clinical infliction of pain on their captives. The crew member's final moments, as his weak fingers scratched uselessly at Cyrion's faceplate, were the final, perfect touch. Such delicious futility. He tasted that desperate fear, its actual tactile sweetness, like nectar on the tongue.

A groan escaped his lips through the tingling rush of chemicals flooding his brain and blood. It was good to be a god's son, even one with a curse. Even when the gods themselves watched a little too closely.

Someone, somewhere, was saying his name. Cyrion ignored it. He had no mind to return to the higher decks and go back to the surgical carving that needed to be done. That could wait. The flood was beginning to fade now, and with it, the tremor in his fingers.

A strange name, that. *The flood.* He couldn't recall when he'd first come to know his gift by that name, but it fit well enough. Latent psychic strength wasn't miraculously rare in the Eighth Legion – or any of the Legions beyond – but his remained a source of quiet pride. Cyrion had never been born psychic, or else his touch of the sixth sense was weak enough to go unnoticed by the extensive tests upon Legion indoctrination. It had simply happened over time, during the years they'd spent in the Eye of Terror. His awareness had blossomed, like a flower opening in the light of the sun.

The wordless whispers began at the edge of his hearing, night after night. Soon enough he could make sense from the hissed phrases, stealing a word here or a sentence there. Each of them shared a single strain of familiarity: they were all fearful utterances, unspoken but still audible, pulsing from those he killed.

In the beginning, he'd merely found it amusing. To hear the fearful final words of those he butchered.

'I do not see why you find this so funny,' Talos had rebuked him. 'The Eye is influencing you.'

'There are those who bear worse curses than I,' Cyrion pointed out. Talos had let it rest, never mentioning it again. Xarl hadn't acted with the same restraint. The stronger the gift became, the less inclined Cyrion was to hide it, and the filthier Xarl found his presence. *Corruption,* Xarl had called it. He'd never trusted psykers, no matter the benevolence of the powers they claimed.

'Cyrion.'

His name brought him back to the present, back to the stink of oily metal walls and newly dead bodies.

'What is it?' he voxed back.

'It's Malcharion,' came the response. 'He... he has awakened.'

'Is this a hilarious jest?' Cyrion hauled himself to his feet with a grunt. 'Deltrian swore there was no progress.'

'Just get up here. Talos warned you about hunting in the ship's bowels when we have work to do.'

'You're as bad as he is, sometimes. Has the war-sage spoken?'

'Not exactly.' Mercutian broke off the contact.

Cyrion started walking, leaving the bodies behind. No one would miss the lower-deck trash that lay in bloody pieces behind him. Hunting in the *Echo*'s deep levels was a forgivable sin, unlike Uzas's occasional mad slayings through Blackmarket and the officer decks, butchering the most valuable members of the crew.

'Hello,' said a soft, quiet voice from nearby. Too low to be human, but unrecognisable in the vox distortion.

He looked up. There, in the chamber's iron rafters, one of the Bleeding Eyes crouched with a gargoyle's patience. Cyrion felt his skin crawl; a rare sensation indeed.

'Lucoryphus.'

'Cyrion,' came the reply. 'I have been thinking.'

'And evidently following me.'

The Raptor nodded his sloping helm. 'Aye. That also. Tell me, little Lord of Smiles, why do you come down here so often to sniff out the excretion-reek of fear?'

'These are our hunting grounds,' Cyrion replied. 'Talos spends long enough down here, himself.'

'Maybe so.' The Raptor's head jerked once, either a flaw in his armour's systems or the result of warp-flawed genetics. 'But he kills for release, for pleasure, for the surge of adrenaline stinging in his veins. He was born a killer, therefore he kills. You hunt to sate another appetite. An appetite that has bloomed within you, not one you were born with. I find that interesting. Oh, yes.'

'You may think whatever you choose.'

The angled, almond-shaped eye lenses showed Cyrion's reflection in miniature. 'We have watched you, Cyrion. The Bleeding Eyes see everything. We know your secrets. Yes we do.'

'I have no secrets to keep, brother.'

'No?' Lucoryphus's laugh was somewhere between a chuckle and a caw. 'A lie doesn't become truth simply because you give it voice.'

Cyrion said nothing. He briefly considered reaching for his bolter. His fingers must've twitched, for Lucoryphus laughed again.

'Try it, Cyrion. Just try.'

'Make your point,' the warrior said.

Lucoryphus leered. 'Why must there be a point to a conversation between kindred? Do you assume every soul is as treacherous as you are? The Bleeding Eyes follow Talos because of that oldest axiom: he breeds trouble wherever he walks. The primarch paid attention to him, and that is an interest still fascinating all these centuries later. He has a destiny, one way or another. I wish to witness that destiny. You, however, have the potential to become a nuisance. How long have you fed on human fear?'

Cyrion breathed slowly before answering, suppressing the tempting flood of chemical stimulants from intravenous feeds in his wrists and spine.

'A long time. Decades. I have never kept track.'

'A very weak breed of psychic vampirism.' The Raptor exhaled a thin breath of steam from his vocabulator grille. 'I am not one to question the gifts of the warp.'

'Then why question me at all?'

He realised his mistake as soon as the question left his lips. Delaying had cost him the edge of opportunity. From the corridor he'd come down, another of the Bleeding Eyes crawled on all fours, blocking the doorway.

'Cyrion,' it said, seeming to struggle with speech. 'Yes-yes.'

'Vorasha,' he replied. It was no surprise when another three Raptors crawled out of the tunnel ahead, their sloping daemon-masks watching him with unblinking scrutiny.

'We question you,' Lucoryphus rasped, 'because while

I would never speak out against the warp's changes, I have much less patience for treachery so close to the prophet. Stability is vital now. He is planning something secret, something he has chosen not to share. We all sense it, like... like a static charge in the air. We walk now in the pressure of a storm yet-to-be.'

'We trust him,' said one of the other Raptors.

'We do not trust you,' finished a third.

Lucoryphus's voice was ripened by a smile. 'Stability, Cyrion. Remember that word. Now run along and witness the war-sage's flawed resurrection. And remember this talk. The Bleeding Eyes see all.'

The Raptors scattered back into the tunnels, worming their way deeper into the ship.

'That isn't good,' Cyrion said to himself in the silent darkness.

HE WAS THE last to arrive, entering the Hall of Reflection almost thirty minutes after the initial summons. The chamber's usual industry was halted in surreal immobility. None of the servitors went about their business, while dozens of low-tier Mechanicum adepts looked on in relative silence. If they communicated with each other, it was via means that the legionaries couldn't discern.

Cyrion walked to First Claw, who stood by the circular bulkhead entrance to one of the antechambers. The barrier itself was rolled open, revealing the stasis chamber within. Cyrion felt something at the edge of his hearing, like the threat of thunder on the horizon. He cycled through his helm's audio receptor modes, picking up the same almost-audible infrasound murmur no matter the frequency.

'Do you hear that?' he asked Talos.

The prophet stood with Mercutian and Uzas, saying nothing. Variel and Deltrian conferred in hushed voices by the adept's central control tables.

'What's wrong?' Cyrion asked.

Talos turned his skulled faceplate to him. 'We are still not certain.'

'But Malcharion is awake?'

Talos led him into the stasis chamber. Their boots sent resonant echoes clanging off the iron walls. Malcharion's sarcophagus remained on its marble plinth, chained in place, supported by hundreds of copper filament wires, power cables and life support tubes. The sarcophagus displayed Malcharion's triumphant death in exquisite detail: gold, adamantine and bronze worked into a vision of a Night Lord victorious, head tilted back to roar at a starry sky. In one hand, the tail-crested helm of a White Scar khan; in the other, the helmet of an Imperial Fist champion. Last of all, his boot rested on the proud helm of a Blood Angels lord-captain, grinding it into the Terran dirt.

'The stasis field is down,' Cyrion pointed out.

'It is,' Talos nodded, crossing to one of the secondary consoles ringing the central plinth. His fingers tapped against several plastek keys. As soon as the final key clicked, the chamber burst with a flood of agonised screaming. The cries were organic, human, but with a tinny edge and an undertone of buzzing crackle.

Cyrion winced, it was that loud. His helm took a couple of seconds to filter the sound to tolerable levels. He didn't need to ask the screams' origin.

'What have we done to him?' he asked. The screaming died as Talos killed the power feed from the sarcophagus to the external speakers.

'That is what Variel and Deltrian are working on. It seems likely that Malcharion's wounds at Crythe have left his mind shattered beyond recovery. There is no telling what he would do if we connected him to a Dreadnought chassis. For all we know, he would turn on all of us.'

Cyrion thought over his next words with exceptional care. 'Brother...'

Talos turned to him. 'Speak.'

'I have supported you, haven't I? You wear the mantle of our commander, but it doesn't quite fit.'

The prophet nodded. 'I have no desire to lead anything. I'm hardly keeping it a secret. Can you not see me doing all I can to restore our true captain?'

'I know, brother. You are the living embodiment of someone in the wrong place at the wrong time. But you are coping. The raid on Tsagualsa was a fine touch, as was sending the Salamanders running at Vykon Point. I don't care what you're planning; the others are either content to trust your judgement, or lose themselves in indulgence in the meantime. But this…'

'I know,' Talos said. 'Trust me, I know.'

'He's a Legion hero. You will live and die by how you treat him, Talos.'

'I am not blind to that.' The prophet ran his hand across the graven image on the surface of the sarcophagus. 'I told them to let him die after Crythe. He'd earned the respite of oblivion. But Malek – a curse upon him, wherever he is – countermanded my order. And when Deltrian smuggled the coffin aboard, it changed everything. He hadn't died, after all. Perhaps I was wrong to believe him too melancholy to survive in this shell, since he'd fought for life when he could so easily have died. We could have used his guidance, Cyrion. He should have stood with us again.'

Cyrion gripped his brother's shoulder guard. 'Tread with care, Talos. We stand on the edge of everything coming unravelled.' He looked at the sarcophagus himself for several long moments. 'What did the Flayer and the tech-adept suggest?'

'Both of them believe he is ruined beyond recovery. They also both concur that he could still be formidable – if unreliable – in battle. Variel suggested controlling Malcharion with pain injectors and focused excruciators.' Talos shook his head. 'Like an animal, collared by unkind masters and trained by beatings.'

Cyrion expected no less from either of those two. 'And what will you do?'

Talos hesitated. 'What would you do, in my place?'

'Truly? I'd flush the organic remains into the void without any of the Legion knowing, and install one of the grievously wounded warriors in his place. Spread the word that Malcharion died during the rituals of resurrection. Then there would be no one to blame.'

The prophet turned to face him. 'How noble of you.'

'Look at the armour we wear. Witness the cloak of flayed flesh worn by Uzas; the skulls hanging from our belts; the skinned faces draped over Variel's pauldrons. There is nothing of nobility in us. Necessity is all we know.'

Talos watched him for what seemed an age. 'Is there a reason for this sudden proselytising?'

Cyrion thought of Lucoryphus, and the Bleeding Eyes' words. 'Just my caring nature,' he smiled. 'So what will you do?'

'I have ordered Variel and Deltrian to see if they can calm him down with synapse suppressors and chemicals. There may be a way to reach him yet.'

'And if that fails?'

'I will deal with that possibility when it becomes an unarguable truth. For now, it is time we played our hand. Octavia's time has come.'

'The Navigator? Is she ready for this?' *Whatever 'this' is,* he added silently.

'Her readiness is immaterial,' said Talos, 'for she has no choice.'

THE ECHO OF DAMNATION rode the tides, powered by plasma fusion, driven by the sentient heart at the ship's core, and guided by the third eye of a woman born of humanity's ancestral home world.

Talos stood by her throne, his own eyes closed, listening to the sounds of the screaming sea. Souls crashed against the hull, mixed in with the very life-flesh of daemons, shaking the warship and rippling over them in an endless, howling tide. He listened, for the first time in decades he truly listened, and heard once more the music of his father's throne room.

A breathy sigh hissed from his parted lips. Gone was the doubt. Gone were the concerns of how best to lead the few warriors that remained to him, and how he should spend the lives of his slaves. Why hadn't he done this before? Why had he never noticed the similarity in sound until Octavia pointed it out? He knew all the tales that warned of listening too close to the warp's song, but they all went blissfully ignored.

The Navigator was sweating, staring into a thousand shades of black. One moment the darkness screamed at her, expressing its pain through souls bursting against the hull. The next, it called to her; nameless things beckoning with the same claws that raked along the ship's metal skin.

The tides writhed with the same coiling chaos found within a nest of serpents. Flashes of sick light winked between the overlapping warp-stuff, either the distant Astronomican or the deceptions of daemons – it didn't matter to Octavia. She aimed the ship for every pulse of light that flickered ahead, crashing through the void-tides with the power and weight behind one of the species' oldest warships. The cold waves of unreality burst apart at their prow, and trembled in their wake, forming shapes no human eyes could ever perceive.

The *Echo* itself remained in the back of her consciousness. Unlike the sullen, contrary soul of the *Covenant*, the *Echo of Damnation* had a great, eager heart. Terra had no sharks, but she knew of them from the Throneworld's archives. Predators within the ancient seas, forever needing to move forward lest they die. That was the *Echo* in a single, simple concept. It desired nothing more than to run with all its strength, breaking through the barriers of the warp and leaving the material realm behind.

You have listened too long and too hard to the warp's call, she chided the ship as sweat ran down her temples.

Burn, burn, burn, it pulsed back. *More strength to engines. More fire in core.*

She felt the ship racing harder in response. Her own instinctive impulses flashed through the neural-sensitive cables plugged into her temples and wrists, curbing the sudden leap in thrust. The *Echo*'s primal excitement snapped back, entering her body through the same ports, sending her into a delicious shiver.

Calm, she pulsed. *Calm.*

The ship's reply was another effort to increase thrust. Octavia could almost see the slave crews in the cavernous chambers of the engine decks, sweating and shouting and dying to feed the generators at the pace demanded of them. For a moment, she thought she could feel them all the way the *Echo* felt them: as a hive of flea-like, insignificant sentience, itching within her bones.

The Navigator pulled back from the mesh of sensation, rejecting the ship's primitive emotions and settling firmer within herself. The cold kiss of her chamber's air supply touched her sweating skin, causing another involuntary shudder. She felt as though she'd been holding her breath under boiling water.

'Starboard,' she whispered into the vox-orb drifting before her face. Its tiny suspensors kept it afloat – a half-skull rendered into a portable vocabulator – and transmitted her words to the crew and servitors on the command deck above. 'Starboard, three degrees, pressurised thrust to compensate for warp density. Axial stabilisers are…'

On and on she mumbled, staring into the darkness, sharing control of the warship with the vessel's crew and its own angry heart.

Outside, the pantheon of ethereal inhumanity raged against the ship's Geller field. The tide itself recoiled, burned and bleeding, each time it broke against the diving vessel. Octavia scarcely spared a thought for the deep, cold intelligences hiding in the endless void. It took all her concentration to focus on the narrow path she was ramming through the Sea of Souls. She could endure the screaming, for she was born to see through the unseeable – the warp held few secrets or surprises for her. But the *Echo*'s eager joy threatened her focus like nothing else ever had; even the *Covenant*'s mulish resistance had been easier to overcome. That required force. This required temperance. It required a lie told to herself: that she didn't share the same savage joy, that she didn't feel the same need to burn the engines unto self-destruction, running faster and diving deeper than any soul – artificial or otherwise – had ever done before.

The *Echo*'s dark delight filtered back through the neural feeds, spicing her blood with excitement's charge. Octavia pulled back from the bond, forcing her breathing to slow as her body reacted to the symbiotic pleasure in the most primal of ways.

Slower, she breathed, sending the word back to the ship's core even as she spoke it aloud. *Geller stability is wavering.*

You are wavering, the *Echo*'s dull sentience pulsed back. *A slave to reason.*

The ship gave another shiver in sympathy to her own. This one was tighter, born of tensed muscles and clenched teeth. It spoke of control and focus, as Octavia's will blanketed the ship's machine-spirit.

I am your Navigator, she whisper-hissed the silent words. *And I guide you.*

The *Echo of Damnation* never communicated with actual language; its pulses of emotion and urges formed words only as Octavia's human mind fought to find meaning in them. Its surrender now never even manifested as false utterances, though. She merely felt it cower back from her surge of willpower, taking its inflicted emotions with it.

Better, she smiled through the tears of sweat. *Better.*

Close now, Navigator, it sent back.

I know.

'Beacons,' she mumbled aloud. 'Beacons in the night.

The blade of light. The Emperor's Will given shape. A trillion screaming souls. Every man and woman and child ever given to the Golden Throne's soul engines, since the dawn of the One Empire. I see them. I hear them. I see the sound. I hear the light.'

Whispering voices slithered into her ears. Deck by deck, the word was being passed, so pathetically slow in its reliance on mortal speech. Octavia had no need to stare at hololithic star maps. She cared nothing for the rattle and clang of deep-void auspex readers.

'All stop,' she whispered through lips bright with spit. 'All stop.'

The hand on her shoulder could have come a minute, an hour, or a year later. She wasn't sure.

'Octavia,' said the low, low voice.

She closed her secret eye, and opened her human ones. Vitreous humour gummed them, leaving them sore as she forced them open. She felt the soft caress of her bandana being draped over her forehead.

'Water,' she demanded, her voice a horse rasp. Her attendants muttered nearby, but the hands bringing the dirty canteen to her lips were armoured in midnight blue. Even the tiniest knuckle-joints gave soft growls.

She swallowed, caught her breath, and swallowed more. With trembling hands, she wiped the cooling sweat from her face, then pulled the intravenous feeds from her arms. The cables in her temples and throat could remain there, for now.

'How long?' she asked at last.

'Sixteen nights,' said Talos. 'We are where we need to be.'

Octavia closed her eyes as she sank back into the throne. She was asleep before Vularai covered her shivering form with a blanket.

'She must eat,' the attendant pointed out. 'Over two weeks... The baby...'

'Do whatever you wish,' Talos said to the bandaged

mortal. 'That is none of my concern. Wake her in six hours and bring her to the excruciation chambers. All will be ready by then.'

SHE WORE HER rebreather again, listening to the sound of her own respiration turned low and throaty. The mask over her nose and mouth stole all sense of taste and scent, leaving only the stale musk of her own breath, tinged with a chlorine edge that stung the back of her tongue.

Talos stood behind her, ostensibly to oversee the moment. She wondered if he'd really remained in order to prevent her from running.

Six hours' sleep wasn't enough, not even nearly enough. Octavia felt her weariness as a physical sickness, leaving her weak and slow, as if her blood beat around her body at a muted rate.

'Do it,' Talos ordered her.

She didn't – at least, not immediately. She walked among the chained bodies, between the slabs on which they lay, weaving through the medicae servitors monotasked with keeping the carcasses alive just a little while longer.

The husks laid out on each table scarcely resembled humans in any real sense. One was a mess of musculature and stripped veins, twitching its final moments away on the surgery table. The flayed ones were little better; neither were those now deprived of their tongues, lips, hands and noses. Ruination was complete on each and every one of them – desecration had never seen such variety. She was walking through a living monument to fear and pain: this was the Legion's imagination given form.

Octavia looked back at Talos, glad he still wore his helm. If she'd seen any pride in his naked eyes in that moment, she would have never been able to tolerate his presence again.

'The Screaming Gallery,' she said, above the muffled

moans and beep of pulse trackers. 'Was it like this?'

The Night Lord nodded. 'Very much so. Now do it,' he said again.

Octavia took a stale breath, moved to the closest table, and removed her bandana.

'I will end it for you,' she whispered to the organic wreckage that had once been a man.

It turned its eyes towards her with the last of its strength, lifted its wet gaze to the Navigator's third eye, and looked into absolute oblivion.

XVIII

A SONG IN THE NIGHT

THE WORLD ARTARION III.

In the Tower of the Emperor Eternal, Godwyne Trismejion watched the astropath writhing against the restraining straps. This was nothing unusual. It was his job to watch over his wards when they dreamed, monitoring them as they sent their somnolent messages to receptive minds on other worlds. He found it amusing – in his own dullish, slow-witted sort of way – that in an empire of a million worlds, the most reliable way to carry a message to another world was to take it there yourself.

Even so, his wards had their roles to play. Astropathic contact saw a great deal of use on Artarion III, as might be expected of any world so heavily populated by guild trade interests.

The astropath started to bleed from the nose. This, too, was within tolerable parameters. Godwyne clicked a steel switch and spoke into his console's vox-input.

'Vital signs for Unon fluctuating within… tolerable…' he trailed off, his eyes locked to the spiking polylithic printout. The readings spiked harsher with each passing second.

'Sudden heart failure, and…' Godwyne looked back to the astropath, seeing the onset of real convulsions now. 'Heart failure and… Throne of the God-Emperor.'

Something wet and red burst against the viewscreen window. He couldn't see through the mess to be sure, but when a purification team entered six minutes later, they would learn it was Astropath Unon's heart and brain, burst by unprecedented external psychic pressure.

By that time, Godwyne was on the edge of panic as he worked at his console, his hands full of vague printed images from the minds of his astropathic wards, and his head full of the wailing sirens as more and more of them died.

'What are they hearing?' he screamed at the chaotic spill of frantic information. 'What are they seeing?'

The Tower of the Emperor Eternal, as a precious and expensive psychic node – warded and strengthened against daemonic intrusion – absorbed all the death and pain taking place within its walls. It didn't distil it or filter it; it merely fused the sudden fears and mortal agonies with the hideous incoming transmission, and beamed the foul whole back into the void.

The notes of the song sailed on through the night, now with a new chorus.

Each world hearing the song would add another chorus in turn.

THE WORLD VOL-HEYN.

On the agricultural world's northernmost archipelago, an Administratum overseer blinked at the spots of blood dropping onto his manuscript. He blinked and looked up, where his advisor – Sor Merem, local provost of the Adeptus Astra Telepathica – was twitching and curling into himself.

The overseer recoiled at the man's fit, activating his hand-vox. 'Inform the medicae division that the Telepathica provost has fallen victim to some kind of seizure.' He almost laughed, seeing the man collapse and smack his head on the table edge on the way down. Bloody drool spurted from his lips.

'What madness is this?' the overseer half-laughed, biting back his unease.

Shouting reached his ears from elsewhere in the building. Other astropaths? Their guardians and keepers? The poor fools 'gifted' with the sacred speech were never stable, never healthy – each one rendered blind and feeble by their soulbinding to the Golden Throne. Shouting in the halls was commonplace as they sent and received their many messages each night. Each one would burn out in under a decade. The overseer didn't relish the fact – it was simply the way of things.

The provost was thudding the back of his head on the stone floor now, beating himself bloody and biting his tongue. The overseer didn't understand. The provost was newly appointed only the previous season. He had many years of use before burning out.

'Merem?' the overseer asked the twitching body. Froth at the man's lips was the only answer. His eyes were wide, terrified by something only he could see.

'Overseer Kalkus,' his hand-vox crackled.

'Speak,' the overseer said. 'I demand to know what's happening.'

'Overseer… the–'

'The what? Who is this?'

Something screamed down the vox connection. It didn't sound human. The overseer would find exactly how true that was in a handful of minutes, when it reached his door.

ON NEW PLATEAU, it came to be known as the Night of the Mad Song, as tens of thousands of hive residents dreamed the same torturous dreams.

On Jyre, the central fortress of the Adeptus Astra Telepathica was destroyed in a riot from within, that spread onto the streets and lasted three weeks before the planetary defence forces quelled the uprising.

On Garanel IV, almost all off-world business within Capital City was brought to its knees by an outbreak of an unnamed contagion in the astropathic guild's sector of the city.

The song carried on into the night.

THE WORLD ORVALAS.

The world itself was largely worthless. Its ore deposits had long since been carved bare, leaving great, dry canyon-scars across the planet's tectonic visage. What few humans remained maintained an astropathic relay station in high orbit. Their sworn duty was as simple as it was vital: to interpret the dreams, images, nightmares and voices of the warp reaching them from other worlds, and relay them onward down the 001.2.57718 Astra Telepathica Duct.

Sixteen minutes after its contingent of psychically-gifted souls received the mortis-cry from several worlds elsewhere along the Duct, the astropathic relay station at Orvalas went dark. No trace of its further existence was ever noted in Imperial record. All five hundred and forty souls aboard were entered into the Adeptus Astra Telepathica's Chronicles of the Lost, at their headquarter bastion on the world Heras, Corosia Subsector, in Ultima Segmentum.

The final astropathic transmissions from Orvalas reached thirty-four other worlds, strengthening the bleak song past its already potent voice.

IT TOOK FOUR hours.

One by one, she killed them with her secret sight. Each of them looked into her hidden eye, and though she never knew what they saw, she knew what would happen. The first howled and reached for her with handless arms, banging its amputated wrists against her face as it died. A single glance at her third eye was all it took. No more lethal weapon existed in all of humanity's long and bloody history. Any sailor of the stars knew that to look into a Navigator's warp eye was to know death. No tales existed of what the doomed ones ever saw in those depths. No one had ever lived to tell of it.

Octavia had her own guesses, though. Her tutors had hinted of their own research, and of archival evidence noted by previous scholars. Her bloodline's priceless mutation allowed her immunity to the warp's taint, but for one without Navigator blood, the third eye was a death sentence. Each of these poor, excruciated remnants looked through the window into Chaos Incarnate. Their minds opened to the horror beyond the veil, and their mortal forms ruptured, unable to contain it.

Some of them simply expired, their spirits at last drifting from the tortured husks that contained them. Others twitched against their restraints, possessing a vitality they'd lacked at any other time, writhing as they died from agonising organ failure. Several of them burst in front of her, drenching her with stinking viscera. Jagged shards of bone cut and bruised her with each disgusting detonation, and the air soon turned thick with the reek. She had blood on her tongue and shit on her face by the time she'd killed the seventh.

By the twelfth, she was drooling herself, trembling, bleeding from her third eye. By the fifteenth, she could barely stand. By the eighteenth, she could no longer recall who she was.

She passed out as she murdered the nineteenth.

Talos didn't let her fall. He gripped the back of her head in his gauntleted hand, forcing her unconscious visage into the faces of those doomed to die. He held her secret eye open with the tip of one finger, slaying wherever he aimed her limp body.

By the end, she was barely breathing. Her attendants rushed to her, but the Night Lord warned them back with a glare.

'I will take her back to her chamber.' He opened his vox-link with a moment's concentration. A rune flashed live on his retinal display. 'Variel, attend to the Navigator in her chambers. She is wounded from her efforts.'

'As you wish,' crackled back the Flayer's reply. 'First Claw awaits you on the bridge, Talos. Will you finally tell us what you've been doing in there for the last four hours?'

'Yes,' Talos replied. 'Yes, I will.'

FIRST CLAW GATHERED around the command throne. The hololithic table's anaemic blue light flickered against their armour as they watched a growing cross-section of the galaxy, increasingly expansive in scope. First, it showed a single system; then several nearby; soon, it was displaying a wide swathe of Ultima Segmentum, with auspex corrosion leaving the picture hazy and indistinct in many places.

'Here.' Talos gestured with the point of his golden sword. The Blade of Angels gently carved through the misty hololithic, in a loose arc that covered hundreds upon hundreds of stars and the worlds enslaved to them.

'What am I looking at?' Cyrion asked.

Talos removed his helm, resting it on the table edge. His black eyes never left the shimmering three-dimensional display.

'A galactic ballet,' he said with a crooked smile. 'More specifically, you are looking at the Zero-Zero-One point Two point Five-Seven-Seven-One-Eight Astra Telepathica Duct.'

'Oh,' Cyrion nodded, none the wiser. 'Of course. How foolish of me.'

Talos pointed to world after world in turn. 'Each Astra Telepathica Duct is as unique as a fingerprint. One might be created by artifice and intent: several worlds being colonised in alignment near stable warp transit routes, allowing the psychic dreamers on each planet to speak across the untold distance. Others are born of chance and happenstance, boosted by the warp itself, or by a simple twist of fate that allows a number of disparate worlds the chance to call to each other across the solar winds.

'The Imperium has hundreds of these ducts,' Talos was smiling now. 'They grow, they fade, they rise and degrade, always in flux. With few other ways to make astropathy even an iota more reliable, there is little other choice. And still, it is an art of casting runestones and heeding whispers from nowhere. Utilising a duct is no stroke of genius. But this one... What we did here, brothers...'

Mercutian leaned forward, shaking his head. 'Blood of the False Emperor,' he swore. 'Talos, *this* was your plan?'

The prophet gave a sadist's smile.

Cyrion watched the arc of stars and worlds for a few more moments before looking at his brothers.

'Wait.' Realisation sank in, running through his blood as an unwelcome chill. 'Wait. You've just sent over a hundred astropathic mortis-cries through an established psychic duct?'

'I have indeed.'

Mercutian's voice had the edge of panic. 'You killed them with... with a Navigator. That's what you were doing in there, wasn't it?'

'It was.'

'This is bigger than us, Talos,' Mercutian said. 'So much bigger than us. I admire you for the ambitious spear thrust at the crag cat's heart, but if this works, the retaliation will wipe us from the face of history.'

Talos's expression never changed.

'Will you stop smiling?' Cyrion asked him. 'I'm not used to it. You're making my skin crawl.'

'What do you anticipate will happen?' asked Mercutian. 'At the very least, this will isolate several worlds for decades. At worst, it will devastate them.'

Talos nodded again. 'I know.'

'Then speak,' Mercutian pressed. 'Stop grinning and *speak*. Our lives could be measured in hours.'

The prophet sheathed his sword again. 'The idea came to me when Deltrian first constructed the Shriek. His craft was to turn fear and pain into a source of power. It made fear into a weapon once more. Terror became a means to an end, rather than the end itself.' Talos met their eyes, lowering all pretence of grandeur. 'I needed that. I needed to focus on a life worth living.'

Cyrion nodded. Mercutian watched in silence. Uzas stared into the shimmering hololithic; whether or not he heard the prophet's words was anyone's guess.

Cyrion turned slightly, realising the entire command deck had fallen silent. Talos was no longer addressing First Claw. He was speaking to the hundreds of mortals and servitors on the bridge, most of whom were now watching the prophet to the exclusion of all else. He'd never seen this side of his brother before. Here was a glimpse of what might yet be – a warrior ready to assume the mantle of leadership; a warlord ready to live up to his vision of what the Eighth Legion once was, and could be again.

And it was working. Cyrion could see it in their eyes. Talos's mix of hesitant confidence and vulnerable fanaticism had them enraptured.

'Tsagualsa,' Talos said, his voice softer now. 'Our refuge, and second home. To find it crawling with vermin left a bitter trail on my tongue. But why punish them? Why destroy these weak, lost colonists? Their sin was nothing more than drifting through the warp to a world that offered cold welcome. That was no crime, except perhaps one of misfortune. And yet, there they were. Millions of them. Lost. Alone. *Prey*, scratching in the dirt. How poetic, to find them here, of all places. Rather than punish them for punishment's sake, we could use them. What better weapon to wield against the Imperium than the souls of its own lost children?'

Talos gestured to the sweep of worlds and suns in the hololithic display. 'Humans die every night. They die in their millions, in their billions, feeding the warp with emotion at the moment of death. Astropaths are no different, except by virtue of degrees. An astropath dies, and a psychic soul cries out that much louder upon final death. The warp boils around those souls, when they are unleashed from their mortal shells.'

The hololithic image turned, refocusing on several worlds not far from the warship's current location. Population and defence data, almost certainly outdated, spilled out in static-blurred lines.

'Purely by excruciating the astropaths, we could have created a song of screams, loud enough to be heard and felt by psychic souls on several nearby worlds. But it wouldn't be enough. The butchery of astropaths is hardly a rarity. How many Legion warbands have done the same over the millennia? I couldn't even begin to guess. Raiders have used the ploy since time out of mind, as a means to cover their tracks. What better way to mask your escape than to stir the cauldron of the warp, thickening the primordial ooze to slow any pursuers? Even with the risk of daemonic contagion, it often works well enough to be worth the risk.'

Talos walked around the chamber, addressing the mortal crew, meeting their eyes in turn. 'All this power and pain at our fingertips. Weapons that can level cities. A warship capable of breaking entire fleet blockades. But that means nothing in the Long War. We can leave scars on steel, but so can any ragged pirate vessel with a battery of macro-cannons. We are the Eighth Legion. We wound flesh, steel and souls alike. We scar memories. We scar minds. Our actions must mean something, or we deserve to be forgotten, left to rot amongst ancient mythology.'

Talos took a breath, his voice growing soft again. 'So I gave voice to the song. The song means something: a truer weapon than any laser battery or bombardment cannon. But how best to twist this silent song into a blade that might bleed the Imperium?'

Cyrion watched the crew's faces. Several of them seemed keen to answer, while others waited with eyes lit by interest. Throne in flames, it was really working. He'd never have believed it possible.

Uzas was the one to answer. He looked up, as if he'd been paying attention all along. 'Sing it louder,' he said.

Talos's lips curled into the same sick smile as before. He looked to several of the crew, as if sharing some jest with them.

'*Sing it louder,*' he smiled. 'We turned our singers into a screaming chorus. Weeks and weeks of pain and fear, condensed into the purity of absolute agony. Then add the torture of others to their own torment. The butchery of thousands of humans is nothing – a drop in the warp's ocean. But the astropaths drank it in. They had no choice but to hear, and see, and feel what was taking place. When the psykers finally died, they expired as husks bloated by genocidal suffering, blinded by the ghosts of the dead all around them. We fed them agony and fear, night after night. They screamed it out as psychic pain. They screamed it out upon the moment of death, right here, into the astropathic duct. World after world is hearing it, even now. The astropaths on those worlds magnify it with their own miseries, adding verses and choruses to the song, sharing it with the other worlds in line.'

Talos paused, the smile finally fading. His eyes slid from all others, now reflecting the bluish gleam of the hololithic.

'All of this was possible because of one final gamble. One last way to make the song louder than we could ever have imagined.'

'The Navigator,' Mercutian breathed. He could scarce give the idea countenance.

Talos nodded. 'Octavia.'

SHE AWOKE TO find she wasn't alone.

One of the Night Lords stood nearby, consulting an auspex reader mounted on his bulky vambrace.

'Flayer,' she said. Her own voice horrified her, to hear it so scratchy and weak. Her hands went to her stomach on instinct.

'Your progeny still lives,' Variel said distractedly. 'Though by all rights, he should not.'

Octavia swallowed the lump in her throat. 'He? It's a boy?'

'Yes.' Variel didn't look up from his scanner, still making adjustments and turning dials. 'Was I unclear? The child is in possession of all attributes and biological distinctions implicit in the term *He*. Thus it is, as you say, a male.'

He looked up at her at last. 'You have a long list of biorhythmic anomalies and physiological deficiencies that need addressing in the coming weeks if you are to regain full health. Your attendants have been briefed in full of the sustenance you require, and the chemicals you are to ingest.' He paused for a moment, watching her with his pale blue eyes never blinking once. 'Am I speaking too quickly?'

'No.' She swallowed again. Truth told, her head was swimming and she was relatively sure she'd be throwing up in the next couple of minutes.

'You do not seem to be following me,' Variel said.

'Just get on with it, you son of a bitch,' she snapped.

He ignored the insult. 'You are also risking dehydration, Kings' Disease, rachitis, and an acute scorbutus flaw. Your attendants are aware of how to treat the symptoms and prevent further development. I have left the relevant medicinal narcotics with them.'

'And the baby?'

Variel blinked. 'What of it?'

'Is it... healthy? What will all of these treatments do to him?'

'What does that matter?' Variel blinked a second time. 'My mandate is to ensure your continuance in serving as the ship's Navigator. I have no interest in the misbegotten fruit of your womb.'

'Then why haven't you... ended it?'

'Because if it survives gestation and infancy, it will eventually undergo implantation to serve in the Legion. I had thought that was obvious, Octavia.'

The Apothecary checked his narthecium readings one more time, and made his way to the chamber door, boots thudding as he went.

'He won't be one of the Legion,' she said to his back, feeling her tongue tingle with a rush of saliva. 'You'll never have him.'

'Oh?' Variel turned enough to look over his shoulder. 'You seem very certain.'

He walked from the room, scattering her attendants before him. Octavia stared at the bulkhead as it whined closed in his wake. Once he was gone, she threw up a thin trickle of sticky bile, and blacked out again, slumped in her throne. That was how Septimus found her, almost half an hour later.

By the time he entered, Vularai and the other attendants had connected the nutrient feeds to the implanted sockets on Octavia's limbs.

'Move aside,' he told them as they barred his way.

'Mistress is resting.'

'I said, move aside.'

Several of them started to reach for their scavenged pistols and the shotguns concealed beneath dirty robes. Septimus drew both of his pistols in a smooth movement, aiming them at two separate hunched attendants.

'Let's not do this,' he said to them.

Before he even knew Vularai was there, he felt the keen edge of her blade at the back of his neck.

'She needs her rest,' the attendant hissed. Septimus had never paid heed to just how snake-like her voice really was. He wouldn't have been surprised to learn her tongue was forked beneath all that bandaging. 'And you are not supposed to be here.'

'And yet here I am, and I am not leaving.'

'Septimus,' came Octavia's weak voice.

All of them turned at the whispered word. 'You woke her,' accused Vularai.

He didn't bother answering. Septimus shrugged her off, and moved to sit by Octavia's throne.

She was pale – as pale as if she'd been born to this life – and she was almost cadaverously thin, but for the swell of her stomach. Blood scabbed her forehead and nose, where it had dried after running down from beneath her bandana. He wasn't sure why, but one of her eyes wasn't opening, and she licked cracked, split lips before speaking.

It must have shown on his face.

'I look that awful, do I?' she asked.

'You... have looked better.'

Her fingertips managed a weak brush along his unshaven cheek, before she sagged back into her throne. 'I'm sure I have.'

'I heard what they did to you. What they made you do.'

She closed her eyes and nodded. When she spoke, only one side of her mouth moved. 'It was quite clever, really.'

'Clever?' he asked, his teeth clenching. *'Clever?'*

'To use a Navigator,' she sighed. 'The secret sight. To rip their souls from their bodies... with the purest, strongest... connection to the warp...' She laughed without breath, doing little more than shivering. 'My precious eye. I saw them dying. I saw them torn loose. Souls cast into the warp. Like mist. Pulled apart by the wind.'

He stroked her hair back from her sweating face. Her skin was ice. 'Enough,' he said. 'It's over.'

'My father told me there was no worse way to die. Nothing more painful. Nothing more damning. A hundred souls, driven mad by fear and torture, killed by looking into the warp itself.' She gave another quivering, breathless laugh. 'I can't even imagine how many people are hearing those mortis-cries now. I can't picture how many are dying.'

'Octavia,' he said, resting his hand on her stomach. 'Rest. Recover your strength. We're getting off this ship.'

'They'll find us.'

Septimus kissed her wet temple. 'They are welcome to try.'

XIX

FALSE PROPHECY

TALOS REFLECTED ALONE, sat in the silence of First Claw's arming chamber. After the activity of recent weeks, he craved the calm.

The *Echo of Damnation* remained in its sedate drift, waiting for its Navigator to recover before they risked the flight back to the Great Eye. Even a short flight was likely to kill Octavia in her current condition, let alone a journey lasting months or years, sailing across most of the galaxy.

Talos was all too cognisant of the fact she'd never sailed into a true warp storm. The Eye was an unwelcoming haven, even for experienced sorcerers. An untested Navigator, especially an exhausted one, was a liability he had no wish to test until he had no other choice.

He still saw the eldar when he closed his eyes. Their lithe figures danced in flickering after-images, shadows against shadows – black and silent one moment, silver and screaming the next.

The eldar. He no longer needed to be asleep to see them. That, too, was a problem. Was Tsagualsa to blame? If that was the case, breathing the carrion world's air had done the opposite of what he'd hoped. Despite gifting him with the inspiration he'd desired, had it also accelerated his degeneration like some cure for cancer that did nothing but fuel the tumours' black spread?

He'd argued with Variel in the apothecarion all those

weeks ago, but the truth had a cold core. He needed no auspex reading or biorhythmic scan to tell him he was falling apart. The dreams were evidence enough. They'd been growing worse since Crythe – more crippling, less reliable – but even that had been manageable. For a time, at least.

No. The eldar dreams were different, because they were more than mere dreams. He no longer needed to be asleep to feel them. The howls and blades of mad aliens were becoming as real as the walls around him, as true as the voices of his brothers.

What plagued him most was the question of why he still saw them at all. Since Hell's Iris, when the dreams had first come, he'd been unashamed in his reluctance to return to the Eye. Now, though, the prophecy seemed void. Xarl couldn't die twice. He'd never been so relieved to be wrong.

It wasn't easy to decide how much to tell the others. Too much, and they'd never follow him. Too little, and they'd yank at their chains, resisting his guidance.

'Talos,' said a shadow at the edge of his vision. Instinct forced him to glance left. Nothing. No figure. No sound. As he exhaled, he heard the clash of a blade against ceramite, as faint and misty as a memory. It could have been coming from somewhere nearby on board the ship; it could have been in his mind.

His brothers' objections coiled amongst the eldar-thoughts. The other legionaries wanted to run right away, heedless of killing the Navigator in the process. Lucoryphus had advocated pushing Octavia as far as they could, then simply trusting the warp's currents to lead them home once she was dead. Voices from among the other claws raised similar desires. Even if the warp carried them elsewhere, the risk was better than remaining here for the certainty of Imperial vengeance.

He'd calmed them down, forcing himself not to show disgust. They sounded craven, either without realising or simply without caring. Imperial revenge would take a great many months to arrive, at best. Warp flight close to the afflicted worlds would be ruined for a long while yet. Then subsector command nodes would have to realise a pattern in the planets affected, which would take months – even years – leaving them here, untouched, with impunity. Even after the pattern was recognised, the Imperium's own disparate worlds would take an unknowable age to seek the song's origin in the telepathic duct.

No, there was nothing to fear just yet. Not from the Imperium, anyway.

'Talos,' another voice whispered. Something black and slender flitted across his vision. He glanced its way to see it vanish.

'Talos,' the air whispered again.

He lowered his head, breathing slowly, perversely enjoying the pulsating throb of veins in his skull. The pain was a reminder that he was awake. A small blessing, but one he was thankful for.

'Talos.' There was a click, followed by a soft metallic whine as a laspistol charged.

With his head still in his hands, he felt the threat of a smile tease the corner of his lips. So it was finally happening. He'd been expecting this for so long now: the seventh slave had changed since the eighth came aboard, and this was a confrontation he'd been anticipating with very little relish.

'Septimus,' he sighed. 'A poor choice of moment to make your move.'

'Look at me, heretic.' The voice wasn't his slave's. Slowly, he lifted his head.

'Oh,' Talos said. 'Greetings, archregent. However did you find yourself here?'

He watched the old man with an almost distracted air. The liver-spotted hands shivered as they held the stolen pistol. Blood flushed the old man's cheeks; blood that in a true warrior would have flooded to the muscles, ready for battle. Here was an old fool thinking with his head, not fighting with his heart. Talos doubted he would even shoot.

'As a point of interest,' the prophet said, 'from the angle of the weapon, you are aiming too low.'

The Archregent of Darcharna, still clad in his filthy robes of state, lifted the pistol higher.

'Better,' Talos allowed. 'However, even if you were to shoot me at this range, it is still unlikely to kill me. Humanity breeds its demigods from hardy stock, you know.'

The old man kept his silence. He seemed caught between the urge to cry, to pull the trigger, or to flee the room.

'I would be intrigued to learn how you are here,' Talos added. 'You should be on Tsagualsa with the others we spared. Did one of the other Claws bring you up here to serve as a slave?'

Still no answer.

'Your silence is vexing, old one, and this conversation grows increasingly one-sided. I would also like to know how you managed to survive several weeks on board without meeting an unpleasant demise in the *Echo*'s halls.'

'One of... of the others...'

'Yes. One of the other Claws brought you aboard as a toy. I had guessed. Now what brings you to this ill-advised assassination, so painfully destined to fail?'

For a moment, just a moment, the old man's face pulled taut, lengthening into something inhumanly elegant that regarded him with soulless and slanted eyes. Talos swallowed. The eldar visage vanished, leaving only the old man.

The archregent didn't reply.

'Did you intend to speak, or did you simply come here in order to aim that useless weapon at me?'

Talos rose to his feet. The gun followed him up, shaking more noticeably now. Without any sign of haste or impatience, Talos took the pistol from the old man's hands. He crunched it in his fist, and dropped the wreckage to the decking.

'I am too tired to kill you, old man. Please just go.'

'Thousands of people,' the archregent whispered through spit-wet lips. 'Thousands and thousands… You…'

'Yes,' Talos nodded. 'I am a terrible creature likely to burn in the eternal fire of your beloved Emperor's judgement. You cannot imagine how many times I have heard similar threats, always whispered by the downtrodden, the powerless, and the desperate. They change nothing, neither the words nor the people that weep them. Is there anything else?'

'All those people…'

'Yes. All those people. They are dead, and you have been broken by what you saw. That is no excuse to whine at me, human.'

Talos picked the old man up by the throat and hurled him into the corridor beyond. He heard the twiggish snap of brittle bones breaking, but couldn't bring himself to care. *Irritating old fool.*

'Talos,' said a voice within the room. His eyes flicked left and right, revealing nothing. He wasn't surprised.

As he lowered himself down again, hanging his aching head, he heard the dream-sounds of rainfall and female laughter drifting back once again.

No, the thought came unbidden, cold and rancid with sudden truth. *The Imperium will not come to answer this atrocity. Someone else will.*

'This is Talos,' he voxed. 'How long has the Navigator been at rest?'

A servitor's voice replied after a seven-second delay. 'Thirty-two hours, fift–'

'That's long enough. Ready the ship to leave the system.'

The next voice was Cyrion's, still on the bridge where Talos had left him in command.

'Brother, even Variel said we shouldn't risk pushing her for a week or more.'

Talos heard a howl behind Cyrion's voice – strangely feral and feminine all at once. It was too clear to be vox corruption, but couldn't possibly be real.

Yet the howl unlocked another memory, granting it like an unwanted gift. *Rainfall.* Talos closed his eyes to focus. *A murderess in the rain. Somewhere... Beneath a storm...*

No, no, no. It was starting to make a sick sense now. He'd avoided taking them to the Eye, unwilling to face the eldar of Ulthwé, refusing to bow to the fate that his brothers would die at their hands. When Xarl had fallen at Tsagualsa, he'd dared to believe the prophecy broken. Surely, once broken, it could be ignored as another false dream.

Surely, his own thoughts mocked him. *Surely we're safe now.*

'Ready the ship to sail the warp,' Talos ordered. 'We need to leave immediately.'

'It will take hours just to prepare the–'

Talos ignored whatever Cyrion was saying. He was already out of First Claw's arming chamber, vaulting the slumped body of the archregent and running through the twisting corridors, sprinting towards the prow.

No, no, no...

'I do not care about the preparations,' he voxed. 'We'll sail blind if we have to.'

'Are you insane?' Cyrion spat back. 'What are you thinking?'

Just a little more time, his racing mind begged. *We have to get away from here.*

He was halfway to Octavia's chambers when the sirens began their careening wail.

'All hands,' came Cyrion's voice over the shipwide address system. 'All hands to battle stations. Eldar warships inbound.'

An Imperial cruiser doesn't merely slip back into reality from passage through the warp; it breaks back into the material universe from a wound in the void, trailing the smoky tides of madness still clinging to its hull. Their passage through the Sea of Souls was a storm of colour, sound, and screaming devilry.

Cyrion had to admit, for all the violence and trauma of such travel, it was at least familiar.

The eldar warships played their own games with the warp. They showed no contrails of clinging ethereal energy, nor did they herald their arrival by vicious detonations in the fabric of space and time. One moment he saw stars. The next, eldar vessels shimmered into being, shadows ghosting out of other shadows, gliding towards the drifting *Echo of Damnation*.

Cyrion knew next to nothing about the metaphysics of eldar void travel, nor was he of a mind to care. He'd heard, at some point, the word 'webway' spoken of in regards to their eerie interstellar wanderings, but the concept meant nothing to him. Meeting the eldar in the past had rarely ended well, and he loathed them even more than he loathed most of his brothers, which made it a very rich hatred indeed. They repulsed him, and it was not a discomfort that he cherished, even perversely.

He saw the warships coming on the occulus, as if space itself had breathed them into being, and he acted on instinct. Being Cyrion, the first thing he did was to swear, loudly and with feeling. The second thing he did was to order the crew to battle stations. The third thing he did was to swear again; a long river of curses that might've made even the primarch blink.

They came on in grand, sweeping arcs, never sailing straight. Each one was forever banking and weaving through the void in dramatic arcs that would have been impressive – as well as impossible – for an Imperial vessel. As he watched the eldar warships dancing with such foul grace, he felt a raw, stale taste on the tongue. Even his acidic saliva glands instinctively reacted to his disgust, for mankind's technology, even flavoured by the taint of Chaos, could never emulate that alien swooping. It was difficult to reconcile what his senses were seeing with what was physically possible in the depths of space.

'You there,' he said to one of the crew. 'Yes, you. Ready the ship for a warp run.'

'Under way, lord. We heard Lord Talos's orders.'

'Good,' said Cyrion, already ignoring the man. 'Activate void shields, run out the guns... All the usual furore, if you please.'

He sat in the command throne – Talos's throne, if he was being perfectly honest – and watched the occulus with a wary eye.

'Should we engage, lord?' one of the uniformed crew asked.

'Tempting. We outsize them both by a measure of magnitudes. But they're likely outriders – hold back for now, focus on getting ready to break into the warp when the Navigator decides to grace us with her attention.'

On the occulus, a distant image resolved behind the first two. This one was much larger, sporting great angled wings of bone and shimmering scales. The glassy serpent-skin sails flashed as they reflected the sun, and the warship gathered speed.

'Another eldar warship entering long range scanning,' the scrymaster called out. 'Capital class.'

'So I see. And we don't outsize that one quite so convincingly,' Cyrion admitted. 'How long until they reach us?'

The hunchbacked Master of Auspex shook his burn-scarred head. 'Difficult to say, lord. A projection based on conventional thrust would be almost thirty minutes. If they keep dancing through the void like this, it could be five, it could be twenty.'

Cyrion reclined, putting his boots up on the throne's armrest. 'Well then, my dear and loyal crew. We have a short while to enjoy each other's company before we die. Isn't that *delightful*?'

* * *

Talos came through the bulkhead in a blur of blue ceramite and a roar of armour joints. Octavia's attendants scattered before him, bolting with all the haste of rats fleeing a hunting cat. Even Vularai flinched back, unsurprised that her query of 'My lord?' went unanswered.

Octavia was already coming around, awoken by the emergency sirens. She jumped in her seat as Talos thudded to a halt, boots hammering into the deck hard enough to shake her throne.

She looked almost dizzy with exhaustion. Despite sleeping for hours on end and having her nutrient feeds tailored to her specific needs, the ordeal of the murders he'd forced her to commit mere days ago still played out in dark patches across her features, as did the long flight to reach this point at the Imperium's edge. Weary circles noosed her eyes, and her clammy skin looked greasy in the chamber's dull light.

She looked up at Talos, the sway of her head on sore neck muscles betraying the migraine going on behind her face.

'Eldar?' she asked, confused. 'Did I hear that correctly?'

'Jump the ship,' he demanded. 'Do it now.'

'I… What?'

'Listen to me,' he growled. 'The eldar are here. They sensed the psychic scream we made – or worse, their witches predicted it beforehand, and they had a fleet lying in wait. More will come, Octavia. Jump the ship now, or we all die.'

She swallowed, reaching for the first of her throne-union link cables. Weakness left her hands shaking, but her voice was firm and clear.

'Where? Where should we go? The Eye?'

'Anywhere but *here* or *there*, Octavia. You have a whole galaxy. Just find us somewhere to hide.'

PART FOUR

VOID STALKER

XX

FLIGHT

THE WARSHIP RAN, again and again and again.

Two days after its initial flight, it sailed back into the true void only to find a blockade of eldar cruisers hanging silently in space, lying in wait. The *Echo of Damnation* came about in a wrenching arc, diving as it rolled, and thrust its way back beyond the physical universe and into the relative safety of the warp.

Three days later, it dropped from its interstellar journeying to drift closer to the world Vanahym, only to find five eldar cruisers already orbiting the world. The alien ships angled their reflective sails as the Night Lord vessel came closer, cutting out of orbit to intercept the Eighth Legion warship.

Again, the *Echo* ran.

The third time it left the warp, it didn't slow down for the eldar blockade. The *Echo of Damnation* surged through the cold tides of real space, broadsides singing into the dark, railing at the alien vessels as it screamed between them. The eldar ships banked and turned with impossible grace, even those with their solar sails shattered by Eighth Legion weapons batteries. The *Echo* outran a fight it couldn't win, concentrating all of its retaliatory fire on holding the xenos warships at bay long enough for a return to the warp.

The fourth, the fifth, the sixth – each successive

emergence met with greater resistance, the farther they flew from their point of origin.

'They're herding us,' Cyrion said after the eighth re-entry and subsequent flight.

Talos had simply nodded. 'I know.'

'We're not going to reach the Great Eye, brother. They won't let us. You know that, don't you?'

'I know.'

A week passed. Two weeks. Three.

On its fourteenth exit from the warp, the *Echo of Damnation* broke the peace of a silent sky. It tore its way back into the material realm, riding a storm of violet lightning and carnelian smoke. This time, there was no rupturing re-entry to the depths of clean space; no pause to gather their bearings and scan for enemies.

This time, the *Echo* ripped into reality and kept running, engines flaring hot. The warship powered its way through the psychotic hues of the Praxis Nebula, diving ever deeper into the immense gaseous cloud. Talos let the engines rage on, powering the ship ahead at hull-rattling speed.

'No eldar,' Cyrion observed.

'No eldar yet,' Talos replied. 'All ahead full. Bury the ship in the nebula, as deep as she'll go.'

The scrymaster called out as his servitors began to chatter. 'Lord Talos, the–'

'The scanner interference,' Talos calmly interrupted, 'is why we're here. I am aware of it, scrymaster.'

First Claw gathered around the central throne, maintaining vigil with their leader. One by one, the other surviving Night Lords walked onto the command deck, their eyes lifted to the occulus, watching in silent unity.

The hours passed.

Talos occasionally let his gaze leave the stars to glance again at the tactical hololithic. Like the viewscreen, the hololithic projection showed stars, a world turning in the void, and nothing else.

'How long?' he asked.

'Four hours,' said Cyrion. He walked by the prow weapons console, looking over the shoulders of the seven uniformed officers stationed there. 'Four hours and thirty-seven minutes.'

'The longest yet,' Talos observed.

'By far.'

The prophet leaned forward in the ornate command throne. The golden Blood Angels blade rested against one of the throne's arms, the prophet's bolter rested on the other. A great high seat of fire-blackened bronze, the throne itself loomed above the rest of the command deck from its central dais.

Talos had always known the Exalted relished being in such a position, lifted above his brethren on the *Covenant of Blood*. The prophet didn't share the sentiment. If anything, he felt detached from his kindred, and the thought wasn't a comfortable one.

'I believe we're clear,' Cyrion ventured.

'Don't say that,' replied Talos. 'Don't even *think* it.'

Cyrion listened to the sounds of the command deck, which had a melody all its own: the grind of levers, the mumble of servitors, the thump of boots. A soothing sound.

'You should rest,' he said to Talos. 'When did you last sleep?'

'I still haven't slept.'

'You're joking.'

Talos turned to Cyrion, his white face drawn, his dark eyes dulled by sleeplessness. 'Do I look as though I'm joking?'

'No, you look as though you died and forgot to stop moving. It's been three weeks now. You're being foolish, Talos. Go. Rest.'

The prophet turned back to the occulus. 'Not yet. Not until we've escaped.'

'And if I summon the Flayer to give you a lecture?'

'Variel has already lectured me on the matter.' Talos

gave a rueful sigh. 'He had charts and everything. In meticulous detail, he noted the strain I was putting on my mind, citing the catalepsean node's operational limit of keeping a Legionary awake for two weeks.'

'A physiology lecture. I sometimes think he forgets you were once an Apothecary.'

Talos didn't answer. He kept watching the stars on the occulus.

Three weeks, the prophet thought. He'd not slept since the endless chase began, when the eldar ghosted out of the void mere hours after he'd murdered the astropaths. How many times had they ripped their way in and out of the warp since then? How many times had they emerged back into real space, only to find yet another eldar squadron waiting for them?

Three weeks.

'We can't keep running, Cyrion. Octavia will die. We'll be stranded.'

Cyrion looked up at Ruven's crucified bones, hanging in state. 'I almost regret the fact you killed the sorcerer. His powers would be a boon now.'

Talos turned weary eyes to his brother. Something akin to amusement gleamed in those black depths.

'Perhaps so,' Talos allowed. 'But then we'd have to suffer through his endless conversation.'

'A fine point,' Cyrion replied. As soon as he finished the words, sirens started to cry out in ululating unity across the deck.

'They've found us,' Talos leaned back in the throne, his voice an exhausted whisper. 'They've found us *again*. Octavia, this is the bridge.'

Her voice sounded as weary as Talos looked. 'I'm here,' she said over the chamber's vox-speakers.

'So are the eldar,' said Talos. 'Ready the ship to run again.'

'I can't keep this up,' she said. 'I can't. I'm sorry, I can't.'

'They'll be on us in twenty minutes at the most. Get us out of here.'

'I *can't*.'

'You've been saying that for over a week.'

'Talos, please, listen to what I'm saying. This will kill me. One more jump. Two more. It doesn't matter. You're killing me.'

He rose from the command throne, walking to the dais rail and leaning down, watching the organised chaos of the bridge below. The hololithic table flickered with ghostly threats sailing closer: six eldar warships, their wing-sails lost in the mist of distortion.

'Octavia,' he said, softening his voice. 'They can't chase us forever. I need a little more from you. Please.'

It took several seconds, but the ship itself gave the answer. Shaking gripped the deck as the warp drive began to amass the energy required to break through one reality into another.

'Do you remember,' her voice echoed across the command deck, 'when I first took control of the *Covenant*?' There was a curious duality in her tone as she bonded with the ship's machine-spirit, an unwholesome unity that made Talos's skin crawl.

'I remember,' he voxed back. 'You said you could kill us all, for we were heretics.'

'I was angrier then. And scared.' He heard her take a breath. 'All hands, brace for entry into the Sea of Souls.'

'Thank you, Octavia.'

'You shouldn't thank slaves,' she replied, her twinned voice resonating around the chamber. 'They'll get delusions of equality. And besides, this hasn't worked yet. Save your thanks for when we're sure we'll survive. Are we running or hiding this time?'

'Neither,' said Talos.

Every eye on the bridge turned towards him. The Legion warriors still on the command deck watched keenest of all.

'We're not running,' Talos voxed to Octavia, well aware that everyone was watching him, 'and we're not hiding. We're making a stand.'

Talos relayed the coordinates through the keypad on the arm of his throne. 'Take us back there.'

'Throne,' Octavia swore, making half the bridge crew wince at the Imperial expletive. 'Are you sure?'

'We don't have the fuel to keep dancing to their song, and we can't break their blockade. If we're being herded like prey, then I'll at least choose where we'll fight back.'

Cyrion came to the throne's side again. 'And if they're waiting for us there?'

Talos looked at his brother for a long moment. 'What do you want me to say, Cyrion? We'll do what we always do: we'll kill them until they kill us.'

WITH THE SHIP in the warp, Talos walked to meet with the one soul he had every reason – yet no desire – to see once again. Sword in hand, he headed down the winding corridors, his thoughts dark and his options even darker. He was going to do something he should've done a long time ago.

The immense doors leading into the Hall of Reflection rumbled open as he stood before them. Menial adepts turned to regard his entrance, while servitors went about their business.

'Soul Hunter,' said one of the robed Mechanicum priests in respectful greeting.

'My name is Talos,' the prophet replied, walking past the man. 'Please use it.'

He felt a hand grip his shoulder guard, and turned to face the one who dared touch him. Such a breach of decorum was most unlike any of the adepts.

'Talos,' said Deltrian, inclining the staring skull that served as his face. 'Your presence, while not a violation of any behavioural code, is unexpected. Our last interaction ended with the agreement you would be summoned if there was any change in the subject.'

The subject, thought Talos. *Very quaint.*

'I am aware of our agreement, Deltrian.'

The robed, chrome cadaver lifted his hand from the

warrior's pauldron. 'Yet you come here armed, a blade drawn in this holy place. In processing your demeanour, only one outcome holds any significant probability.'

'And that would be?'

'You have come to destroy the sarcophagus, and slay Malcharion within it.'

'Good guess.' Talos turned away, heading into the annexed chamber where the war-sage's ornate coffin was being held.

'Wait.'

Talos halted, but not because Deltrian ordered it. His shock froze him in his tracks, the blade still held in a loose fist. He took in the sight before him: the ornate sarcophagus linked and chained into place, mounted on the ceramite shell of an armoured Dreadnought. The blue aura of weak, focused stasis fields still played around the war machine's limbs – locking them into immobility.

'Why have you done this?' Talos didn't look away. 'I gave no orders to prepare him as a Dreadnought.'

Deltrian hesitated before speaking. 'The later rituals of resurrection require the subject's installation within the holy shell.'

Talos wasn't sure what to say. He wanted to object, but knew nothing was likely to move Deltrian to see any kind of sense. His surprise doubled when he saw another figure was already in the chamber. He sat with his back to the wall, idly squeezing the trigger of a chainaxe, listening to the blades whine.

'Brother,' the other Night Lord greeted him.

'Uzas. What brings you here?'

Uzas shrugged. 'I come here often, to watch him. He should come back to us. We need him, but he doesn't want to be needed.'

Talos breathed, low and slow, before addressing Deltrian. 'Activate the vox-speakers.'

'Lord, I–'

'Activate the vox-speakers or I will kill you.'

'As you command.' Deltrian walked on his stick-thin legs, clicking his way over to the primary control console. Several levers cranked with unhealthy grinding sounds.

The chamber filled with screaming. Breathless, animalistic, exhausted screaming. Somehow, it sounded like an old man – that degree of ancient, weary weakness.

Talos closed his eyes for a moment, though his helm stared ahead, as remorseless as ever.

'No more,' he whispered. 'I am ending this.'

'The subject is biologically stable,' Deltrian vocalised louder, to speak over the screaming. 'He has also been rendered into a state of mental stability, as well.'

'You think this sounds like mental stability?' The prophet still hadn't turned around. 'Can't you hear the screaming?'

'I can hear it,' Uzas interrupted. 'Bitter, bitter music.'

'I am indeed aware of the vocalised pain response,' Deltrian said. 'I believe it indicates–'

'No.' Talos shook his head. 'No. Don't try that with me, Deltrian. I *know* there's something human inside you. This isn't a "vocalised pain response". It's screaming, and you know it. Lucoryphus was right about you: no mind could conceive of the Shriek and be as truly detached as you claim. You understand fear and pain. I know you do. You are one of us, whether you wear ceramite or not.'

'The "screaming" then,' Deltrian allowed. For the first time, there was a nuance of tone in his voice: an iota of displeasure. 'We have brought him to a state of mental stability,' he continued, 'relatively speaking.'

'And if you deactivated the stasis locks on the machine-body?'

Deltrian had to pause again. 'It is likely that the subject would kill us all.'

'Stop saying *the subject*. This is Malcharion, a hero of our Legion.'

'A hero you mean to murder.'

Talos rounded on the tech-priest, the blade flaring to electric life in his hand. 'He has already died twice. A fool's hope allowed me to let you play your games with his corpse, but he is not coming back to us. I see that now. It is wrong to even try, for it goes against his final wish. You are no longer allowed to toy with his remains when it keeps him locked in some eternal, dead-minded agony. He deserves better than this.'

Deltrian hesitated again, processing through potential responses, seeking one to appease the ship's master in this uncomfortably mortal outburst. During the short pauses, the screaming continued unabated.

'The subject – that is to say, Malcharion – can still serve the Legion. With applied excruciation and the correct pain control, he would be a devastating presence on the battlefield.'

'I've already refused that path.' Talos still hadn't deactivated his sword. 'I will not tolerate abuse of his body, and in his madness he'd be just as likely to shoot our own forces.'

'But I can–'

'*Enough.* Throne in flames, this is why Vandred lost his mind. The infighting. The bickering. The claws killing one another with knives in the dark. I may not have desired this idiotic pedestal my brothers have placed me upon, but I am here now, Deltrian. The *Echo of Damnation* is *my* ship. We may be running, we may be doomed, but I will not die without a fight, and I will not meet my end condoning this disgusting indignity. Do you understand me?'

Deltrian didn't, of course. This all sounded so very mortal to his audio receptors. Any actions based on emotion or mortal chemical processes were to be purged and ignored.

'Yes,' he said.

Talos laughed, little more than a bitter bark of amusement against the backdrop of the Dreadnought's screams. 'You're an awful liar. I doubt you even recall what it means to have any regard or trust in another soul.'

He turned his back on the priest, hauling himself up the sarcophagus, climbing it one-handed. The power sword crackled with a buzzing drone as it came close to brushing the stasis fields.

Talos stared at the image of Malcharion wrought in precious metals – his lord, his true lord before the years of Vandred's reign – resplendent in that ancient moment of ultimate glory.

'How different all of this might've been,' Talos said, 'had you lived.'

'Do not do this,' Deltrian vocalised his final objection. 'This course of action violates the tenets of my circle's oath to the Eighth Legion.'

Talos ignored him. 'Forgive me, captain,' he said to the graven image as he raised his blade.

'Wait.'

Talos turned, but only from surprise at who'd spoken. He remained as he was, halfway up the Dreadnought's armoured body, ready to sever the power feeds linking the life support machinery to the sarcophagus.

'Wait,' Uzas said again. The other Night Lord still hadn't risen to his feet. He tapped the blade of his axe on the decking, *tap-tap... tap-tap... tap-tap*. 'I hear something. A pattern. A pattern in the chaos.'

Talos turned to Deltrian. 'What does he mean?'

The tech-adept was so confused by the exchange that he almost shrugged. Assuming a less-human behaviour instead, he emitted a spurt of negative code.

'Clarification required. You are querying me as to the meaning of your own brother's words, in the expectation I can provide some insight?'

'I take your point,' said Talos. He dropped from the sarcophagus, boots thudding onto the deck. 'Uzas. Speak to me.'

Uzas still tapped the axe in a soft, clanging rhythm. 'Beneath the screams. Listen, Talos. Listen to the pattern.'

Talos glanced at Deltrian. 'Adept, can you not scan for what he might be speaking of? I hear only the screams.'

'I have sixteen slave processes running continual diagnostics.'

Uzas looked up at last. The bloody palm-print over his faceplate caught the chamber's dull light. 'The pattern is still there, Talos.'

'*What* pattern?'

'The... the pattern,' Uzas said. 'Malcharion lives.'

Talos turned back to the sarcophagus. 'Honoured adept, would you do me the service of explaining exactly what constitutes your order's ritual of resurrection?'

'That lore is forbidden.'

'Of course. Then maintain the secrets, simply... be vague.'

'That lore is forbidden.'

The prophet almost laughed. 'This is like drawing blood from a stone. Work with me, Deltrian. I need to know what you are doing to my captain in there.'

'A combination of synaptic enhancement pulses, electrical life support feeds, chemical stimulants and invasive physiological stabilisers.'

'A long time since you played Apothecary.' Uzas's grin was obvious from his tone. 'Shall I run and find the Flayer?'

Talos almost smiled despite himself, at hearing his lost brother making a jest. 'That sounds close to several of the methods we use in excruciation, Deltrian.'

'This is so. The subj–Malcharion has always been a troubling project. Awakening him requires an unusual degree of effort and focus.'

'But he's awake now,' Talos said. 'He's *awake*. Why maintain the ritual?'

Deltrian emitted an irritated blurt from his throat vocaliser.

'What in the warp's many hells was that?' Talos asked.

'A declaration of impatience,' the adept answered.

'How very mortal of you.'

Deltrian made the sound again, louder this time. 'With respect, you are speaking in ignorance. The rituals of resurrection do not cease purely because the subject is physically awakened. His mind is not cognisant of his surroundings. We have awakened his physical remnants, allowing him to bond with the holy war machine. But his mind is still lost. The ritual proceeds in order to refuel and restore his anima.'

'His... what?'

'His sense of self-awareness and capacity to reason in response to stimuli. His conscious sentience, as the manifestation of his living spirit.'

'His soul, you mean. His mind.'

'As you say. We have brought forth his brain and body, but not his mind and soul. There is a difference.'

Talos breathed in stale, recycled air through his teeth. 'I had a dog once. Xarl used to poke it with sticks.'

Deltrian froze. Although his eye lenses remained focused and unmoving, his internal processors raced for some kind of comprehension to find purchase with the current conversation.

'Dog,' he said aloud. 'Quadrupedal mammal. Family Canidae, Genus Canis, Order Carnivora.'

Talos was watching the sarcophagus again, listening to the screams. 'Yes, Deltrian. A dog. This was before Nostramo burned, before Xarl and I joined the Legion. We were children on the streets most nights, little knowing of the lawless madness taking hold of the world outside our city. We thought we lived at the heart of the gang warfare. That delusion came to be almost amusing, in time.'

Talos's tone never changed as he continued. 'The dog was a stray. I fed her, and she followed me forever afterwards. A mean bitch, never shy to show her teeth. Xarl would poke her with sticks when she slept. He found it hilarious to have the dog waking up, barking and snapping her jaws. He kept poking her once, even when she was up and barking at him. After a few minutes of his teasing, she went for his throat. He got his arm up in time, but she savaged his hand and forearm.'

'What happened to the dog?' Uzas asked, surprising Talos with the curiosity in his voice.

'Xarl killed her. He broke her head open with a tyre iron the next morning, while she was asleep.'

'She didn't wake up barking that time,' Uzas observed, in the same strange, soft tone.

Deltrian hesitated before replying. 'The relevance of this adjacent conversational pathway eludes me.'

Talos inclined his head to the sarcophagus. 'I am saying he's already awake, Deltrian. What have you done since he awoke? You told me he needed to be stabilised, but the fact remains: he's awake now. What have you been doing?'

'The rituals of resurrection. As stated: synaptic enhancement pulses, electrical life support feeds, chemical stimulants and invasive physiological stabilisers.'

'So you've filtered maddening chemicals and electrical stimulants through the body of a warrior wounded unto death, who has already demonstrated his symbiosis with the sarcophagus doesn't follow standard patterns.'

'But...'

'He's awake now, and in his madness, he's trying to go for your face. You've poked him with sticks, Deltrian.'

Deltrian mused on that. 'Processing,' he said. 'Processing.'

Talos was still listening to the screaming. 'Process faster. My captain's screams aren't music to me, Deltrian.'

'At no juncture has the subject registered within acceptable levels of higher cognitive function. If he had, then the rituals of resurrection would immediately be terminated.'

'But you said, Malcharion's reawakenings never followed conventional patterns.'

'I...' Deltrian, for the first time in centuries, began to doubt his findings. 'I... Processing.'

'You process that,' said Talos, walking away. 'Sometimes, Deltrian, it pays to share your secrets with those you can trust. And it isn't always a curse to think like a mortal.'

'A potential flaw occurs,' Deltrian vocalised, still watching the reams of calculations playing out on his retinas. 'Your supposition breaks the established and most holy ritual for a guess based primarily on emotion. Should your assumption prove incorrect, the damage to the subject physiology may be irreparable.'

'Does it seem as if I care?' Lightning danced down the golden blade as Talos drew near the central control console. He glanced across it, at the army of dials, scanning screens, thermal gauges, levers and switches. This was what pumped poison and pain into the body of his captain.

'Shut this down,' he said.

'Negative. I cannot allow such an event to come to pass, based on something as flawed as mortal supposition and a metaphor centred on the interrupted sleep of a quadruped mammal. Talos. Talos, do you hear me? Deactivate your sword, my lord, please.'

Talos raised the blade, and Uzas started laughing.

'*NO.*' Deltrian vocalised a piercing, weaponised burst of sound that would deafen any mortal and render them incapacitated. Talos's helm left him immune to such theatrics. He'd used the same scream himself as a weapon too many times to fall for it now. '*TALOS, NO.*'

The blade fell, and the repellent union of the power field and the console's delicate machinery bred an explosion that hurled debris across the chamber.

TALOS ROSE TO his feet in the silent aftermath, and his first thought was a bizarre one: Uzas was no longer gunning the chainaxe's trigger. Through the thin smoke, he saw his brother standing by the wall, and Deltrian halfway across the chamber floor.

The stasis fields were still active, imprisoning the

Dreadnought's limbs, generating a hum severe enough to make the prophet's teeth itch. But the screaming had ceased – the sterile chamber felt somehow charged by its absence, akin to the richness of ozone in the air after a storm.

Talos watched the towering war machine, waiting, listening – his senses keen for any change at all.

'Talos,' Uzas called.

'Brother?'

'What was your dog's name?'

Keza, he thought. 'Be silent, Uzas,' he said.

'Hnnh,' the other Night Lord replied.

The Dreadnought didn't move. It didn't speak a word. It stood in silence, finally, *finally* dead.

'You killed Malcharion,' Uzas said as he walked closer. 'That was always your intent. All those things you said... You wanted to help him die, no matter what else you said.'

Victory had a foully hollow taste. Talos swallowed it back before speaking. 'If he lived, so be it. If he died, then the torture would end and we'd have complied with his final wish. But either way, I was ending it.'

Deltrian circled the ruined control console, his auxiliary arms deployed and picking up chunks of smoking debris.

'No,' he was saying. 'Unacceptable. Simply unacceptable. No, no, no.'

Talos couldn't keep from smiling an awkward, bitter smile. 'It's done.' The relief was palpable.

'**Talos,**' said a voice, avatarically guttural, loud enough to make the deck rumble.

In the same moment, the chamber's doors opened on grinding hydraulics. Cyrion entered, tossing a skull into the air and catching it each time it fell. Clearly it was one of the skulls from his armour, the chain broken and rattling at his hip.

He stopped, took in the scene – Talos and Uzas standing together, staring at the Dreadnought; Deltrian standing with all arms deployed, staring in the same way as the legionaries.

'Talos,' repeated the booming, vox-altered voice. **'I can't move.'**

Cyrion laughed as he heard the voice. 'Captain Malcharion is awake again? Wasn't that worthy of a shipwide message?'

'Cyrion...' Talos managed to whisper. 'Cyrion, wait...'

'Cyrion,' the Dreadnought intoned. **'You're still alive. Wonders will never cease.'**

'It's a fine thing to see you again, captain.' Cyrion walked over to the Dreadnought's chassis, looking up at the sarcophagus chained into its armoured housing. He caught the skull one more time.

'So,' he said to the immense war machine. 'Where should I begin? Here's a list of what's taken place while you slumbered...'

XXI
DEAD WEIGHT

THE LAST WARRIORS of the Tenth and Eleventh Companies had gathered in the *Echo of Damnation*'s war room. For seven hours, none of them moved, all remaining around the prophet and the war-sage. Occasionally, one of the warriors from the other claws would speak up, adding their recollections to those spoken by Talos.

At last, Talos released a long, slow breath. 'And then you awoke,' he said.

The Dreadnought made a grinding sound deep within its innards, akin to a tank slipping gears. Talos wondered if that was the equivalent of a grunt, or a curse, or simply clearing your throat when there was no longer a throat to speak of.

'You did well.'

Talos almost flinched at the sudden proclamation. 'I see,' he said, purely from a need to say something, anything at all.

'You seem surprised. Did you expect my anger?'

Talos was acutely aware of the others watching him. 'I had expected to kill you at best, or awaken you at worst. Your anger – either way – hadn't occurred to me.'

Malcharion was the only thing in the room standing truly motionless. Though the others remained in place, they'd shift their posture from time to time, or tilt their heads, or share quiet words between claw-kin.

Malcharion was monumental in his stillness, never breathing, never moving at all.

'I should kill that accursed tech-priest,' he growled.

Across the chamber, Cyrion chuckled. Convincing Malcharion not to annihilate Deltrian for the traumatic and agonising resurrection had taken the two brothers some time. Deltrian, for his part, had been mortified – albeit in his subtle and unemotional way – at the failure of his resurrection rituals.

'But the eldar…' Talos wasn't sure how to finish the sentence.

'With no officers, you've managed to keep us alive this long, Talos. Reclaiming the *Echo* was a fine gesture, as well. The eldar's trap is meaningless. The only way to avoid it would have been to continue existing on the fringes, accomplishing nothing, making no difference to the galaxy. How many worlds will have fallen dark from your psychic scream?'

He shook his head, unsure of the specifics. 'Dozens. Perhaps a hundred. There is no way to know without accessing Imperial archives once the dust has settled on every afflicted world. Even then, we may never know.'

'That is more than Vandred ever did, even if it wasn't done on the field of battle. Do not be ashamed for fighting with your mind instead of your claws, for a change. The Imperium knows *something* happened out here. You've sown the seeds of a subsector legend. The night a hundred worlds fell dark. Some will be silent for months. Some will be lost to warp storms for years. Some will never be heard from again – the Imperium will no doubt arrive to find them reaved clean of life by the daemons loosed upon them. I confess, Talos, you are colder than I ever imagined, to dream up such a fate.'

Talos fought to turn the subject away from himself. 'You say the Imperium will know something happened here, but the eldar already know. For them to have reacted as fast as they did, their witches must have peered into the future and seen something in the tides of alien prophecy.'

The Dreadnought moved for the first time, turning on its waist axis to look over the gathered Night Lords.

'And this troubles you?'

Several heads nodded, while other warriors replied with 'Yes, captain.'

'I see what you are all thinking now.'

The Night Lords looked back at their captain, incarnated in his hulking shell, a towering monument to a life lived in devoted service.

'You do not wish to die. The eldar herd us into a final fight, and you fear the call of the grave. You think only of escape, of living to fight another day, of preserving your lives at the cost of all else.'

Lucoryphus hissed before speaking. 'You make us sound craven.'

Malcharion turned to the Raptor, his armoured joints grinding. **'You have changed, Luc.'**

'Time changes all things, Mal.' The Raptor's head jerked to the side, with a whine of servos. 'We were the first on the walls at the Siege of Terra. We were the blades of the Eleventh before we were the Bleeding Eyes. And we are no cravens, Captain of the Tenth.'

'You have forgotten the lesson of the Legion. Death is nothing compared to vindication.'

The Raptor gave a harsh croak, his equivalent of a laugh. 'Death is still an ending I would rather avoid. Let us teach the lesson and live to teach it again another day.'

The Dreadnought gave a rumbling growl in response. **'The lesson wasn't learned if you have to teach it twice. Now stop whining. We'll face these aliens down before we worry about dying at the day's end.'**

'It's good to have you back, captain,' said Cyrion.

'Then stop sniggering like an infant,' the Dreadnought replied. **'Talos. What is your plan? It had better be grand, brother. I have no desire to die a third time in anything less than glory.'**

Several of the gathered legionaries shared a grim chuckle.

'That was no joke,' Malcharion growled.

'We didn't take it as one, captain,' said Mercutian.

The prophet activated the tactical hololithic. A dense spread of asteroids filled the space above the projection table, densest in the void above a shattered sphere. At the heart of the cluster, a pulsing rune showed the *Echo of Damnation*.

'We're safe for now, within the Tsagualsan asteroid field.'

Malcharion made the gear-grinding sound again. **'Why is the asteroid field so dense in this region? Even allowing for drift patterns, this is different to what I remember.'**

Lucoryphus gestured to the hololithic. 'Talos shattered half of the moon.'

'Well.' Cyrion cleared his throat. 'Perhaps a fifth of it.'

'You have been busy, Soul Hunter.'

'How many times must I drag you back from the grave and tell you to stop calling me that?' Talos keyed in another set of coordinates. The hololithic shrank, zooming out to show Tsagualsa itself, and a host of other flickering runes ringing the world and its wounded moon.

'The enemy fleet is gathering beyond the field's perimeters. They're holding off from coming in after us, and are refraining from attacking the several thousand souls we left alive on the planet itself. For now, they seem content to wait, but this is it. The noose has tightened. Each time we sought to run forward, they forced us back. They know we have no choice but to fight. Our backs are to the wall.'

He looked around the war room, meeting the eyes of his last living brothers. The warriors of Tenth and Eleventh Companies, now grouped into four final claws.

'You have a plan,' Malcharion rumbled. It wasn't a question this time.

Talos nodded. 'They've tightened the noose to force us into a fight, true enough. They have the firepower to annihilate the *Echo of Damnation*, without a shadow of doubt. More of their vessels are arriving every hour. But we can still surprise them. They're expecting us to cut out of our hiding place and make a last stand in the void. I have a better idea.'

'Tsagualsa,' one of the other Night Lords said. 'You can't be serious, brother. We stand a better chance in the void.'

'No.' Talos refocused the hololithic. 'We don't. And this is why.' The flickering image resolved to show a spread of Tsagualsa's polar region, and the jagged remnants of a structure that had once rivalled the sky with its towers. Several of the gathered legionaries shared quiet words, or shook their heads in disbelief.

'Our fortress scarcely stands,' Talos said. 'Ten thousand years haven't been kind to the spires and battlements. But beneath the remains…'

'The catacombs,' Malcharion growled.

'Exactly so, captain. Auspex scans show the catacombs are largely unchanged. They still reach for kilometres in every direction, with entire sections of the labyrinth immune to orbital bombardment. A fight on *our* terms. If the eldar want us, they're welcome to come down into the dark. We'll hunt them as they hunt us.'

'How long can we last down there?' Lucoryphus asked, his vox-voice crackling.

'Hours. Days. Everything depends on the force they deploy to chase us. Assuming they land an army and flood into the tunnels, we'll still bleed them more savagely than we could in a fair fight. Hours and days are both longer than lasting a handful of minutes. I know which one I'll choose.'

The warriors were leaning forward now, hands resting on weapons. The atmosphere had turned, all reluctance filtering away. Talos continued, addressing the claws.

'The *Echo of Damnation* is unlikely to survive even the brief run to the planet's atmosphere. Once we break from the densest region of the asteroid field, the eldar will be on us like a second skin. Everyone who intends to survive must be ready to evacuate the ship.'

'**And the crew? How many souls aboard?**'

'We're not certain. Thirty thousand, at least.'

'**We cannot evacuate that many, nor can we afford essential crew members leaving their stations. What will you tell them?**'

'Nothing,' replied Talos. 'They'll burn with the *Echo*. I'll remain on the bridge until the last moments, so the command crew doesn't realise the Legion is abandoning them to die.'

'**Cold.**'

'Necessity. There's more. This is our final stand, and we damn ourselves if we hold anything back. First Claw will remain with me, to arrange our final surprise for the eldar. The rest of you will make planetfall via drop-pods and Thunderhawks as soon as you can. Lose yourself beneath Tsagualsa's surface, and be ready for what follows. Remember, even if we survive this, the Imperium is coming. They will find the survivors we left in Sanctuary, and spread the story of our deeds. The eldar care nothing for the populace. They're here for our blood.'

Fal Torm of the newly-gathered Second Claw gave a wicked chuckle. 'Suddenly you're talking of survival. What are the odds of us actually surviving this, brother?'

Talos's only reply was a singularly unpleasant smile.

HOURS LATER, THE prophet and the Flayer walked together through Variel's personal apothecarion. The facilities here were more specific in scope, with far fewer attendant slaves and servitors to get underfoot.

'Do you realise,' Variel asked, 'how much work you are asking me to simply cast aside?'

Cast aside, thought Talos. *And Malcharion calls me cold.*

'That's why I've come to you,' he said. As he spoke, he ran his hand along the mechanical arm of a surgical machine, imagining it in motion, in sacred use. 'Show me your work.'

Variel led Talos to the holding chambers at the apothecarion's rear. Both warriors looked in, where the Flayer's charges huddled in their bare cells, chained to the walls by collars around their throats.

'They look cold,' Talos noted.

'They probably are. I keep them in aseptic containment.' Variel gestured at the first of the children. The boy was no older than nine, yet his flesh showed the ragged pink scars of recent invasive surgery along his chest, back and throat.

'How many do you have?'

Variel didn't need to consult his narthecium for exact figures. 'Sixty-one between the ages of eight and fifteen, adapting well to the various stages of implantation. A further one hundred and nine of harvestable age, yet not ripe for implantation. Over two hundred have died so far.'

Talos knew those kinds of figures well enough. 'Those are very good survival rates.'

'I know that.' Variel almost sounded piqued. 'I am skilled at what I do.'

'That's why I need you to keep doing it.'

Variel entered one of the cells, where one of the children lay on his front, unmoving. The Flayer turned the boy over with the edge of his armoured boot. Dead eyes stared back up.

'Two hundred and thirteen,' he said, and gestured for a servitor to drag the infant's body away. 'Incinerate this,' he ordered.

'Compliance.'

Talos paid no heed to the servitor as it went about its funereal work. 'Brother, listen to me for a moment.'

'I am listening.' Variel didn't stop keying in notes on his vambrace, recording yet more details.

'You cannot stand with us on Tsagualsa.'

That made him stop. Variel's eyes – ice-blue to Talos's black – lifted in a slow, sterile stare.

'You tell a hilarious jest,' the Flayer said, utterly without warmth.

'No jest, Variel. You are holding the key to a significant piece of the Legion's future. I am sending you away before the battle. Deltrian's ship is capable of warp flight. You'll be going with him, as will your equipment and your work.'

'No.'

'This is not a debate, brother.'

'*No.*' Variel tore the flayed skin from his pauldron, revealing the winged skull beneath. The symbol of the Eighth Legion stared back at Talos with hollow eye sockets. 'I wear the winged skull of Nostramo, the same as you. I will fight and die with you, on that worthless little world.'

'You owe me nothing, Variel. Not anymore.'

For once, Variel looked close to stunned. 'Owe you? *Owe you?* Is that how you see our brotherhood? A series of favours to be repaid? I *owe you* nothing. I will stand with you because we are both Eighth Legion. Brothers, Talos. Brothers unto death.'

'Not this time.'

'You cannot–'

'I can do whatever I wish. Captain Malcharion agrees with me. There is no room on Deltrian's vessel for more than ten additional warriors, and even that is better devoted to relics that must be returned to the Legion. You and your work must be preserved above all.'

Variel took a breath. 'Have you ever realised how often you interrupt those you are speaking with? It is almost as irritating a habit as Uzas constantly licking his teeth.'

'I'll bear that in mind,' Talos replied. 'I'll work on this alarming character flaw in the many years of life I have left. Now, will you be ready? If I give you twelve hours and as many servitors as you need, can you ensure your equipment is loaded aboard Deltrian's ship?'

Variel bared his teeth in an uncharacteristic angry smile. 'It will be done.'

'I've not seen you lose your temper since Fryga.'

'Fryga was an exceptional circumstance. As is this.'

Variel pressed his fingertips to massage his closed eyes. 'You are asking much of me.'

'Don't I always? And I need you to do something else, Variel.'

The Apothecary met the prophet's eyes again, sensing something disquieting in the other Night Lord's tone. 'Ask.'

'Once you're gone, I want you to find Malek of the Atramentar.'

Variel raised a thin eyebrow. 'I am never returning to the Maelstrom, Talos. Huron will have my head.'

'I don't believe Malek will have remained there, nor do I believe the Atramentar would willingly join with the Blood Reaver. If they boarded a Corsair vessel, it was for another reason. I don't know what that reason was, but I trust him despite what happened. Find him if you can, and tell him his plan worked. Malcharion lived. The war-sage resumed command, leading the Tenth again in its final nights.'

'Is that all?'

'No. Give him my thanks.'

'I will do all of that, if you wish. But Deltrian's ship will not get far without needing to refuel. It is too small for long-range flight. We both know this.'

'It doesn't have to get far. Not at first. It just needs to get away from here.'

Variel gave a grunt of displeasure. 'The eldar may chase us.'

'Yes. They may. Any other complaints? You're wasting what little time I can give you.'

'What of Octavia? How will we sail the Sea of Souls without a Navigator?'

'You won't,' Talos replied. 'That's why she's going with you.'

HE COULD HAVE guessed her reaction would be somewhat less polite than Variel's. Had he bothered to predict such a thing, he'd have been quite correct.

'I think,' she said, 'I'm sick and tired of doing what you tell me.'

Talos wasn't looking directly at her. He walked around her throne, casting his gaze across the fluid pool, remembering the chamber's previous occupant. She'd died in filth, broken apart by the bolters of First Claw. Despite a memory that bordered on eidetic, Talos found he couldn't recall the creature's name now. *How rare.*

'Are you listening to me?' Octavia asked. The tone of her voice, so exquisitely courtly, drew his attention back.

'Yes.'

'Good.' She sat in her throne, one hand cradling her swelling stomach. Her near-emaciation made the pregnancy all the more prominent.

'What are the chances that Deltrian's ship will even make it to safety?'

Talos saw no sense in lying to her. He looked at her long and hard, letting the seconds pass by to the rhythm of her heartbeat. 'Your chance of survival is almost amusingly small. But a chance, nevertheless.'

'And Septimus?'

'He is our pilot and my slave.'

'He's the father of–'

Talos held up a hand in warning. 'Be careful, Octavia. Do not mistake me for a being able to be moved by emotional pleas. I have skinned children before their parents' eyes, you know.'

Octavia clenched her teeth. 'So he's staying.' She wasn't sure why she said it, but it came out in a spill, nevertheless. 'He'll follow me, somehow. You can't keep him here. I know him better than you do.'

'I have not yet decided his fate,' Talos replied.

'And what about you? What's your "fate"?'

'Do not speak to me in that tone of voice. This is not the Imperial Court of Terra, little highness. I am not impressed or awed by a haughty tone, so save your breath.'

'Sorry,' she said. 'I'm... just angry.'

'Understandable.'

'So what will you do? You're just going to let them kill you?'

'Of course not. You saw what happened when we tried to run, how we battered our prow against blockade after blockade. They won't let us run to the Great Eye. The noose started to close around us the moment I let out the psychic scream. We make our stand here, Octavia. If we leave it any longer, we'll lose our last chance to choose where this war will be fought.'

'You're not answering my question.'

'We're going to die.' Talos gestured to her bank of wall monitors, each one showing a different angle outside the ship – each one an eye staring upon the millions of rocks drifting in the void. 'How can I be clearer? How can it be more obvious? Outside this asteroid field, alien warships wait for us to make our move. We're dead, Octavia. That's all there is to it. Now ensure you are ready to leave the ship. Take whatever you wish, it matters nothing to me. You have eleven hours before I never want to see you again.'

He turned and left, shoving aside two of her attendants that didn't scatter quickly enough. She watched him walk away, tasting freedom on her tongue for the first time since she was captured, and unsure whether the taste was as pleasant as she remembered.

The door opened with smooth traction, revealing his master in the entrance arch.

Septimus looked up, Uzas's helm still in his hands. He'd been making the final repairs to the left eye lens socket.

'Lord?' he said.

Talos walked in, filling the humble chamber with a chorus of snarling joints and the ever-present hum of live armour.

'Octavia leaves the ship in eleven hours,' the Night

Lord said. 'Your unborn child goes with her.'

Septimus nodded. His eyes never left his master's faceplate. 'With respect, lord, I had already guessed.'

Talos walked around the room, casting his attention here and there, never lingering for long on one thing. He took in the half-repaired pistols on the desk; the sketches of schematics; the charcoal drawings of his lover Octavia; and the clothing left in messy heaps. Above all, the small space bled a sense of life, of personality, of being the sanctum of one specific living soul.

A human's room, Talos thought, reflecting on the empty lifelessness of his own personal chambers – chambers resembling the quarters of any other Legionary, except for the prophecies scrawled on the iron walls. *How different they are to us, to leave their imprint so sternly on the places they live.*

He turned back to Septimus, the man that had served him for almost a decade now.

'We must speak, you and I.'

'As you wish, master.' Septimus put the helm down.

'No. For the next few minutes, we will forget the roles of those who serve and those who are served. For now, I am neither *master*, nor *lord*. I am Talos.' The warrior removed his helm, looking down with his pale features calm.

Septimus felt the mad urge to reach for a weapon, unnerved by this strange familiarity.

'Why do I feel like this is some frightening prelude to slitting my throat?' he asked.

The prophet's smile never reached his dark eyes.

OCTAVIA AND DELTRIAN weren't getting along, which was a surprise to neither of them. She thought he was unbearably impatient for such an augmented creature, and he thought she smelled unpleasantly of the biological chemicals and organic fluids involved in mammalian reproduction. Their relationship had started with those first impressions, and gone downhill from there. It was a relief for both of them when she went to her quarters for her final preparations before flight.

She strapped herself into the uncomfortable throne in the belly of Deltrian's squat insectoid ship. Her 'chamber', such as it was, offered a single picter-screen and barely enough room to stretch her legs.

'Has anyone ever sat here and tested this equipment?' she asked as a servitor slid a slender neural spike into the modest and elegantly-crafted socket at her temple. '*Ouch.* Careful with that.'

'Compliance,' murmured the cyborg, staring with dead eyes. It was all the answer she received, which didn't surprise her, either.

'You push until it clicks,' she told the lobotomised slave. 'Not until it comes out my other bloody ear.'

The servitor drooled a little. 'Compliance.'

'Throne, just go away.'

'Compliance,' it said for a third time, and did exactly that. She heard it bumping into something in the corridor outside, while the ship shook on the deck with final armament loading. Octavia's box of a room had no porthole windows, so she cycled through the external picter feeds. Image after image of the *Echo*'s main hangar deck flickered across the screen. Thunderhawks were being loaded with full payloads, and drop-pods were winched into position. Octavia watched with emotionless eyes, not sure what to feel. Was this home? Would she miss all of it? Where would they even go, if they managed to get away?

'Oh,' she whispered, watching the screen. 'Oh, shit.'

She paused the scrolling feed, keying in a code to tilt one of the imagefinders on the ship's hull. Loader buggies and crew transports ferried back and forth; a lifter Sentinel, stolen from some long-past raid, clanked its way past, steel feet thumping on the deck.

Septimus, with a beaten leather bag over one shoulder, was speaking with Deltrian by the main gangramp. His long hair covered his facial augmetics, and he wore a subtly armoured bodysuit beneath his heavy jacket. A machete was sheathed at his right shin, and both pistols hung low at his hips.

She had no idea what he was saying. The external viewfinders didn't offer sound. She watched him slap Deltrian on the shoulder, which the stick-thin cadaver of chrome didn't seem to appreciate, if his recoil was anything to go by.

Septimus made his way up the gangramp, and vanished from view. The screen showed Deltrian return to directing his loader servitors, and the endless flow of machinery being brought aboard.

She heard the knock at her bulkhead door almost immediately after.

'Tell me you've got your bandana on,' she heard him call through the metal.

She smiled, reaching a hand to check, just in case. 'You're safe.'

The door opened, and he dumped his gear the moment he'd closed it behind him. 'I was dismissed from service,' he said. 'Just like you.'

'Who'll fly *Blackened* down to the surface?'

'No one. There are only enough squads for three gunships. *Blackened* has been loaded into this ship's conveyance claws already. Talos has bequeathed it to Variel, full of his apothecarion equipment and relics from the Hall of Reflection. It's to be returned to the Legion in the Eye, if we ever make it that far.'

Her smiled faded, the sun going behind the horizon. 'We're not going to make it that far. You know that, don't you?'

He shrugged, evidently sanguine. 'We'll see.'

WORD HAD SURELY spread throughout the ship of the upcoming battle, but the *Echo* was a city in space, with all the various multitudes such scope implied. On the highest crew decks, the battle to come was a matter of focus – the officers and ratings knew their parts to play, and went about their duties with all the professionalism of those aboard an Imperial Navy warship.

On the lower decks, as one ventured deeper into the ship's innards, the battle was either a matter of prayer, ignorance, or helpless muttering. The thousands who fed the ship with their blood and sweat, toiling in the reactor chambers and the weapon battery platforms, had no wider understanding of the situation beyond the fact a battle would soon be fought.

Talos went alone to the primary hangar deck. Tenth Company's surviving warriors were already on board their drop-pods, while their Thunderhawks were loaded with wargear to be ferried down to them on the surface. Servitors stood in idle silence here and there, waiting for the next order that would engage their limited response arrays.

The prophet crossed the quiet landing bay, to where Deltrian was descending down his ship's gangramp.

'All is in readiness,' Deltrian vocalised.

Talos regarded the adept with unblinking red eye lenses. 'Swear to me you'll do as I say. Those three sarcophagi are priceless. Malcharion will stand with us, but the other three tomb-pods have to reach the Legion. They are relics beyond price. They cannot die here with us.'

'All is in readiness,' Deltrian said a second time.

'The gene-seed matters most of all,' Talos pressed him. 'The gene-seed supplies in storage must reach the Eye, at all costs. Swear to me.'

'All is in readiness,' Deltrian repeated. He had scant regard for the swearing of oaths. In his view, promises were something sworn by biologicals seeking to use hope in place of calculated likelihood. In short: an agreement made on flawed parameters.

'Swear to me, Deltrian.'

The tech-priest made an error sound, vocalising it in a low burr. 'Very well. In an effort to end this vocalisation exchange, I give my oath that the plan will be followed to precise parameters, to the best of my ability and capacity to oversee the efforts of others.'

'That'll do.'

Deltrian wasn't quite finished. 'Estimates suggest we will remain in the asteroid field for several hours after your departure before we know for certain if every xenos vessel is giving chase. Auspex unreliability is a factor. Drift jamming is a factor. Alien interference is a factor. The logistics of–'

'There are many factors,' Talos interrupted. 'I understand. Hide as long as you need to, and run when you can.'

'As you will it, so shall it be.'

The tech-priest turned, then hesitated. Talos wasn't moving away.

'Do you linger here in the desire that I will wish you luck?' Deltrian tilted his leering skull of a face. 'You must be aware that the very idea of fortune is anathema to me. Existence is arbitrary, Talos.'

The Night Lord held out his hand. Deltrian's eye lenses focused on the offered gauntlet for a moment, soft whirrings in his facial structure giving away the fact his eyes were refocusing.

'Intriguing,' he said. 'Processing.'

A moment later, he gripped the legionary's wrist. Talos gripped the adept's, returning the Eighth Legion's traditional warrior handshake.

'It's been a privilege, honoured adept.'

Deltrian searched for the appropriate response. He was an outsider, but the ancient formal words, traditionally spoken between warriors of the Eighth Legion on the eve of hopeless battles, came to him with an alacrity he found surprising.

'Die as you lived, Son of the Eighth Legion. In midnight clad.'

The two broke apart. Deltrian, as dead to patience as he was to subtlety, immediately turned and walked up the gangramp, heading into the ship.

Talos hesitated, seeing Septimus at the top of the ramp. The slave raised his gloved hand in farewell.

Talos snorted at the gesture. *Humans. The things emotion forces them to do.*

He acknowledged his former slave with a nod, and left the hangar without a word.

XXII

GAUNTLET

THE ECHO POWERED through the asteroid field with no concern for ammunition reserves or void shield charges. The smaller rocks crashed aside, repelled by the ship's crackling shields as the cruiser rammed the asteroids out of the way. The larger rocks died in invisible detonations, as the warship's guns pounded them into rubble.

It didn't turn to avoid any impacts. It didn't slow down, or manoeuvre, or deploy drones to break up any debris in its path. The *Echo of Damnation* was done hiding. It tore its way from its volatile sanctuary, every cannon along its sides and spine swinging forward, ready to cry out in anger for the final time.

On the bridge, Talos watched from his throne. The command crew, mortals all, were almost silent in their focused devotion. Servitors relayed printed reports, several of them emitting slow rolls of inked parchment from augmetic jaws. The prophet's eyes never left the occulus. Beyond the twisting rocks, past even those that weren't yet bursting apart under the *Echo*'s weapons fire, the alien fleet lay in wait. He saw them moving through the void in a tidal drift, disgustingly harmonious, their glittering solar sails tilted to catch the distant sun's weak light.

'Report,' Talos said.

The responses came from every section of the

command deck. Calls of 'aye' and 'ready' hailed back in an orderly verse. To coin Deltrian's phrase, all was in readiness. There was nothing he could do now beyond wait.

'Alien fleet moving to intercept. They're positioned in the clearest paths through the rest of the asteroid field.'

He could see that well enough. The smaller vessels, shaped of contoured bone, remained around their motherships – lesser fish feeding from sharks – but the bigger cruisers moved with a speed no less impressive. They came about in fluid arcs, sails banking, running to head off the *Echo of Damnation* as soon as it left the densest sector of the asteroid field.

He didn't like how they moved; not only because of the grotesque agility far beyond human capability, but because outrunning and outgunning this fleet was already impossible, and they were making it look like outmanoeuvring them was an equal fiction.

'Forty-five seconds, lord.'

Talos leaned back in the throne. He knew full well there was a chance he'd never get off this deck alive. The run to the planet was looking to be the hardest part; slaughtering these skeletal alien wretches in the Tsagualsan catacombs would be a delightful treat by comparison, and one that almost made his mouth water.

'Thirty seconds.'

'All targets marked and locked,' called out the weapons overseer. 'We'll need a full minute of uninterrupted bearing to unleash the entire first volley.'

'You'll have it, Armsmaster,' Talos replied. 'How many targets will that hit?'

'If the aliens behave as eldar fleets usually do, rather than running alongside us for a broadside exchange... Fifteen targets, my lord.'

Talos felt his lips twitch behind his faceplate, not quite a smile. *Fifteen targets in one volley.* Blood of Horus, he'd miss this ship. She'd been a beautiful twin sister to the *Covenant,* and it would be churlish to begrudge the armament improvements performed by the Corsairs in the centuries they'd claimed her.

'Twenty seconds.'

'Give me shipwide vox address.'

'Done, lord.'

Talos drew a breath, knowing his words were being heard by thousands upon thousands of slaves, mutants, heretics and serfs across the ship's myriad decks.

'This is the captain,' he said. 'I am Talos, of the bloodline of the Eighth Primarch, and a son of the sunless world. A storm like no other bears down upon us, ready to break against the ship's skin. Survival rides on your blood and sweat, no matter the deck you toil upon. Every life counts in the minutes to come. All hands, all souls, brace for battle.'

'Five seconds, lord.'

'Start the Shriek.'

'Aye, lord.'

'First volley as planned, then fire at will.'

'Aye, lord.'

'Lord, we're clear of the Talosian Density. Enemy fleet is moving to eng–'

'*Open fire.*'

THE ECHO OF DAMNATION ran with all its heart, streaming plasma flame in contrails almost beautiful in their devastating heat.

The wider asteroid field's presence was one of the many unwelcoming aspects that made Tsagualsa such a secure haven for so many years after the Heresy. It was significantly less of a hazard to navigation than the denser debris around the shattered moon, but the eldar ships still ghosted and looped around any loose rock rather than risk impact.

The *Echo of Damnation* took no such care. It ploughed ahead, relying on its void shields and forward weapons array to ram aside any impending threats.

Their initial dives were somewhat less graceful than their previous void dancing, for their prey was playing a different game. The *Echo* obeyed no conventional logic, never once turning for better angles with its weapon batteries, making no adjustments to its flight vectors. The warship wasn't where the alien vessels expected it to be, nor was it going where they'd prepared for it to go. By simply carving its way through the asteroid field, the *Echo* was sacrificing an insane amount of ammunition and shield power, knifing directly towards the world ahead.

The eldar ships ready to engage, laying in wait throughout the clearer routes in the debris field, now found themselves far away from the path of their fleeing prey.

'Is it working?' Talos asked. He could see it working – it was obvious in the way several alien vessels were coming about at speed to adjust their attack runs – but he wanted to hear it, nevertheless.

The officers stared down at their consoles, none more keenly than those stationed at the auspex hololithic projectors.

'The eldar fleet is struggling to come about to our trajectory. Several cruisers are already failing their intercept courses.'

'It's working.' Talos remained in the throne, resisting the desire to pace the deck. The ship shook with the firing of the guns, and the hammering shivers of rocks pounding against the void shields. 'We're outrunning almost half of them.'

The alien ships were elongated, contoured things – all smooth bone and shining wing-sails. He suspected the distant sun made the eldar warships sluggish, starved of the heat they needed on their solar sails, but he hardly had a wealth of experience in the function of alien vessels. With the eldar, everything always felt like guesswork.

'Xenos vanguard ships entering maximum weapons range.'

Talos thought of his brothers in their drop-pods, and

the gunships warmed and waiting in the landing bays. On the occulus, the coin-sized grey sphere of Tsagualsa grew by the second. Proximity alarms wailed at each and every asteroid that went spinning aside from the inexorable advance, and servitors slaved to their stations chattered at the threat of incoming warheads.

For no reason he could adequately explain, Talos felt a smile creeping across his face. A crooked, sincere smirk of inappropriate amusement.

'Lord,' called out one of the auspex officers. 'Alien torpedoes are resistant to our interference.'

'Even to the Shriek?' He knew it was calibrated to Imperial technology, but even so, he'd been hoping it would make a difference.

'Several have lost their bearings, others are ploughing into the debris field. But more than three-quarters are still on target.'

'Time to impact?'

'The first will be upon us in less than twenty seconds.'

'That's good enough. All hands, brace for impact.'

Soon enough, the hull's rattling became shaking, and the shaking in turn became violent convulsions. Talos felt the creeping of some new and unwelcome unease worming its way up his backbone; how many times had he been aboard a warship in a void battle? A difficult question. One might as well ask how many breaths he'd drawn over the centuries. But this was different. This time, he was the one guiding the ship's path. He couldn't just leave it in Vandred's hands and focus on his own lesser conflicts.

Malcharion should be here. Talos quashed the treacherous thought, true as it might be.

'Shields holding,' a servitor chattered nearby. 'Two-thirds strength.'

Talos watched the grey world growing as the *Echo of Damnation* cried out around him.

'Come on,' he whispered. 'Come on.'

* * *

THE EIGHTH LEGION warship hammered her way onward, ramming through the asteroids lying in her path.

The eldar captains were hardly novices in void warfare, nor could any of their craftworld home on the edge of the Great Eye ever be truly surprised by the tactics of an Archenemy warship. Solar sails aligned across the fleet as the alien cruisers swam through their haunting, beautiful attack runs, filling the rocky void with flashing streams of pulsar fire.

Individually, each pulsar beam was as thin as string against the background of infinite black, but they streaked across the void in a cobweb of shining force, raining and lashing against the *Echo*'s suffering void shields.

The *Echo of Damnation* rolled as it ran, offering its broadsides and spinal batteries to the enemy. Return fire burst from the Eighth Legion cruiser – corruption bursting from suppurated wounds – as the warship lashed back with its own guns. Such was their grace, several of the eldar vessels seemed to shimmer out of existence, vanishing from the path of incoming fire. Others took the onslaught, letting it starburst across their shields, secure in the knowledge that the *Echo*'s flight forced it to devote the majority of its armament to clearing a way through the rocks.

The first alien ship to fall was a minor escort ship bearing a name no human could accurately pronounce. Certainly, none of those present on the *Echo of Damnation* cared to try, yet they cheered and laughed when it broke apart before their eyes, ruined by a barrage of plasma and hard-shell fire from the spinal batteries.

A lucky shot, and Talos knew it. Nevertheless, his skin prickled at the sight.

The second xenos vessel died as much from the random tides of fate as from Night Lord malice. With no time to turn, the *Echo of Damnation* poured all of its forward fire into a huge asteroid ahead. Its lances carved into the frozen stone, splitting the rock along fault lines in time for the ship's shielded prow to ram straight into the surface. As the asteroid broke apart, scattering from the crackling and protesting shields, spinning rocks tumbled in all directions. The eldar fleet, for all their arcing agility, were hampered by the oppressing rocks all around. Even as they scattered to fly aside, several of them took incidental damage from the spreading rubble.

Talos gave a crooked smile as one of the heaviest chunks crashed into the slender form of a swooping enemy warship. The debris shattered a solar sail into nothing more than beautiful diamond glass, before grinding into the vessel's body of supernatural bone. The ship twisted, suffering and straining, before diving directly into another asteroid ahead.

'Even if we die here,' the Night Lord chuckled, 'that was worth seeing.'

'Three minutes until we pass Tsagualsa, lord.'

'Good.' The smile died on his lips as he remembered the betrayal to come. Given the ship's trajectory and the overwhelming force against them, many of these poor souls had surely already guessed the only way this could possibly end.

'Should we ready the ship for warp flight?' asked one of the closest officers. Talos heard it in the man's voice; the officer had surrendered his hope, and sought to hide his unrest. The prophet admired him for that. Cowardice had no place on this bridge.

'No,' Talos replied. 'Do you genuinely believe we will make it to safety?' The ship shuddered around them, forcing several mortal crew members to cling to railings and consoles. 'Even with this successful run, do you believe we'll evade them for much longer?'

'No, lord. Of course not.'

'A wise answer,' Talos told him. 'Focus on your duties, Lieutenant Rawlen. Don't worry what will come after.'

* * *

Septimus and Deltrian stood in the modest, cramped chamber that the tech-adept announced, with no trace of pride or shame either way, as *Epsilon K-41 Sigma Sigma A:2*'s bridge.

He'd also demanded Septimus leave the deck, to which the human had replied in Nostraman, with something dubiously biological about Deltrian's mother.

'I'm a pilot,' he added. 'I'm going to help fly this thing.'

'Your augmetic aspects, while impressive, are far too limited for you to interface with the machine-spirit of my vessel.'

He gestured to the rocks quivering on the unreliable hololithic. 'You trust servitors and a machine-spirit to fly out of *this?*'

Deltrian made an affirmative sound. 'More than any human. What... what a strange query.'

Septimus had relented, but remained on the bridge by the pilot-servitor's throne.

The slave and the adept, along with the two-dozen servitors and robed crew, were watching the hololithic projection that served as tactical map and occulus alike. Unlike the *Echo*'s holo-imagery, Deltrian's was watery and flickered at intervals that pained Septimus's human eye. Looking through his bionic took away the ache, and helped resolve some of the flickering interference. Only then did he realise it was a projection designed to be viewed by augmetic eyes.

The ship itself was a rounded, bloated beetle of a vessel, bristling with defensive turrets, with almost three-quarters of its length given up to the drive engines and warp generators. Bulkheads sealed those areas of the ship off from the habitable areas, and Septimus had seen several of the adepts wearing rebreather masks while entering and leaving the engine decks.

The entire vessel was cramped to the point of madness. To make room for the vessel's armour, weapons systems and propulsion, every tunnel was a narrow walkway, and every chamber was a squat box featuring the essential systems and enough room for a single operator. The command deck was the most spacious area of the whole ship, and even that offered no room to move if eight people were present at once.

Septimus watched the ship's identifier rune pulsing on the hololithic, attached to an asteroid as it hid from the aliens' scanners. Far across the field of malformed rocks, the rune signifying the *Echo* was a speck among a nest of angry signals.

'The *Echo* is almost there,' he said. 'They're going to make it.'

Septimus turned his head at a familiar sound. Variel walked in, his armour joints humming with every movement.

'Tell me what's happening,' he demanded, as calm as ever.

'It doesn't look like they know we're here,' Septimus let his eyes drift back to the hololithic.

'Tell me about the *Echo*, idiotic mortal.'

Septimus had the grace to force a smile, abashed at the obviousness of his mistake. 'They're going to make it, Lord Variel.'

The Apothecary showed no emotion at the use of the honorific, just as he never showed any emotion the many times Septimus had or hadn't used it before. Such things were less than meaningless to him.

'Am I to assume we will be departing soon?'

Deltrian nodded, doing his best to simulate the human movement on a neck not designed to flex in such subtle ways. Something locked at the top of his spine, and he had to take a moment to will the vertebrae coupling to loosen.

'Affirmative,' he vocalised.

Variel moved to where Septimus stood, watching the hololithic himself. 'What is that?' he gestured to another runic signifier.

'That...' Septimus reached down to the servitor pilot's console, and adjusted the hololithic display with a few tapped keys. '…is the Genesis Chapter's strike cruiser we destroyed months ago.'

Variel didn't smile, which was no surprise to Septimus. His pale blue eyes blinked once as he regarded the hololithic image of the broken cruiser, its hull left open to the void. He reached down to magnify the image, taking in the absolute devastation where the warship lay dead at the heart of the Talosian Density, among the thickest cluster of asteroids above the broken moon.

'That was a particularly satisfying kill,' the Night Lord noted.

'Aye, lord.'

Variel glanced at him with those disquieting eyes. After almost ten years in service to the Eighth Legion, Septimus would have gambled on nothing being able to unnerve him anymore. Variel's eyes seemed to be a rare exception.

'What is wrong with you?' the Apothecary asked. 'Your heart rate is elevated. You reek of some moronic, emotional excitement.'

Septimus inclined his head to the hololithic. 'It's difficult to watch them fight without us. Serving the Legion is all I've done for most of my adult life. Without that… I'm not even sure I know who I am.'

'Yes, yes. Fascinating.' He turned to Deltrian. 'Techpriest. A question, to alleviate my boredom. I want to listen to the eldar's communications. Can you leech their signal?'

'Of course.' Deltrian deployed two of his secondary limbs, letting them arch over his shoulders to work on a separate console. 'I have no capacity to translate eldar linguistic vocalisations.'

That caught Variel's attention. 'Truly? Curious. I'd thought you'd be more enlightened than that.'

'An adept of the Mechanicum has more pressing matters to attend to than the mumblings of wretched xenos-kind.'

'No need to become irritated,' Variel offered a

momentary smile, as false as it was brief. 'I speak several eldar dialects. Just leech the signal, if you are able.'

Deltrian paused before pulling the last lever. 'Explain your mastery of the alien tongue.'

'There is nothing to explain, honoured adept. I dislike ignorance. When the chance to learn something arises, I take it.' He looked over at the robed figure. 'Do you believe the Red Corsairs only battled the corrupt Imperium? We fought the eldar countless times. Captives were not unknown, either. You have one chance at guessing who extracted information from them through excruciation.'

'I see.' Deltrian accepted the answer with another attempt to simulate a nod. His spinal column, made of various precious metals reinforced by tiny plates of ceramite, clicked and whirred with the movement. As he engaged the lever, the bridge was flooded by sibilant alien whispers, distorted by vox crackle.

Variel spoke a word of thanks, and returned his attention to the hololithic. Septimus stood with him, his attention alternating between the unfolding battle and Variel's pale face.

'Stop looking at me,' Variel said after a minute had passed. 'It is getting annoying.'

'What are the eldar saying?' Septimus asked.

Variel listened for another half-minute, not seeming to pay overmuch attention. 'They speak of manoeuvres in three dimensions, comparing warship movements to ghosts and beasts of the sea. It is all very poetic, in a bland, worthless and alien way. No casualty reports yet. No sound of any eldar captains shrieking as their souls are cast adrift.'

It was suddenly clear to Septimus what Variel was really listening for. First Claw had been right; Variel really was one of the Eighth Legion, no matter the origins of his gene-seed.

'I…' the Apothecary started, then fell silent. The eldar voices whispered on in the background.

Septimus drew breath to ask, 'What are they–'

Variel silenced him with a glare, his pale eyes narrowed in suspicious concentration. The slave crossed his arms over his chest, waiting and hoping for an explanation, but hardly expecting one.

'Wait,' Variel finally breathed, closing his eyes to better focus on the alien tongue. 'Something is wrong.'

XXIII

A FATE DENIED

OCTAVIA WAS DOING something she'd not dared in a long while. She was using her gift for pleasure, not for duty or necessity.

The Sea of Souls was not a source of easy indulgence, and her childhood was littered with a thousand tales told of Navigators who looked too long, too deep, into the warp's tides. They never saw anything the same afterwards. One of the Mervallion family's own scions – her cousin Tralen Premar Mervallion – was locked beneath the family spire in an isolation tank where he could do himself no more harm. The last time she'd seen him, he'd been floating in the murky fluids of an amniotic pool, leashed by restraint straps, now the proud and laughing owner of a ragged hole in the middle of his forehead where his third eye had been. She shivered at the memory, seeing the bubbles spilling up from his laughing mouth. He always laughed now. She'd hoped whatever fuelled his manic amusement offered some kind of solace, but she wasn't naive enough to believe it.

She didn't like to think of Tralen. Navigators were said to die from the removal of their warp eyes. It seemed there were some few, rare exceptions to that vile rule.

It had taken long enough to calm her nerves before risking her needless viewing, but with her human eyes closed and her bandana pulled free, the rest took no time at all. In truth, it was almost frighteningly easy – a similar sensation to falling from halfway up a difficult climb – but she knew she had the strength to pull herself back.

Octavia, once Eurydice of House Mervallion, might not have been born to a bloodline blessed as strong Navigators, but experience aboard the temperamental, wilful vessels of the Eighth Legion had honed what skills she possessed. She couldn't help but wonder, as she gazed into the infinite black tides, how she would perform on the aptitude judgement arrays back on Holy Terra now. Had she grown stronger, or was it merely a matter of familiarity and confidence?

She'd never know. The odds of her ever setting foot on the Throneworld again were millions to one. That thought didn't seem as bleak as it once had. She wasn't sure why.

Curiosity forced her hand now, though. A less selfish, more perverse curiosity than dwelling on her own fate. *Seeing* into the Sea of Souls was as simple as opening her third eye. She didn't need to be in the warp, though she knew some Navigators did. Few of them could compare the use of their gift with absolute common ground. Her father could only see into the warp with all three of his eyes open. She'd never known why; they all had their personal habits.

When she *saw*, she merely stared with her secret sight, watching the shadowy ebb and flow of the half-formed nothingness, shapeless yet tidal, formless yet serpentine. Shamans and witches from the primitive ages of Old Earth would consider it no different than a ritual allowing them to look into the layers of their mythical Hell.

But when she *searched*, she couldn't help but hold her breath each time, until her hammering heart and aching lungs forced her to breathe again. She was aware, on some logical level, that she was projecting her sight through the unholy tides, perhaps even casting a fragment of consciousness into the ether – but Octavia cared little for the metaphysics at play. All that mattered was what she could find with her second sight.

In the madness of the eldar blockades, they'd run again and again, flowing through the tides along the path of least resistance. Talos's psychic scream left the warp raw and abused, its veins swollen and its rivers in turmoil. She'd guided the ship as best she could, riding the winds rather than fighting too hard and risk the *Echo* breaking apart. All the while, she'd been caught between two states, seeing the sundered warp and feeling her hand resting on her swelling stomach.

Now, free from the pressure of navigating the warp, she was free to stare into it. Octavia stared harder, her sight reaching deeper, past the hundred shades of black outside the Astronomican's light, seeking any source of light between the conflicting clouds.

For the first time, she started to see what Talos had done. The colliding waves of daemonic matter bled before her eyes, riven by savage wounds and leaking into one another. She watched them splitting and reforming, meshing and dividing, birthing screaming faces and dissolving them just as quickly. Hands reached out from the thrashing tide, melting and burning even as they gripped the outstretched claws of other nearby souls.

Octavia steadied herself, staring deeper. The wounded warp – *no*, she realised, *not wounded…. energised* – stretched on and on, the bleeding rivers meeting to become a bleeding ocean. How many worlds were choking in this invisible storm? How much terror would this spread?

She could hear her name in the crashing waves. A whisper, a scream, a plaintive cry…

Octavia pulled back. Her eye closed. Her eyes opened.

For a moment, fascination at what Talos had spread through dozens of solar systems gripped her more than the fear of having to fly through it. The warp was always in eternal flux, and in the hours after the scream first sounded, it had boiled with rejuvenation. Now, however, she was preparing to guide an unfamiliar ship into unsailable seas.

The Navigator replaced her bandana, retied her ponytail, and stretched in the uncomfortable throne, trying to ease the pressure on her backbone. She gave an idle thought for her attendants stationed outside the door, no doubt cramped in the narrow corridor. She missed Hound with a dull ferocity, and that in itself was painful to admit. More than that – *and how I hate to confess this, even to myself* – she wished Septimus was with her. He was incapable of ever saying the right thing, but even so. His self-conscious smile; the edge of amusement in his occasional glances; the way he slouched into his throne no matter how dire the threat seemed…

What a stupid, stupid place to fall in love, she thought. *If that's what it even is.*

As Octavia shuffled in her seat, her eyes widened in sudden shock. As if afraid to touch her own flesh, she rested a hesitant hand on her stomach, where for the first time she felt the new life moving within her.

WHEN THE SHIELDS died, Talos never moved in his throne. The crew – those standing, at least – were thrown from their feet in the sudden resurgence in violent shaking that gripped the ship. Two legless servitors fell from their installation sockets, mouths opening and closing as their useless hands worked at the floor, mimicking motions on consoles they could no longer reach.

'Shields down, lord…' called out one of the officers.

No, really? Talos thought.

'Understood,' he replied through gritted teeth.

'Orders, sire?'

The prophet had watched the grey world grow until it became a swollen orb taking up the occulus with its dreary, pockmarked visage.

Close now. So very close.

'Damage report,' he ordered.

As if the ship's heaving wasn't report enough. As if he

needed some other confirmation that they were being cut apart in record time by alien pulsar fire. This many eldar ships, with that much firepower… the *Covenant of Blood* had never had to withstand that much damage in its distinguished career. The *Echo of Damnation* was enduring it for the first, and the last, time.

The officer, Rawlen, couldn't tear his wide eyes from the console screen. 'There's… Lord, there's too much to…'

'Are we in drop-pod range for a surface assault?'

'I…'

Talos vaulted the railing and landed with a crashing thud next to the officer. He turned to the screen himself, calculating the scrolling runes into some semblance of sense. With a snarl, he turned to the vox-mistress.

'Deploy the Legion,' he growled over the chaos taking hold around them.

The woman, uniformed and branded in service to the Red Corsairs, started hitting key commands on her desk. 'Legion deploying, lord.'

'Vox-links,' he demanded. 'Vox-links now.'

'Vox, aye.'

The voices of his brothers rasped their way across the shaking bridge, half-lost in the storm of noise and fire.

'This is Talos to all Legion forces,' he shouted. 'Soul count. Report affirmative deployments.'

One by one, they called back to him. He heard the exultant yells of his brothers in their drop-pods as they reported back: 'Second Claw away,' 'Fourth Claw deployed,' and 'Third Claw launched.' The occulus re-tuned to show several Thunderhawk gunships blasting from the hangars for the final time, engines flaring white hot as they raced out into the stars.

Malcharion's bass rumble heralded the war-sage's departure.

'I'll see you on the carrion world, Soul Hunter.'

Three more confirmations followed, each with the same machine-growl voices. The occulus flashed back to show a scene from some mythical hell, fiery tides washing over the viewscreen like liquid flame.

'We're in the atmosphere,' yelled one of the officers. 'Orders?'

'Does it matter?' another screamed back.

'Pull the ship up!' one of the helmsmen shouted to the others.

Even Talos had to clutch at a railing as the *Echo* gave a horrendous kick, lurching into an uncontrolled dive. He didn't want to imagine how little of the ship was still in one piece – not after running that insane gauntlet.

The western bridge doors opened on grumbling hydraulics, showing Cyrion silhouetted by fire in the doorway.

'Are you mad?' he voxed. 'Hurry the hell up.'

Now or never, thought Talos. He sprinted up the dais to his command throne, needing to hold the armrest to stay on his feet. The melting view on the occulus showed thin clouds, then stars, then the ground, all in an endless, random cycle.

With his free hand, he pulled his sword from its place locked at the throne's side, and sheathed it on his back.

'You should be in the drop-pod,' he voxed back to Cyrion.

'I wish I was,' his brother replied. 'The ship's backside just fell off.'

'You're joking.'

'No engines. No joke. We're in freefall.' Cyrion was gripping the door frame, as human crew flooded around him, trying to flee the bridge. 'Come *on*,' he urged.

Talos ran to him, keeping his balance despite the humans falling underfoot and the deck seeming to disregard all pretence of physics.

Their swords didn't stay sheathed for long. As they forced their way through corridors turned thick with the press of panicked human bodies, both blades fell and carved, hewing a way through the living forest. Blood joined the sweat-stink and fear-scent, aching in Talos's senses. Through the screams, he was dimly aware that he was butchering his own crew, but what did it matter? They'd be dead in moments, anyway.

Cyrion was breathing heavily, kicking out at the humans to break legs and backs as often as he lashed out with his gladius.

'We're going to die,' he breathed over the vox, 'and it's your fault for waiting so long.'

Talos cleaved his sword through a mortal's body, splitting the human from neck to pelvis and shouldering through the falling pieces.

'You didn't have to come back just to whine at me.'

'I didn't have to, no,' Cyrion allowed. 'But no one should die without being reminded of their mistakes.'

'Where in the infinite hells are you?' came Mercutian's voice over the vox.

Talos disembowelled one of the fleeing crew from behind, hurling the biological wreckage aside. He was sweating beneath his armour, already feeling the strain of the endless chopping through the panicked humans blocking the tunnels. A horde of them, hundreds – and soon to be thousands – were fleeing for the escape pods. Exhaustion wasn't a factor; he could carve all day and all night without rest. The problem was purely one of time.

'Launch the drop-pod,' Talos voxed. 'Mercutian, Uzas, get down to Tsagualsa.'

'Are you insane?' Mercutian's strained reply came back.

'We're closer to the command deck's escape pods. Just go.'

Cyrion pulled his gladius from the spine of a uniformed deck officer, his own breath starting to come through ragged. 'If there are any escape pods left after these vermin have run away, that is.'

'Ave dominus nox, Talos. We'll see you in the catacombs.'

Talos heard the massive grind of the drop-pod's clamps disengaging, and Uzas's joyful howling. Their descent through the atmosphere carried them out of vox range in a matter of heartbeats, silencing Mercutian's curses and Uzas's laughter in the same second.

Talos and Cyrion butchered their way onward.

The whispering continued. A chorus of soft voices exchanged words and laughter, each of them like silken mist on the ears, even through the hiss of vox distortion.

Variel had been listening to it for almost half an hour, his casual interest becoming keen attention, quickly evolving into rapt focus. Septimus watched the Apothecary more often than he watched the hololithic now. Variel's colourless lips never stopped moving, softly mouthing the alien words as he translated them in his mind.

'What are–' Septimus tried again, only to be silenced by a raised fist. Variel made ready to backhand him if he spoke again.

'Deltrian,' the Apothecary said after several heartbeats had passed.

'Flayer,' acknowledged the adept.

'The game has changed. Get me within vox reach of Tsagualsa's surface.'

Deltrian's eye lenses rotated and refocused in their sockets. 'I request a reason for a course of action in utter opposition to our orders and planned processes.'

Variel was still distracted, listening to the breathy purring of eldar language. Septimus thought it sounded like a song of sorts, sung by those who hoped no one hears their voices. It was beautiful, yet it still made his skin crawl.

'The game has changed,' Variel repeated. 'How could we have known? We couldn't. We could never have guessed this.' He turned around the humble command deck, his ice-blue eyes looking through everything, alighting on nothing.

Deltrian was unfazed by Variel's distant murmurs. 'I restate my request, altering the terms to make it a demand. Provide adequate reasoning, or cease your vocalisation of orders you have no authority to give.'

Variel finally fixed his gaze on something – specifically, Deltrian, in his red robes of office, with his chrome skull face half-hidden in the folds of his hood.

'The eldar,' said Variel. 'They whisper of their own prophecies, of the Eighth Legion bleeding them without mercy in the decades that follow. Do you understand? They are not here because of Talos's psychic scream. They have never once spoken of it. They speak of nothing but our foolishness and their need to sever the strands of an unwanted future from the skeins of fate.'

Deltrian made an error-abort sound, in his equivalent of a dismissive grunt. 'Enough,' the adept said. 'Alien witchery is irrelevant. Xenos superstition is irrelevant. Our orders are all that remains relevant.'

Variel's eyes were distant again. He was listening to the aliens' sibilant voices sing in their whispery tongue.

'No.' He blinked, staring at the adept once more. 'You do not understand. They seek to prevent some future… some event yet to come, where Talos leads the Eighth Legion in a crusade against their dying species. They chant of it, like children offering prayers in the hope of a god taking pity upon them. Do you hear me? Are you listening to the words I speak?'

Septimus backed away as Variel walked to stare down at the seated adept. He'd never seen Variel's blood up like this.

'They fight to prevent a future that frightens them,' he said through clenched teeth. 'One they cannot allow to come to pass. These ships… This is a vast risk for them. A colossal gamble. They've backed us into a corner, using ships crewed by spirits, saving their precious alien lives for the final blow. *That* is how much they need Talos dead.'

Deltrian repeated the negative sound. 'Purely supposition based on xenos whisperings.'

'And if they're right? The Prophet of the Eighth Legion will rise at the end of the Dark Millennium and bleed the Ulthwéan eldar far beyond what their dwindling population can sustain. Are you so blind and deaf to everything outside your work that you can't hear my words? Listen to me, you heathen warlock: in these futures they've seen, he brings the Legion itself against them. These alien dogs believe he *unites* the Eighth Legion.'

Loader Primaris Marlonah secured herself in the restraint throne, shaking hands fumbling with the buckles. *Click*, went the first lock. *Click*, went the second. She didn't know it, but she was mumbling and swearing to herself as she worked.

Dumb luck had found her on the primary crew decks rather than at her station when the battle took a turn for the worst. She'd been on her way back to the starboard tertiary munitions deck, after an emergency discharge from the apothecarion in the wake of another malfunction in her augmetic leg.

The limb itself was still a bit of a bitch. She doubted she'd ever get used to it, no matter what the sawbones said.

The sirens screamed before she'd even managed to hobble halfway back to her duty shift. These weren't the rapid pulses of a call to battle stations, or the long caterwauling of pre-warp flight readiness. She'd never heard this siren before, but she knew what it was the moment it started screaming.

Evacuation.

Panic flooded the decks, with crew running in every direction. She'd been close enough that even her limping run kept her ahead of the pack, but the corridors leading to the pod bays were choked by the many dozens of souls that had been even faster, even closer, or even luckier.

When her time had come, she was a trembling, sweating wreck that fairly spilled into the last throne inside the pod. Outside the pod's closing doors, people were shouting and beating on the walls. Some were trampling each other. Others were stabbing and shooting, desperate to get to the pods before the ship's remains made one brutal bitch of a crater in the grey landscape.

Even through her relief as the last buckled *click*, she felt the ache of sympathy for those still trapped outside, hunting for pods. She couldn't look away from their faces and fists, pressed to the dense glass.

As she watched, mouthing the word 'sorry' to each pair of eyes she met, the clamouring faces were swept aside in a blur of cold blue and wet red. Blood smeared across the viewing glass, while shadows danced beyond, just out of sight.

'What the...' one of the other crew members stammered from his seat in the opposite restraint throne.

The door shuddered in a way no amount of beating fists and yelled curses had managed to inflict. The second time was worse: it shook to its reinforced hinges.

It came away the third time, letting in a burst of sickeningly hot air, and revealing a scene from a carcass pit.

Two of the masters stood outside, ankle-deep in the dead, their blades dripping with blood. One of them hunched down to enter the confines of the pod. No thrones remained untaken, and even if they had been free, none of the Legion could fit their bulky armoured forms into a human restraint throne.

There was no debate, no hesitation. The Night Lord rammed his golden sword through the chest of the closest human, ending any resistance, and dragged the spasming body from its seat. The harnesses snapped as the Legionary pulled with one, hard tug, before hurling the body outside into the corridor to lie amongst the slain.

The second Legionary entered, his armour joints snarling as he mimicked the first murder. The second man to die shamed himself by weeping and begging before he was cut apart. Two of the restraint thrones followed, torn from their moorings and hurled out into the corridor. The towering figures meant to empty the pod in order to create the room they needed to stand within it.

Marlonah was scrambling to unlock her restraints when the third man was killed and thrown outside.

'I'll get out!' she was yelling. 'I'll get out, *I'll get out* – I swear I will.'

She looked up as the hunched shadow fell across her, blocking out the dim red illumination from the central emergency light.

'I know you,' the master growled in his vox-voice. 'Septimus argued with one of the human surgeons to grant you that leg.'

'Yes... Yes...' She thought she was agreeing. In truth, she had no idea whether she was even speaking aloud.

The Night Lord reached to slam the reinforced door closed, leaving the bloodbath on the other side.

'Go,' he growled to his brother.

The other warrior, who was forced to stand stooped in the same half-crouch, reached to the central column and pulled the release levers – one, *crunch*; two, *crunch*; three, *crunch*.

The pod lurched in its cradle, and the whine of its propulsion systems became a forlorn roar.

When the escape pod fell, Marlonah felt the floor drop out from under her in the same moment that her stomach tried to find a new home in her throat. She wasn't sure if she was screaming or laughing as they rattled their way down to safety, but in actuality, she was doing both.

DELTRIAN HAD TO admit, he was struggling to make a decision. Talos had demanded a set process of actions from him, but the Apothecary (while grotesquely emotional) made a persuasive case.

And yet it still came down to practicalities and probability. Deltrian knew this better than anyone.

'To process the odds of this vessel surviving a direct

engagement with the enemy fleet requires a calculation few biological minds would be able to comprehend. Suffice to say, in terms you will understand, the odds are not in our favour.'

Had he been able to smile sincerely rather than as a natural by-product of a metallic skull for a face, Deltrian would probably have grinned in that moment. He was extremely proud of his mastery of understatement.

Variel wasn't moved, nor was he amused. 'Focus the cogs and gears that rattle behind your eyes,' he said. 'If the eldar are so fearful of this prophecy coming to pass, then it means there's a chance Talos *does* survive the war down there. And *we* are that chance. My brother has a destiny beyond a miserable death in the dust of this worthless world, and I mean to give him the chance to seize it.'

Deltrian's emotionless facade didn't even alter. 'Talos's final orders are all that remain relevant,' he stated. 'This vessel is now the gene-seed repository for over one hundred slain legionaries of the Eighth. This genetic material must reach the Great Eye. That is my oath to Talos. My sworn promise.' Those last words made him acutely uncomfortable.

'You run, then. I will not.' Variel turned back to Septimus. 'You. The Seventh.'

'Lord?'

'Ready your gunship. Get me down to Tsagualsa.'

XXIV

CATACOMBS

Ten thousand years ago, the fortress stood defiant as one of the last great bastions of Legiones Astartes invincibility in the material universe. The coming of the Primogenitors made a lie of that claim. The centuries since had been no kinder. Jagged, eroded battlements thrust up from the lifeless earth, broken by ancient explosives and the bite of a million dust storms.

Little remained of the fortress's great walls beyond hills of rubble, half-swallowed by the grey soil. Where the battlements still existed, they were toothless and tumbledown things, devoid of grandeur, brought low to the ground with the passing of the years.

Talos stood in the grey ruins, watching the *Echo of Damnation* die. Grit in the wind crackled against his armour as he stood in the open, surrounded by defanged, fallen walls. The warship made an agonisingly slow dive towards the horizon, shedding wreckage as it burned, trailing a thick plume of smoke.

'How many were still on the ship?' asked a female voice at his side. Talos didn't glance down at her; he'd forgotten Marlonah was still there. The fact she'd even considered the question was the starkest difference between them both in that moment.

'I don't know,' he said. The truth was that he didn't care. His masters had made him into a weapon. He felt no guilt at the loss of his humanity, even when it caught him by surprise in times like these.

The *Echo of Damnation* went down behind the southern mountains. Talos saw the flash of its reactor flare going critical, lighting the sky like a second sunset for a single, painful heartbeat.

'One,' he counted. 'Two. Three. Four. Five.'

A roll of thunder broke above them, fainter than the voice of a true storm, but all the sweeter for it.

'The *Echo*'s final cry,' Cyrion said from behind.

Talos nodded. 'Come. The eldar will be on us soon.'

The two warriors walked past their downed escape pod, through the uneven remnants of the landscape left by the erosion. Marlonah kept pace as best she could, watching them hunting through the broken buildings and ruined walls, seeking an uncollapsed tunnel that would lead deeper into the labyrinth.

After several minutes, they came across an empty Legion drop-pod, its paint seared off during descent, and its doors open in full bloom. It had shattered through a weak roof in what had once been a large domed chamber. Little else but two walls and a span of arcing ceiling remained, like the filthy ruins discovered by xeno-archaeologists on long-dead worlds. What was left of their grand fortress looked like nothing more than the remains of a dead civilisation, unearthed millennia after a great extinction.

Marlonah heard the clicking of the two warriors conversing over their helm voxes.

'Can I come with you?' she mustered the courage to ask.

'That is unwise,' Cyrion told her. 'If you wish to live, your best chance at survival is making the three-week journey south, towards the city we allowed to survive. If the scream was loud enough, the Imperium will come one night, and save those souls.'

She didn't know what any of that meant. All she knew was that there was no way she'd survive walking for three weeks with no food and no water, let alone make it through the dust storms.

'Cy,' said the other Night Lord. 'Does it matter if she follows us?'

'Fine then.'

'Descend into the catacombs if you wish, human,' said Talos. 'Just remember that our own lives are measured in mere hours. Death will come quicker than in the desert of dust, and we cannot afford to linger with you. We have a battle to fight.'

Marlonah tested her aching knee. The bionic was throbbing where it joined to her leg.

'I can't stay up here. Will there be places to hide?'

'Of course,' Talos replied. 'But you'll be blind. There's no light where we're going.'

SEPTIMUS LISTENED TO the engines whining into life. Nowhere else was as comfortable for him as the very seat he now occupied – the pilot's throne of the Thunderhawk gunship *Blackened*.

Variel sat in the co-pilot's throne, still unhelmed, staring off into the middle distance. Once in a while, he'd absently reach to run a thumb along his pale lips, lost in thought.

'Septimus,' he said, as the engines cycled live.

'Lord?'

'What are the chances of us reaching Tsagualsa undetected?'

The serf couldn't even begin to guess. 'I... know nothing about the eldar, lord, or their scanning technology.'

Variel was clearly still distracted. '*Blackened* is small, and the void is close to infinite in scope and span. Play to those advantages. Stay close to the asteroids.'

Septimus checked the bay doors ahead. Beyond the gunship and several stacks of what Deltrian insisted was essential equipment, there was precious little room in *Epsilon K-41 Sigma Sigma A:2*'s only landing bay. Even the Thunderhawk was loaded with vital supplies and relic machinery from the Hall of Reflection, denying any room for extra crew. Deltrian was less than thrilled to see it departing.

There'd been no time to speak with Octavia. A short vox message to her private chamber was all he'd been able to arrange, and he'd barely known what to say, anyway. How best to tell her he was probably going to die down there, after all? What would reassure her that Deltrian would protect her once they reached the Great Eye?

In the end, he'd mumbled in his usual awkward tone, in a mixed mess of Gothic and Nostraman. He tried to tell her he loved her, but even in that inspiration deserted him. It was hardly an elegant declaration of emotion.

She'd not replied. He still didn't even know if she'd received the message at all. Perhaps that was for the best.

Septimus triggered the launch cycle, closing the forward gangramp. It shut beneath the cockpit with a mechanical slam.

'We're sealed and ready,' he said.

Variel still seemed to be paying little attention. 'Go.'

Septimus gripped the control levers, feeling his skin prickle as the engines shouted harder in sympathy. With a deep breath, he guided the gunship out from the confined hangar bay, and back out into the void.

'Have you considered the fact you might be wrong?' he asked the Flayer. 'Wrong about Talos surviving, I mean.'

The Apothecary nodded. 'It has crossed my mind, slave. That possibility is something else that interests me.'

TIME PASSED IN darkness, but not silence.

Talos viewed the subterranean world through a red veil, his eye lenses piercing the lightless corridors without strain. Tactical data in tiny white runes scrolled in an endless stream down the edges of his vision. He paid no heed to any of it, beyond the healthy signals of his brothers' life signs.

Tsagualsa had never been home. Not in truth. Returning to walk its forgotten halls bred a certain uneasy melancholy, but nothing of sorrow, or of rage.

The human serf hadn't remained with them for long. They'd outpaced her limping stride in a matter of minutes, ghosting through the corridors as they tracked their brethren's vox-signals. For a time, Talos had heard her shouting and weeping in the dark, far behind them. He saw Cyrion shiver, surely a physical reaction to her fear, and felt the acid tang of corrosive saliva on his tongue. He didn't like to be reminded of his brother's corruption, even as subtle and unobtrusive as it was.

'She'd have been better off on the plains,' Cyrion voxed.

Talos didn't reply. He led the way through the tunnels, listening to the vox-net alive with so many voices. His brothers in the other Claws were laughing, making ready, swearing oaths to bleed the eldar dry before they finally fell themselves.

He smiled behind his faceplate, amused by all he heard. The remnants of Tenth and Eleventh Companies were on the edge of death, cornered like vermin, yet he'd never heard them sound so alive.

Malcharion reported that he was alone, walking through the tunnels closest to the surface. When the claws protested and argued they should fight alongside him, he'd cursed them for fools and severed his vox-link.

They found Mercutian and Uzas before the first hour fully passed. The former embraced Talos, wrist-to-wrist in greeting. The latter stood in mute inattention, breathing heavily over the vox. They could all hear Uzas licking his teeth.

'The other Claws are getting ready to make their stands in similar chambers.' Mercutian gestured to the northern and southern doorways – open now that the doors themselves had long since rotted away to memory.

Talos took his brother's point: the two entrances would make the chamber relatively easy to defend compared to many others of comparable size, while still giving them room to move. He followed Mercutian's second gesture, indicating a crawlspace high in the western wall that had once been an access point to the maintenance ducts. 'When they fall back, they'll move through the service tunnels.'

'Will we fit?' Cyrion was checking his bolter with meticulous care. 'They were built for servitors. When we left this place, half the ducts were too small for us.'

'I've scouted the closest ones,' said Mercutian. 'There are several dead ends where we can't make it through, but there are always alternate routes. Our only other choice is to dig through the countless collapsed tunnels.'

Talos took in the whole chamber. It had once belonged to another company, used as a training hall. Nothing remained of the room's former decoration. When viewed through the red wash of his eye lenses, Talos saw nothing but bleak, bare stone. The rest of the catacombs looked no different. The entire labyrinth was the same naked, hollow ruin.

'Our ammunition?'

Mercutian nodded again. 'Already done. The servitors who came down in the other pods landed close to the claws. As for gunships, it's less obvious which ones made it down. Our mules are down here, and safe. I'll take you to them; they're idling in a chamber half a kilometre to the west. With so many tunnels collapsed between here and there, it's quicker to take the maintenance ducts.'

'They made it, then,' Cyrion said. 'A slice of precious luck, at last.'

'Many didn't,' Talos amended, 'if the vox is anything to go by. But we've smuggled enough ammunition down here to give the eldar a thousand new funeral songs.'

'Is our primary cargo intact?' Cyrion asked.

For once, it was Uzas who answered. 'Oh, yes. I'm looking forward to that part.'

As First Claw made their way in ragged, hunched formation, clattering their way down the service ducts, Talos heard the first report of battle over the vox.

'This is Third Claw,' came the voice, still coloured by laughter. 'Brothers, the aliens have found us.'

SEPTIMUS HUNTED FOR the right touch. Speed was of the essence, but he had to fly close to every asteroid – hugging them, staying in their shadows wherever possible, before sprinting to the next closest. Beyond that, which was easily enough to worry about already, he was careful not to push the engines too hard in case the eldar vessels now stationed in high orbit above the fortress had the capacity to detect their presence via heat signature.

They'd only been flying for ten minutes when Variel closed his eyes, shaking his head in gentle disbelief.

'We have been boarded,' the Flayer said softly, to no one in particular. Bootsteps from behind forced Septimus to crane his neck to look over his shoulder. The gunship slowed in response to his wavering attention.

Three of Octavia's attendants stood by the doorway leading into the confined cockpit. He recognised Vularai at once; the others were most likely Herac and Folly, though their ragged cloaks and bandaged hands meant they could be almost anyone.

Septimus looked back at the windshield, bringing the gunship in a slow bank around another small rock. Smaller dust particles ceaselessly rattled against the hull.

'You stowed aboard before we left?' he asked.

'Yes,' said one of the males.

'Did she send you?' Septimus asked.

'We obey the mistress,' replied the one who was probably Herac. In fairness, they all sounded similar, too. Voices didn't always make it any easier to tell them apart.

Variel's unwholesome blue eyes fixed on Vularai. The attendant was wrapped in a thick cloak, and though she wore her glare-goggles, the bandaging around her face and arms was loose and hanging in places, revealing pale skin beneath.

'That deception would fool a disinterested Mechanicum menial,' Variel said, 'but it is almost tragically comical to attempt the same with me.'

Vularai started to unwrap her bandaging, freeing her hands. Septimus risked another glance over his shoulder.

'*Fly.*' Variel's eyes were enough of a threat. 'Focus on your duty.'

Vularai let the wrappings fall at last, and cast aside the heavy cloak. She reached up to her face, removed the glare-goggles and checked her bandana was in place.

'You're not leaving me alone on that piece of crap ship, with that mechanical abomination,' said Octavia. 'I'm coming with you.'

DELTRIAN MADE HIS way to Octavia's chamber in the vessel's bulbous belly, seeking to contain any traces of irritation from manifesting in his movements or vocalisations.

When he'd given the order to his servitor-pilots to make their way through the asteroid field, all had been well.

When he'd calculated the best prospective location to risk entering the warp without attracting attention from eldar raiders *or* risking a hull breach from accidental collision during acceleration and reality dispersion, all had still been well.

When he'd ordered the warp engines to begin opening the tear in the fabric of the material void, all had still been well.

When he'd ordered Octavia to ready herself, and received no reply of confirmation… he encountered the first flaw in an otherwise perfect process.

Repeated attempts to contact her elicited the same response.

Unacceptable.

Truly, utterly unacceptable.

He'd ordered the vessel back into hiding, and started to make his way down to her chamber himself.

A handful of her attendants scampered aside from his hurried advance down the corridor. That in itself would have been curious to anyone that knew the Navigator well, but Deltrian was not such a soul.

His thin fingers overrode the lock on her bulkhead, and he stepped into the cramped chamber, standing before the cabled throne.

'You,' he said, preparing to initiate a long and accusatory tirade, centred on themes of obedience and duty, with subsidiary aspects of self-preservation to appeal to her biological fear of corporeal demise.

Vulari sat back in Octavia's throne with her boots up on the armrest. Without her bandaging, she was a wretched thing – anaemic flesh showed the veins underneath, swollen and black like cobwebs beneath the thinnest skin. Her eyes were watery, half-blinded by cataracts, and ringed by dark circles.

For several seconds, Deltrian catalogued a list of visual mutations in the woman he was seeing before him. Her warp-changes seemed subtle by some standards, but the overall effect was a fascinating one: beneath her thin flesh, it was possible to see the shadow of bones, veins, muscle clusters and even the beating silhouette of her heart, moving in disharmony with her swelling, contracting lungs.

'You are not Octavia,' he vocalised.

Vularai grinned, showing scabby gums populated by cheap iron teeth. 'What gave it away?'

TALOS WAS LAST to enter the chamber. The prophet panned his gaze around the empty hall again, alighting at last on the only other living souls. Fifteen servitors stood in slack-jawed repose, too dead of mind to be considered truly patient. Almost all of them had their arms replaced by lifter claws or machine tools.

First Claw moved over to the stowage crates the lobotomised slaves had hauled down into the depths.

Talos was the first to pull something forth. He held a massive cannon in his gauntlets – a lengthy, multi-barrelled weapon rarely used by the Eighth Legion.

With a glance at the closest servitors, he dumped the cannon back in its crate. It rested atop a ceramite breastplate, densely armoured and proudly displaying its aquila shattered with ritual care.

'We don't have long,' he said. 'Let's get this started.'

XXV

SHADOWS

THEY GHOSTED DOWN the corridor, blacker than the shadows that shielded them. His eyes weren't what they once were – relying on movement as much as shape – but he watched them draw nearer, moving in a haunting, sinuous unity he could only call alien. *Alien*. While the term was accurate, even as the creatures bore down on him, he felt the term lacked a certain poetry.

He knew little about this xenos breed. They burst the same as any human under the grinding hail of autocannon fire, which was reassuring but hardly a surprise. Watching them shatter and crumble in wet showers told him very little he didn't already know.

Had he been able, he'd crouch over one of their corpses, peeling the broken armour back, and learn all he needed in a feast of flesh. With the taste of blood on his lips, his enhanced physiology would infuse him with instinctive knowledge about the fallen prey. In an existence he still barely understood, the pleasure of tasting fallen foes' lost lives was one of the things he missed most of all.

Eldar. He admired them for their disciplined silence even as he found their bending grace repulsive. One of them, evidently unprotected by its fragile interlocking plates, burst across the left wall in a wet slap of gore and clattering armour.

He couldn't kill them all with the sluggish cannon

that served as his arm. Several of the aliens ducked and weaved beneath his arc of fire, conjuring chainblades into their thin-fingered hands.

The Night Lord laughed. At least, he tried to. He gagged on the pipes and wires impaling his mouth and throat, while the sound emerged as a gear-shifting grind.

With no hope of outrunning them, he still needed to step back to brace himself. The feeling of them chopping and carving at his vulnerable joints was an unusual one – without pain, without *skin*, the sensation became an almost amusing dull scrape. He couldn't make out individual figures when they were this close, but the corridor lightning-bolted with sparks from the blades chewing into his connective joints.

'Enough of that,' he grunted, and lashed down with his other fist. The servos and cable-muscles of his new body lent strength and speed beyond anything he'd known in life. The fist hammered into the stone floor, shaking the entire corridor and breeding a rain of dust from the ceiling. The alien wretch caught beneath his downswing was a pulped ruin, smeared across the ground.

Malcharion turned on his waist axis, lashing out again, crushing with his fist even as it spewed liquid fire from its mounted flamer. The aliens weaved back, but not fast enough. Two died beneath his pounding fist; one wailed as it dissolved in the torrent of corrosive fire.

The Dreadnought breathed in deep, inhaling the scent of the now empty corridor. Instead of cold air filling his lungs with the scent of murder, he felt the oxygen-rich fluid of his coffin bubbling with his breath, and smelled nothing at all beyond the chemical stink-taste of his tepid confines.

When he shivered, it translated as his metal body juddering, reloading his autocannon with a *clunk* and a *click*. When he sighed, it left his sarcophagus as a machine's snarl.

Temptation almost made him open the vox-net again,

but the fawning regard of those he'd once commanded was an irritant he had no desire to deal with. Instead, he hunted alone, stealing what pleasure he could from how things had changed.

Malcharion moved around the slender corpses, his waddling stalk shaking the tunnel with each tread. Without hope of stealth, he had to play a different game.

'Eldar...' he growled. **'I come for you.'**

LUCORYPHUS CROUCHED ATOP the ruined battlements, watching the sky. He could hear his brothers eating the eldar behind him, but hadn't partaken himself. He'd eaten their flesh before, and felt no compulsion to repeat the experience. Their blood was thin and sour, and their skin lacked any of the salty richness found in a mouthful of human meat.

The leader of the Bleeding Eyes wasn't sure where the eldar were appearing from. Despite maintaining a vigil of the sky and refusing to descend into the catacombs, he'd seen no sign of alien landing craft. Yet they kept appearing, here and there, moving from behind broken walls or manifesting atop fallen spires.

The fortress ruins spread for kilometres in every direction. He knew his Raptors couldn't cover all that ground alone, though he drove them hard, making the attempt. What confused him most of all was that the aliens didn't seem to be appearing in the numbers he'd been expecting. They had enough ships in the void above to land an army. Instead, he was witnessing small fire teams and scout parties descending into the labyrinth, and butchering those few that remained on the surface.

The thrusters on his back gave a sympathetic whine in response to his musing.

'Ghost ships,' he said.

Only one of the Bleeding Eyes bothered to look up from their meal. 'You speak?' Vorasha hissed.

Lucoryphus gestured upward with a deactivated lightning claw. 'Ghost ships. Vessels of bone and soul in the void. No crew but the ghosts of dead eldar.'

'Ulthwé,' Vorasha said, as if that was agreement enough.

'Silent ships, piloted by bones, captained by memories. An unbreakable armada in the heavens, but on the ground?' His head jerked with a muscle tic. 'They are not so strong. Not so numerous. Now we know why they owned the heavens, but fear the earth.'

The Raptor breathed slowly, inhaling the planet's unhealthy air through his mouth grille. Mist rose with each exhalation.

'I see something,' he said.

'More eldar?' asked one of the pack.

'A shadow within another shadow. There,' he pointed to the overhang of a rotted stone building. 'And there. And there. Many somethings, it seems.'

When the challenge came, it was given in a tongue Lucoryphus couldn't understand, shouted from a throat he ached to slit. The eldar warrior knelt atop a wall two hundred metres away, a crescent blade in one hand, and great eagle wings arcing up from his shoulder blades.

As soon as the cry carried across the air, another four winged figures revealed themselves, each one crouched atop a broken tower or ruined wall.

'Bleeding Eyes,' Lucoryphus whispered to his kin. 'At last, some prey worth hunting.'

UZAS AND MERCUTIAN were first. With none of the Mechanicum's blessings or prayers, it took significantly less time for them to get ready. While they waited, Talos and Cyrion stood watch in the northern and southern tunnels, listening to the sounds of battle carrying over the vox.

'Armour primed,' Mercutian voxed to Talos. 'Uzas is ready, too.'

'That took almost half an hour,' Cyrion noted. 'Still not a rapid process, even without the Machine Cult's ramblings.'

'It's fast enough,' Talos replied. 'Mercutian, Uzas, cover us.'

Talos waited until a low, industrial grinding sound echoed down the tunnel. The fall of each bootstep was a roll of thunder.

'Your turn,' came Uzas's vox-altered growl. The new helm was a muzzled and tusked visage, sporting eye lenses of ruby red and a painted daemon skull. The armour itself emitted a constant, guttural hum, and was wide enough to fill half the corridor on its own.

'How does it feel?' Talos asked his brother.

Uzas stood straighter, against the war plate's natural hunch, and the power generators hummed louder. In one hand, he held a new-model storm bolter, the aquila markings defiled by scratches or melted away completely. His other arm ended in a power fist, the thick fingers crunching closed in reverse bloom.

On one shoulder, the broken draconic symbol of the Salamanders Chapter was buried beneath a bronze icon of the Eighth Legion, hammered into place by thick steel rivets.

'It feels powerful,' said Uzas. 'Now hurry. I wish to hunt.'

SHE ANSWERED HIM, shriek for shriek and blade for blade. The Bleeding Eyes took to the air on howling thrusters, filling the sky with filthy exhaust fumes in their pursuit of their prey. The eldar, armoured in contoured war plate of innocent blue, replied to the hateful shrieking with war-calls of their own – each one a piercing, dismissive cry.

The fight was an ugly one; Lucoryphus knew how it would play out the moment they first clashed. The eldar ran and the Raptors gave chase. Most of the alien skymaidens were armed with slender, tapered laser rifles, spitting out coruscating stabs of energy. They needed distance to use them, while the Raptors filled the sky with the clatter of short-range bolt pistols and the desperate whine of slashing chainblades eating air and going hungry.

The first to fall from the sky was his brother Tzek. Lucoryphus heard the death rattle over the vox – a choking gargle from bloody lungs and a ruptured throat – followed by the spiralling whine of engines failing to fire. The Raptor twisted in the air, keeping his own foe back by lashing out with his clawed feet, just in time to see Tzek's body crash into the uneven ground.

The sight caused his tongue to ache, filling his mouth with hissing ichor. Tzek had been with him down the many years of twisted time, since the first night of the Last Siege. To see such a noble soul broken by alien filth made him angry enough to spit.

The eldar leaned back, hawkish wings vibrating with a melodic chime as she flipped in the air, swooping as true and elegantly as a bird of prey. The gobbet of corrosive slime missed her completely.

Lucoryphus followed her, engines roaring and breathing smoke in opposition to her musical glide. Each cut from his claws sliced nothing more than air, as the alien bitch danced back, diving and arcing aside, seeming to soar on thermals.

The Raptor released the frustrated scream he could no longer contain. Either the wind stole much of its potency, or her sloping, crested helm inured her to burst eardrums, for she ignored it completely.

She soared higher, spinning through the sky, her blade trailing electric fire. Lucoryphus of the Bleeding Eyes chased her, his fanged maw screaming as loudly as his protesting engines.

Her grace counted only when she danced through the air; in a straight and honest chase, he had her dead. They both realised it in the same moment. Lucoryphus caught her from behind, carving through her wings with his lightning-kissed claws. They cleaved through the alien-forged material, crippling her in mid-flight.

With another war cry, she twisted in the air, bringing her sword to bear even as she started to fall. The Raptor parried her blade, letting it rasp against his charged talons. His free hand gripped her throat, keeping her aloft and in his arms for a precious second more.

'Goodnight, my sweet,' he breathed into her faceplate. Lucoryphus released her, letting her tumble from the sky in mirror of Tzek's ignoble demise.

His laugh died as soon as it began. She'd not fallen more than three seconds before one of her kin caught her at the end of a swooping dive, angling down to bear her to the ground.

'I think not,' the Raptor hissed, leaning forward into a dive of his own. He could hear them over the wind, shouting to one another in their babbling tongue. He had to bank sharply to avoid her pistol spitting its jagged light back up at him, but with the eldar's erstwhile saviour encumbered, they had no chance of outrunning the Raptor's second assault. Lucoryphus hit them both like a bolt from above, latching his claws into both torsos and tearing the two figures apart.

He screamed at the effort it took, his rapturous shriek echoing across the sky. The wingless maiden went one way, falling and spinning down through the air to crash in a mangled heap, smeared over the ground. The male fell in similar reflection, blood raining from the wounds in his breastplate. His wings quivered, seeking a final flight, but the drying blood on Lucoryphus's claws told the last of that particular tale. The Raptor sneered as the eldar struck the earth, flopping over the rocks as he came to pieces in the tumbling impact.

He was still smiling when he turned in time to see Vorasha die next. His brother fell back from a mid-air grapple, his body raining meat and shards of armour-plating as it plummeted. The eldar who'd shot Vorasha at point-blank range turned in the air, bringing his rifle up to aim at Lucoryphus.

The Raptor leader tilted forward and boosted closer, another shriek leaving his scarred lips.

Talos led First Claw through the corridors in a new kind of hunt. With no need to heed any caution, the four Terminators thudded their way onward in a loose phalanx, unfamiliar weapons aimed at the ready.

'This will take some getting used to,' Cyrion voxed. He was still bemused at the aquila showing on the edge of his retinal display. In Deltrian's many modifications and reconfigurings, he'd evidently not managed to scrub that detail from the armour's internal systems.

Talos was distracted by the vox-net; the reports of Second and Third Claws engaging the enemy higher up in the catacombs, and the Bleeding Eyes' savage curses as they fought on the surface. He tried not to wonder what Malcharion was doing – the captain had decided to die alone, and he couldn't find flaw with that desire. First Claw would have to split up soon enough. Once unified resistance became impossible against greater numbers, it would come down to murder in the dark, and every soul for himself.

He'd never worn Tactical Dreadnought war plate before, and the sensation was a surprising one. His battle armour was as familiar as his own skin, and as comfortable as clothing once wearer and suit bonded over time. Terminator plate was a different beast from tusked helm to spiked boots; every muscle in his body felt revitalised, stinging with strength. He'd expected to feel sluggish, but the range of motion and speed of movement was little different from the times he'd trained out of his armour. The only disconcerting aspect was the forward-leaning hunch, leaving him always on the edge of breaking into a run.

Talos had tried running. It resulted in a quicker, more forceful tread that was somewhere between a stagger and a sprint. Compensatory servos and stabilisers wouldn't allow him to pitch forward and fall, though the shift in the centre of his balance still felt unusual after so many centuries crusading in his modified Mark V plate.

One of his hands was an armoured glove the size of a legionary's torso – the power fist active and rippling with a passive force field. The other clutched a heavy rotary cannon, his finger resting on the curved trigger. They didn't have much ammunition for the assault cannon. When First Claw scavenged the suits from the Salamanders, they soon learned the Imperials had used most of their reserves. He carried his double-barrelled bolter locked to his thigh, ready to draw it the moment he dumped the empty cannon.

Mercutian reached with his oversized power fist, tapping at the ornate tusks Deltrian had grafted to the muzzle of his bullish helm.

'I once saw Malek of the Atramentar head-butt someone with his tusks,' he said. 'I'd like to try that.'

Talos held up a fist for silence – or as close as they could come to silence while in suits of armour rumbling like the idling engines of four battle tanks.

A hail of razor-edged discs sliced out from the corridor ahead, followed by the advancing forms of eldar warriors. They hesitated in their tracks when they saw what was stalking towards them. Several of them scattered, while others fell back, still firing. Talos heard the shuriken projectiles clattering against his armour, with the same tinkling sound of glass shards breaking on the floor.

In reply, he squeezed his trigger, filling the tunnel with the distinctive flashing roar of an Imperial assault cannon. Suspensors in his elbow, wrist and the gun's grip counterbalanced any recoil, letting him aim without distraction, but his retinal feed had to dim to compensate for the brightness of the muzzle flash.

First Claw stood in disbelief ten seconds later. Talos tilted the cannon to get a better look at its steaming, reddening barrels.

'Now *that's* a cannon,' said Cyrion, as the four of them waded through the organic mess left in the corridor. 'Can I use it for a while?'

MARLONAH WASN'T SURE what she was hearing anymore. Sometimes the stone hallways echoed with what sounded like distant gunfire, other times it seemed like nothing more than the wind, weaving through the dark at her side.

She had a lamp pack – no crew member on an Eighth Legion vessel would walk a ship's halls without one – and she knew the power cell would be good for another few hours at least. What she didn't know was what to do, or where to go.

Does is make a difference? What does it matter if I die down here or on the plains?

She still had her stub gun, for what it was worth – a primitive little slug-thrower compared to a Legiones Astartes bolter, make no mistake. It'd be fine for shooting herself in the head before she died of thirst, but it wasn't much use if she walked into a battle. Slaves weren't permitted weapons on the *Echo of Damnation*, but the thriving black market trading going on in every level of life took care of that. The Legion never enforced such a law anyway, for they feared no uprising. She suspected they enjoyed a little spice to the challenge when they hunted crew members for sport, as well.

Marlonah wasn't sure how long she'd been alone before the thumping started. She made her way through the deserted catacombs, sending her torch beam ahead, letting it cut the blackness as best it could. All sense of direction had long since abandoned her. Sound echoed strangely down here, to the point she wasn't even sure whether she was heading towards the thumping or avoiding it completely. It never seemed to fade or grow any stronger.

She never saw what knocked the lamp pack from her grip. A breath of air passed by the back of her neck, and a rough impact against her hand sent the torch clattering to the ground. For a split second, its spinning beam sent insane shadows against the walls: the silhouettes of witch-thin figures with elongated, inhuman helms.

Marlonah went for her gun before the torch had fallen still. That, too, left her hand with what felt like a kick to her fist.

The second time she felt the breath, it was against her face. The voice emerging from the darkness was as unwelcomingly soft as velvet on bleeding skin.

'Where is the Prophet of the Eighth Legion?'

She aimed her fist at the voice in the blackness, but her punch met nothing but air. A second, third and fourth swiped through the same nothingness. She could hear the subtle movement and breathing of something dodging her in the dark, betrayed by the smooth scrape of armour plates sliding with every weave.

A hand bolted around her throat, collaring her with thin fingers sheathed in cold iron. She managed a single blow against the unmoving arm, before she was slammed back against the wall. Her boots scrabbled against the stone, unable to reach the ground. Her rough augmetic leg made clicking, whirring sounds as it struggled to find the floor.

'Where is the Prophet of the Eighth Legion?'

'I've lived my whole life in the dark,' she told the unseen voice. 'Do you think *this* scares me?'

The collar of fingers tightened enough to cut off her breath. She wasn't sure if the thumping was getting louder, or if she was being deceived by her own rising heartbeat.

'Filthy, blind, poisonous, cancerous mon-keigh animal. Where is the Prophet of the Eighth Legion? Thousands of souls remain at stake while he draws breath.'

Marlonah thrashed in the stronger grip, beating her fists against the armoured arm.

'Stubborn creature. Know this, human: the silent storm approaches. The Void Stalker comes.'

The clutch at her throat vanished as fast as it appeared, dropping her to the ground. The first thing she thought, as she heaved the stale air back into her body, was that her heartbeat hadn't lied. The thumping was all around her now, the thudding crunch of steel on stone. It sent trembles through the ground beneath her, and the wall against her back.

Marlonah scrabbled for her lamp wand, chopping its thin blade of illumination around the chamber. She saw stone, and stone, and stone, and... something immense, and dark, and leering down at her with rumbling joints.

'What are you doing down here?'

HE CAME IN too hard, at a bad angle, and tumbled across the dusty ground. It took a moment to haul himself back up to all-fours, and another two attempts to stand straight. His metallic foot-claws splayed to compensate, digging into the soft dust.

The pain was... quite something. He tasted blood with each breath, and the ache of his muscles put him in firm mind of the three nights he'd been racked by Lord Jiruvius of the Emperor's Children.

That hadn't been a pleasant war. Losing it had felt even worse.

Lucoryphus hadn't landed far from the last eldar. He walked over to her prone form, noting the trail of bloody fluid leaking from several of his armour joints. His war plate was an interesting display of battle cartography, marked by laser burns and punctures from the aliens' short bone-daggers.

The Raptor rolled the sky-maiden's corpse with his foot-claw. Her slanted eyes, as lifeless as sapphires and much the same colour, stared up into the grey heavens. On her chest was a smooth red jewel, named by her kindred as a soulstone. Lucoryphus tore it from the armour and swallowed it whole. He hoped her immortal spirit would enjoy its fate to dwell forever within his bowels.

'Soul Hunter,' he voxed at last.

The prophet's voice was flawed by distance distortion and gunfire crackles. 'I hear you, Lucoryphus.'

'The Bleeding Eyes are dead. I am the last.'

He heard Talos give a grunt of effort. 'It grieves me to hear that, brother. Will you join us down here?'

The Raptor looked to the fallen walls, the remnants of once-great battlements. Storm clouds were gathering above them – an anomaly on this weatherless world.

'Not yet. Something comes, Talos. Watch yourselves.'

XXVI

STORM

THE RAIN STARTED the very moment her boots touched the Tsagualsan soil.

Lucoryphus watched her from his tenuous perch, crouched on what remained of a long stretch of battlement wall. Five eldar soulstones sat cold in his guts. When he closed his eyes, even just to blink, he was certain he could hear five voices screaming in a lamenting dirge.

How curious, he thought, as she manifested. She stepped from a heat shimmer in the air itself, falling a dozen feet to land on her toes, with arms outspread. Her armour consisted of silver plating, shaped like slender musculature over a black bodysuit that shimmered like fish scales. In one hand was a staff – scimitar-bladed at both ends and wet with slow ripples of liquid lightning. In her other fist, she clutched a throwing star the size of a battle shield, ending in three hooked dagger blades. The fire that danced along the alien steel was black, forged through a craft Lucoryphus wasn't certain he wished to know.

Her face was shielded by a silver death mask, sculpted in the cold-eyed image of a screaming goddess. A high, long crest of black hair flowed down her shoulders and back, somehow immune to the wind sending dust-wraiths haunting through the ruins.

Everything about her radiated wrongness, even to a

creature as warp-touched as he. For several seconds, the heat haze remained around her, as if she were at risk of being rejected by reality.

This is no eldar maiden, the Raptor knew. *Perhaps she was, once. Now... she is something much more.*

Lucoryphus's claws tightened on the stone as the eldar war-goddess flew across the ground in a blurred sprint, her feet barely gracing the earth. One moment she was a silver blur in the ruins; the next she was gone, either vanished into thin air or descended underground – Lucoryphus wasn't certain.

'Talos.' He opened the vox-link again. 'I have seen what hunts us.'

SECOND CLAW HAD survived for over three hours in a series of running gunfights, repelling wave after wave of alien attackers. The only lights to flash down the tunnels and illuminate the chambers came from the staccato flicker of weapons fire, or the rare clash of opposing energy fields when a power sword met another of its kind.

Yuris was limping from the blade wound to his thigh. He knew his brothers would leave him behind soon. It wasn't a matter of needing to talk them into abandoning him, nor did it come down to something as noble as self-sacrifice. They'd leave him behind because he was getting slower, and getting weaker. His life had become a liability to theirs.

The Night Lord caught his breath with his back to a wall. He locked his bolter to his thigh for a moment, reloading it with a crunching smack, and only a single hand.

'My last,' he voxed to the other two survivors. 'I'm out of ammunition.'

'We'll fall back to the reserve crates,' replied Fal Torm. The truth was implicit in the other warrior's words: they would fall back to the ammunition reserves, but they'd almost certainly leave him behind. If Yuris's death bought them a few more seconds, then all the better.

'You're hurt worse than you're admitting,' said Xan Kurus. The backswept wings on Xan Kurus's helm had been shattered off hours before, broken away by an alien blade. 'I can smell your lifeblood, and hear the strain in your hearts.'

Yuris couldn't catch his breath. It was difficult to inhale, forcing air into a throat that felt too tight.

Is this what dying feels like?

'I'm still standing,' he voxed back. 'Come. Let's move.'

The three survivors of Second Claw retreated further into the dark, breaking into a ragged run. Mere hours before, Yuris had led nine other souls. Now he was the high and mighty lord over two warriors, both of whom were preparing to abandon him the moment the opportunity presented itself.

As with humans, all eldar were not created equal. Yuris had learned that at great cost. The ones with weak projectile rifles and thin armour of black plate and mesh weave – they died like weak children and shot with all the skill expected of any hive-born member drawn from humanity's urban dregs. But the others... The shrieking witches and the sword-killers...

Six warriors dead in three hours. The alien maidens would dissolve out of the dark, weaving past any gunfire, and lock blades with the Night Lords in a storm of blows. Whether they killed or not didn't seem to change their behaviour; as soon as the first blade clashes were done, they'd break away and flee back through the tunnels.

The howling was the worst part of every charge – they'd scream a dirge long and loud enough to wake the forgotten dead of this accursed world. Each howl knifed a sliver of ice right into the back of his head, doing something to his brain, slowing his reactions enough to leave him straining to parry every blow.

Ah, but Second Claw hadn't gone down easy. They were the hunters, after all. Yuris had slit three of the maidens' pale throats himself, grappling them from behind and ending them with a quick, sawing caress of his gladius.

Back and forth it went: charge, defend, hunt, slice, retreat…

Yuris stumbled in his run, his hand resting on the wall for balance. He'd run ahead of his brothers, but that soon became limping alongside them, and at last, limping and lagging behind.

'Goodbye, Yuris,' Xan Kurus voxed from up ahead. Fal Torm didn't even stop – he carried on at a dead sprint.

'Wait,' Yuris said to Xan Kurus. 'Wait, brother.'

'Why?' Xan Kurus was already running again. 'Die well.'

Yuris listened to his kindred's bootsteps growing fainter. His stumbling run devolved into a simple stagger, and he crashed against the wall, sliding down to his knees.

I don't want to die on Tsagualsa. The thought rose, sourceless and unbidden. Was Tsagualsa truly a worse place to die than any other?

Yes, he thought. *The carrion world is cursed. We should never have returned here.*

The ancient superstition brought a painful smile to his bloody lips. And what did it matter? He'd served, hadn't he? He'd served loyally down the centuries, and ripped pleasure from a galaxy that had never been able to deny him. *Until now…*

Yuris tried to grin again, but blood spilled from his mangled lips in a black gush.

No matter. No matter. It was a fine thing, to be alive and to be strong.

His helm tipped forward as that strength finally faded, seeping out with his blood.

'Yuris,' the vox crackled.

Begone, Fal Torm. Run ahead, if you wish. Let me die alone and in peace, bastards.

'Yuris,' the voice repeated.

He opened his eyes without realising they'd been closed. Red-tinted vision returned, showing his cracked breastplate and the stump where his left hand had been less than an hour before.

What? he asked, and had to make a second attempt to speak it out loud. 'What?' he voxed.

His retinal display feeds were white blurs of scrolling gibberish. Blinking twice brought them back into resolution.

Xan Kurus's life signals registered as a flatline. As did Fal Torm's.

That cannot be. Yuris forced himself to his feet, biting back a groan at the agony of his broken knee and missing hand. His armour's damage prevented it from flooding pain inhibitors into his bloodstream, only compounding his torment.

He found his last two brothers in the hallways ahead, and shook with suppressed laughter. Both bodies were sprawled across the stone floor, their ruination exacting and complete. Xan Kurus and Fal Torm were both cleaved in half at the waist, their bodies separated from their legs. Blood decorated the floor in patternless blotching.

Neither of them had a head. Their helms were free of their severed necks, released to roll against the wall once the corpses fell.

Yuris couldn't bite back the laughter. Despite abandoning him, they'd died before him, anyway. Even through the pain, the notion appealed to his sense of poetic justice.

The blade that killed Yuris struck first in the back, driving through his lower spine and bursting from the layered armour over his belly. Foul, glistening ropes of offal followed it out, as his insides tumbled in a sick heap at his boots.

Yuris managed to remain standing for another couple of heartbeats before the blade struck again. He saw it this time; a blur of spinning silver and burning black, slashing through the air quicker than a blink. It cleaved into his ripped stomach and tore out from his lower back, and this time Yuris fell to the ground with a cry and a crash.

For one grotesque moment, he found himself on his back, reaching with his one remaining hand to drag himself back over to his legs.

Then she was above him. The creature Lucoryphus had warned them about. His racing, firing, dying mind screamed at him to act. He had to vox the others. He had to warn them she was already down here.

But that didn't happen. He said nothing. He warned no one. Yuris opened his mouth, only to choke a hot flood of bile and blood down his neck.

The silent witch-queen lifted the spear cradled in her other hand, and lifted it high above. She said a single word in crude Gothic, her accent spicing it almost beyond recognition.

'Sleep.'

For Yuris, blessed blackness dawned at last, with the fall of an alien blade.

THE FIRST HOWLS had caught him unprepared. He wouldn't make that mistake again.

When First Claw linked up with Faroven's Third Claw, both squads readied to hold an expansive network of chambers for as long as they could, replete with annex rooms, fall back tunnels and defensible junctions.

'Have you seen Malcharion?' was Faroven's first question.

'He still hunts alone,' Talos had replied.

The screaming maidens came in the wake of those words. After fighting the weakling warriors of the last few hours, the shrieking assault had been an unpleasant change in pace and tactics. Still, it had at least stopped Cyrion from pining to use the assault cannon.

The first howls had caught them unprepared. Before the blade-witches attacked, they shrieked their mournful cries, using the song itself as a weapon. Immunity to fear meant nothing in that song's shadow – Talos felt his blood run cold, felt his muscles slowing, felt sweat break out at his temples, as his body reacted the way any terrified mortal's flesh might.

The sensation had been... incredible, almost intoxicating in its unnatural force. Like nothing he'd ever felt in all the long decades of his life. No soul enhanced by gene-seed could feel terror, yet even though the creeping doubt never touched his mind, the physical sensation of feeling fear still forced a laugh from his throat. To think *this* was a pale reflection of what he inflicted on those he killed? To sense it first-hand?

How educational, he'd thought, grinning his crooked grin. The amusement was admittedly dampened by the deadness in his limbs, and short-lived enough to burn away in his anger a moment later.

But the aliens were among them by then. They cut and cleaved and carved with their mirrored blades, savaging the ranks of the last two Night Lord claws left standing. They danced as they killed, as though performing some inhuman dance to music only they could hear. Each of their helms was sculpted into a shouting death mask, open mouths projecting the psychically amplified shriek.

A lovely trick, he thought, hating himself for admiring anything an alien breed could create.

As the prophet deflected a descending sword with the back of his armoured glove, he fancied – in his fever – he could sense the song's edges himself. The crash of blades on ceramite was the rapid clash of soft drums; the grunts and cries of his dying brothers became the rhythm beneath it.

'Be silent,' he snarled, backhanding the alien wretch with his power fist. Her shrieking ended along with her life: with a wet crack against the stone wall behind.

The eldar were gone as quickly as they'd come, fleeing back into the tunnels.

'They're not howling now,' Cyrion had laughed.

Talos hadn't laughed. Three of Third Claw lay dead, cut to pieces by the banshees' blades. Only one of the eldar had fallen; the one he'd smashed aside with his fist.

Talos walked his careful, crunching way across the chamber. As he drew near, he saw her fingers twitch.

'She still lives,' Faroven warned.

'So I see.'

Talos pressed his boot down on her hand, the gears grinding in his knees. It took no effort at all – the Terminator suit made it no harder than drawing breath – to crush her hand into a bloody smear of paste.

That woke her up, and she woke up screaming. He dragged the helm from her head, and the psychic cry died, leaving an almost-human moan in its place.

Talos rested the assault cannon on her chest.

'I know you,' she said in awkward Gothic, as though the words tasted foul. Her slanted eyes narrowed, showing the lush green of long-lost forests. 'I am Taisha, Daughter of Morai-Heg, and I know you, Soul Hunter.'

'Whatever your alien witchery has told you,' his voice was a vox-altered snarl, 'is meaningless. For you lie at death's edge, and I am the one to kick you over it.'

Trapped with her arm ruined beneath his boot, she still managed to smile through agony's breathless panting.

'You will cross blades with the Void Stalker,' she grinned with bloody gums. 'And you will die on this world.'

'And who is the Void Stalker?'

Her answer was to lash out with a kick. He'd tortured eldar countless times before – they never broke under excruciation, and never whispered a word they didn't wish to speak.

Talos lifted his boot and walked away.

'End her,' he voxed, not caring who did the deed.

* * *

Lucoryphus wasn't ashamed of the feast. Just as the Eighth Legion scavenged wargear from the slain, so too did the Bleeding Eyes scavenge flesh.

He knew if Talos or any of the others saw him pulling apart his brothers' bodies to devour the meat within, they'd be unlikely to see it in such generous terms, but with events unfolding as they were, that hardly seemed to matter.

And it wasn't as if Vorasha and the others needed their flesh anymore. Lucoryphus was careful, between mouthfuls, to save their gene-seed. No ceremonial extraction for a fallen Raptor, and no emotional butchery at a brother's hands. Lucoryphus pulled the fleshy nodes out with handfuls of meat around them, and stored them in a cryo-canister at his thigh.

Then went right back to devouring the dead in the rain.

He looked up every now and again, his bare face tingling in the unfamiliar feel of wind as he scanned for signs of eldar arrival. What scraps of chatter he caught from the vox sounded as though the subterranean hunts were no longer of interest. They were all as good as dead.

He wasn't even sure why he was taking the Bleeding Eyes' gene-seed. Some traditions were tenacious, even in the face of death.

When he heard the gunship's engine, his instinctive reaction was to tense, claws activating as he turned to face the growing sound. Without his helm's vision cycles, his sight suffered at a distance. He needed movement to follow, motion to track, else he was close to blind past a hundred paces.

Lucoryphus was reaching for his helm when the gunship reached him, hovering overhead, breathing engine wash downward and blasting dust across the ruins. He watched without expression as the gangramp opened, and felt no pulse of surprise at the figure that dropped from the sky.

The Night Lord landed with a smooth thud, and voxed

back up to the gunship. 'I am down. Land on the battlements over there. Stay away from any eldar ground forces. If you are engaged from the air, run. That is all I desire from you. Understood.'

The gunship banked without the pilot replying, thrusters flaring as it obeyed.

'Lucoryphus of the Bleeding Eyes,' said Variel.

'Variel the Flayer.'

'I have never seen you with your helmet off.'

Lucoryphus replaced his helm, fixing the daemon's visage back over his face.

'You look like a drowned corpse,' Variel noted.

'I know what I look like. Why are you here?'

Variel let his gaze drift around the ruins. 'A fool's hope. Where is Talos?'

Lucoryphus gestured with his claw, the blades angled down. 'Beneath.'

'I cannot reach him on the vox.'

'Contact breaks down. They're deep under, and fighting.'

'Where is the closest entrance to the catacombs?'

Lucoryphus gestured again. The Apothecary started walking, his own dense bionic leg making a *thunk, thunk, thunk* on the dusty soil. Pistons hissed in his cybernetic knee.

Lucoryphus followed, dropping to all fours in a graceful prowl that never failed to impress Variel for its unexpected elegance.

'How did you get past the blockade?' the Raptor asked.

'There is no blockade. Two-dozen vessels wait in high orbit, with little sign of landing craft. We didn't even detect a sensor sweep. It took hours to reach this far, but twenty vessels cannot keep an entire world in their eyes. You may as well ask a blind man to count each rock that makes up a mountain.'

Lucoryphus said nothing as they passed Vorasha's mutilated, half-eaten body. Variel wasn't so silent.

'In a time now considered myth, cannibalism was

considered good for the body and soul.' He looked at the Raptor for a moment. 'If we survive this, I would like a sample of your blood.'

'Not a prayer.'

Variel nodded, expecting that answer. 'You are aware, Lucoryphus, that such degrees of *livor mortis* and bacterial decomposition on your face and throat would simply not manifest on a living being? Your biology is in a stage of autolysis. Your cells are eating themselves. Does the feasting on fraternal flesh regenerate the process?'

Lucoryphus didn't reply. Variel continued nevertheless. 'How then do you live? Are you dead, yet still alive? Or has the warp played a greater game with you?'

'I no longer know what I am. I haven't known for centuries. Now tell me why you're here.'

Above the forgotten fortress, the storm finally showed its strength. Lightning lit up the grey sky, while heavier rain lashed down on their armour. Variel's flayed shoulder guard, the skinned face of a brother he'd slain long ago, seemed to be weeping.

'Talos.'

He didn't reply. Teeth clenched, he kept the cannon's trigger pulled tight, streaming out tracer fire to illuminate the dark tunnel. The numeric runes on his retinal display depleted away, shrinking by the second, even as the cannon's spinning barrels began to glow a brighter red with the pressure of overheating.

'Talos,' the voice crackled again. 'Don't move too far ahead.'

The assault cannon eased off with a descending whine. He bit back a harsh reply, knowing it would make no difference. Cyrion was right; still, the frustration remained. The hunt had changed once more. When the eldar stopped coming to them, they'd taken the fight to the eldar.

Talos stalked to a stop, letting the stabilisers and

servos in his leg armour settle once more. The cannon hissed in the cold air, while dead aliens lay strewn at his feet.

Cyrion and Mercutian stomped closer, filling the tunnel with their whirring joints and pounding footsteps. Both of their storm bolters showed defiled Imperial aquilas. Both weapons also had smoking barrels.

'I'm almost out of ammunition,' voxed Mercutian. 'It's time to get back into our battle armour and split up. The butchery was enjoyable, but they're avoiding us as a pack.'

Talos nodded. 'I'll miss the armament.'

'As will I,' Mercutian replied. 'And I've lost count how many of these wretches we've killed. I lost count at seventy, at the last intersection. This group makes…' Mercutian panned his storm bolter across the destroyed, bloody bodies. 'Ninety-four.'

'These are nothing more than dregs.' Cyrion turned his tusked helm towards Mercutian. 'But the shrieking maidens? I've not managed to hit one, yet.'

'Nor I,' said Talos. 'Not since the first one. The weaker ones die like vermin. The howling ones are a breed apart.'

Uzas came last of all, his armour washed by blood. Instead of tusks, his helm sported a brutal, curved horn from the bridge of the faceplate's nose.

'They are warrior-priestesses of their war god's daughter.' First Claw turned to look at him, none of them saying a word for a moment. 'What?' Uzas grunted. 'I have excruciated eldar captives in the past, just as you have.'

'Whatever they are, we should get back to Third Claw.'

'*Talos.*'

The prophet hesitated. No name rune flashed on his retinal display. 'Variel?'

'Brother, I am in the ruins above with Lucoryphus. We must speak.'

'No. Please let this be a foul jest. I ordered you away for a reason, fool.'

Talos listened to his brother's explanation, as hurried and fragmented as it was. He took several long moments to reply.

'Back to Third Claw,' he ordered the others. 'Variel, do not descend into the ruins. The tunnels are infested with eldar.'

'Are you returning to the surface?'

Talos wasn't even sure of that himself. 'Just stay hidden.'

The howling maidens returned as soon as First Claw rejoined Faroven and the Third. Faroven was down to four warriors; their slain brethren were left in the corridors, while the remnants of the claw moved as a unified pack.

This time, the Night Lords were ready. Pursuing their prey through the corridors for the last couple of hours had fed their hearts in a way forming defensive lines never could.

The aliens spilled through the Eighth Legion's ranks, blades blurring and hair-crests flowing. Talos caught a growled 'We're outnumbered,' from one of his brothers, but the press of limbs and blades made the details hopeless.

The two maidens before him both screamed at once, raising their blades. He felt the same ice crawl through his muscles, dragging him back, slowing him down.

Two... can play... that game...

The Night Lord released a scream of his own – a roar from three lungs and an enhanced respiratory system, heightened tenfold by the vox-speakers in his snarling helm. The surviving Night Lords heard the cry and took it up a heartbeat later.

He'd used his cry to shatter windows and deafen crowds of humans to soften them up for the kill; now he used it in opposition to those who sought to turn his own weapon against him.

Three of the maidens' swords shattered outright. Several of the alien warriors lost eye lenses to splitting cracks as the harmonious, savage scream reached its apex. In the same moment the Night Lords' cry hit its crescendo, the eldar's howl died a sudden death.

Talos killed the first of the warriors before him with a fist around her head, crushing the skull and bones of her shoulders before hurling her away. The second died while still staggering back from the shout, cut to pieces by the final hail from his assault cannon. He dropped the empty weapon and reached for his relic bolter, drawing in breath to scream a second time.

With the tide turned, with the maidens stumbling back and succumbing to the butchery they'd inflicted on the legionaries, a new sound invaded the warriors' senses.

Uzas hammered his fist into one of the alien's stomachs, breaking her breastbone and spine in the same blow. As she fell against him on strengthless legs, he lowered his head and rammed his helm-horn through her torso.

'Do you hear that?' the others were voxing.

'Footsteps.'

'Those aren't footsteps. They're too fast.'

He couldn't hear a thing beyond the beating of his hearts, and the blood rain streaming down his helm and shoulders. It took two heaves to shove the twitching body off his horn. His neck gave a stiff crackle as he stood up straight again.

Then he heard it. And Talos was right. It was footsteps.

'I know what that is,' he said. The steps had the rhythm of a racing heartbeat, soft against the stone yet still echoing down the hallways, loud as the winds of the warp.

Talos stood above two slain maidens, blood dripping from his curled fingers. The only sound was the footsteps, now all the screeching had fallen still.

'What is it?' he asked.

'A storm in flesh, with a rain of blades. She Who Stalks the Void.' Uzas ran his tongue across his teeth, tasting the acid on his gums. 'The Storm of Silence.'

XXVII

VOID STALKER

She came from the darkness, just as her sisters had done. Varthon was the first to see her, and shouted a warning to the others. The cry died in his throat as soon as it started, ended by the spear blade punched through his breastplate, bursting both of his hearts in a single blow. A full metre of the black spear thrust out from his spine for a single moment, until the weapon slid back from his flesh with vicious patience.

She watched each of them as she let the body fall, while a flatline tune played out in every Night Lord's helm.

Every figure moved at once. The legionaries lifted their bolters and opened fire, each of them unleashing a torrent of explosive shells and none of them coming close to striking her.

Flatline wails rang in Talos's ears as he fired at the dancing, flickering figure. Centuries of training and battle aligned with the targeting processors in his Terminator plate and retinal display, guiding his aim as much as instinct. The storm bolter bucked and banged in his grip, spitting shells in a tide that only relented when he had to reload.

He backed away, crunching another magazine home. All of them were reloading out of sync, all sense of unity and covering fire gone in a moment. Talos saw, in one blurry scan of the chamber, how their bolter fire had savaged every single wall without once hitting their prey.

Jekrish White-Eyes died next, his head cleaved clean from his shoulders. As the body started to topple, Talos lifted his fist to block his brother's spinning helm from hitting him. It clanged aside, dropping to the floor. He was already firing at the black blur, aiming in the places instinct and his targeting reticule said she'd be. More stonework died in detonation craters and splintering chips.

She didn't even slow down to kill. The spear reaped right through Gol Tatha's waist, severing him from his legs. In the same second, Faroven died halfway across the chamber, a three-bladed throwing star forged of alien iron and black fire cracking his head down the middle. Both bodies fell, twinning their thuds as they struck stone.

Mercutian cried out, his bulky suit of armour arching its back as he cursed. Talos caught a flicker of movement in his visor display as the spear lanced back out from his brother's back. Mercutian staggered forward, only prevented from falling by the artificial ironclad muscles in his armour's joints. His storm bolter boomed once more, before spilling from his grip.

When the throwing blade hit Uzas, it crashed against his horned helm, sending ceramite chunks clattering off the walls. He didn't stagger as Mercutian had; he tumbled one step and dropped to his hands and knees, heavy enough to send tremors through the floor. Talos saw blood drip to the dark stone ground, pooling between Uzas's shaking hands.

'Talos...' crackled the vox.

'Not now.'

'Brother,' said Variel, 'when are you returning to the surf–'

'Not now!'

He followed the blur with his storm bolter, just as it danced behind Korosa, the last soul standing in Third Claw. Korosa turned, as fast as a genhanced human body was capable of moving, lashing out with his howling chainsword. In the single second it took Talos to draw aim, Korosa was lurching backwards, blood gouting from his severed arm. He made it two steps before the spear's backswing disembowelled him, spilling a wet slop of innards down the front of his war plate.

Talos fired over Korosa's shoulder. The single *crack* and the throaty burst that followed were the sweetest sounds he'd ever heard. He saw the blur resolve into a female figure, as tall as any of them in their Terminator ceramite, falling back with her head snapped to the side.

Mercutian was struggling to reach for his dropped bolter and Uzas was still down, but Cyrion aligned his aim the same moment Talos fired again. A silver crescent arc blurred before her, detonating shell after shell before they could touch her. It took the prophet's eyes a couple of precious seconds to adjust to the speed, before he realised she was blocking their incoming fire with the blade of her spear.

She couldn't shatter them all. A withering spit of shells crashed against her black-and-bone armour, sending her reeling again.

Talos broke off to reload. Cyrion did the same, a second later. Both of them froze with their bolters empty, staring at the damaged wall where she'd been a moment before.

Korosa crashed to the ground, breaking the sudden silence.

For a long moment, Cyrion turned in place, unwilling to believe she was gone. Other, less intrusive sounds filtered back into being: Mercutian's choking breaths, Uzas's pained grunts, and the hiss of cooling bolter muzzles.

'I can't see her,' Cyrion voxed over their squad link. 'And I'm out of ammunition.'

'As am I.' Talos resisted the need to check on Uzas and Mercutian, never taking his eyes from the walls as he turned, back-to-back with Cyrion.

'She's still here,' said Cyrion. 'She must be.'

'No.' Talos gestured with his power fist. A trail of blood spatters led from the chamber, back into the tunnels. 'She's running.'

Cyrion threw his empty storm bolter away, discarding it without care. 'We should be doing the same.'

THE SERVITORS AWAITED them, still silent in their dead-minded reverie. Talos was first into the chamber, gesturing for the augmented slaves to attend him.

'Get me out of this armour.'

'Compliance,' uttered twelve voices at once.

'And me,' said Mercutian. Unhelmed now, he spat blood onto the floor. It started dissolving the stone at once.

'Compliance,' said the rest of the servitors.

'Make it quick,' Cyrion voxed, taking guard with Uzas at the entrance archway. Mercutian threw him his storm bolter as the servitors closed around. Cyrion checked the ammunition feed on his retinal display, and readied the weapon. Despite his wound, Uzas stood straight and speechless; the only sound registering from him was the tidal flow of his slow breathing. His helmet was a cracked ruin, baring most of his bloodstained face beneath. Unfocused eyes stared into the tunnel, as did the twin barrels of his storm bolter.

'I'll miss this armour,' Cyrion said. 'Uzas and Mercutian are only still alive because of this war plate. That spear went through battle armour like a knife through flesh.'

Mercutian muttered a reluctant agreement. He was struggling to stand, and each movement brought a fresh muscle cramp, with another pulse of pain slithering up his spine.

'I'm not going to make it much further,' he said, needing to spit the blood from his mouth again.

The servitors' machine-tools went to work – drilling; unscrewing; prising plates clear. Talos felt himself breathing easier with each layer that came free. 'None of us are,' he said. 'We didn't come down here to win.'

Uzas chuckled at that, but said nothing more.

'Brother?' Talos voxed. 'Uzas?'

The other Night Lord turned his broken helm, bloody features looking back at Talos. 'What is it?'

The Terminator shoulder guards were machined free, coming loose with a series of crunches and clicks, and carried away by the servitors. Talos met Uzas's eyes, black to black, sensing something had changed in his brother's face but unable to decide what.

'Are you well?'

'Aye, brother.' Uzas turned back to his guard duty. 'Never better.'

'You sound well. You sound very... clear.'

'I imagine I do.' Uzas's armour gave a slow growl as he glanced at Cyrion. 'I feel clearer.'

The servitors were removing Mercutian's power fist when his legs gave way. He stumbled, needing to lean against the wall to remain standing. Blood was running from the corner of his mouth.

'Leave me behind when you go,' he said. 'My spine's aflame, and it's spreading to my legs. I can't run like this.'

Cyrion was the one to answer. 'He's right, anyway. It's time to split up, Talos. She'll go through us like a cold wind if we hunt her as a pack.'

Uzas gave another guttural chuckle. 'You just want to hide.'

'Enough of your perspective, drooling one.'

Mercutian bit back a growl. 'Enough talk of splitting up. Leave me, and get the prophet back to the surface. Variel's come for a reason, fools. Talos can't die here.'

'Shut up, all of you.' Talos breathed deep as the helm was lifted clear. 'Uzas, Cyrion, be silent and watch the tunnels.'

* * *

Malcharion's hunt was slower, but no less purposeful. He made his way through the tunnels, backtracking when he encountered a collapsed passageway or a hall too narrow and low for him to traverse.

'This was once a laborium. The Legion's Techmarines worked here. Not all of them, of course. But many.'

Marlonah limped alongside the colossal war machine. Her torchlight flickered and died yet again, and this time, smacking it against her thigh didn't bring it back to life. For several seconds she stood in the darkness, listening to the dusty ghosts of the forgotten fortress.

'Our Techmarines and trained serfs constructed servitors in a ceaseless horde. Captives. Failed aspirants. Humans harvested from a hundred worlds, brought here to serve. Can you imagine that? Can you picture the production lines filling this bare hall?'

'I... I can't see anything, lord.'

'Oh.'

Light returned with a crack. A lance of illumination burned from the Dreadnought's shoulder.

'Is that better?'

'Yes, lord.'

'Stop using that word. I am no one's lord.'

Marlonah swallowed, looking around where the beam of light pointed. 'As you wish, lord.'

Malcharion made his slow, grinding way across the large chamber. **'It is all so different now. This is no longer my home, and it is no longer my war. One last hunt, though. For all of the pain, it was worth it to hunt one last time.'**

'Yes, lord. If you say so, lord.'

The Dreadnought whirred on its waist axis, coming about to a new direction and stomping that way when its legs realigned. Sparks briefly lit up the tarnished armour-plating. Their last few run-ins with the masked aliens had left their mark on the war machine's iron body. Still, he'd slaughtered them all before they could come anywhere near her.

'Are you alive, lord? I mean... You speak of death and resurrection. What are you?'

The Dreadnought made an awkward gear-grinding sound. **'I was Captain Malcharion of Tenth Company, called war-sage by my primarch, who found my long treatises on warfare to be pointless, but amusing. He lectured me more than once, you know. Told me to serve with the Thirteenth, where my wit would be more welcome.'**

She nodded slowly, seeing her breath mist in the air. 'What's a primarch?'

Malcharion made the same gear-shifting noise again. **'Just a myth,'** the vox-speakers boomed. **'Forget I spoke.'**

For a time, they stood in silence. Malcharion tuned back into the vox, listening in contemplative quiet to the words of Variel, Talos, Lucoryphus and the last surviving members of his company. The arrival of the Flayer was a surprise, as was the presence of the gunship he brought. Beyond that, they all seemed to be dying just as they'd desired: falling only after reaving countless enemy lives, watering the stones of their ancient castle with the blood of their foes one last time.

Perhaps it wasn't glorious, but it was right. They weren't the Imperial Fists, to stand in gold beneath the burning sun and scream the names of their heroes to the uncaring sky. This was how the Eighth Legion fought, and how all sons of the sunless world should finally die – screaming their anger, alone, down in the dark.

He thought for a moment of the lie he'd told the human by his side; the lie that he relished this last hunt. He was perversely thankful for the chance to witness his former brethren meet their ends as true sons of the Eighth, but he cared nothing for shedding the cursed blood of these foolish xenos heathens. What grudge did he bear against them? None. None at all. Killing them was only a pleasure to teach them the ways of the Eighth, and the flaws of their inhuman arrogance.

He considered it unlikely they could kill him with

their scattered, weakling war parties. Perhaps twenty or thirty of them with better blades might be able to overwhelm him, but even then...

No.

He'd meet his end in this cold tomb, already interred within his coffin, finally falling into silence when the Dreadnought shell ran out of power. It could be ten years. It could be ten thousand. He had no way of knowing.

Malcharion shut off the vox, and once more considered the human by his side. What was her name again? Had he even asked? Did it matter?

'**Do you want to die down here, human?**'

She hugged herself against the cold. 'I don't want to die at all.'

'**I am not a god, to forge miracles from nothingness. Everything dies.**'

'Yes, lord.' Again, the silence. 'I hear more whispers,' she confessed. 'The aliens are coming again.'

The immense cannon on the Dreadnought's right arm lifted and made the clanking reloading sounds that were already becoming so familiar to her. The whispers were already growing stronger. She could almost feel the warmth of breath stroking the back of her neck.

'**My chronicle already ends in glory. Captain Malcharion, reborn in unbreakable iron, slaying Raguel the Suffer of the Ninth Legion for the second time, before at last passing into eternal slumber. That is a fine legend, is it not?**'

Even without understanding the meaning of the words, she felt their significance. 'Yes, lord.'

'**Who would ruin their legend with one last, untold tale? Who would cast aside the slaughter of an Imperial hero in favour of saving a single human from death in the infinite dark?**'

Malcharion never gave her time to answer. His weapons rose even as he pivoted, and filled the chamber with echoing, deafening gunfire.

* * *

First Claw stood ready, surrounded by inactive servitors and priceless, precious suits of Terminator war plate that would never see sunlight again.

Talos sheathed his gladius along his shin, locked his empty bolter to his thigh, and drew the Blade of Angels. His skull-painted faceplate – marked with the forehead rune depicting the title he so often hated – regarded his brothers in turn.

Mercutian's breathing came in ragged growls, sounding wet over the vox, but he stood straight enough to hold his heavy bolter. He regarded the others through a dispassionate helm, crested by twin curved horns.

Uzas wore his palm-printed helmet of ancient design, his chainaxe in one hand, his gladius in the other. His cloak of skinned flesh was draped over one shoulder in grim, regal contrast to the skulls hanging from his armour.

Cyrion readied his chainsword and his bolter, the lightning bolt markings of his faceplate looking like jagged tear trails.

'Let's end this,' he said. 'I was bored of being alive, anyway.'

Talos smiled, though he'd never felt less amused. Uzas said nothing at all. Mercutian nodded, his words coming after a grunt.

'We'll get you to the surface, brother. Then when Variel's had his chatter, we'll get back to skinning that alien harpy.'

'Simple plans are often the best,' Cyrion noted.

Talos led them from the chamber, leaving their abandoned relics and mindless slaves to waste away in the dark.

XXVIII

A TRUTH NEVER TOLD

AFTER AN HOUR, it became a hindrance. After two, a problem. In the third hour, they were barely moving at all.

'Just leave me,' Mercutian said, supported on Talos's shoulder. He was dragging them back, slowing them down. Talos knew it. Cyrion and Uzas knew it, and Mercutian knew it better than any of them.

'Leave me,' he kept saying.

'Leave the cannon,' Talos replied. 'It isn't helping.'

Mercutian clutched the heavy bolter tighter. 'Just leave me. I'll cut down any of the xenos wretches that come here to find me. If they're behind us, I'll buy you some time.'

Cyrion walked alongside Talos and the limping warrior. Over a private link, he took a deep breath. 'We should leave him, brother.'

Talos didn't even glance Cyrion's way. 'You should be silent.'

'We're going to die, Talos. That's why we're here. Mercutian is already dying, and the head wound Uzas is wearing doesn't look like it's left him all in one piece, either. His skull is bare to the bone, and we left one of his eyes back in the chamber where Third Claw died.'

Talos didn't argue. 'Uzas is worrying me as much as Mercutian. He seems… cold, distant.'

'To say the least. Come, what does it matter if Variel

overhead a whisper of alien witchery? We're dead men. If we don't die here, we'll die in orbit.'

Talos didn't answer at once. 'The gunship slipped in. It can slip out. You heard what Variel said about the wraithships. The game has changed.'

'And you believe him? You think you're destined to live on, and unite the Legion?'

'I don't know what I believe.'

'Very well. If you're not supposed to die here, what visions of the future have you seen beyond tonight?'

'None.'

'There's your answer. You die here. We all do. Don't let our last hunt fail because we had to limp and flee like wounded dogs. We should find her while she's wounded, not let her come to us in another ambush. It's not our way.'

Talos shook his head as he adjusted Mercutian's weight on his shoulder. 'Enough, Cy. I'm not leaving him. And I have to get to Variel.'

'Your trust in the Flayer is your own flaw to fight. Don't drag our lives into it. If you're really turning your back on our last hunt, then Mercutian is *still* right. You want to reach the surface, and he's slowing us down.'

Talos narrowed his eyes as he walked. 'Sometimes, Cy, you make it easy to see why Xarl hated you.'

'Is that so?' Cyrion snorted. 'Don't hide behind his ghost as if he'd smile and nod and cheer you on for the sentiment. Xarl would be the first to leave him behind. You know that as well as I. It would be one of the few things he and I ever agreed on.'

Talos had no answer to that.

'Brothers,' Uzas said, with serene calm. 'I hear her. She comes, sprinting through the black.'

First Claw redoubled their efforts. Cyrion took Mercutian's other side, helping the wounded warrior limp onward.

'Talos,' Mercutian grunted.

'Shut up. Just move.'

'Talos,' he snapped. 'It's time. Throne in flames, Soul Hunter. It's time. Leave me. *Run.*'

SHE CAME FROM the darkness again, eldritch blades in bone-armoured fists. The throwing star burned black with warp-tempered fire; the spear hissed like fresh iron in a forge trough, spitting-hot to the touch.

One figure stood in the hallway before her. She smelled the chemical reek of its weapon oils and the dirty blood leaking from its wounds. She'd marked this one. She knew the scent of his life.

A lone mon-keigh from their unclean warrior caste, abandoned by his kindred to bleed out the last of his life alone. How little these creatures knew of loyalty or nobility.

As she drew near, she saw him strain to lift his weapon, and heard a single word in one of the human species' filthy tongues.

'Juthai'lah,' said the dying soul of the warrior caste.

MERCUTIAN DRAGGED IN cold air through his mouth grille. The target locks on his retinal display struggled to align on the advancing witch-queen, as though reality itself resisted her presence.

He blinked to clear his vision, braced back against the weight of his bolter cannon, and lifted the muzzle to aim down the hallway.

She walked closer, and still he couldn't lock onto her. To the hells with augmented targeting then. Back to simple purity.

Mercutian breathed the word aloud into the corridor, uncaring whether she knew its meaning or not.

'Preysight.'

His bolter kicked in his fists a second later, hammering in anger and filling the narrow tunnel with explosive shells.

* * *

THE SURVIVORS RAN.

Their boots pounded onto the stone as they sprinted, never once looking back. Genetically enhanced muscles bunched and moved within the fibre-bundle cabling that augmented their strength, while three lungs and two hearts worked to capacity inside their heaving chests.

Talos vaulted a pile of rocks, his boots crashing down on the other side and never missing a stride. His eye lenses flickered runic sigils between eighty-four and eighty-seven kilometres per hour. Those figures sank lower each time he was forced to slide and skid around a corner, or leap up and kick off from an adjacent wall at a junction in order to maintain a semblance of speed.

They'd been running for a full seven minutes before Talos cursed under his breath. At the edge of his retinal display, the three remaining life signs became two, and a flatline whined its way across the vox.

MERCUTIAN TREMBLED AS he died in her grip. Even through his fading vision, he noted the damage done to her helm and breastplate – the armour was cracked, letting some of her stinkingly ripe alien blood trickle through. He'd only managed to graze her a handful of times with over forty shells from his heavy bolter, but the detonations left her charred and wounded, even if he'd failed to cripple her as he'd hoped.

'*Sleep,*' she caressed him with her voice, somehow mocking despite its gentleness.

Mercutian gripped the spear that impaled his chest, and *pulled*. He slid half a metre closer to her, feeling the horrendous, squealing scrape of the metal pole grating against his destroyed ribcage and burned flesh.

'*Sleep,*' she said again, laughing this time. A full-throated and melodious laugh, that only ground Mercutian's teeth together even harder. He gripped again, and pulled a second time. He barely moved – strength was fleeing him, along with his blood.

She whipped the spear back, and the pain of the

withdrawal was worse by far than the *crack* of it going in. With nothing to support him, he crumpled to the ground on dead legs, his armour crash reverberating through the tunnel.

For a moment, he lay foetal, trying to suck in air that wouldn't come. He was drowning without being underwater, his vision already greying at the edges.

She walked past him. The sight of her boots swishing past were a catalyst, shocking him back to his weakening senses. In his preysight, she was little more than a thermal blur, but training allowed him to make out the details he needed.

With a roar of effort and pain mixed into one screamed song, Mercutian moved as fast as he ever had in his life, and faster than he ever would again. The gladius in his hand rammed through the back of the maiden's leg, bursting through the front of her shin, and sticking fast. She cried out in kind, spinning to ram her spear down through his chest a second time.

Mercutian grinned up at her as his last breath left him. He spent it speaking a final sentence, meeting the witch-queen's eyes.

'*Now* try running…'

Lucoryphus landed in a haze of spreading dust. Variel ignored it, breathing the recycled air within his sealed suit as he stood in the rain.

'I see them,' the Raptor said. 'They surfaced to the west, on the battlements.'

Variel immediately started to run. He heard Lucoryphus laughing, and the Raptor's engines cycling back up to power. The Apothecary had a handful of seconds before Lucoryphus struck him from behind, grabbing his shoulder guards, and lifted him off the ground.

Variel – who had no love for flying, but even less affection for any of the Bleeding Eyes – clung on in undignified silence as the ruins passed below.

* * *

His first sighting of Variel wasn't actually when the Apothecary was dropped rather crudely onto the battlements from above. It was when his eye lens display acknowledged his Badabian brother's proximity, and linked a third vital sign feed to join Uzas and Cyrion's. Xarl's name rune, along with Mercutian's, were silent and faded by comparison.

Lucoryphus touched down with considerably more grace, his claws gripping the ramparts of the crooked, leaning battlement wall.

Talos approached the Apothecary as Variel was picking himself up. 'I want answers, Variel, and I want them now.'

'My explanation may take some time. I can call the gunship.'

'Septimus and Octavia are truly here? On this world?'

'That, also, will take time to explain.'

'We are short of many things, brother: ammunition; hope; warriors. You can add time to that list. Where's *Blackened*?'

'The battlements, to the north. Perhaps four minutes' flight.'

Talos re-tuned his vox to the familiar channel he never thought he'd contact again. 'Septimus.'

'Lord? It's good to hear your voi–'

'Get the gunship in the air, and fly over the central ruins. We are proceeding there now. Don't land until we call you in – it's too dangerous for you to remain on the ground any longer than you have to. Do you understand me?'

'Aye, lord.'

'And if by chance you catch an eldar maiden in armour of bone in your gunsights, I would appreciate you shooting her into red mist.'

'Uh… as you say, lord.'

Talos severed the link, and looked back to the others. 'Scatter into the ruins until the gunship comes in. Don't let her find you. Now move. Variel, you're with me. Start explaining.'

* * *

Cyrion sprinted through the rain. Erosion had left this stretch of ruined battlements a mere seven metres above the ground, which Cyrion cleared in a casual drop down to ground level. His boots crunched on the rocky earth, and he broke back into his run.

Taking cover in the ruins of the gigantic fortress was hardly difficult; even on the surface, weathering had left an abandoned city of rubble and tilted walls on the grey plains. He ran for several minutes, stopping at last when he reached a slope of rubble that had once served as a barracks wall, next to the battlements.

The Night Lord started to climb, his gauntlets punching and clawing handholds in the stone where it was too smooth to grip in the rain.

'Cyrion,' said a voice. Not over the vox. Over the rain. It was that near.

Cyrion looked up. Uzas crouched at the top of the wide wall, looking down at him. The painted palm-print was smeared over his ancient faceplate, untouched by the cold rainfall.

'Brother,' Cyrion replied. A pregnant pause reached between them. Cyrion hauled himself the rest of the way up. Uzas rose to his feet, and backed away. His chainaxe and gladius were still in his fists.

'Let us speak,' Uzas said. The storm heaved harder, lightning splitting the sky above them both.

'Talos told us to split up.'

Uzas never turned his red eye lenses away. 'Talos. Yes, let us speak of Talos.' His voice had never sounded so clear – at least not in the centuries since the Great Heresy. Cyrion couldn't help but wonder just what the head wound had done.

'What of Talos?' he asked.

Uzas gunned the trigger of the chainaxe for a moment. Raindrops sprayed from the whirring teeth.

'Talos has lost his patience with me many times in the decades since we fled Tsagualsa. Yet he has always treated me fairly. Always defended me. Always remembered that I am his brother, and that he is mine.'

Cyrion rested his hand on his sheathed chainsword. 'Aye. He has.'

Uzas tilted his head. 'But you have not.'

Cyrion forced a laugh. It sounded as insincere as it was.

'Cyrion, Cyrion, Cyrion. I have been thinking, as I look down at these red hands of mine. I bear the sinner's red hands because of my many, many rampages through the mortal crew of the *Covenant*. The voidborn's father was the last, wasn't it? That foolish, fearful old man, who would sweat and weep and cringe every time we walked near.'

Uzas took a step closer to Cyrion. 'How did his fear taste, Cyrion? How did it taste when you killed him? Was it still tingling on your tongue when you stood by and let the others blame me?'

Cyrion drew both blades as Uzas took another step closer. 'Lucoryphus told you, then.'

'Lucoryphus told me nothing. I have been playing the past through my mind these last hours, and the conclusion was simple enough. No one else would have found the old fool a tempting target. None of the others would have been able to taste his cowardice the way you could. And any of them would simply confess to Talos what they'd done. But not you, *oh no*. Not the perfect Cyrion.'

Cyrion glanced behind. He was close to the wall's edge now, and the long drop down to the rubble that came with it.

'Uzas...'

'I've been so blind, haven't I? Answer me this, Cyrion. How many times did you slay to sup on the crew's fear, and stand by while I was blamed? As I pull through the broken memories, I can recall my true hunts, and too many instances of losing control. But nothing like the amount I've been blamed for.'

'Don't seek to blame me for t–'

'*Answer me!*' Uzas pulled his helm clear, hurling it

aside and facing Cyrion barefaced. His scarred, stitched, broken-angel features were contorted by hate. Blood still painted one side of his head, and one eye socket stared hollow, still not quite wedged shut by the wound. *'How many of your sins have damned me?'*

Cyrion smiled at his brother's slipping control. 'Over the centuries? Dozens. Hundreds. Take your pick, madman. What do a few more souls matter in the harvest you've reaped alone?'

'It matters because I am punished for your sins!' Spit sprayed from Uzas's lips as he screamed. *'The others despised me! How much of that blame can be laid at your feet?'*

'The others are dead, Uzas.' Cyrion kept his voice calm, cold. 'What they believed no longer means anything. You damned yourself in their eyes by forever screaming about your Blood God each time you drew a blade in battle.'

'I. Never. Worshipped. Anything.' Uzas aimed the chainaxe at his brother's head. 'You never understood it. The Legion raises icons to the Powers when it suits them. Whatever the cost, wars must be won. I am no different. *No different!'*

'If you say so, Uzas.'

'Do you know how many times my thoughts have cleared, only to be confronted by a brother enraged at me for slaying some vital member of the crew?' Uzas spat over the side, his face even more hideous now the rain had washed away the blood. His skull showed where the left half of his head had suffered the skin being ripped away. *'I killed dozens, yet bore the blame for hundreds!'* He raised the weapons in his fists, displaying his red gauntlets. 'These are your marks of shame, Cyrion. I wear them because you are too weak to do so yourself.'

The rage bled from him as abruptly as it had risen. 'I… I will tell Talos. And you will confess what you've done. He must know the depths of your… appetite. The things it has forced you to do.'

'If you say so,' Cyrion repeated, 'brother.'

'Forgive my anger. The wrath is difficult to bite back, some nights. I know the feel of the warp's caress, as surely as you do. I feel for you, my brother. I truly do. We are more alike than either of us has ever admitted.'

Uzas sighed and closed his eyes. A smile – the first sincere smile in centuries – spread across his broken face.

Cyrion moved the moment Uzas's eyes closed. He lashed out with both blades at once, aiming for the pale flesh of Uzas's throat. The other Night Lord flinched, barely blocking with his own weapons, and hit back with a kick that rang against his brother's breastplate like a tolling temple bell. Cyrion staggered, boots loose on the edge, and plummeted from view without a sound.

Uzas howled, a full-throated cry to the unquiet sky, his clarity shattered and his vision bathed red. The heaven's thunder melted into his throbbing heartbeat, and the rain in his eyes stung like his own acid-spit. He took a running leap, chainaxe snarling, and threw himself after his treacherous brother.

HE HEARD THE howl, but saw no source.

Lightning forked the sky again, a pulse of daylight's brightness bathing the ruins for a single second. For a moment, the toppled walls and spires resembled a dead city, and the legs of Titans.

Talos stopped running. He slowed to a halt, looking around with narrowed eyes, ignoring the pointless data streaming across his eye lenses.

'No,' he said, to no one but himself. 'I've seen this before.'

The lightning flashed again, drenching the ruins in short-lived light. Again, in the fragmentary sight, he saw Titans formed from the tilting walls, and tanks revealed as lifeless stone when the blinding brightness faded.

He leaned against –

Flash!

– the hull of a Land Raider –

– the stone wall of a fallen building, and looks for signs of his brothers. He sees Cyrion, half-buried in a mound of rubble, almost a thousand metres away by the testimony of scrolling retinal tactical data.

He watches another struggling figure emerging from the wreckage, and his visor locks onto Uzas, approaching Cyrion's prone form from behind.

And, at last, he knows where he's seen this.

It was never at Crythe. I read my own vision wrong. Uzas... He kills him here. He kills Cyrion here.

He broke into a run, the golden sword's power field flaring to life.

CYRION WINCED AT the pain in his thigh, feeling fairly certain his leg was broken by the twenty-metre fall. His helm's display was a haze of static, stealing any chance of checking his bio-readings, but having lost an arm in battle and feeling a haunting sense of familiarity in the sensation now, he felt he could make a fair guess.

He tried to claw his way free of the rubble. He had to get away from–

'Cyrionnnnn.' The low growl lingered on the final syllable, lost in drooling confusion. He heard Uzas scrabbling across the rocks behind, and thrashed in the rubble's grip, pulling himself half-clear. He could hear footsteps, heavy and swift, but couldn't twist to see.

The shadow above him lengthened across the rocks, as Uzas raised the axe. Cyrion was still reaching for his fallen sword when the blade descended.

UZAS STIFFENED, THE chainaxe falling from loose fingers to clatter onto the rubble. He looked down, no longer seeing Cyrion trapped beneath him, his eyes drawn to nothing but the golden sword extending through his chest.

I know that sword, he thought, and started laughing. But no breath meant no laughter, and he did nothing more than wheeze through bloody lips. The golden blade was already cleansed of his blood, washed clean by the rain. Even so, the cold droplets aggravated the shimmering energy field, breeding a buzzing aura around the steel, spiced with sparks.

He sighed, almost in relief, as the sword slid back out. Surprisingly, he felt nothing in the way of pain, though the pressure in his chest was mounting to the point he feared his hearts would rupture.

He turned to face his murderer. Talos stood in the rain, red eye lenses offering nothing of mercy.

Talos, he tried to say. *My brother.*

'You...' The prophet readied the blade again, clutching it in two hands. 'I trusted you. I argued again and again and again for your life to be spared. I swore to the others you were still inside there somewhere. Still a shred of nobility, waiting to be reborn. Still a fragment of worth, deserving of hope.'

'Talos.' He tried to say again. *Thank you.*

'You are the foulest, basest, most treacherous creature ever to the wear the winged skull of Nostramo. Ruven was a prince by comparison. At least he was in control of himself.'

Talos... Uzas's vision swam. He blinked, and upon opening his eyes, he found he was looking up at his brother towering over him. Had he fallen to his knees? *I... I...*

'Wait...' Uzas managed to say. He was appalled and amused in equal measure by the weakling's whisper his voice had become. 'Talos.'

The prophet kicked him in the chest, sending him toppling onto his back. His head cracked on the jagged rocks, but he didn't feel any pain beyond the press of cold stone.

No more words would come. Every breath sent black blood, deliciously warm, spilling over his chin.

He saw Talos rise above him, the golden sword spitting sparks in the storm. 'I should have killed you years ago.'

Uzas grinned, just as Mercutian had grinned, at the moment of death. *You probably should have, brother.*

He saw Talos turn and move away, out of sight. Variel replaced him, the Apothecary's icy eyes staring down with polite disinterest. Drills and saws deployed from his narthecium gauntlet.

'His gene-seed?' Variel asked.

Talos voice carried back from nearby. 'If you harvest it from him, I will kill you, too.'

Variel rose to his feet with one last dispassionate look, and moved away as well. The last words Uzas heard were those spoken by Cyrion, grunting as he was pulled from the rubble.

'He came at me from behind, screaming his endless devotions to the Blood God. My thanks, Talos.'

XXIX

ENDINGS

THE GUNSHIP CAME in low across the battlements, thrusters roaring as it hovered. Heat-shimmer turned the air as murky as water beneath the flaring jump jets. Steam rose from their armour, all traces of rainfall evaporating away.

Cyrion was limping, but able to stand unaided. Variel and Lucoryphus remained unharmed, but Talos hadn't spoken since he'd butchered his brother. He was a silent presence in the group's core, meeting no one's eyes as they climbed the ramparts, and avoiding eye contact afterwards.

Cyrion moved back and looked up to the sky beyond the gunship's scissoring searchlights, letting the rain wash across his painted faceplate.

'Have you noticed that it always rains here when we lose a war? The gods have a curious sense of humour.'

None of the others said a word in reply. Talos spoke, but it was only to Septimus.

'Bring her down. Be ready for immediate dust-off.'

'Yes, lord.'

The gunship kissed Tsagualsa's lifeless soil. Slowly, too slowly, the gangramp started to descend.

'This world is a tomb,' Talos said softly. 'For the Legion, and the hundreds of eldar that died down there tonight.'

'Then let's leave,' Cyrion hardly sounded impressed,

'and die in orbit, in defiance of the Flayer's moronic superstition.'

'All claws, all souls of the Eighth Legion, this is Talos. Answer me if you still breathe.'

Silence replied, thick and cold, over the vox. True to his words, he felt as though he was shouting across a graveyard.

Even Malcharion is dead. The thought made him shiver.

'Variel,' he said, as the ramp lowered fully. 'It isn't me.'

The Apothecary hesitated. 'I do not understand.'

For a moment, Talos just watched his own retinal display. Xarl. Mercutian. Uzas. All faded. All silent. All gone.

'It isn't me. I doubt any prophet will rise to unite the Eighth Legion, but if one does, it will not be me. I couldn't unite a single Claw.'

'Well,' Cyrion interrupted, 'we were a difficult group at the finest of times.'

'I mean it, Variel. It isn't me. It was never me. Look at me, brother. Tell me you believe *I* could unite tens of thousands of murderers, rapists, traitors, thieves and assassins. I don't think like them. I don't even want to be one of them, anymore. They damn themselves. That was always the Legion's flaw. We damned ourselves.'

'Your loyalty to your brothers does you credit, but you are speaking while affected by mourning.'

'No.' Talos shook his head, taking a step back. 'I'm speaking the truth. One of the many, many writings that remain with us from the era after the Heresy speaks of this "prophet". We call it the Crucible Premonition, though it was never shared past a few captains. And whether it's a destined fate or not, I am not that prophet.'

Variel nodded. Talos read the look in his brother's pale eyes, and smiled. 'You've considered the alternative,' he said, and it wasn't a question. 'I can tell.'

'The concept has remained with me since I ran the tests on your physiology.' Variel inclined his head to the gunship. 'A child that grows with your gene-seed implanted within its body will have all the makings of a powerful seer.'

'You're guessing.'

'I am. But it's a good guess.'

Cyrion cursed at them from the ramp. 'Can we leave, if we're going at all?' Lucoryphus crawled up the ramp, but Talos and Variel remained as they were.

'My father said something to me, in the hours before he died. Words for my ears alone; words I've never shared before tonight. He said: *"Many will claim to lead our Legion in the years after I am gone. Many will claim that they – and they alone – are my appointed successor. I hate this Legion, Talos. I destroyed its world to stem the flow of poison. I will be vindicated soon, and the truest lesson of the Night Lords will be taught. Do you truly believe I care what happens to any of you after my death?"*'

The Apothecary stood motionless, as Talos took a breath. 'Sometimes, I almost know how he felt, Variel. The war drags on for an eternity, and victory comes at an agonising pace. Meanwhile, we endure betrayals; we hide; we run and flee; we raid and ambush and skin and flay and kill; we loot our own dead; we drink the blood of our enemies; and suffer the endless tide of fratricide. I killed my own mother without knowing her face. I have killed nineteen of my own brothers in the last century alone, almost always in idiotic battles for possession of this sword, or over matters of bruised pride. I have no wish to unite the Legion. I *hate* the Legion. Not for what it is, but for what it made me become.'

Variel still said nothing. Rather than seeming lost for words, he simply seemed to lack any desire to speak at all.

'There's one thing I want,' said Talos. 'I want that alien witch's head. I want to plant it on her spear at the heart of these ruins.' Talos turned away from the gunship, walking away. 'And I mean to have it. Stay in the air, Variel. Land once it's over. Whether I live or die this night, you are welcome to my gene-seed come the dawn.'

Cyrion left the ramp, following Talos. 'I'm coming with you.'

Lucoryphus's head jerked with a muscle tic in his neck. He briefly rose to his clawed feet, and stalked after the others. 'I will join you. One more dead eldar will bring the Bleeding Eyes to two score. I like the sound of that number.'

Variel stood by the gunship, fighting the urge to follow. 'Talos,' he said.

The prophet looked over his shoulder in time to see blood burst from Variel's body. The Apothecary shouted – the first time Talos had ever heard an utterance of such volume from the Flayer's lips – and reached his hands to his bloody mouth, as if he could stem the flow of lifeblood gushing from his lips.

The black spear pulled out, staggering him as it withdrew from his back and cleaved through both of his legs on the backswing. The bionic leg gave crackling sparks of protest as its sundered systems tried to restore balance. His human leg bled, and bled, and bled.

The three Night Lords were already running, weapons alive in their fists.

'Get in the air,' Talos yelled into the vox. 'Consider it your final order.'

The gunship immediately rose, unsteady on its whining thrusters.

'You dismissed me back on board the *Echo*, Talos. I don't have to follow your orders, do I? Come with us.'

'Don't die with us, Septimus. Run. Anywhere but here.'

Talos was the first to reach the eldar maiden, as she was releasing the first notes of her paralysing shriek. He charged with a raised sword, telegraphing his intent to give a two-handed cleave. At the last second, as her spear came around to offer a perfect parry, he launched up and thundered a kick to the front of her facemask. Her head snapped back, the howl ended as her helm cracked, and she caught herself in a graceful handspring to avoid falling to the floor.

Talos landed hard and rolled back to his feet, the golden blade coming up again. He grinned at the sight of her deathmask split down the middle by a brutal faultline crack.

'You have no idea how satisfying that was,' he told her.

'You,' she said in mangled Gothic. Her helm's vocaliser grille was damaged, deforming her speech. *'Hunter of Souls.'*

He met her again, blade on blade, their power weapons resisting one another like opposing magnetic fields.

'I'm so tired of that name,' Talos breathed. He headbutted her, shattering the mask a second time. He saw her eye – her alien eye, slanted and unlovely – through the crack.

Cyrion and Lucoryphus came at her from opposite sides. The former had his chainblade parried by the three-knived throwing blade in her other hand; the latter missed with both lightning claws as the maiden danced out of the warriors' triangle, flipping and leaping aside.

She stumbled as she landed, the first sign of gracelessness in her movements, and they all heard the rasping hiss of pain. Blood sheeted her left leg from the shin down. Whatever had wounded her had done a beautiful job of hobbling her. Wounded, she was barely faster than them.

Lucoryphus wasn't part of First Claw, and lacked the unity of purpose that showed so clearly in the other two brothers. He leapt ahead of them with a roar that wouldn't have shamed a Nostraman lion, clawed fingers curled and aiming for her heart.

The spear met him in the chest, annihilating his breastplate and casting him to the ground. Even as the maiden rammed her spear one-handed through the prone Raptor's stomach, she was hurling her throwing star.

Cyrion's enhanced reactions were honed from centuries of battle, and years of training even before that.

In his lifetime, he'd blocked solid-slug bullets on his vambrace, and weaved to avoid laser fire without feeling its heat. His reflexes, like all of the warriors within the Legiones Astartes, were so far beyond human that they bordered on supernatural. He was already moving to dodge aside before the blade left her fingers.

It wasn't enough. Not even close. The spinning knives took him in the chest, crunching deep as they bit, and black fire burst across his armour.

The witch-queen held her hand to recall the throwing star. As it flashed through the air, Talos broke it in half with a swing of his power blade. The maiden tried to wrench her spear back out of Lucoryphus's belly, but the Raptor gripped the haft in his metal claws, keeping it lodged inside his body and the stone ramparts beneath.

The prophet was on her a heartbeat later. She weaved aside from the first swing, and the second, and the third, leaping back and dodging each ponderous carve. Despite moving faster than the human eye could follow, his heavy swings wouldn't land.

On another flip, her wounded leg gave out again. Talos swept her leg out from under her as she staggered to recover her balance, and at last Aurum struck home. The golden sword cleaved through her right arm, severing the limb close to the elbow.

She shrieked, then – an unamplified shriek of pain and frustration that sounded almost mortal. Dirty alien blood hissed and crackled as it burned away on the blade.

Her reply was a firm-fingered chop to the soft armour at his throat, crunching the cables there and thudding into his larynx hard enough to kill a human outright. It was enough to make him fall back, raising his blade defensively, struggling to catch his breath.

Talos felt his head snap to the right from a blow he never saw coming, and had a brief glimpse of Lucoryphus on his back, like some kind of iron-skinned helpless testudeen reptile, turned over on its shell.

The sword flew from his grip, kicked from his hand by a bloodstained boot. Another kick smashed into the scarred aquila on his chestplate, hurling him backward, barely keeping his balance. The combat narcotics flooding his muscles did nothing; he couldn't block her, he couldn't dodge her – he could scarcely even see her.

'Preysi–'

His own sword interrupted him as it crashed against his helm. Pain flared white-hot, cobwebbing out from his temple in the same moment his arc of vision halved. Before he could even process the notion he'd been blinded in one eye, the blade hammered home again. It slid into his chest with a loving lack of haste, stealing all breath, all energy, all thought, beyond one truth.

She killed me with my own sword.

He laughed without a sound, spraying flecks of blood into his helm. When she dragged the blade free, he first thought she'd cast it aside; instead, she broke it across her knee.

The pain burrowing through his chest finally embraced his spine, clinging with fervour. That's when he fell – but only to his knees. Somehow, that was worse.

'So falls the Hunter of Souls,' she said, pulling her helm off to stare down with slanted, milky grey eyes. She'd have been beautiful, had she not been so disgustingly inhuman. One of her ears twitched in the rain, as sensing a sound only she could hear.

He rose to his feet again, removed his own helmet, and looked out at another vision finally coming true.

The details were close. Not perfect, but so very close. His fevered mind had coloured places with ancient memory, making the fortress appear still standing in desolate glory, rather than the tumbled ruin he saw now.

But the rest was so clear, he had to smile. Talos took a step closer to her, and stooped despite the flare of agony in his chest, reaching to pick up the broken blade.

'In my dreams,' he breathed, 'you still had your helm on.'

She nodded – a slow and grave acknowledgement. 'In the dreams of Ulthwé's seers, they saw the same. Fate is fluid, Hunter of Souls. Some futures cannot be allowed to pass. There shall be no Prophet of the Eighth Legion. There shall be no Night of Blood, when the Tears of Isha are drunk by your thirsting brethren. You die here. All is well.'

He held a hand to his ruptured chest, feeling the aching beat of at least one heart. His breathing was tight, but his redundant organs had come to life, sustaining him past mortal death.

The maiden walked to pull her spear from Lucoryphus's chest. The Raptor made no movement beyond a limp twitch.

As she moved back to him, her black spear in her remaining hand, dream and reality melted together, becoming one at long last.

XXX

LESSONS

The prophet and the murderess stood on the battlements of the dead citadel, weapons in their hands. Rain slashed in a miserable flood, thick enough to obscure vision, draining down the wall's sides. Above the rain, the only audible sounds came from the two figures: one human, standing in broken armour that thrummed with static crackles; the other an alien maiden in ancient and contoured war plate, weathered by an eternity of scarring.

'This is where your Legion died, is it not? We call this world *Shithr Vejruhk*. What is it in your serpent's tongue? *Tsagualsa*, yes? Answer me this, prophet. Why would you come back here?'

Talos didn't answer. He spat acidic blood onto the dark stone floor, and drew in another ragged breath. The sword in his hands was a cleaved ruin, its shattered blade severed halfway along its length. He didn't know where his bolter was, and a smile crept across his split lips as he felt an instinctive tug of guilt.

Malcharion would not be proud, he thought.

'Talos.' The maiden smiled as she spoke. Her amusement was remarkable if only for the absence of mockery and malice. 'Do not be ashamed, human. Everyone dies.'

He couldn't stand. Even pride has limits over what it can force from a body. The prophet sank to one knee, blood leaking from the cracks in his armour. His attempt at speech left his lips as a grunt of pain. The only thing he could smell was the copper stench of his own injuries. Battle stimulants ran thick in his blood.

The maiden came closer, even daring to rest the scythe-bladed tip of her spear on his shoulder guard.

'I speak only the truth, prophet. There's no shame in this moment. You have done well to even make it this far.'

Talos spat blood again, and hissed two words.

'Valas Morovai.'

The murderess tilted her head as she looked down at him. Her long, ember-red hair was dreadlocked by the rain, plastered to her pale features. She looked like a woman sinking into water, serene as a saint while she drowned.

'Many of your bitter whisperings remain occluded to me,' she said. 'You speak… "First Claw", yes?' Her unnatural accent struggled with the words. 'They were your brothers? You call out to the dead, in the hopes they will yet save you?'

The blade fell from his grip, too heavy to hold any longer. He stared at it lying on the black stone, bathed in the downpour, silver and gold shining as clean as the day he'd stolen it.

Slowly, he lifted his head, facing his executioner. Rain showered the blood from his face, salty on his lips, stinging his eyes. He didn't need to wonder if she was still smiling. He saw it on her face, and loathed the kindliness of the gesture. Was it sympathy? Truly?

On his knees, atop the fallen battlements of his Legion's deserted fortress, the Night Lord started laughing.

Neither his laughter nor the storm above were loud enough to swallow the heavy sound of burning thrusters. A gunship – blue-hulled and blackly sinister – bellowed its way into view. As it rose above the battlements, rain sluiced from its avian hull in silver streams.

Heavy bolter turrets aligned in a chorus of mechanical grinding, the sweetest music ever to grace the prophet's ears. Talos was still laughing as the Thunderhawk hovered in place, riding its own heat haze, with the dim lighting of the cockpit revealing two figures within.

'I saw this,' he told her. 'Didn't you?'

The alien maiden was already moving. She became a black blur, dancing through the rain in a velvet sprint. Detonations clawed at her heels as the gunship opened fire, shredding the stone at her feet in a hurricane of explosive rounds.

One moment she fled across the parapets, the next she simply ceased to exist, vanishing into shadow.

Talos didn't rise to his feet, uncertain he'd manage it if he tried. He closed the only eye he had left. The other was a blind and bleeding orb of irritating pain, sending dull throbs back into his skull each time his two hearts beat. His bionic hand, shivering with joint glitches and flawed neural input damage, reached to activate the vox at his collar.

'I will listen to you, next time.'

Above the overbearing whine of downward thrusters, a voice buzzed over the gunship's external vox-speakers. Distortion stole all trace of tone and inflection.

'If we don't disengage now, there won't be a next time.'

'I told you to leave. I ordered it.'

'Master,' the external vox-speakers crackled back. *'I...'*

'Go, damn you.' When he next glanced at the gunship, he could see the two figures more clearly. They sat side by side, in the pilots' thrones. 'You are formally discharged from my service.' He slurred the words as he voxed them, and started laughing again. 'For the second time.'

The gunship stayed aloft, engines giving out their strained whine, blasting hot air across the battlements.

The voice rasping over the vox was female this time. *'Talos.'*

'Run. Run far from here, and all the death this world offers. Flee to the last city, and catch the next vessel off-world. The Imperium is coming. They will be your salvation. But remember what I said. We are all slaves to fate. If Variel escapes this madness alive, he will come for the child one night, no matter where you run.'

'He might never find us.'

Talos's laughter finally faded, though he kept the smile. 'Pray that he doesn't.'

He drew in a knifing breath as he slumped with his back to the battlements, grunting at the stabs from his ruined lungs and shattered ribs. Grey drifted in from the edge of his vision, and he could no longer feel his fingers. One hand rested on his cracked breastplate, upon the ritually-broken aquila, polished by the rain. The other rested on his fallen bolter, Malcharion's weapon, on its side from where he'd dropped it in the earlier battle. With numb hands, the prophet locked the double-barrelled bolter to his thigh, and took another slow pull of cold air into lungs that no longer wanted to breathe. His bleeding gums turned his teeth pink.

'I'm going after her.'

'Don't be a fool.'

Talos let the rain drench his upturned face. Strange, how a moment's mercy let them believe they could talk to him like that. He hauled himself to his feet, and started walking across the weathered, sunken battlements, a broken blade in hand.

'She killed my brothers,' he said. 'I'm going after her.'

HE MOVED FIRST to where Cyrion lay. The throwing star had left almost nothing of his chest, its black fire eating much of the bone and meat of his sternum and the organs beneath. He removed Cyrion's helm with a careful touch brought on as much by his own wounds as respect for the dead.

Talos blinked when Cyrion's hand gripped his wrist. His brother's black eyes rolled in their sockets, seeing nothing, trailing raindrop tears in mimicry of the lightning bolts on his faceplate.

'Uzas,' Cyrion said. One lung quivered in the exposed crater of his chest. One heart still gave a weak pound.

'It's Talos. Uzas is dead.'

'Uzas,' Cyrion said again. 'I hate you. Always hated you. But I'm sorry.'

'Brother.' Talos moved his hand before Cyrion's eyes, with no reaction. The blindness was complete.

'Talos?'

He took Cyrion's hand, gripping his arm wrist-to-wrist. 'I'm here, Cy.'

'Good. Good. Didn't want to die alone.' He sank back against the stone, relaxing in his hunched lean. 'Don't take my gene-seed.' He reached up a hand to touch his own eyes. 'I... I think I'm blind. It's the wrong kind of dark here.' Cyrion wiped a trickle of spit from his lips. 'You won't take my gene-seed, will you?'

'No.'

'Don't let Variel take it, either. Don't let him touch me.'

'I won't.'

'Good. Those words you said. About the war. I liked them. Don't pass my gene-seed on. I'm... done with the war... as well.'

'I hear you.'

Cyrion had to swallow three times before he could speak again. 'Feel like I'm drowning in spit.'

He wasn't – it was blood. Talos said nothing about it, either way. 'Septimus and Octavia got away.'

'That's good. That's good.' Cyrion drooled blood through a loose smile, his body starting to twitch with the onset of convulsions.

Talos held him still as he shivered, saying nothing. Cyrion filled the silence, as he always did.

'I'm dying,' he said. 'Everyone else is dead. The slaves escaped. So...' he breathed out slowly, '...how are you?'

Talos waited for the last breath to leave his brother's lips before gently closing Cyrion's eyes.

He took three things from the body – no more, no less.

* * *

LUCORYPHUS WAS A motionless husk. Talos gave the corpse a wide berth, making his way to Variel.

The Apothecary was far from dead. The prophet caught up with him as he crawled, straining and legless, across the stone. Becoming crippled from the knees down hadn't improved his demeanour at all.

'Don't touch me,' he said to Talos, who promptly ignored him. The prophet dragged him to the ramparts, a little more shielded from the rain.

Several compartments of Variel's narthecium were open, their contents dispensed, mostly into the Apothecary's bloodstream.

'I won't die,' he told Talos. 'I have staunched the flow of blood, eliminated the risk of sepsis and other infections, applied synthetic skin and armour sealant, while also–'

'Shut up, Variel.'

'Forgive me. The stimulants in my system are volatile and strong by virtue of their emergency requirements. I am not used to–'

'Shut up, Variel.' Talos clasped his brother's arm, wrist-to-wrist. 'I'm going after her.'

'Please do not endanger your gene-seed.'

'In truth, you'll be fortunate if it survives intact.'

'That grieves me.'

'And if you ever escape this cursed world, leave Cyrion's gene-seed untouched. Let him rest in peace.'

Variel tilted his head in the rainfall. 'As you wish. Where is the gunship? Will it be returning?'

'Goodbye, Variel. You'll do the Eighth Legion proud. I do not need to be a prophet to know that.' He gestured to Variel's belt, at the pouches, the bandolier and ammunition straps. 'I will take those, if you do not mind.'

Variel allowed it. 'How will I leave Tsagualsa if the gunship does not return me to Deltrian's vessel?'

'I have a feeling some of the Legion will come one night, to see what happened here for themselves.'

'A guess?' Variel started tapping keys on his vambrace.
'A good guess,' Talos replied. 'Goodbye, brother.'
'Die well, Talos. Thank you for Fryga.'

The prophet nodded, and left his last living brother in the rain.

She came for him when she could no longer hear the cold iron hunter-craft in the air, when distance had at last swallowed its engine-roar. She moved from the shadows, sprinting down the battlements, her spear held loosely, with perfect balance, in her remaining hand.

Silken hair streamed back in a sword-dancer's tail, kept out of her eyes as she ran. Ulthwé's banshee shrine had needed her, and to Ulthwé's banshee shrine she'd come. The division between the craftworld's seers was an unfortunate one, as was the separation of forces that followed.

Few of the other Path shrines would walk with her, no matter their respect for the armour she wore and the blades she bore. They would not leave Ulthwé so undefended, and thus, the armada had been a thin and hollow enterprise, populated by wraiths, with few able to risk setting foot on the unholy world.

Losses this eve had still been grievous. Ulthwé could ill afford to lose so many to the blades of blasphemers, but the Hunter of Souls was fated to fall, before he could become the Bane of Isha at the dawning of the Rhana Dandra.

So it was written. So shall it be.

In all the years since her most recent Becoming, few events had shown the portents aligning as fiercely those speaking of this very night. The very rightness of her actions, and the gravity of her cause, leant speed and strength to her aching limbs.

This time, he was hunting her, in his own slow, limping way. The blade in his hands rang with ancient resonance, the crude metals used in its forging dating back to the Humans' Hubris, when their arrogance burst open the Gate of Sha'eil like a great eye in the heavens. She did not fear it. She feared nothing. Even her damaged accoutrements would manifest whole once more, when the fates aligned.

She ran faster, the rain cold on her skin, the blade high in her hand.

Talos offered no resistance.

The black spear cleaved through him, finishing the work his own sword had started in her hands. He didn't smile, or curse, or whisper any last testament. She kept him at arm's length, the impaling spear forcing him back.

As the sword dropped from his grip, Talos opened his other hand. The grenade in his fist activated the moment his fingers slipped from the thumb-plate. It exploded, triggering the three grenades he'd taken from Cyrion, the two he'd taken from Variel, and the power generator on his back.

With the exception of the fire that incinerated half of an alien immortal's physical form, Talos Valcoran of Nostramo died much the same way he'd been born: with black eyes open, staring at the world around, and silence on his lips.

Marlonah limped into the rainstorm, closing her eyes and letting the cool water rinse her body of hours of sweat. She felt like weeping. Running her hands through her soaking hair was a pleasure she couldn't put into words.

The Dreadnought preceded her, but took no similar joy. The war machine dragged one leg, scraping sparks with every step and leaving a mangled engraved path along the ground. Its armour-plating was blackened in places, melted to sludge and hardened again in others, or riddled with silver shuriken discs like misaligned fish scales. His joints no longer whirred with confident, heavy grinding – they crackled and sparked and clanked, as gears and servos slipped across each other's loose teeth, finding only occasional purchase.

The construct walked onward, out onto the battlements, both its arms lowered and loose. Dozens of cables linking the sarcophagus to the main body were severed, either venting vapour, leaking fluid, or simply dried up completely.

She didn't know how many of them Malcharion had killed during their journey and ascent. They'd come at him with chainswords, with knives, with pistols, with rifles, with laser weapons and projectile-throwers and claws and spears, and even rocks and curses. He showed the impact of every single one of them on his ruined adamantite hull.

'I heard a gunship...' the Dreadnought growled. 'I... I will contact it. Talos's human slaves. They will come back for you. Then. Then I sleep.'

On the battlements ahead of them, she saw the devastated body of a legionary slumped against one wall, his armour burned black and every joint melted and fused. Smoke rose from the corpse, tangling with the downpour.

Closer to where they walked, one of the alien maidens still moaned and crawled across the stone. She only had one arm, the other lost to savage burn wounds, and one leg that ended below her thigh. The other was nowhere to be seen. All hair was seared from her body, as was most of her flesh. She writhed and groaned and bled, shivering and twitching in the rain.

'Jain Zar,' she whisper-croaked, struggling to speak with a scorched tongue. *'Jain Zar.'*

Impossibly, the only unharmed part of her body was her left eye, which watched Marlonah with sour, sentient malice.

'Jain Zar,' the dying alien rasped again.

Malcharion crushed the living wreckage under his armoured foot, smearing it across the battlements. He lifted a protesting arm on whining joints, to gesture to the legionary's corpse.

'I... have to finish everything... for that boy.'

EPILOGUE PRIMUS
NAMES

The slaves huddled together in the darkness, the male cradling the female. It wouldn't be long now. Their confines shivered as the shuttle rose, labouring on its way back into the atmosphere.

The evacuation began five days before, when the Navy's first envoy made planetfall. A hundred other refugees sat in the near-dark, speaking in quiet voices, several weeping with relief, others with fear. The people of Darcharna had never left their world. Even those taught to cherish the distant Imperium as their saviour were bound to be frightened now they were finally in the empire's less than tender care.

The slaves had spent two long months in the Last City. Two months of lying to blend in with the other survivors; two months of hiding her third eye; two months of hoping Variel wouldn't appear in the doorway of their scavenged shack. She dreamed of that confrontation all too often, picturing his red eye lenses, hearing the snarl of armour joints. She always woke the moment his gloves of cold ceramite stroked across her belly.

But he never came.

In quiet moments, she still recalled Talos's words: 'If Variel escapes this madness alive, he will come for the child one night, no matter where you run.'

But where was he? Had he fled Tsagualsa with Deltrian after all? She didn't dare believe they were safe from Variel's knives, but she was beginning to hope.

Octavia's hands rested on her stomach. The baby would be with them soon – a month or two at most. She wondered if he'd be born in the void, like that poor girl on board the *Covenant*, or if she'd first breathe the air of whatever world they'd call home once they'd lied their way through Imperial processing.

He'd agreed to act as a manual worker from one of the smaller southern cities. She was going to claim descent from the planet's original Navigators, from the colony fleet four hundred years before. It still amused her, in her calmer moments, to think that with Navigator biology, her story was technically the more likely one. She doubted she'd have any difficulty with whatever dubious authority finally processed the survivors of Darcharna. As a Navigator – precious as she was – they'd be likely to send her to a stronghold of the Navis Nobilite in a nearby sector, but pilgrims and refugees were one of the Imperium's many lifebloods. Losing themselves among the teeming billions would be no trouble.

They'd be fine, she knew, as long as the Inquisition didn't get involved.

Octavia nodded to Marlonah across the cargo hold. She nodded back, returning a nervous smile. It'd been good to have her around these last months, and she shared Octavia's amusement that all three of them only still lived because the Legion had – at various points – saved their lives. Such bizarre behaviour from soul-sworn murderers. Even after a year and more in their company, she'd never understood any of them.

Well. Perhaps Talos.

For the first time in longer than she cared to remember, she let let her thoughts drift to the future.

'I just had a thought,' she said, in a strange voice.

Septimus kissed her sweaty forehead. 'What is it?'

'What's your name?' she asked.

'What do you mean?'

'You *know* what I mean. Your real name, before you were the seventh.'

'Oh.' Septimus smiled, and though she had no hope of seeing it in the dark, she heard the grin in his whisper. 'Coreth. My name was Coreth.'

Eurydice – once Octavia – tasted the word, then turned to taste his lips. 'Coreth,' she said, her mouth against his. 'Pleased to meet you.'

EPILOGUE SECUNDUS
THE MONTHS OF MADNESS

[EXCERPT BEGINS]
...from the rogue trader vessel *Quietude*, that the eldar of Segmentum Obscura name that specific date "the Night of Sacred Sorrow", with no record of...
[EXCERPT ENDS]

[EXCERPT BEGINS]
...personally report contact lost with subsector guild interests on thirty-seven worlds, nine of which still remain dark. We await the reports of scout vessels and Imperial Navy forces in the area, but...
[EXCERPT ENDS]

[EXCERPT BEGINS]
...don't trade there, anymore. Rumours of warp storm geneses, and temperamental tides. It's not worth the money in repairs. The *Iago*'s Navigator went blind...
[EXCERPT ENDS]

[EXCERPT BEGINS]
...without confirmation of this "sizeable Archenemy fleet" on the Eastern Fringes, it is a fool's crusade to petition for...
[EXCERPT ENDS]

* * *

[EXCERPT BEGINS]
...Golar, the second world of the system of the same name, simply no longer exists in any habitable capacity. The population of the capital city was recorded in the last referenced census as four million. Extensive planetary tectonic activity left the city...
[EXCERPT ENDS]

[EXCERPT BEGINS]
...which is why, if you will heed the archival data, you will see fluctuations in the quality of astropathic contact, alongside severe...
[EXCERPT ENDS]

[EXCERPT BEGINS]
...is meaningless. Tell the Mechanicus representative that we've scryed the region *twice* now, at a cost in fuel and crew lives I struggle to tally without a cogitator...
[EXCERPT ENDS]

[EXCERPT BEGINS]
...in the region of one of the dead worlds, but no recognised Imperial tongue...
[EXCERPT ENDS]

[EXCERPT BEGINS]
...*Viris colratha dath sethicara tesh dasovallian. Solruthis veh za jass*...
[EXCERPT ENDS]

EPILOGUE TERTIUS
PROPHET OF THE EIGHTH LEGION

1

THE PROPHET LOOKED up as the bulkhead opened on squealing hinges. He wasn't surprised to see who stood there.

'Apothecary,' he said without a smile. 'Greetings.'

The Apothecary avoided all eye contact. 'It is time,' he said.

The prophet rose to his feet, hearing the healthy grind of his armour joints. 'I presume the others are already waiting?'

The Apothecary nodded. 'They will join us on the way. You are ready?'

'Of course.'

'Then let us go. The council is already in session.'

As they walked the winding, twisting hallways at the heart of the *Sun's Scourge*, screams and moans sounded in the distance, on the many decks below. The prophet let his gauntleted hand brush along the ornate steel walls.

'I will claim a ship like this one night,' he said.

'Is that a prophecy,' the Apothecary replied, 'or a hope?'

'A hope,' the prophet confessed. 'But it seems likely, if all goes well tonight.'

The two of them continued walking, their armoured boots thudding on the decking. Soon enough, they were joined by a third figure. This one wore the same midnight-blue ceramite, though its helm was a sloping, snarling daemon mask. Twin tear trails graced its face, painted in scarlet and silver. The figure crawl-walked on all fours, hunched over and loping along behind them like a loyal hound.

'Variel,' the newcomer said in a burst of crackling vox. 'And hail to you, prophet.'

Variel said nothing, though the prophet inclined his head in greeting. 'Lucoryphus,' he said. 'Have you spoken to the other Bleeding Eyes?'

'Yes. Over three hundred of the cult have attended the gathering. I spoke with several Bleeding Eye leaders among the other warbands. A dozen other cults are also in evidence. All is well. A gathering of the rarest significance, I believe.'

'True enough.'

They walked on, heading deeper. Variel occasionally checked the readings from his narthecium gauntlet, adjusting dials seemingly on a whim. The prophet didn't bother to ask what was occupying the Apothecary's mind. Variel's thoughts were forever his own; he was not a man that enjoyed sharing counsel.

The three figures soon joined another two; both of these stood in hulking suits of Terminator war plate, their tusked, horned helms lowering in respectful greeting. The Legion's winged skull stood proud on their curving shoulder guards.

'Malek,' said the prophet. 'Garadon. It is good to see you again.'

'It's nothing,' Garadon said. An immense war maul was slung over one shoulder.

'We would be nowhere else,' Malek added. His massive gauntlets carried the scythe-like claws retracted in armoured housings.

'Not meeting with the other Atramentar?' asked the Raptor, now crawling above them, hanging on the ceiling.

'That can come after this,' Malek replied. 'The survivors of the old First Company have precious little to say to one another, these nights. Meetings always degenerate into duels over their warlords' respective strengths.'

'The cults are the same. As are the Legions themselves.' Lucoryphus seemed amused by the idea. 'Your decades in the Maelstrom were ill spent if you believed anything would change.'

'The Maelstrom,' Garadon chuckled. 'An entertaining guess. How little you know, screecher.' Malek simply snorted, not quite an argument, and left it at that.

Malek and Garadon fell in alongside the prophet, flanking him as they marched three abreast down the labyrinth of corridors. Variel allowed himself to drift behind. The prophet's entrance should be alongside two of the Legion's most respected Atramentar warriors. He had no wish to debate the point.

They came, at last, to the council chamber at the very heart of the ship. The sound of raised voices and cursing could be heard even through the sealed bulkhead.

'Do they scream or laugh?' Lucoryphus rasped.

'Both,' said Malek, hauling the door open.

The group stalked into the chamber, joining one of the largest gatherings of Eighth Legion commanders in ten thousand years.

2

For almost three hours, the prophet simply listened in silence. His attention drifted from figure to figure around the central table, drinking in the details of their armour, their terror markings, their warpaint and the stories scratched across ceramite in burn marks, scars and dents.

The Legion's gathered lords and sorcerers were as divided as ever. Many called out for allegiance, no matter how temporary, to Abaddon's rising Crusade. This would be the Thirteenth, and the first with a goal to truly wound the Imperium's fortress world of Cadia beyond recovery. Others called out for patience and discretion, letting the Black Legion bear the brunt of the initial assaults while the Night Lords devoted themselves to raids away from the front lines.

Still more would hear none of it, refusing to join the Black Crusade, no matter the prize or threat of retribution. They were souls who'd abandoned the Long War, living only for themselves and the glory they could claw from existence as raiders.

The prophet didn't judge any of them, no matter their choices – courageous or craven, wise or wasteful, all of them were his brothers, for better or worse.

Talk turned to individual assaults. What fleets could strike where. What slivers of tactical intention the Despoiler had revealed so far. How best to capitalise on it for success against the Imperium, or as a means of betraying the Black Legion and cannibalising false allies in the name of spoils.

When the prophet finally spoke, it was a single word.
'No.'

3

THE NIGHT LORDS didn't fall silent immediately. Several arguments raged too hot, too loud, for an immediate quiet to descend. Instead, those nearest the prophet turned to him with cautious eyes. The lords and their honour guards – some of warriors, some of Terminators, some of Raptors – watched with sudden and cold interest, as the unknown lord spoke at last. Thus far, he'd not even named himself, yet many of those present recognised the warriors at his side.

'What did you say?' asked the nearby lord whose tirade the prophet had interrupted.

The prophet stepped forward, taking a place at the table. 'I said "No". You asserted that you will stand triumphant at the coming battle in the Alsir Divide. You will not. You will die aboard your command ship, mutilated and screaming in rage. Your final thoughts will be to wonder where your legs and right arm have gone.'

The lord hissed something low and vile through his helm's vocaliser. 'You threaten me?'

'No, Zar Tavik. I do not. But I have seen your death. I have no reason to lie.'

The named lord barked a laugh. 'No reason? Perhaps by keeping me away, you hope to secure the victory there for yourself.'

The prophet lowered his helm, conceding the point. 'I am unwilling to argue. Where you die means nothing to me.'

Silence was spreading around the table now, as infectious as a foul scent. One of the other commanders, a Raptor in silvered war plate, turned his daemon mask to the prophet.

'And how do I die, seer?'

The prophet didn't even turn to look at the Raptor. 'You die here, Captain Kalex. This very night. Your final thoughts are of disbelief.'

There was a moment's hesitation. Kalex's claws closed around the hilts of his sheathed chainswords.

'And how could you possibly know such th–'

The Raptor crashed back from the table, blood spattering those nearest him. Malek of the Atramentar lowered a double-barrelled bolter, smoke coiling from its brazen mouths.

'As I said,' the prophet smiled.

Lords nearby were edging away from him now; some in caution, others readying weapons. Kalex was one of the few to lack an honour guard. No warriors pulled iron in a bid to avenge him. Instead, a tense silence flooded the chamber, rippling out from the prophet and his brothers.

'Many of us will fall in the coming Crusade, whether we swear allegiance or abstain entirely.'

'Seize the moment…' Lucoryphus's voice came over the vox.

The prophet pointed to lord after lord, each in turn.

'Darjyr, you will be betrayed by the Word Bearers at

Corsh Point, when they leave you to face the Imperial blockade alone. Yem Kereel, you will fall in the last charge at the Greson Breach, against the Subjugators. You will be succeeded by your lieutenant, Skallika, who will be killed three nights later, when his Land Raider is toppled by a Titan and overrun by Guard platoons. Toriel the White Handed, the Legion will consider you lost to the warp when you leave here, swearing never to fight under what you call Abaddon's "slave mark". The truth is close; you are attacked by one of your own Claw leaders while under way in the warp, and as you lose your hold on your ship's path, the Sea of Souls floods into your warship.'

On and on, the prophet spoke, until a full third of the gathered warriors had been named as doomed to die in the coming Black Crusade, or while they abandoned it.

'This war will cost us. We will pay in blood and souls, night after night. But the price will be victory. The Imperium's defences will be broken, and we will never need to sneak and fight our way from the Eye again. The empire's throat shall be forevermore bared to our blades. That is what Abaddon offers us.'

'He's offered us the same thing before,' one of the lords called.

'No,' Lucoryphus hissed. 'He hasn't. The other Crusades were merely *crusades*. The Despoiler left the Eye to achieve whatever Black Legion madness he wished to achieve. This one is different. It will be a war. We will break Cadia, and forever after be free to raid the Imperium at will.'

The prophet nodded to the Raptor's words. 'Some of us have remained Legion brothers down the centuries. Others have splintered from the Legion in all but name, while still others among us have cast aside the colours entirely. I see several warbands now wearing the colours and honours of their own factions, for they've been strong enough to rise from the old ranks and claim mastery over their own paths. Yet we are all bonded by the fact that this Crusade, this Thirteenth Uprising, will be the war we've waited for. The more of our blood we add to the tides, the greater our triumph.'

'But so many deaths…' Another lord nearly spat the words. 'The price is high, if you even speak the truth.'

'I see these deaths in thick, spiteful dreams each time I close my eyes,' the prophet said. 'I dream of nothing else. I see the death of every single warrior bearing Eighth Legion blood in his veins. Just as our primarch knew he was destined to fall – just as our sorcerers suffer visions of their own deaths, and the demises of those near them. But my soul-sight goes… further. Your worlds of birth mean nothing. If we are connected by gene-seed, then I have watched your last breaths. If you have Eighth Legion blood beating through your veins, then I have seen you die. Most are vague, indistinct endings, ripe for change with a twist of fate. A few may be ironclad, the same in a hundred visions, and all that remains is for you to sell your lives dearly. But most are not. Fate is not etched in stone, brothers.'

Silence reigned now, almost majestic in its oppressive totality. Variel and Lucoryphus stepped closer, alongside Malek and Garadon, as the prophet drew breath to speak again.

'Do you know what one of the greatest threats to victory will be in Abaddon's Final War?' he asked the gathered warleaders.

'Each other,' several of them joked at once. The prophet waited for the laughter to die down.

'For once, no. The Imperium will claim an ally of desperate strength, and one we cannot afford to leave at our backs. What ancient detritus is caught within the Great Eye's eternal grip? What haven of alien filth still holds out against the forces of the Enlightened Legions?'

'Ulthwé,' said one lord.

'The Black Eldar,' said another. Disgruntled murmurs started up, just as the prophet knew they would. The Eighth Legion – like all of the Eye's forces – had lost their fair share of warriors and warships over the millennia due to the interference of the accursed Ulthwé eldar.

The prophet nodded again. 'Craftworld Ulthwé. They came for Tenth Company once, decades ago. They chased the Tenth across the stars, feverish in their need to end a single life before prophecy could become truth. They failed in that quest, though they never knew it. Their witches and warlocks scryed a future they could not allow to come to pass: a future where the Prophet of the Eighth Legion rallied his kindred to bring fear and flame upon their precious craftworld in an unrelenting storm. These creatures, with their species so close to extinction, fear damnation more than anything else. *That* is where the Eighth Legion will strike first. *That* is where we will devote our initial assault, raining bloodshed and terror onto the eldar, drenching their dying craftworld in the tears of the slain.'

'And why should we?' called Lord Hemek of the Nightwing. 'Why should we spill eldar blood, when we have hordes of Imperial Guard to slake our thirsts?'

'Revenge,' argued another. 'For vengeance.'

'I need no vengeance against the eldar,' said Hemek. His Legion-crested helm was resplendent with its wings of black-veined cobalt. 'We all carry our own grudges, and mine have nothing to do with Ulthwé.'

The prophet let the arguments rage for a few minutes.

'This is getting out of hand,' Variel privately voxed.

'Let me handle it,' the prophet replied. He raised his hand for silence. Peace was a while coming, but the others eventually fell silent.

'I have seen you die,' he said. 'All of you. All of your warriors. These fates may be promised by destiny, but destiny can always be denied. The eldar cannot be allowed to join this war with their forces untouched. None of you can imagine how many of us will die. These are losses I would spare the Eighth Legion from suffering, if you will heed my words.'

'My sorcerers speak of the same ill omens,' one of the other lords announced. 'Their warpsight afflictions are hardly as reliable as Talos's visions once were, but they have served me well in the past.'

Several voices rose in agreement. Clearly, it was a sentiment many shared within the councils of their own warbands.

'And you are?' the prophet asked politely.

'Kar Zoruul, of what was once Fortieth Company. On the guidance of my sorcerers, I was already planning to assault the eldar, as were several of our brother warbands.'

Hemek wasn't convinced. 'So you come to bring us a warning of the eldar?'

All or nothing, thought the prophet.

'The eldar are a threat to be considered now,' he said, 'but they are not the true reason I came here. What matters is what comes after. Some of you have already met Abaddon, while others will meet with him in the coming months, as his Crusade gathers potency. To survive, to break the Imperium's back and enter the Emperor's final nights, we must join this war, no matter our reservations. The future holds great things for us, my brothers. The Last Age of the Emperor is drawing to a close, as the Dark Millennium ends. This is it, my lords. With the Legions and their forces no longer contained in the Eye, we stand on the edge of final victory.'

More silence, for several moments. The prophet smiled behind his faceplate; it was enough to get them thinking. This wasn't a war he expected to win in a single night. Slowly, slowly, he'd win them to his side, offering counsel and aiding them in avoiding the bitter fates awaiting them.

'There was talk,' Toriel the White Handed said softly, 'that Talos survived the carrion world. It was said Malek and Garadon returned to stand by him, and here we see both of those honoured Atramentar among us. How much of this is true, Variel?'

The Apothecary didn't answer. He merely turned to the prophet.

'Does it matter?' Lord Darjyr snorted. 'Why should we believe this thin-blooded wretch? I scent the changes in you, young one. Your gene-seed is old, but it has scarcely ripened within you. You are an infant, standing in the shadows of gods.'

'You do not have to believe what I say.' The prophet smiled behind his faceplate. 'It makes no difference to me, or to my kindred.'

'You are not Talos, then? This isn't some trick?'

'No,' the prophet replied. 'I am not Talos, and this is no trick.'

'Tell us your name,' demanded one of the others, one of those not named to die in the coming months.

The prophet leaned on the central table, red eye lenses panning across them all. His armour was a scavenged mesh of conflicting marks, each ceramite plate showing carved Nostraman runes. His breastplate bore the image of an aquila, its spread wings ritually broken by hammer blows. Over one shoulder was a sweep of pale age-browned flesh, flayed into a cloak with thick black stitches. Skulls and Imperial Space Marine helms hung on bronze chains from his belt and pauldrons, while two weapons were sheathed at his hips: the first was a double-barrelled bolter, inscribed with ancient writings and depicting the name *Malcharion*; the second was a relic blade stolen from the Blood Angels Chapter a forgotten number of centuries ago. Its once-golden length was discoloured silver, evidence of a recent reforging.

The prophet's helm was a studded, brutal affair with a skull-painted faceplate, and sweeping ceremonial Legion wings rising up in an elegant crest. The skull's eyes wept black lightning bolts, as if the bone itself was cracked. In the centre of its forehead, a single Nostraman rune gleamed black against the bone white.

He removed the helmet slowly, making no sudden moves, and regarded them all with a youthful, unscarred face. Dark eyes glinted in the chamber's low light, drifting from warrior to warrior.

'My name is Decimus,' the Night Lord replied. 'The Prophet of the Eighth Legion.'

ACKNOWLEDGEMENTS

Thanks to my editor Nick Kyme, as usual, for his patience – above and beyond the call of duty this time. Thanks as well to Laurie Goulding, Rachel Docherty and Nikki Loftus for their keen eyes and sage advice.

A portion of this book's proceeds will go to Cancer Research UK and the SOS Children's Villages charity, for orphans in Bangladesh.

ABOUT THE AUTHOR

Aaron Dembski-Bowden is a British author with his beginnings in the videogame and RPG industries. He's written several novels for the Black Library, including the Night Lords series, the Space Marine Battles book *Helsreach* and the *New York Times* bestselling *The First Heretic* for the Horus Heresy. He lives and works in Northern Ireland with his wife Katie, hiding from the world in the middle of nowhere. His hobbies generally revolve around reading anything within reach, and helping people spell his surname.

'Aaron Dembski-Bowden is heretically good.'
Dan Abnett

WARHAMMER 40,000

THE EMPEROR'S GIFT

New York Times bestselling author
AARON DEMBSKI-BOWDEN

An extract from The Emperor's Gift
by Aaron Dembski-Bowden

On sale June 2012

A BLUR OF pain and fire. A storm of noise and cancerous colours. Liquid nothingness, yet with a spiteful sentience in its tides, manifesting enough solidity to grip at your arms and legs as you fell through it.

Before I could focus my concentration enough to repel the sensation back, we–

Appeared in perfect arrangement, all five of us ringing the regent's throne. Our weapons were still raised – five wrist-mounted storm bolters aiming ten barrels at the convulsing ruler of Draufir. His robes rippled, echoing the fleshcrafting beneath.

The sonic boom of our arrival shattered almost all thirty of the great stained glass windows, letting even more sunlight spill into the throne room. The white mist, now poisoned to warp-red and arterial crimson, lingered in coiling tendrils. Even as it dispersed, it stroked at our armour, dulling the polish.

The regent, flushed and mutable in his spasms, bleeding pus from his tear ducts, actually managed to gasp at our appearance. Stupefaction and fear halted his change.

Galeo spoke without speaking. The weight of his psychic proclamation was enough to grind my teeth together.

+In the name of the Emperor of Mankind, we do judge thee diabolus traitoris. The sentence is death.+

We closed our hands into fists, and five storm bolters boomed in the harmony of absolute rhythmic unity.

The regent's physical form burst across the five of us, painting silver armour with vascular, stringy viscera. Bones shattered and crumbled, blasting apart, cracking off our helms and breastplates. A partially articulated ribcage crashed back onto the throne.

+Peace.+

We ceased delivering sentence, but did not lower our weapons. Smoke rose from ten barrels, adding a rich, powdery chemical scent to the surgical reek tainting the raised dais.

Only the regent's shadow remained. It twisted in the centre of the circle we had formed, writhing and clawing at nothing as it sought to build a physical form from the air.

+Dumenidon.+

The warrior named drew his blade in a sharp pull. Each of us added our emotions – our disgust, our revulsion, our hatred – to his own, layering our surface thoughts around his clear, clean rage. The touch of our minds spurred his anger deeper, blacker, into a wrath intense enough to cause him physical pain.

But he was strong. He let his own body and brain become the focus for our psychic force, channelling it along the length of his blade. Psychic lightning danced down the sacred steel, raining fragile hoarfrost to the marble floor.

All of this, from our arrival to the focus of killing energy, happened in the span it took Annika's heart to beat five times. I know that because I heard it. It formed a strangely calming drumbeat to our execution.

Despite barely being able to see it, Dumenidon

impaled the crippled shadow with a deep thrust. His blade instantly caught fire. This time, the burst of gore was ectoplasmic and ethereal in nature. Slime hissed against our warded aegis armour plating, failing to eat into the blessed ceramite.

The creature's shriek rang in our ears, shattering the few windows our teleportation arrival hadn't.

Thus ended the reign of Regent Kezidha the Eleventh.

I turned to Inquisitor Jarlsdottyr, finding her in a canine crouch halfway down the steps leading up to the throne. A hundred silk-robed courtiers stared at us. Fifty armed palace guards did the same. None of them moved. Most of them didn't even blink. This was not quite the gala ballroom event they had been expecting.

'And them?' I asked her. My voice was a rasp-edged growl from my helm's vox grille.

'Skitnah,' she said, her lips forming a Fenrisian snarl. Skitnah. Dirty. Foul. Tainted.

We raised our weapons again. That sent them running.

'I will cage the vermin,' said Malchadiel. He raised his arms as if pushing at the chamber's great double doors, even from this distance. The rest of us opened fire, scything down those fleeing slowest, or who dared raised arms against us. Insignificant las-fire scorched my armour, too sporadic and panicked to be worthy of concern. A crosshaired targeting reticule leapt from robe to robe, flickering white with screeds of biological data. None of it mattered. I blanked my retinal display with a thought, preferring to fire free.

The nobles of Draufir hammered on the throne room doors, crushing each other in their attempts to escape. Fists beat against the solid bronze, forming a revolting cacophony in their fear. As they wept and screamed, they burst like bloated sacks of blood and bone under explosive bolter shells.

I spared a glance for my brother Malchadiel, who stood rigid, hands taloned by his efforts. Psy-frost rimed his splayed fingers, crackling into ice dust with each fractional movement. The doors held fast, and I wondered if he was smiling behind his mask.

Less than a minute later, all guns fell silent and blades slid back into sheaths. Malchadiel lowered his hands at last. The immense bronze doors creaked as they settled back onto their hinges, at the mercy of gravity and architecture once more, rather than my brother's will.

Stinking, opened bodies lay in ruptured repose along the carpet, and a world's worth of aristocratic blood ran across the floor. Annika was toe-deep in a spreading lake of it, clutching her bolter in her hands. Red stains flecked her face in a careless impression of tribal tattoos.

'It's the smell I hate most,' she said.

They do say Fenris breeds cold souls.

Order from *blacklibrary.com*
Also available from

GAMES WORKSHOP

and all good bookstores